Praise for Spider Robinson

"Robinson's strong points include a punchy, clear-eyed style...a near-tangible concern with community, responsibility and creativity, and a willingness to take risks with offbeat ideas."

—SCIFI.COM

"Robinson's writing [is] potentially addictive and...full of earthy delight."

—PUBLISHERS WEEKLY

"If I didn't think it understated his achievement, I'd nominate Spider Robinson...as the new Robert Heinlein....He writes as clearly about computers as he does about karate chops."

—THE NEW YORK TIMES BOOK REVIEW

THE Crazy YEARS

Spider Robinson

BENBELLA BOOKS
Dallas, Texas

The Crazy Years
Copyright © 1996–2004 Spider Robinson

BenBella Books
6440 N. Central Expressway
Suite 617
Dallas, TX 75206
Send feedback to feedback@benbellabooks.com
www.benbellabooks.com

Printed in the United States of America

10 9 8 7 6 5 4 3 2 1

Library of Congress Cataloging-in-Publication Data

Robinson, Spider
    The crazy years / Spider Robinson — BenBella Books ed.
        p. cm
    ISBN 1-932100-35-0
    I. Title
    PS3568.O3156C73 2004
    814'.54—dc22

                                                            2004018608

Interior design and composition by John Reinhardt Book Design
Cover design by Melody Cadungog

Distributed by Independent Publishers Group
To order call (800) 888-4741
www.ipgbook.com

This book is dedicated with thanks to my friend and colleague Shannon Rupp, who stopped me in the middle of a rant one day and said, "Don't tell *me*—write it down and sell it to the *Globe and Mail*."

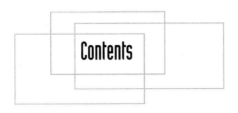

Contents

Present Imperative, or Social Mahooha

Environmental Floss

Extreme Forms of Argument

"It claims to be fully automatic—but actually, you have to push this little button, here . . ."

Lagniappe

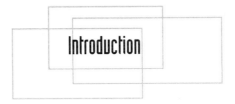

Introduction

I F MEMORY SERVES (and, increasingly, it only stands and waits), I first met Spider Robinson somewhere in cyberspace in 1999. He e-mailed me to find out if I'd provide a blurb for a book of his, and I e-mailed back to say that I wouldn't.

That probably doesn't sound like much of a foundation on which to build a friendship. Well, a lot you know.

Spider prefaced his request with an apology for making it, and I explained my refusal as a matter of policy, and we said a number of nice things about each other's work and placed one another on our respective mailing lists. And, let me tell you, I came out way ahead on that deal. What Spider got was a slew of tour schedules, book offers and other drivel from the LB Institute for Perpetual Self-Promotion (of which you too can avail yourself, Dear Reader, by signing up at www.lawrenceblock.com, all free and worth every penny). What I got was an advance peek at each of Spider's columns, always accompanied by a note advising me to let him know if I wanted to be spared further installments thereof.

Why on earth would I want to get off that list? I have never for one moment entertained such a notion. Au contraire, mon frere. What I did almost immediately was open a Spider Robinson folder and save each column as soon as I'd finished reading it. I didn't want to let go of them. Now I suppose I could delete the folder, as I've got the columns (including a couple I somehow missed) right here in book form. But I think I'll let them have hard drive space as well.

The man's entertaining, provocative and of a wholly original turn of mind and phrase. Moreover, he's evidently incapable of writing an awkward sentence. (Oh, I suppose he could do it if he tried. But not if he didn't.)

But you know all that.

And there's the real challenge in writing this introduction. I am, inevitably, preaching to the choir, because who else is going to show up? However heroic an effort the publisher might make (and, for a small press, every effort is heroic), the likelihood of the book being plucked off the shelf by someone unacquainted with Spider's work is as remote as Tierra del Fuego

and as unlikely as Michael Jackson. (Yes, I know, people do get to TdF—I've been there myself—and MJ does exist, albeit in a parallel universe.)

In point of fact, the members of this volume's audience are very likely better versed and more deeply steeped than I in the man's work. I've read (and have now reread) the columns, and I've read a couple of the Callahan books, but many of you have read *all* of the Callahan books, and read them over and over and over, and can (and, alas, do) quote them verbatim, and at some length, upon the slightest provocation.

All things considered (well, at least as many of them as I can think of), I can't flatter myself into believing that anything I can write here will induce anyone to buy the book, or render the experience of owning and reading it one whit more pleasurable than it would be without my participation. Saying things about the columns is pointless. They're not "The Waste Land," for God's sake. You don't have to tunnel like a badger to root out their hidden meanings. And a good thing, too.

We don't need no steenkin' badgers.

Still, I have to say something. I am, after all, getting paid for these words, so it's my job to furnish a reasonable number of them. Pointing out the excellent qualities of the man and his work does seem beside the point, but what else am I qualified to do?

Let me see. I've only met the man once, if you rule out encounters through the e-mail ether and the no less intimate contact two human beings achieve through sympathetic reading of one another's work. In July of 2001, my wife and I flew to Vancouver, where we were to embark on a two-week Alaska cruise on the *World Discoverer*. Spider and his wife met us, and we walked around downtown Vancouver a bit, had lunch somewhere and found that we liked each other as well face to face as we had at a distance.

Later, we found we had an interesting friend in common, a dear man and brilliant writer named Larry Janifer. I had known Larry back in the late fifties and lost touch with him for years; Spider knew him later in life. Larry moved to Australia, where I was curiously unable to see him because his phone was always busy because he was always on-line. Every few hours he would phone and leave a message at my hotel, and I would call back, and his line would be busy again.

Then health problems led Larry to move back to the States, where he died. And, now that I think about it, I'm not sure just what that has to do with anything, but Larry played a formative role in my career and, I gather, in Spider's, and he's too little remembered these days, so I figured this was a good place to mention him.

I tried to dedicate a book to Spider once. The book was *Tanner's Tiger,* and it hadn't borne any dedication when Gold Medal published it in 1968.

A few years ago Subterranean Press brought out a handsome hardcover first edition, and I seized the opportunity to dedicate it to someone, and picked Spider, because the book takes place in Canada, and so, generally, does Spider.

When my author's copies arrived, I plucked one off the stack, ready to inscribe it to the dedicatee.

No dedication.

Well, these things happen. As far as I'm concerned, *Tanner's Tiger* is dedicated to Spider Robinson, whether it says so or not.

And that, Dear Reader, is as much as you need to hear from me. Turn your attention, I entreat you, to the essays that follow. And if you can get past the "My crows. . ." groaner, you can handle anything.

Lawrence Block
Greenwich Village
January 2004

The Crazy Years: A Mission Statement

I N 1939, THE GREATEST SCIENCE FICTION WRITER who ever lived, Robert Anson Heinlein, produced one of the first of the many stunning innovations he was to bring to his field: he sat down and drew up a chart of the history of the future, for the next few thousand years.

The device was intended as a simple memory aid, to assist him in keeping straight the details of a single, self-consistent imaginary future, which he could then mine as often as he liked for story ideas. But because Heinlein was who he was, his famous Future History came, over the next six decades, to have an uncanny—if nonspecific—predictive function. That is, no specific event he wrote of came to pass exactly as he invented it, but he was simply so smart and so well educated that, more often than not, he correctly nailed the general shape of things to come. He was, for instance, just about the only thinker in 1939 to seriously predict a moon landing before the twenty-first century—and he invented the water bed.

And in Heinlein's Future History chart, the last decades of the twentieth century—the ones he wrote about and discussed as seldom as possible— were clearly and ominously marked: "the Crazy Years."

I discussed this with him several times before his death in 1988. He had decided—half a century in advance—that a combination of information overload, overpopulation and Millenial Madness were going to drive our whole culture slug-nutty by the end of the century. One of his characters summed it up by describing the Crazy Years as "a period when a man with all his gaskets tight would have been locked up."

This book is dedicated to the notion that Heinlein was right: that future generations will look back on us as the silliest, goofiest, flat-out craziest crew of loonies that ever took part in the historical race from womb to tomb; that never before in human history has average human intelligence been anywhere near as low as it is today; and that no culture on record has ever behaved as insanely as this one now does routinely. And if Heinlein is right, before long I'll be comfortably esconced in a padded cell, my frayed nerves soothed by powerful calming drugs.

Information Overload

Braindrain Wave

FIRST PRINTED FEBRUARY 2002

SINCE POUL ANDERSON, one of the most lyrical and learned sf writers of all time, left us a few years ago, I've been digging out old favorite books of his and re-reading them. I doubt I'll live long enough to finish the task; Poul was almost as prolific as his friend Isaac Asimov. The worst book he ever wrote was above average. The one I looked for first, however, *Brain Wave*, is missing; I probably lent it unwisely.

I haven't read it in forty years, but it stuck: it was one of the first ten books I ever read. It posits a vast force field or zone of some kind in space, which has the effect of inhibiting intelligence—and through which the solar system has been traveling for thousands of years. One day in the late twentieth century, the solar system finally emerges . . . and every living thing on earth suddenly becomes exponentially smarter. This turns out to present as many challenges as opportunities—are you ready to negotiate with your pet, for instance?

In real life, however, I'm beginning to suspect the exact opposite has occurred. Available evidence strongly suggests the planet is currently entering an intelligence-suppressing field. How else to explain, for instance, the Israeli-Palestinian lunacy? Peace damn near broke out there, for a while . . .but fortunately stupider heads on both sides prevailed, boys were taught to throw rocks at armed men, girls trained to blow themselves apart in crowds of innocents and the region was again made safe for mothers insane with grief.

And speaking of moronic perverters of Islam....Nine years after the first attempt on the World Trade Center failed utterly, al-Qaeda finally developed a genius planner—one Mohammad Atta. But the genius's plan had him be the first one killed—for no reason at all. His superiors saw no problem with this either: they let their one and only genius suicide without objection.

And what bloodcurdling follow-up atrocities have they produced since the towers fell? Besides trying to hide behind starving cripples, then leaving their Taliban host/protectors holding the bag while they ran like roaches, I mean. Well, they masterminded two diabolically horrid new schemes and darned near pulled them off, too.

First, they scoured the earth for the stupidest, clumsiest man alive, incompetent to operate a Zippo, trained him to dress and behave as suspiciously as possible and then entrusted him with a bomb which, even if it had detonated, would not have brought the plane down. Somehow, the scheme went wrong.

Next, they apparently gave four Moroccan Muslim militants a baggie containing four kilos of potassium ferrocyanide and sent them to Rome in a nice inconspicuous group. The Italian cops recently rolled them up like a cheap rug; they were cleverly carrying around, to save themselves the trouble of memorizing them, several maps of the Eternal City with its water pipes and reservoir highlighted.

My point is not that al-Qaeda has suddenly become unusually stupid. It has always been unusually stupid, and only once unusually lucky. My point is that the United States of America has become unusually stupid. Rambo, brandishing his howitzer in all directions and bellowing his war cry, is menaced by a mouse. The mouse knew a lion, once, but the lion's dead now. Kicking in doors indiscriminately all around the world to find the mouse, and trashing the finest Constitution and Bill of Rights on earth to punish him, is as profoundly stupid as, say, announcing to the world with childlike candor that henceforth you plan to lie to it any time you think advisable. And what could possibly be stupider than that, eh?

How about an example from right here in Canada? I've been chided in the past for citing monumental stupidities by Palestines, Israelis and Americans...but only trivial, local stupidities by Canadians. Why, I've been asked, can't Canada get a fair shake in the idiocy Olympics? My critics will be glad to hear we have a shot at the gold, having produced what some judges believe is the most appallingly stupid case of journalistic irresponsibility in recent memory. In response to one US government agency's recently announced intention to spread disinformation—admittedly a piece of world class stupidity in itself—one of our large metropolitan newspapers ran a lengthy article that assembled slanted factoids, scurrilous Internet rumors, illogical innuendo and obvious outright nonsense to "prove" that President Bush himself bombed the World Trade Center and Pentagon, and pinned it on al-Qaeda to give himself an excuse to kill all the Arabs and steal all the oil. The piece is presented with an absolutely straight face, and only in the last paragraphs are you told the punchline: if America says it can lie, hey, maybe we're lying too. Tee hee.

My heart sank as I read it: it was perfectly obvious to the meanest intelligence that many readers were going to miss the satirical intent. The majority of them, it would appear: a week later, responses were printed...and sure as hell, three out of five readers believe the piece was serious. One says he faxed it to all his friends, another calls it "brilliant and complete" and the third says it restored her faith in the possibility of freedom of speech in this country.

I have to agree with her: even composing enemy propaganda is now apparently acceptable, if you smirk as you do it. Or is that word too harsh? Publishing lies that blame Bush for 9/11 will, inarguably, give aid and comfort to our enemy, in time of war (albeit undeclared); the only question then is whether aspirations to humour constitute adequate excuse for putting Canadians at increased risk. I certainly won't collaborate: I've pointedly not named the writer or newspaper and won't while it's still possible to download the article with a few mouse clicks. But I've given plenty of clues; anyone who really wants it, and is bright enough to be trusted with it, can find it.

For my next magical trick, I've actually got something even more shamefully stupid than crafting propaganda for terrorists as a joke—and again, Canada gets the discredit. You probably think I mean that doctor who refuses to treat smokers, but he's already been adequately savaged by my distinguishable colleague Rex Murphy. I've got something worse: a pack of doctors who've sunk a knife into the broken hearts of some grief-stricken parents and twisted it, claiming the noblest of motives.

They're highly respected, accomplished doctors from the Hospital for Sick Children with the University of Toronto and the University of Maryland School of Medicine. Their goal happens to be the same as that other doctor: they yearn to become heros who helped save the planet from wicked tobacco. But not by doing anything so strenuous as, say, learning how to prevent or cure nicotine addiction. Demonizing the addicts is so much easier. And how better to demonize addicts than to make everyone think they're baby killers?

All it takes is bogus science. So these heros inspected the lungs of fewer than four dozen infants who died of SIDS, formerly called "crib death," looking for nicotine (only). Sure enough, sometimes they found some. There, they announced triumphantly to the press: We've proved smoking parents cause SIDS. Ma'am, you killed your child.

Of course, they'd proved nothing of the sort. No one knows the cause(s) of SIDS. Even if one accepts the ridiculous proposition that anything a zealot finds in a corpse's lungs must be what killed it, there was another small problem with the logic: very often, the parents of the dead infants with nicotine in their lungs were both nonsmokers. Oops.

Easily fixed: The doctors simply told the press, on zero evidence, that those parents are liars. No point checking with their insurance company, which usually tests for nicotine: just brand them as lying junkies. Make the data fit the theory.

These disgraces to science didn't stop with simply blaming the bereaved, shaming the shattered: some are actively urging other well-intentioned nimrods to kidnap smokers' children! "If Children's Aid Societies step in to protect children who are undernourished, maybe we have to step in when babies do not breathe clean air," the lead "investigator" blithely told this newspaper. A spokesperson for the Ontario Association of Children's Aid Societies agreed they're seriously considering doing just that. To between one fifth and one quarter of all parents. On the basis of a single unreplicated study of forty-four infants that proves nothing.

Doctors, if I can manage to find any molecules of alcohol, caffeine, cannabis, chocolate, sugar or any other enjoyable substance that some yahoo wants banned as a health menace in the lungs of any of your children, may I come to your houses with armed backup and apprehend the kids for their own safety?

The competition in international imbecility is heavy. How about those al-Qaeda geniuses who paid a fortune for weapons-grade plutonium that turned out to be medical waste, barely radioactive enough to make a Geiger counter snicker? Or all the Hindu and Muslim extremists pissing on Ghandi-ji's memory in India, each desperate to prove their religion is the most barbaric? Or Prince Philip's boffo Australian debut as a comedian, making spear-chucker jokes to aboriginals? Or the Pope's controversial debut as a Russian televangelist? But by God, Canada can hold its head as low as anybody. We've all entered the stupidity zone together.

Says Who?

FIRST PRINTED OCTOBER 1996

What are the facts? Again and again and again—what are the facts? Shun wishful thinking, ignore divine revelation, forget what "the stars foretell," avoid opinion, care not what the neighbors think, never mind the unguessable "verdict of history"—what are the facts, and to how many decimal places? You pilot always into an unknown future; facts are your only clue.
—ROBERT HEINLEIN, *TIME ENOUGH FOR LOVE*

THE FIRST AND MOST OBVIOUS problem is that it's getting harder to tell a fact from a factoid—let alone a factoid from pure mahooha.

Witness the public humiliation of poor old Pierre Salinger, who was unwary enough to trust data he'd gotten from the Internet and publicly proclaim that Flight 800 had been shot down by the US Navy. (A theory which, at a minimum, requires one to believe not one sailor on the hypothetical offending vessel harbors the slightest desire to be rich and famous, and the captain has no enemies.) It has always surprised me to meet people who believed, "It must be true: I read it somewhere," and in my lifetime I have been equally surprised to find people who believed, "It must be true: it was on TV." I find myself astonished again now that I'm meeting people who tell me, "It must be true: I downloaded it."

The Internet, as presently constituted, is anarchy. Information ka-ka. Garbage in, garbage out. There are no fact-checkers. There is no peer review. Any fool who fancies him or herself an information guerilla can publish any gibberish he or she likes. Therefore all Internet "facts" not supported by checkable references have the same value: zero.

Our culture appears to be packed with people desperately eager to lay down a kilobuck or two, fill their desktops with large cranky gear and devote hundreds of hours of skullsweat—to gain access to an endless cornucopia of suspect data. And, since it arrives via the highest of high tech, treat all of it

9

as revealed truth. We're piloting on the basis of the most up-to-the-minute rumors. This strikes me as a recipe for the first global riot.

But the Internet is not the problem; only its latest avatar. No matter how information comes to us, it takes hard work and careful analysis to decide how much it's worth. Okay, we can automatically discount anything on government stationery or paid for by any political party or interest group. Sure, we can be suspicious of any announcement from anything calling itself an institute. Sooner or later *Time* or *Newsweek* will report on something of which we have personal experience, and we'll get a sense of how much faith can be placed in them. And when I receive (and I swear I did) a junkmail from some psychic advisors that begins, "We hope this did not reach you too late," I can tell at once that it has reached me about forty-five years too late.

But what are we to do when, for example, we read the flat assertion that, "Children born to women who smoked dope while pregnant cannot make decisions. They cannot learn," in a November 20 *Vancouver Sun* Op-Ed column by one Connie Kuhns? Let's even suppose for argument that some shred of documentation had been offered, some study cited, some scientist named—suppose we'd been given facts, rather than a claim they exist. How are we to check the facts? Required: at least an hour in a good library (or navigating cyberspace) just to find the cited study and read it. (And even after reading the whole thing, how many of us possess the necessary intellectual training to tell a good study from a statistical massage?) Another half hour to assess the professional competence of the author(s). An hour, minimum, wading through fat indexes of technical journals to learn whether the claimed result is reproducible or unique to the claimant. More work will be required to trace who funded the study and where they got their money. Then, for context, you have to step back and derive for yourself the ratio of anti- to pro-marijuana studies that receive funding—and a dozen other threads. It was kind of Ms. Kuhns to spare us all that tedious work—but in consequence only those of us who chance to actually know any children of mothers who smoked pot while pregnant can tell she is speaking pernicious nonsense.

Bad data are dangerous, whether cybernetic or semantic. We all know that some downloaded programs contain viruses, bits of bad programming that instruct the host computer to do self-destructive things, and that the wise hacker practices safe surfing. But Richard Dawkins pointed out that ideas are very like viruses. If I think up a good idea and tell it to you, it takes over a little of your brain's processing power, forces it to make a copy of itself and encourages you to pass it on to others. The stronger the idea, the faster and farther it replicates itself, until—if it be vigorous enough—it saturates the whole infoculture. An early hacker named K'ung Fu-Tse, for instance, wrote some viruses that have survived for millennia. Such proto-nerds as Muhammad, Buddha and Jesus programmed infobots so powerful that they continue to crash operating systems and reformat whole hard drives to this day. A really good idea can spread like chicken pox through a daycare center.

So can a really bad one. As Heinlein said, "The truth of a proposition has nothing to do with its credibility—and vice versa."

We need some real-life equivalent of Disinfectant, the clever little program written by John Norstad of Northwestern University which con-stantly guards my Mac against infection by corrupting ideas. Information hygiene requires a cultural Crap-Detector that will allow us to practice safe sentience.

And so we come at last to the second, less obvious and more serious problem, which I will have to leave for another day:

Nobody wants one. Not enough to pay for it. Deep down, we don't re-ally care if the stories we download from the Net are true, as long as they're good stories and support our preconceived prejudices. These are, after all, the Crazy Years.

The Mahooha Filter

FIRST PRINTED FEBRUARY 1997

EDGAR PANGBORN, one of the most lyrical writers science fiction (or fiction) has yet produced, worked in a time when one could not use, in print, the common euphemism which literally refers to male bovine excrement. (A term which subsequently became acceptable for a time, but is now once again politically incorrect in that it ignores the valuable contributions of female ruminants.) One can scarcely discuss the human condition in any thoughtful way without mentioning the substance in question rather frequently. So Mr. Pangborn was forced to invent a euphemism for a euphemism, and he selected the splendid word "mahooha." I recommend its resurrection.

One of the more invigoratingly difficult challenges of life in the Crazy Years is learning how to strike a balance between keeping an open mind and being a sucker. One should not dismiss new ideas out of hand...but neither should one accept old ideas out of hand. One ought to be deeply suspicious of anything that Everybody Knows—and just as suspicious of Secret Truths known only to Pierre Salinger.

Indeed, there seems little to choose between them. Mr. Salinger is prepared to believe in an airtight conspiracy made up on the spot by a shipful of randomly selected sailors. The rest of the media, to a person, seem equally prepared to believe that in Colorado it takes six months to get back the results of a simple DNA match. Whether it comes vouched for by the *New York Times* or from some anonymous text-only Web site, mahooha is still mahooha.

We navigate an uncharted sea of suspect data gathered by unreliable sensors. Riches and reefs alike await us in the dark—and in the end we really have only intuition to guide us. There is no shortage of lookouts. There are too many, all shouting at once, all warning of contradictory dangers. What is needed is a Mahooha Filter.

One may not wish to discriminate—but one must become discriminating, or drown in mahooha. There just isn't enough time to run down every bit of information offered and rate its reliability. A way must be found to safely reject whole sheaves of data, by their smell alone.

So one adopts certain rules of thumb. Here are some I have found useful:

I routinely ignore:

- Anyone who uses the word "Jehovah." This one is actually not a value-judgment; it's simply beyond my control. Speak to me of Jehovah, and with the best will in the world, my eyes glaze over. If this be the reflex that will send me to Hell, blame He who hardwired it into me.
- Any newscaster who pronounces "nuclear" as "nucular."
- Any newscaster.
- Any Pro-Life advocate who has not adopted and raised at least one unwanted child, to adulthood and through college. No excuses for economic hardship; no excuses, period. Put up or shut up.
- Any antismoking zealot who cannot, at a minimum, identify and explain the principal logical fallacy in the famous Wertheimer study of sidestream smoke.[1]
- Any antinuclear zealot who is not familiar with the comparative health records of the U.S. Navy nuclear submarine service (which permits smoking in enclosed airspace) and the general public.
- Any critic (as distinct from reviewer) who is not a credentialed practitioner of the art in question—e.g., any book critic who has never been published in that genre, or any film critic who has never been professionally engaged in film-making.
- Any reviewer (a distinctly different trade from critic), regardless of credentials, who gives away the ending or the big plot twist. This is, indeed, the only sin a reviewer can commit.
- Any conspiracy theory involving more than three living principals or more than a hundred dollars.
- Any work of art with an exclamation point in the title.
- Any press release from a political party or candidate.
- Any press release, including—especially!—my own.
- Anything purporting to be science fact that is broadcast on the Arts and Entertainment Network, especially if narrated by Leonard Nimoy.
- Any and all psychic friends who have a question.
- Any claim that something pleasurable is unhealthy. Tell me broccoli causes cancer, I'll listen. (This one is finally moot, since every conceivable pleasurable human activity has now been claimed to be bad for you.)

---

[1] The Wertheimer study of sidestream smoke is in fact nonexistent—I made it up to prove to myself that anti-smoking zealots never actually look at any data they didn't make up themselves. In nearly ten years, not *one* has ever caught me at it. Instead, *to a man*, they mumble something about flaws in Wertheimer's critics' methodology. They bullshit, in other words.

Finally, I would like to propose an international telephone number—a sort of People's Mahooha Filter. Remember the old TV game shows with applause-meters, measuring audience reaction by decibels? Let's set up a North American Mahooha Foundation with broad police powers. Each day the foundation will select from the news whatever event, action, verdict or pronouncement is, in the opinion of the trustees, the day's most profoundly stupid. Then the rest of us get to phone in—at our own expense, to keep us honest—and literally give it the Laugh Test.

If enough of us are moved to pay long distance rates to howl with laughter at, say, the woman in Philadelphia who is presently suing the pharmacy that sold her a popular contraceptive jelly, because she ate it on toast but got pregnant anyway (I swear, this is true), she has to shut up and go away. If we all roar at the sight of Pepsi and Coke wasting billions on a perfectly useless advertising-battle, they have to spend the money lowering prices instead. See how it could work?

I realize this system would require at least a couple of constitutional amendments—but wouldn't it be worth it?

A Tale of Two Charlies

FIRST PRINTED APRIL 2001

O N THE FRONT PAGE OF THE *Toronto Globe and Mail*'s April 18, 2001, newspaper, a twenty-two-year-old Chinese student said, "[Americans] have attacked our plane and killed our heroic pilot. All the world has seen this act—it is proof that the USA is an aggressive power." China's official website overflowed with similar loud clucking. Reading it, I couldn't help but think of my colleague Dean Ing's splendid story "Very Proper Charlies" . . .and of Charlie's chickens, the first ones I ever met socially.

I moved to Canada to become a small farmer in Nova Scotia under the tutelage of my college roommate Charlie Daniels (no, not the singer), bringing along my bachelor's degree in English in case the Sears catalog in the outhouse ever ran out. Today Charlie's the chiropractor in Yarmouth, but back then he owned a spread on the Bay of Fundy, with a big garden, a couple of ducks . . . and a coopful of chickens who, between them, could barely muster enough intellectual wattage to make a penlight flicker. I found them outstandingly stupid—and remember, I was born and raised in New York City, where Olympic records in that category have been set. Charlie told me classic dumb-chicken stories: the ones who gaped up at a rainstorm until they all drowned, and so forth. My favorite was the cautionary tale of the breeder who'd finally developed a strain of chicken that would reliably lay at least an egg a day apiece; the only problem was, they were literally too dumb to eat. The extra egg money all went to pay for force-feeding and anorexia counseling.

If you were to test a flock of such chickens, and select the one whose mates call her "Dopey," you'd find even she's too smart to believe a fully-loaded twenty-four-passenger propellor-driven aircraft can possibly, conceivably, under any set of circumstances even a TV writer could dream up, sideswipe and destroy a one-man fighter jet flying at a safe distance. You simply cannot believe such a preposterous thing and be bright enough to eat. It doesn't pass the laugh test. A pubescent pullet can see that the subsequent reaction of America has not been that of an aggressor seeking war.

Yet a large fraction of the human race is apparently either that stupid . . . or willing to publicly pretend they are, if that will furnish a flimsy excuse to vent rage at the capitalist barbarians who supply their Nikes, Cokes and Big Macs. Many members of the oldest and greatest civilization on this planet today seem to need a scapegoat for their own frustrations so badly they'll publicly declare black is white, if that's what it takes to pick a quarrel. The student quoted above knows perfectly well the world saw nothing and knows he's heard testimony from only one of the twenty-five surviving witnesses: the officer whose clear failure to control his notorious hotdog pilot Wen Wei allowed this mess to happen.

Believing or purporting to believe that disgraced officers's absurd self-serving account is one of the dumbest things the usually-wise Chinese people have done so far in this millennium. I believe it derives directly from the dumbest thing they did in the last one: forcibly limiting their birthrate while utterly ignoring the huge cultural preference for boy babies. As anyone could have predicted, by now this has generated an enormous cadre of combat-age males for whom there are no mates. That's a recipe for war: the only motivations for it that make any sense to me at all are stupidity or aggressive intent.

Anyone capable of believing the Chinese government's version of the F-8/EP-3 collision is, I submit, dumber than most chickens. And any leader who thinks inciting a few billion chickens to anger with lies is a safe or sane—much less ethical—course of action is even dumber. Start a stampede in a flock that size and the entire coop will be torn up when and if the dust ever settles.

Which brings me to Dean Ing—once a science fiction writer like me, latterly the author of bestselling high-tech thrillers. Dean's a results-oriented man. Back around 1965, for example, he built himself a car, for fun. You can't buy one as good today; nobody can. With a standard VW engine, the original Magnum got over fifty mpg on the highway, did fifty-five mph in first gear and featured extras like roll-cage, crash harness good to seventy gees and energy absorbing bumpers; Dean persuaded Traveler's Insurance to give him a special rate by crashing it into a wall at thirty mph a few times for them. He's improved it a lot, since.

I haven't re-read Dean's classic near-future tale "Very Proper Charlies" in twenty years, but I've never forgotten its magnificent premise. The leaders of the media finally agree worldwide terrorism has become such a serious threat to civilization itself that extraordinary measures to stop it are required. Better, they all figure out at long last that terrorism requires them, the news media—that it cannot work without their cooperation. So they decide not to play.

It's quietly agreed that henceforth, terrorist violence will still be given major coverage as before...but the spin of that coverage will now be to induce laughter. Terrorists will always be depicted as proper Charlies: bumbling incompetents, jargon-spouting nitwits, psychotic illiterates, scruffy unlaid losers barely competent to light the fuse and retire in correct sequence. Camera angles will always be unflattering; bios will highlight the terrorists' most humiliating past fiascos—they'll basically be treated the way Bill Clinton was, in other words.

The beauty of it is, all Dean's journalists actually do is tell the unvarnished truth for once: describe stupid people as stupid people. Vividly. Dean believed that since the media usually slant the story anyway, maybe we have a duty to do so ethically and not let ourselves be hijacked and coopted by would-be social hackers. C.S. Lewis said, "The Devil cannot abide being mocked." Maybe we can best fight suicidal folly by mocking it.

If you haven't noticed, I've been trying it for the last thousand words.

And Now the News . . .

FIRST PRINTED AUGUST 1996

I N THE EARLY FIFTIES, the great sf writer Theodore Sturgeon wrote to his friend Robert Heinlein that he was both broke and blocked; he literally could not think of a story to save his life. Robert's reply was typical of him: a cheque . . . and several pages of story ideas. All of them made money for Ted—but one in particular inspired a very prescient and powerful story.

Heinlein had said, "Write about the neurosis that derives from wallowing daily in the troubles of several billion strangers you can't help . . . ."

From this seed, Sturgeon created "And Now The News—" (available in several collections and anthologies). His protagonist is a simple, good man with an obsessive addiction to the news—he takes every paper sold, subscribes to current affairs magazines, keeps news on the radio and TV at all times. When asked why, he quotes John Donne: "Every man's death diminishes me/for I am part of mankind." Over time, his obsession deepens; he makes a desperate attempt to go cold turkey . . . and events ensue so astonishing I honestly don't think it'll spoil the story for you if I give away the kicker here: In the end, the guy tells his shrink he's finally found a viable solution to his problem: he's going to go out there and diminish mankind right back. The last line is, "He got twelve people before they cut him down."

This was forty years before the Unabomber.

If Earth is one big starship, the news media constitute its intercom. And almost nothing comes over the intercom but damage reports. Tragedies way over on the other side of the vessel, malfunctions in inaccessible compartments, tales of distant madness and mutiny, conflicting rumors of collision hazards in our path . . . and constant reminders that, first, our acceleration is increasing beyond design expectations, and second, there is no Captain, and the wheel is being fought over by vicious ignoramuses. Is it any wonder morale is so rotten on this starship?

Pessimism has become the very hallmark of sophistication. Only a dullard would go see a movie known to have a happy ending these days. Every Hollywood sci fi future is either a nightmare . . . or dismissed as a fairy tale.

We, the richest and luckiest humans who ever got to gripe for seventy or eighty years, are coming to subconsciously expect—in some perverse way, to crave—the imminent End of All Things. And so we find ourselves obsessed with damage reports, like a man staring in fascination at the slow progression of gangrene up his leg.

No rational person can blame the media for this: we demand it of them. We won't pay for good news. We insist on knowing the worst, even when we're helpless to do anything about it. God knows why. Attempts have been made to establish cheerful media, which would scour the planet to tell you everything that went right today, every averted tragedy, miraculous serendipity or realized dream that might give you hope, lighten your load…and they all went belly-up. There is no media conspiracy to depress people. But there is a media conspiracy to feed ourselves and our families, and that means we must sell you what you want to buy.

I don't propose that the media lie or suppress facts or strain for Panglossian slants—but if we're going to convey the truth and nothing but the truth, we ought to shoot for the whole truth. Every news outlet needs a regular feature, given equal weight with the day's lead story, titled, "Silver Lining." The massive resources of the newsgathering industry could—and should, as both public- and self-service—manage to come up with one story a day that made us feel a little less like diminishing mankind right back. And it wouldn't hurt to quadruple the comics section, while we're at it.

I've experienced five decades. With all its plagues, wars, disasters and injustices, the one just past (in which computers got friendly, the Berlin Wall came down, the Soviet Union peacefully folded its cards, nuclear apocalypse receded for the first time in my life, smallpox was annihilated, Mr. Mandela walked free, perfect music reproduction became trivially cheap, Geraldo's nose was broken on camera and the Beatles put out two new singles) has been hands down the best. Yet it was back in 1965-75, a decade when just about everything that could possibly go wrong did, that a significant fraction of us last seemed to believe we could change the world.

Hope—belief in the possibility of beneficial change—is a scarce and precious resource and has been throughout history; every society that ever ran out of it died. Our hope is battered daily by the barrage of bad news and by the defeatist attitude it engenders: the cynical compulsion to deconstruct every comforting myth, to find (or if necessary invent) feet of clay for every hero, to explain away every hopeful event as a cursing in disguise.

Granted, we can't hide our heads in the sand. It is my obligation as a crewman of Starship Earth to listen to the intercom regularly. But it's also my obligation to turn the damn thing off when it starts to impair my morale. That means triaging my newspaper, removing CNN and Newsworld from my remote-menu and zapping the network news fungus whenever it appears. (You'd be surprised how little you miss that way: after a dogged, relentless effort to ignore the OJ Simpson story, I find I still know far more about it than the jury was allowed to.) It's possible to have too much information to do your job.

Fear is a subtle and potent drug, and it has its uses. Daily news is civilized man's analog for the exhilaration of facing the sabertooth: a daily hit of bracing fear. But dosage is crucial: at high concentrations (particularly if mainlined: taken by television), evil side effects start to set in. You cannot kill the sabertooth. There is nothing one can do about any of the horrors in the news (purely local bunfights excepted), except fret... and at some point panic, yield to despair. And when there are enough panicked, despairing people on the starship, the Crazy Years come.

Time we all turned to the funny pages. It's important to remember something else Robert Heinlein once said: "The last thing to come out of Pandora's Box was Hope."

Substance Abuse

Bean Counting

FIRST PRINTED JULY 2000

S TEP RIGHT UP—I'm going to make you rich!

Or at least offer you the opportunity to make yourself rich, and maybe part of the Third World as well—and I mean rich enough to influence the planetary economy, change the destiny of nations and seriously impress Bill Gates. I've been granted one of those sudden flashes of stupendous insight that used to hit Nikola Tesla[1] like a meat hammer between the eyes at regular intervals...and I'm going to give it to *you*! And all I want in return, for my commission, is enough cash to buy back the Northern Songs catalogue from that treacherous (but probably *not* pedophilic) little rat-bastard Michael Jackson as a birthday present for Sir Paul McCartney.

I'm not saying it'll be a cakewalk. Some trivial developmental work still needs to be done, I admit, before you can start soliciting investors and planning your IPO. Minor engineering details, really—I'd take care of it myself if I weren't so busy just now. But basically the plan is sound, and most of the really hard work has already been done since World War II.

Want to hear about it?

A brief preliminary lecture is necessary, and forgive me if I go on a bit, because—now that I've quit tobacco for good—I'm speaking here of my number one all-time favorite legal drug. A jones I share with billions of hu-

---

[1] Inventor of the kind of electricity we actually use.

mans—and nearly all writers. I'm using it as I type this... and almost wish, as I have almost wished for twenty-seven years, that I had some sort of IV setup to drip it directly into my veins and spare me full use of my hands. (But I don't *really* wish that... because, as with most addictions, the ingestion ritual is more than half the fun. That's exactly why my idea is worth gigabucks.)

Perhaps you use the stuff yourself: coffee, it's generally called. We junkies refer to it as "black gold," "java," "jamoke," "joe" or "that which makes life endurable." I once had to quit a perfectly good spiritual commune because I was unable to persuade my fellow hippies that coffee is in fact Far Out. Keep your *kensho* and leave me my Kenya AA!

Okay, I'll stop rhapsodizing. I forgot: you're waiting to get rich.

All coffee trees belong to the genus *coffea*. There are many species of *coffea*, but most authorities will assure you there are only two of any significance: *coffea arabica* and *coffea canephora*.

Both, unfortunately, are a real bitch to grow.

Arabica yields by far the best-tasting coffee... and is one of the most feeble, finicky crops on earth. It wants steep slopes at least one or two thousand meters above sea level and no more than twenty-five degrees north or thirty degrees south of the Equator, with plenty of rainfall (though not enough to wash it away), but lots of sunshine too. As if that weren't enough, the damn plant is susceptible to about a zillion parasites, diseases and blights. But it produces superb cherries: small, and with a distinctly pleasant aroma even before they're dried and roasted. But "small" is the point to remember.

Canephora, commonly called "Robusta," is, as that name implies, hardy... but only in comparison to Arabica. You can get it to grow below a thousand meters—in rare cases, even at sea level—but it's still finicky, and vulnerable to all sorts of things. And its beans are far less valuable: suffice it to say they use Robusta to make—shudder!—instant coffee. (Or to mix Arabica with, for a cheapo blend.) About a decade ago a coffee-grower in Queensland, Australia, explained to me why this is so.

Gebhardt Keyserlingck is an infuriating genius who lives in a castle he built for himself and his family in the bush just outside of Daintree in northern Queensland. He's a genius because he somehow managed to raise a couple of acres of Arabica coffee trees there, at sea level, on a gentle slope—which any expert will tell you is quite impossible. Some of the best coffee I ever tasted, too. The infuriating part is that he refuses, for philosophical reasons I just don't grok, to ship so much as a bean of it to anywhere, at any price: if you want Geb's coffee you must go to Daintree and buy it from him. I haven't had a sip in ten years, damn it!

Anyway, he keeps a couple of Robusta trees to help him lecture tourists, and once he showed me Arabica and Robusta cherries side by side I understood why they use the latter for instant (and for even lesser uses like "coffee" flavoring for ice cream, etc.). The Robusta coffee cherry is *huge*. The ones I saw ranged from grape to walnut size. Dried down to beans, they'd be at least twice as big as the coffee beans you're used to seeing.

Perhaps you grasp the problem. When you roast a Robusta bean, *by the time the inside is done, the outside is burnt.* It just plain *has* to produce a coffee that's inferior in taste and aftertaste.

That's why almost nobody ever even *talks* about the *third* most common species of coffee: *coffea liverica*, or Liberian. Its cherry is even bigger than Robusta's.

A shame…because Liberian coffee will grow just about anywhere it's warm, at any altitude, under any conditions, despite drought or neglect.

In fact, it more or less insists on doing so. In Liberia (after which it's named), for instance, it's considered a damn nuisance, a weed to be fought, about as popular as kudzu is in the southern US. Liberian coffee grows wild in many countries—on the Ivory Coast, throughout Equatorial Africa, in Cameroon—and these happen to be some of the very poorest places on this planet.

Think how wonderful it would be if you could somehow make *coffea liverica* commercially worthwhile. Coffee's one of the biggest, most lucrative legal industries there is. It's presently owned by a few incredibly rich men who seized control of it from the starving peasants who actually grew the stuff *long* before modern education and communications technology gave said peasants even a hope of negotiating on a level playing field. If Liberian coffee suddenly became valuable tomorrow, perhaps the Liberian growers would be more sophisticated than was poor old Juan Valdez—enough to retain a measure of control, this time.

Ah, but the damn Liberica bean is even worse than Robusta—just *way* too big for conventional roasting methods. Roast the outside properly: the inside is underdone. Roast until the inside's done: the outside's burnt. Try and compromise: get a cup of mud.…

I see that this is running long—and worse, I'm out of coffee. So on reflection, I think I'm going to just give you a single word, and then leave the rest as an exercise for the student. I realize this one word is not by itself the full answer, that it raises almost as many problems as it solves. But I believe those problems are all quite soluble, if you imagine my scheme *in combination with* conventional methods. And I do think this one word should be sufficient to show you where I'm going, point you in the right direction. If you can't take it from there yourself…well, maybe you don't really *deserve* to be one of the wealthiest people on the planet.

Reflections of a Recovering Nicotinic

FIRST PRINTED JULY 2000

MY NAME IS SPIDER, and I'm a nicotinic. It's been one year since my last drag. Thank you.

I once went eighteen months without buying a pack. But I cheated often. I've quit smoking dozens of times in forty years... and whatever the duration, I always cheated, at least occasionally.

I haven't had a single puff since Quit Day. Not one. On New Year's Eve, I wandered into a restaurant washroom and saw a full pack of my old brand abandoned on the sink. Not a soul present. I did what I'd come to do and got out, without a second glance.

Twain said, "Quitting smoking is easy. I've done it hundreds of times." But this time is different, for me. This time I believe it's going to take. (Knock wood.) I'll always be a nicotinic, the way an alcoholic will always be an alcoholic... but this time I think I'm going to get over and forever remain an addict who doesn't use anymore. It's *so* hard to get that tiger to sleep, I don't want to risk waking him again.

The thing is, I never was that smart before.

Why this time, then? One obvious answer is increasingly strident medical advice. But I had serious lung trouble much of my adult life, and it wasn't enough to break my addiction. Neither was the surgery that finally corrected matters... even though it's reputedly one of the most painful procedures a patient is apt to survive.

Sudden late-life onset of character is another possible explanation, I suppose. But I doubt it.

I assign the credit to bupropion, marketed in Canada as Zyban and in America as Welbutrin. Originally developed as an antidepressant, it had problems in that regard, and its makers were about to scrap it when they discovered that it seemed to help smokers kick. I've tried several vaunted stop-smoking programs, hypnosis, acupuncture, vitamin megadose, gum and many other methods. Zyban did it for me.

I began taking it with almost zero faith in it. I'd been on two other antidepressants, years earlier, and they'd done nothing to alleviate nicotine craving. Quite the reverse: they'd brought me back from a place where I was so despairing I couldn't even be bothered to smoke. Also, both had undesirable "side effects."

Zyban had no perceptible effects whatsoever. No ringing in the ears, no dry mouth, no funny smell in the urine, no dullness of affect, no erectile difficulty, no metallic taste—nothing. But I had a much easier time kicking tobacco than ever before. And even since weaning myself from the Zyban, I've had far fewer and milder cravings than usual.

Your mileage may vary. Two of my best friends, also longtime recidivists, quit the same week I did, using the same drug. One's still clean . . . the other says he's just about ready to try again. Also, I'd be a lot happier if the makers of the miracle drug had even a vague theory as to how it works—they still don't. But I offer my experience for whatever help it may be, to you or a loved one.

So what's it like to be tobacco-free for a year?

Downside first. To my surprise, my nose has not gotten even slightly better at detecting pleasant smells . . . but it *is* doing a *vastly* better job of acquainting me with unpleasant ones. I can barely stand the smell of my own body and excrement, now, let alone the many stinks of the world. (Irony: My first novel featured a mad scientist who enhanced everyone's sense of smell until technological civilization collapsed.) The improved sense of taste I'd expected from previous quittings has likewise failed to materialize this time: food tastes no better than usual. Sigh. Yet I've somehow managed to gain the usual twenty-five pounds. Requiring the usual total-wardrobe-replacement. If I have any more wind than last year, I don't notice it.

Upside: My chest never hurts anymore. My mouth never tastes like an ashtray. I never run out of smokes . . . or even pat my pockets to check. I'm saving money. I'll live longer, unless I don't. The federal and provincial governments have lost roughly twenty-five opportunities a day to rob me at gunpoint. Air travel is now an almost endurable torture. And the cataclysmic post-quitting clinical depression that antismokers never warn you about has, for once, failed to arrive. Is that because I began with an antidepressant this time? Perhaps in another twenty-five years the Guesswork-in-a-White-Coat that calls itself modern medicine will have an answer.

Best of all, I'm now more certain than ever of my motives in believing most antismoker zealots to be fascists. I quit in spite of them, not because of them. More than ever I despise their outrageous lies about the "deadly dangers of sidestream smoke"—and the venal weasels in government who, with their encouragement, have publicly gang-raped a legal industry, relentlessly mugged and insulted one out of every five Canadians and paved the way for endless further curtailments of liberty—and the medical establishment which has evinced *zero* interest in making cigarettes safer, preferring to punish the addicted. I no longer suffer personally at the hands of health Nazis, but I still want them horsewhipped out of polite society—quickly, before they do any more damage.

And they've done far more than poor old Joe Camel ever did. Ever since we foolishly began empowering them ten or fifteen years ago, the rate of teenage smoking has relentlessly climbed, year after year. Everything they've tried having failed, they now propose to do it harder. Here's how clueless they are: they actually believe kids will be *repelled* by huge gross color photos of diseased lungs on cigarette packs! Or they claim to. Perhaps they're just trying to assure themselves lifetime occupation, berating and bullying yet another generation.

If they had anything approaching a conscience, they'd recall the advice of Aesculapius to the would-be do-gooder—"First, do no harm"—and would (finally) shut the hell up. But I'm not holding my breath. . . .

Mugging the Poor for Their Own Good

FIRST PRINTED AUGUST 2000

'D HOPED THAT BY QUITTING TOBACCO I might eventually be able to quit the anger that comes with the territory these days. Perhaps, I thought, all I had to do was foreswear heresy and the ongoing Inquisition would come to seem less odious. It hasn't worked out that way.

Nicotine-free for over a year, I still feel my blood simmer when I read, in the *Globe and Mail*, of the World Health Organization's new report urging every government on earth to massively increase tobacco taxation—to promote public health. This august body of humanitarians purports to believe "millions of lives could be saved" in the Third World by reducing poor people's excess liquidity with a simple cashectomy: picking their pockets for their own benefit. I don't think anyone bright enough to blink could possibly really believe that. Yet the report was delivered in a public place with a straight face. Imbecility seems far too kind an explanation; I think we have to go with insensate greed and/or monstrous hypocrisy.

The study was co-sponsored by the WHO and ... the World Bank, that famed champion of the world's poor. It was fed to the media at some assemblage of health-bullies and other busybodies calling itself the "World Conference on Tobacco"—in Chicago, where the international airport does not even permit smoking *outdoors* anymore. "By 2030," the report alleges, "some seventy percent of tobacco deaths will be in low-income and middle-income countries. And in rich countries, smoking is increasingly concentrated among the poor and is responsible for much of their ill health and premature mortality." Gosh, isn't it good to know that someone in an expensive suit is looking out for all those poor peasants and fishermen, willing to take the time to protect them all from their own needs and choices?

How could these do-gooders help it, though? The logic is utterly compelling. Tobacco may be legal, but it is evil ... because it's addictive. Its users are helpless slaves, powerless even to moderate their intake. But—follow closely, here—we're pretty sure they'll *learn* to control this uncontrollable addiction, somehow, if you'll just let us raise the obscenely high taxes on it even higher. And keep the money. For research.

We all know every time a drug bust temporarily raises the street price of heroin, poor people stop using it. Right? They'll often turn down an offer to take part in a major felony, specifically because they fear it might bring them so much money they'd be able to afford drugs.

Perhaps you've never been a smoker and can't fathom why people would endure so much public abuse and expense to smoke something that doesn't even get them high. Let me try to explain, and maybe you'll see why the WHO/WB report is so wicked.

Tobacco's secret, magic gift is solace. Simple solace. Smoking doesn't make you feel GOOD, exactly; there's rarely any real pleasure in it. What it does is make you feel just a little *better*. Not quite as bad as a moment ago. Reliably, 100 percent of the time, twenty to sixty times a day, you can light up a cigarette and maybe your problems and sorrows will all remain, but at least you've scratched that one urgent itch for the next few minutes. You've taken action and bettered your lot, however briefly or illusorily.

You can't eat twenty to sixty meals a day, or even snacks, without becoming a blimp. You can't have sex that often without dying, not at my age anyway. You can't knock back beer in anything like that quantity and hope to have a sex life... or a job. If you smoke crack sixty times a day, you'll be dead soon and useless until then. But tobacco takes decades to kill, doesn't inhibit competence... and *always* does the trick: makes its user feel just a little less lousy than the moment before.

O World Bank and World Health Organization—ye patricians in grey suits and UN politicians in phony white medical coats—here's a news flash for you: *the poor have the greatest need for that kind of solace.* They have damn little else. You make your living on their backs: you cannot persuade me you honestly believe raising the cost of that pitiful solace will brighten or lengthen their lives. You cannot convince me 42 million poor people will quit smoking, abandon the only comfort you have left them, if you raise the price by ten cents a pack. I resent the implication that I look that gullible.

I think some folks behind that report realize perfectly well that raising tobacco taxes even higher will accomplish exactly what it *always* has: massive widespread smuggling. I suspect they've concluded there's serious money to be made by adding yet another front to the perpetually lucrative Worldwide War on Drugs—that far too much tobacco money is going to the people who merely cultivate, grow, harvest, cure, purify, blend, roll, filter, package, distribute and advertise the stuff—that every new black market is a bonanza for old white people and the young lawyers and cops who work for them.

I'm certain they know nothing about how to discourage kids from taking up smoking: the more money we let them extort for that purpose, the more teens light up, year after year. They know nothing about how to help an adult quit smoking—any progress in that field has come from pharmaceutical companies, by accident. And they demonstrably have less than zero interest in the one thing that a fifth of the world's population (the people they claim to represent) earnestly want and desperately need: safe cigarettes. A better nicotine delivery system. Solace that doesn't kill, even over decades, doesn't require a life of crime to afford and doesn't create a criminal subculture to seduce and destroy their children.

As songwriter Randy Newman had the poor cry to Heaven, "Oh Lord, if you can't help us, won't you please, please, let us be?"

Big Nanny's New Clothes

FIRST PRINTED MARCH 1998

WHAT COULD BE MORE SATISFYING than the sight of the forces of righteousness and rectitude scurrying about like doomed rats, fleeing a lethal flood of escaped facts, frantically trying to slap together a levee of lies to protect their position as the Good Guys of Fascism? Can there be a sight funnier than an expert hemorrhaging credibility the way the *Hindenburg* leaked hydrogen, while stoutly denying he has a problem? Gasbags everywhere are presently in the process of deflation—and just try and find one with the intellectual honesty to admit it.

On March 9, 1998, the *Vancouver Sun* ran a small story on the leaking of a major new study by the World Health Organization. The seven-country study, run by two of the most respected scientists on the planet, and "one of the largest ever to look at the link between passive smoking...and lung cancer," clearly and unmistakably shows (like the majority of such studies) that so-called secondhand tobacco smoke *does not* cause lung cancer. In fact, it seems to have a slight *protective* effect. Understandably, the WHO, which has spent years and megabucks on anti-tobacco campaigns, decided to suppress these results and tried to limit publication to a single report in an unnamed scientific journal. But someone, apparently afflicted with a sense of personal honour, let the cat out of the bag.

Next day, the *Sun* ran a follow-up—on the *second* section's front page, but *above* the fold—in which representatives of Big Nanny (as I call the worldwide conspiracy to Do Good At Gunpoint) counterattacked. The study was "misleading." And had been "leaked by agents of the tobacco industry." And contradicted "a mountain of evidence" to the contrary.

Particularly incensed, a fellow identified as a "Vancouver-Richmond Health Board associate medical health officer" told the *Sun*, "The connection between second-hand smoke and lung cancer is well documented by everyone from Health Canada to the US Environmental Protection Agency to the WHO itself...." He conceded that "a small number of studies came to no conclusion...but that's quite different from suggesting they proved there is no connection."

This chap may be competent, and he may be truthful—but in this instance it's hard to see how he could be both. If he has even casually examined the subject, he knows perfectly well that the US Environmental Protection Agency *has never conducted a single study of second-hand smoke*. In arriving at its 1993 assertion that second-hand smoke causes "3,000 lung cancer deaths per year" in America, the EPA relied, instead, on thirty existing independent studies—*none* of them funded by the tobacco industry. *Twenty-four of those studies found no statistically significant connection between second-hand smoke and illness*, but the EPA chose to ignore those and *add together the conclusions* of the six studies that did. Of those, the *worst* purported to show that constant exposure to second-hand smoke posed a danger approximately equal to that of drinking two glasses of milk a day, and slightly less than the danger of living in an industrialized society.

This is the "mountain" of evidence the new WHO study contradicts. The new study is "misleading" only if you were determined to lead people into ignorance for their own good. And it was "leaked by the tobacco industry" only if you are capable of making yourself believe the World Health Organization is riddled with tobacco-company moles. Big Nanny could not possibly say such things with a straight face... *unless* she were emotionally committed to the position that she intuitively knows what is best for other, sillier people, and inconvenient facts be damned.

The truth is out, friends. The self-righteous swine who have persuaded you to gang up on a quarter of your fellow citizens have just lost their *only* valid argument. If you are enjoying the discomfiture of millions of addicts forced into constant withdrawal too much to stop now, by all means continue to harass them. But you can no longer even pretend you are doing so in self-defense. Have the decency in future to admit that you are doing it for the same reason our ancestors robbed and murdered Native peoples, the same reason we hound pot smokers and heroin users alike into lives of crime, the same reason the *only* thing anyone has ever gotten all the organized religions to agree on is the demonization of homosexuals—because it is primevally satisfying to attack a minority. Let's face it: witch-hunts are *fun*.

But you might want to bear in mind that every time society agrees to legitimize a lynch-mob, it endangers itself. The disgusting weapons you've agreed to permit the anti-tobacco forces to employ cannot be reclaimed and put back in the armory after the pogrom is over. If governments and packs of lawyers can bully and rob one cartel, they can bully and rob any cartel. When the same noble thugs and vultures currently circling over the tobacco industry have finished picking its bones and turned their attention to *other* "morally questionable" industries (alcohol, coffee, chocolate and refined sugar spring immediately to mind, along with certain segments of the music business), you may regret having given them carte blanche to run other peoples' lives for their own good, because once given it cannot be recalled.

The same week the new WHO report hit the fan, the forces of Big Nanny issued a public invitation to get in line for the gang-bang—excuse me, the class-action suit—they have planned for the tobacco industry, and helpfully supplied a phone number you can call if you have ever been in the same room with a smoker and would like some free money. I can only hope you agree with me that, like a tired old hooker in the harsh light of morning, Big Nanny was a lot more seductive with her clothes on. Naked, stripped of her best lie, she is a pretty ugly sight.

Terminal Improvement

FIRST PRINTED MARCH 1997

WHAT'S THE ONLY THING a newspaper columnist wants *more* than a week in Key West in March? A legitimate excuse to mention it in his next column. Add an opportunity to ride one of his favorite hobby-horses, and you have a happy man.

Back in 1997—back when I was a smoker—I was that fortunate fellow. And I felt like it...until I boarded the aircraft.

Oh, I knew I had a long ride without a cigarette ahead. But as I sat there in the Benson & Hedges Smoker's Lounge in the new Vancouver Airport, gulping my last puffs, I reflected that at least the journey was not non-stop: there'd be an opportunity to stoke my nicotine reserves back up again during the change-over in Chicago, and that would get me through the long second leg.

You know where the Smoker's Lounge was back then in O'Hare Airport? It was called the parking lot. As far as possible from where long-distance fliers change planes: two full concourses away. There is no provision for smokers anywhere in that vast complex. (This, of course, was before they banned smoking even *outside* the airport.) The last time I had passed through O'Hare, smoking was permitted in the bars. But the bars were apparently getting packed full of smokers who ordered nothing...so they made the whole airport nonsmoking. All the smokers (who happen to have sufficient time) got the healthy exercise of a trek the entire length of the airport, twice, with a wasted security check on the way back in.

My luck was good: I was *just* able to sprint all the way to the free world, suck down a lungful of solace and race all the way back before my flight lifted. And indeed the run seemed to have done me good; I noticed how pale and wan my spouse looked by comparison. I steeled myself for the long flight to come, anticipating the classic symptoms of nicotine withdrawal plus jet-lag: excitability, hyperirritability, racing thoughts, etc.

To my surprise, I deplaned in the same condition as my nonsmoking beloved: apathetic, thick-witted and headachey. A quick smoke in the parking lot was no help; neither was a good sleep. It was at least two days before

I felt "right" again. Ah, well, I thought, getting old. You're in Florida in March; quit complaining.

We had a lovely time in Key West. And then we headed home.

I knew the first leg would be the longest, going back, but didn't mind. I was utterly content after a blissful vacation. Besides, the layover in O'Hare this time—five hours!—would be more than adequate for as many smoking hikes as I wanted.

Our vacation bliss was gone when we reached O'Hare. Headache, fatigue, mental torpor. My wife and I sat by what would eventually be our gate and read. Newspapers. Only twice could I work up the energy to make the half-mile trek for a smoke—on arrival, and just before re-boarding. By that point I was so groggy I was having trouble spotting the logical fallacies in *USA Today* editorials. And it was on that final smoke-break that I met the two flight attendants.

They emerged from the terminal to find themselves—like everyone who left a terminal those days—in a dense cloud of smoke from the dozen or so of us clustered around the ashtray just outside the door, mixed with the exhaust of a hundred taxis and buses. They both smiled, and they both took in deep breaths of blue-grey air, and they chorused, "Thank God—fresh air again!"

Of course I took this for sarcasm. But one of them saw my face and said, "No, really. Compared to what we've been breathing for the last eight hours, this is fresh air." I lifted an eyebrow, and she and her friend explained. And things began to click into place.

Remember back when the anti-smokers first demanded every flight be smoke-free? Ever wonder, as I did, why every single airline caved in without a whimper, risked offending up to forty-five percent of their customers and degrading pilot performance? They did so *because it allowed them to cut back inboard air circulation by over fifty percent, saving them a medium-sized fortune in jet fuel.* Why circulate the air if the customer can't *see* it, and smell it?

Result: every passenger—and crew member—of every flight now spends the entire journey in a poorly-ventilated Petri dish of shared viruses and bacteria. And deplanes, quite often, with symptoms resembling those of CO_2 poisoning. The flight attendants have noticed this, and many of them are mad as hell and have formally complained to their union, which is agitating to have the airflow turned back up again, and have you heard a lot about that on *your* eleven o' clock news? I haven't. "And it's even worse in the terminals, now," my informant said, "but of course there's probably nothing we can do about that...."

Several years ago I was invited aboard the nuclear submarine *USS John*

C. *Calhoun*, and was shown everything except the reactor room and the upper third of the Trident missiles. A fascinating day. Finally my host pointed to a massive device that looked like God's boiler. "That's my station," he said, "the carbon monoxide scrubber." Like an idiot, I said, "You mean carbon *di*-oxide scrubber." He smiled forgivingly. "There are two of those, much bigger than this little thing." I suddenly recalled that I had seen sailors smoking all over the boat. "You mean they installed a monster unit like this just so the men can smoke?" I asked. "God, no," he said. "Cigarettes are no problem at all—if your air circulation isn't good enough to deal with cigarette smoke without help, it just isn't good enough, period. Most of the CO we scrub is transistor-exhaust: over a year or so, it builds up."

We civilian passengers, and the professionals who fly us around, receive much less concern for our welfare. A large fraction of us are in drug withdrawal, and the rest are poisoning themselves—and us—to keep us there, all in the name of public health.

Where There's No Smoke...

FIRST PRINTED AUGUST 1996

A LOT OF ESSAYS COULD BE WRITTEN dissecting the current plague of antismoking hysteria, but this is not one of them. This one is an attempt to make the whole problem go away.

Purely for purposes of (postponing) argument, let us stipulate that second-hand tobacco smoke in the restaurant or workplace actually represents a health threat which ought to be considered significant by any rational being who operated an internal combustion engine to get there. My question is, why are we all arguing about second-hand smoke...when there is no need to have any?

I own an ingenious device called a SmokeTrapper. It is distinctly different from any other "smokeless ashtray" sold. This is the difference: it works.

Where can you buy this wondrous gizmo?

Well, you can't. Not anywhere. Apparently the mighty North American industrial plant was unable to produce the parts at competitive rates, so SmokeTrapper got theirs from Japan. There was a little wobble in the dollar/yen exchange rate a few years back—and the firm went navel-uppermost, just as their moment in history was arriving.

Every other such device currently on the market fails on the same fundamental principle: they all try to suck smoke down through a filter underneath the ashtray. This results in a widget that looks much like a standard ashtray—and is about as useful. Smoke doesn't want to *go* down. Some genius finally noted this—and designed a widget that sucks smoke *up* through a filter. His or her concept looks very little like an ashtray.

But the Centers for Disease Control states that it removes over ninety-three percent of the total smoke from each cigarette.

What does this complex high-tech wonder consist of? Start with a ceramic cup, with a notch in its top edge. Roll a sheet of stainless steel into a cylinder, cut a square port low in one side and fit the cylinder snugly over the cup, so that the notch shows through the port. Plug the upper end of the cylinder with a plastic housing containing a removable filter-puck, a standard computer fan, two C batteries (with optional AC input) and an off-on switch. Fit burning cigarette into notch, throw switch: no smoke. Total size: equivalent to a Big Gulp. Weight: about the same as a portable CD player. Noise: quieter than your computer. Smell: zero, if you change filters regularly.

Before I quit, I used mine while doing public readings and signings, during panels at conventions, performing in coffeehouses, visiting the homes of friends who are genuinely allergic—and never received a single complaint. Most often, nobody noticed unless I drew attention to it. I used another in my bedroom, the cigar version: a broad flat base with a slot to hold a cigar instead of a cup with a notch. (As a fringe benefit, since there's no point in using it unless you keep the cigarette resting in the slot between puffs, you can't fall asleep with a cigarette in your hand.)

I called the company when they went broke and bought up all the filters they had left in stock—but by the end I was reduced to cracking open old ones and recharging them with aquarium charcoal. The representative I spoke with said the defunct company would be overjoyed to peddle their patents (US Patents 4043776-239540) for just about any reasonable offer. But they had no way to underwrite a search for more venture capital; it never happened.

I've been trying ever since to publicize the idea. A number of years ago, for instance, when Vancouver was debating its resolution to totally ban smoking in all public places (my, has that been a godsend to the restaurant industry just outside of town!), I called up the reporter who was covering the resulting bun-fight for one of our local dailies and suggested there was no reason for it. This was an intelligent and ethical man, a nonsmoker who nonetheless seemed to feel uneasy at seeing a large fraction of his fellow citizens harassed and demonized and his city's restaurant trade damaged. When I described the SmokeTrapper, he became very excited, and promised to arrive the next day with a photographer.

He called back two hours later. His editor had killed the story. "He said it would constitute advertising."

"For whom?" I screamed.

"Well, I asked that, too," he admitted—and then changed the subject. He hung up quickly, clearly embarrassed and ill at ease.

Fanatic anti-smoker editor? Possibly. But perhaps that editor simply saw no advantage to his paper in preventing a good bun-fight.

My modest proposal is this: why don't we set up a crown corporation to buy up the SmokeTrapper patents and produce the little dinguses by the millions? Every restaurant, office building, airport and hospital in the land needs at least three dozen, right now. Every smoker needs at least a couple. I was overjoyed to pay about $60 apiece for mine, some years ago—and I believe a responsibly-run firm could make us all a huge profit selling them much cheaper than that today. (The price of computer fans has come down, for one thing.) There's even more money in the filters, in the long run: believe me, it's tedious rolling your own. The market is planetary.

Let us fill the land with SmokeTrapper clones. Take the torches away from the mob, and let there be a little peace around this castle again.

Imagination Has Its Downside

FIRST PRINTED JANUARY 1998

R EAL PROBLEMS, you can grapple with. It's imaginary problems that'll give you fits.

A rumor begins that a bank is unsound. The rumor is false: the bank is sound, the problem imaginary. But the bank will close soon anyway. It's impossible to reason with the unreasonable.

Outrage over rumors that some tobacco companies may have experimented with higher nicotine yields is another example. "Those monsters want to make tobacco even more addictive!" What can you possibly say to people who believe tobacco could be more addictive?

Go to the airport departures area: observe us addicts in our pitiful ghetto outside the door. Why are we all puffing so deeply, one cigarette after another? Because we all know the higher the nicotine level in our bloodstreams, *the longer it will be before we feel the craving another cigarette.* Raise the patient's morphine dose, it takes him longer to ring for the next shot. Increase the nicotine content, we'll smoke *less.*

Why would a tobacco company want its customers to smoke less? Perhaps because they're rational. Customers who smoke fewer cigarettes will continue buying them for many more years, remain healthy enough to pay for them and annoy their superstitious nonsmoking neighbors less. Lower the risk (presently one chance in sixteen of death), and more potential customers may choose to take it. If this spoils anyone's image of tobacco executives as mindless monsters, inhuman evil slimeballs, gleeful death-peddlers—good.

The ideal cigarette, for everyone, would be *high* in nicotine, while as low as possible in the *harmful* ingredients: the tars. Sadly, the tobacco companies haven't found a way to make such yet.

Happily, I know a way. Sadly, it'll never happen. It would raise imaginary problems.

Harvard Medical School just released a definitive study of a possible alternative nicotine delivery vehicle. They tracked thousands of subjects, for more than twenty years and conclusively proved this substance is absolutely medically transparent. Smoking fifty cigarettes of it a day for twenty years has *no* significant effect on lung cancer rate, emphysema rate, asthma rate, measured lung function or overall death rate. Sprinkle nicotine on it, and all the smokers could live long happy lives, harming no one. Extremely happy lives, if they like. It's called cannabis.

Even someone determined to believe smoking marijuana is bad for an adult (and these days, you have to be determined enough to ignore nearly *all* the available evidence) must concede that we can grow cannabis with no psychoactive ingredient—hemp clothing is sold everywhere. So why don't we grow a lot more, steep it in nicotine and make safe cigarettes?

Too intelligent. Instead let's lynch a few tobacco executives, and then tell all the dying addicts, "Sorry—we couldn't help you any, but at least we avenged you." We've solved an imaginary problem.

Science in Fishnet Stockings

FIRST PRINTED JULY 1997

J UST BECAUSE A BLOKE in a white coat says it doesn't make it so. An "expert" is just an ordinary person a long way from home.

And these are hard times for many experts. Funding for scientific research is at its lowest level this century (which is to say, ever). At present, if you want to consult an astronomer or a theoretical physicist, your best bet is to call a cab.

So says Dr. Hale, the astronomer of Hale-Bopp (and other) fame. He complains loudly about the huge number of unemployed scientists in North America today. Even he, with all his accomplishments, has been unable to secure steady employment or ongoing funding. He claims we misled an entire generation of students into believing there were careers in science waiting for them after graduation...and now many are waiting tables or pushing brooms.

I asked two scientist friends if their experience in Canada bore out Hale's charge. "God yes!" Guy Immega, the roboticist, exclaimed. "Every time I advertise an entry-level position with my company, two dozen Ph.D.'s apply, all hungry." "Are you crazy?" said Ray Maxwell, the mechanical engineer. "The outfit I work for is *desperate* for qualified professionals; we'd settle for bright grad students." Clearly much depends on what *sort* of scientist you're talking about. But Guy and Ray agreed that Hale was right in essence: that overall, there are probably more unemployed scientists in Canada today than there were scientists in all the world a century ago—and that the ones who are employed often must work with drastically shrinking budgets.

And there are only so many cabs to be driven.

Most scientists want to be moral, ethical beings. Their trade has *never* been a really good way to get rich. But ethics and morality are for those with full bellies. Throughout history, one consequence has *always* followed economic collapse. When times get *really* hard, it's time to get out the fishnet stockings.

At least, this is the only excuse I can devise for the folks at Scripps

Research Institute in La Jolla, California, Complutense University of Madrid in Spain and the University of Cagliari (I swear) in Italy, who jointly released a shocking report on marijuana last week. At first I thought their findings were being slanted by the media...but close examination shows the media simply printed what they were told, without thinking about it, as usual.

I am *not* discussing the virtues or drawbacks of marijuana here. I am only addressing what we did and did not learn about it from the report in question—because what its authors did is very interesting. We've all seen Street-Hooker Science, in which the scientist simply fakes data supporting whatever predetermined conclusion someone is willing to fund. That is not—quite—what we're dealing with, here. This is more like Call-Girl Science.

Let's start at the beginning. Neuropharmacologists Friedbert Weiss and George Koob (we could almost stop there, but we won't) decided to examine whether marijuana might be addictive, because, they say, they noted that 100,000 people in the US alone seek treatment for marijuana dependence every year.

Stipulating for argument this dubious figure, we're talking about four hundredths of one percent of the population. Now consider that 100,000 in comparison to just the Americans who regularly smoke cannabis—let's accept the lowball estimate of twenty-five percent of the country. Now we find that a whopping sixteen hundredths of one percent of regular users either *feel* they have a problem, or are required (by a judge, lover, parent, employer, etc.) to *say* they do. (A *much* higher percentage of *aspirin* users report real medical problems, such as bleeding.)

Terrified by this pandemic, Weiss and Koob sprang into action...and soon were joined by visiting colleagues from Spain and Italy. Hearken now to just what they did. First, they (well, their graduate students) collected impressive data which *proves*—beyond a shadow of a doubt—that a person who smokes marijuana feels good. That would have been plenty for, say, Pasteur or Koch, but the team pressed on. Next they amassed more data *proving* just as inarguably that a person who's been smoking cannabis regularly for a long time, if forced to stop, will probably feel bad for awhile. Hold on, the best is yet to come: the conclusion. "Therefore," they said, "marijuana is a gateway to heroin."

Aren't you breathless? They didn't fudge a single datum. They simply neglected to do any *quantifying* of the data...for example, by *comparing* the unhappiness they chose to call marijuana "withdrawal" with that experienced by someone who cannot get his morning coffee, nightly Aero bar, hourly cigarette or thrice-daily shot of heroin. Every number in their report, I'll wager, is truthful. It's only in the words, at the end, that mahooha appears—in the implied assertion that the data and the conclusion have anything to do with one another. You tell me: is that more, or less, honest than simply cooking the data would have been?

The other way science can wear fishnet stockings, besides outright lying or card-palming, is by keeping its mouth shut. Any scientist who sees that report knows it's garbage; how many have said so publicly? (Years ago, when it made good anti-tobacco ammunition, several scientists gleefully proved that a cigarette smoker who switches to a brand with lower nicotine will smoke more, to maintain his addiction. Where are all *those* folks, now that the evil swine who call themselves public health authorities in both the US and Canada have openly announced their scandalous intention to lower the nicotine content of cigarettes? Why aren't ethical scientists loudly pointing out the obvious: that this genocidal madness will force smokers to smoke *more*...killing us even sooner and robbing us even worse in the meantime to compensate?)

It's a silent cry for help, I tell you. People with excellent brains are fronting for morons and thieves—because it's the only game in town—or keeping silent for fear of losing their grant to political correctness. We live in the only society in the past 200 years too dumb to know basic research *always* pays off, in cash. These are truly the Crazy Years.

Buzzed High Zonked Stoned Wasted

FIRST PRINTED NOVEMBER 2002

'M IN A UNIQUE POSITION to pin British Columbia Premier Gordon Campbell's drug troubles on New York State, all the way back in the sixties. Unfortunately, I can't prove a word of it.

At the end of that dizzy decade, I was an impoverished State University student living on dishrag soup and scraped icebox. By good fortune I caught the eye of a powerful official in the administration, who got me into the Work-Study Program—something very like being named A Friend of Ours by certain Italian-Americans in the adjoining state of New Jersey. The Work-Study Program was a wonderful boondoggle in which one provided part-time unskilled sinecure labor to the university and got paid at full-time executive assistant rates, with the tacit understanding that most of it would eventually come back to the system in tuition, fees and taxes. The more I think about it, it was *exactly* like being a friend of Tony Soprano's.

I did a lot of different things for my pay—most of them ridiculous and none remotely onerous. I sang folk music in dormitory lounges. I ushered at rock concerts. When everyone else left for vacations, I prowled the deserted campus with a flashlight, a walkie-talkie, a hat that looked just like a police officer's and a shillelagh up me sleeve. For one preposterous and absurdly lucrative semester I was, personally, the entire fire alarm system for a whole quadrangle—long story.

But mostly what I did for the state was type. This was not just before personal computers, it was also before cheap photocopying. It was possible to make at most three copies of a typed document, using something you don't want to know about called "carbon paper." I typed bazillions of words, either on triple-sandwiches of paper and carbon paper, or on something you don't even want to *think* about called a "mimeo stencil"—all while unaware I was enduring the basic training and developing the iron carpals that would enable me to survive as a freelance writer.

One day I had to type up the results of a study conducted by something called the New York State Narcotics Addiction Control Commission. Google search yields no mention of it after 1988, nor can the search engine at the New York State home page locate any reference to it, so I presume it's either extinct or renamed. NYSNACC was born the same year I was, a branch of the corrections bureaucracy tasked with frightening citizens about drugs.

To that end, it decided to compare the effects of alcohol and marijuana on driving performance.

The study was large, well-funded and unusually intelligently designed. First they established five levels of intoxication for each of the two drugs—I can't remember the terms they used, but basically it came down to Buzzed, High, Stoned, Zonked and Wasted. (Sounds like Cheech and Chong's attorneys.) They brought experienced volunteers into the lab and quantified what dosages would reliably bring them to each level. Then they had the volunteers spend weeks driving a course intended to test their driving competence—first cold sober, for a baseline, and then at each of the five levels for each drug, all this under honest double-blind conditions. Finally, they'd have the proof that cannabis really *was* a menace to—

Perhaps you're already wondering at this point why you've never heard of this study. Or why in the forty years since, apparently nobody else in the anti-drug industry has ever had the same idea.

I'm not wondering, because I'm one of the few people who ever got to see the results.

With alcohol, you'll be unsurprised to learn, driving performance began to suffer immediately at Buzzed—the equivalent of one beer. By level two, the subject was already legally drunk, significantly impaired. By level four, he was a crash test dummy that vomits, and at level five he was a very large amoeba. At each level, he would typically insist that he was completely unimpaired.

With marijuana, level one subjects showed slight but distinct *improvement* in their driving.

Peripheral vision expanded slightly, reaction time improved and subjects became alert, observant and acutely cautious. These positive effects declined at level two, but did not disappear until level three. By level four, the pot subject drove about as badly as the drunken subject had at level one. At every level, he tended to *over*estimate his own impairment.

PLEASE PLEASE PLEASE *don't toke and drive on my say so*: I can't prove these results ever existed—and more importantly, since they were never replicated I have no way of knowing if they were even accurate! Maybe those researchers were bozos, or pro-marijuana guerrillas. That's the point. Nobody knows.

Faced with evidence suggesting the state might have a moral responsibility to furnish moderate amounts of marijuana to drivers on demand, someone apparently made the no-brainer decision. Instead of being published, those results I typed, plus the several cubic feet of raw data, were filed forever in some enormous anonymous government warehouse, two aisles over from the Lost Ark of the Covenant. No anti-drug agency ever reconsidered the topic, as far as I can find, and nobody else ever got funded.

So I say Gordon Campbell should try to pin the blame for his drunk-driving scandal (at least) on New York. Here in Canada we de facto have no law against marijuana possession at the moment; our courts have scrapped the law we had and nobody seems to be breaking their neck to craft a new one. The country seems poised on the trembling verge of outright decriminalization, like England, Portugal and several other nations. If only the state of New York had not kicked dirt over that study forty years ago, who knows? Even the US might already be there by now... and if it were, British Columbia's premier might not have gotten in hot firewater and landed himself in the Campbell Soup. Maui and his home province are, after all, both world renowned for their cannabis: martinis would have been doubly politically incorrect. If nothing else, we'd have understood why he was grinning for his mug shots.

Flinging Phlegm at the Flim Flam in Flin Flon

FIRST PRINTED AUGUST 2002

RECENTLY I WENT IN HOSPITAL for a test which required injecting me with a radioactive drug. I told them, as I always do, that drugs invariably hit me harder than most people, and they nodded and shot me up with the standard dose, as always, and I vomited nonstop for the next eight hours. One of these days I'll write on why donning a white uniform induces deafness—but not today.

This essay's about what they did for my nausea that day, which was nothing. They shot me up with four successive drugs, starting with Gravol (a standard dose) and working up to the mightiest antinausea drug in the pharmacopoeia, without effect. I retched continuously until it was simply not possible for my stomach to clench anymore; then, thank God, I was able to persuade them to stop helping me and let me go home. My problem soon vanished. My impulse to vomit uncontrollably only returned today, when I sniffed the latest mound of media manure from Health Minister Anne McLellan.

There's a memorable moment in Casablanca when Claude Rains, as Captain Reynaud, calls down a raid on Rick's Place, announcing, "I'm shocked—shocked!—to discover that gambling is taking place in this club." What makes the line immortal is that, as it leaves his lips, he's accepting his winnings. Total, bald hypocrisy, naked as a kick in the groin.

In that precise spirit, I'm shocked—shocked!—to discover that Ms. McLellan is a typical contemporary Canadian politician. That is, a protean pile of adjustable principles prepared to call excrement strawberry jam if the alternative is to risk offending a triggerhappy Texan. Her bashful confession that the Manitoba Marijuana Mine she's been overseeing in Flim Flam—excuse me, Flin Flon, Manitoba—has really been a giant 6 million-dollar dribble-glass joke, along with the recent police persecutions of Compassion Clubs across Canada, demonstrate that her government has sold out every suffering citizen who believed they could look to it for relief from pain, nausea or other debilitating symptoms.

So if you believed two years of promises that medical marijuana would soon be made available to sick people who need it desperately . . . what have you been smoking? The cowboy-bootlickers we allow to pick our pockets have already made it clear they feel little obligation to provide even Third World medical care for any of us, so why would they make an exception for troublemakers antisocial enough to acquire diseases that require Ottawa to grow a conscience?

What they meant by the best possible medicine was, the best medicine Dubya says we can have.

You'll also be stunned to hear Ms. McLellan's been able to find a few doctors either shameless enough to pretend to believe, or perhaps dim-witted enough to actually believe, that marijuana's safety and efficacy have not been known fact for over a century, established repeatedly in every reputable study from the LaGuardia Commission in the US and the LeDain report in Canada to the most recent reports from the World Health Organization and Harvard. A Dr. Raju Hejela of Kingston, for instance, told the *Globe and Mail*, "a single joint is as harmful as ten cigarettes," a preposterous falsehood. Fortunately, for anyone with interest, Internet access can find the true facts effortlessly, as former health minister Allen Rock did. (Try it yourself—please!)

The *Globe* has also reported on Alison Myrden of Burlington, Ontario, one of 806 registered sufferers who've been jerked around by their alleged representatives for the last two years. She now knows that "burueaucratic compassion" is an oxymoron, like "ministerial honour." For the rest of her life, according to Dr. Hejela and Ms. McLellan, she'll be much healthier downing thirty-two pills and 600 milligrams of morphine a day (!) for her MS than she would have been if she'd been able to use a few natural flowers without fear of arrest.

There was a time when this country had the guts to tell America to go to hell when it was dead wrong. Back in the 1960s we were led by a man who actually had the stones to tell the US that any of its children who had a problem with being forced to murder strangers in Asia were welcome here. Canada gained immeasurably thereby: in prestige, in pride and in immigrants who've made a powerful positive contribution ever since.

Today America tolerates, like a cancer on its heart, a cult of armed hypocrites who pretend to believe marijuana is a dangerous drug like heroin, PCP or crack, and who on the basis of that flagrant lie have spent decades imprisoning not tens, but hundreds of thousands of decent people for possession of a plant that causes laughter...and incidentally assured themselves steady income and low-risk thrills. In God's name, why are we enabling these foreign parasites—at the cost of torturing our own citizens? Why not align ourselves with societies with rational marijuana policies, like the Netherlands, England or Portugal?

Every sentient being in Canada knows marijuana is not a "drug" any more than coffee is. Every child we try to educate about the real dangers of real drugs knows the very first words out of our mouths are a lie. How long will we go on like this, spending vast sums we can't afford to pay armed bullies to persecute our own children for giggling too much and our infirm and elderly for seeking relief from chronic misery?

It's not the money I mind so much—it's the minutes. Horrid minutes of churning awfulness that will seem to last a million years each to every poor nauseous patient who has to rely on the present government for compassion. Every day it remains illegal here to supply pot to sick people legally entitled to smoke it, this nation is in disgrace.

There's nothing nobler than alleviating suffering. And nothing wickeder than failing to, out of cowardice or ignorance.

———

The above was originally published as a column in the *Toronto Globe and Mail*.

In a letter rebutting that column, the Dr. Raju Hajela I quoted, a white coat and past president of the Canadian Society of Addiction Medicine (and someone who laymen walking past might easily take for someone who knows what he is talking about), wrote, "...marijuana smoke produces fifty percent more tar and contains seventy percent more benzopyrene *than the same weight of tobacco*. Marijuana smokers generally take a two-thirds larger puff volume, one-third greater depth of inhalation and a four-fold longer breath-holding time than tobacco smokers. So it is easy to see how researchers arrive at the estimate of joint/cigarette harm at about 1:10...."

There's little chance of my getting Dr. Hajela to concede that he's spouting mahooha; it's likely he honestly believes it himself, and if so, his mind slammed shut a long time ago. Few in his profession agree with him, and even civilians with no interest in marijuana are liable to have personally encountered the evidence he declines to see.

Yes, it is easy to see how researchers arrived at that estimate. They either checked their integrity at the door, or never learned to do arithmetic. In the first place, as the good doctor surely must know, the average joint *contains about one tenth as much pot by weight as the average cigarette contains tobacco*. Only wasteful showoffs smoke joints as fat as a cigarette; knowledgable hipsters have always rolled 'em needle-thin. So if I were to accept his 1:10 ratio, I would find no difference between the two and would be forced to conclude that marijuana is no more harmful than a product sold legally all over the planet.

Unless I factored in something *else* that even a senator knows perfectly well: the average marijuana smoker typically takes no more than four to five puffs on his slender joint. I haven't been a tobacco smoker for quite a while, so I just went to a public place and took an informal survey: the average cigarette smoker takes at least ten tokes. Now marijuana looks *half* as dangerous as tobacco, using Dr. Hajela's figures.

But he has somehow apparently failed to notice that even the heaviest—and richest!—pot smokers consume no more than ten or twelve joints a day, whereas heavy tobacco users smoke forty to sixty cigarettes a day. Now his own figures have pot being less than one *tenth* as dangerous as tobacco, at worst.

If, that is, one is ignorant enough to assume that "tar is tar." A specialist like Dr. H must be aware, and simply forgot to mention, that tar molecules come in different kinds, with different shapes and sizes, *and radically different properties*. Some kinds of tar molecules, especially large ones, are handled quite easily by the lungs' natural self-cleansing mechanisms; that's why it is possible to live in an industrialized society. Others, like tobacco tars, fall between the cracks and don't get flushed. Marijuana tar has a quite large molecule: the gross differences between it and tobacco tar are so pronounced as to be immediately obvious to the layman—simply on sight and feel, no microscope or training required.

Next, one of my favorite shibboleths: "Chemically, tetrahydrocannabinol (THC) in marijuana is a hallucinogen that interferes with perception and is addictive." Let's skip details, like there being several kinds of THC, only two of which are believed to be hallucinogenic—that is, imagination-enhancing—and there being several other known or suspected hallucinogens in pot, such as cannabinol (CBN) and cannabidiol (CBD). Such facts might confuse the doctor as badly as the concept that thoughtful humans occasionally need to interfere with perception. Let's jump to the big buzzword at the end: "addictive."

I'll stipulate there may be marijuana addicts in Canada, and there may be many in therapy for it. I do not wish to seem unsympathetic. I won't speculate on how many of them are actually addicted to receiving treatment and would, if marijuana were magically eliminated from the biosphere, become addicted to something else within a week. What I will do is insist that the misfortune of sixteen hundredths of one percent of the populace is insufficient reason to deprive their fellows of the medical benefits, or even just the recreational joys and comforts, of marijuana—much less put thousands of them in jail or worse.

Robert A. Heinlein once wrote, "I shot an error in the air; it fell to earth... *everywhere*." Reefer has been demonized for so long that there ex-

ist many people who have dedicated their lives to exorcising it and are used to taking their income from preaching about its horrors. Perhaps we need some sort of Intellectual Welfare system to provide support for those whose ideas, however well-intentioned, have been discredited by the advance of knowledge. God knows there are a few surviving Marxists around who could use it too.

O Canada

Citizen Keen

FIRST PRINTED SEPTEMBER 2002

I T'S HARD TO EXPLAIN why it took me so long to apply for Canadian citizenship. Even for one as preternaturally lazy as myself, a quarter of a century is a long time to put off paperwork. It certainly was no reflection on Canada; I've known since the day I first set foot on Canadian soil that I was home at last. (I knew it when I discovered that the old friend I'd come to visit in Nova Scotia literally had no way to lock his home from the outside. "Lock my door?" he said, astounded. "Suppose somebody came by while I was away; how would they get in?")

Nor am I trying to make some kind of veiled anti-American statement. I proudly retain my American heritage, and my firm belief that one day the USA will live up to each and every one of its magnificent ideals. They may be a little hot under the collar down there at the moment, but they have cause; eventually they'll settle down and act a lot more humanely than many another nation might in their place.

The real reason I took so long to make the step from Landed Immigrant to Citizen, I think, came to me only minutes after I took the oath, as the full implications began to soak in: now that I have the vote, all that mahooha going on in Ottawa and in Victoria is *my* fault. For years I've been able to throw up my hands and say, "Don't look at *me*, cobber—nothing *I* can do about it." No more.

Why then did I finally do it? I think it had something to do with the fact that last year I bought a house, the first thing I've ever owned more expensive than my guitar. I seem to have put down a root. I actually am landed; it seemed time to start calling myself that.

Whatever the reasons, I filed my application. In the fullness of time I was invited to come downtown and be tested on my fitness to become a Canadian, and provided with a thick booklet containing the minimum basic facts of history, geography, economy and culture that a citizen ought to know. I took it seriously, memorized the booklet. The test turned out to be a boat race: a multiple choice affair that could probably have been aced by an aardvark with Alzheimer's. I passed.

I want to say that my Canadian Citizenship Ceremony was a genuine gasser. They did a proper job: solemn without being oppressive, light without being frivolous, inspirational without being risible. All the officials and helpers present were alert, genuinely friendly and infinitely patient—and nearly all were volunteers. Provision was made for attending family and friends, photo ops were provided and everything went flawlessly.

Waiting for each of us new citizens at our assigned numbered chair was a small maple-leaf lapel button and a copy of the lyrics of "O Canada" in both English and French. (It's a close call, but I'd say they're slightly dippier in French.) There were only a couple of speeches, short and sound; then we stood and each spoke our name aloud in turn—"I, Spider Robinson…"— then collectively we swore or affirmed allegiance to Her Majesty (pretty nice girl; not a lot to say) in English and French, received our Citizenship Certificate and picture-ID Citizenship Card from Judge Sykora, sang "O Canada," heard one last very short speech and that was basically it. My friends and I went out to Milestones for eggs benny and coffee, and now here I am back home on my island, feeling a sudden strange compulsion to buy a Celine Dion CD. But I will be strong.

The only downside to the whole thing is that I'll never show anyone except very insistent border guards my new Canadian Citizen ID Card. The photo was taken shortly after I was maimed in a tragic shaving accident, and my entire nude chin is exposed. Not a pretty sight. It makes my driver's license photo look good.

I estimate that, at fifty-three, I was one of the ten oldest people there. Two were under seven. Altogether 103 of us took the oath or made the affirmation, and eight were Caucasian… if you count Russians as Caucasians, which seems only fair since the Caucasus is in Russia. Judge Sykora specifically listed the countries our group came from: Albania, Bosnia-Herzegovina, Ukraine, South Africa, China, Taiwan, Japan…. On and on and on the list went. Nobody but me was from an English-speaking nation, the US or England or Scotland or Ireland or Australia or New Zealand. None-

theless everyone in the room spoke exceptionally good English...save one old Chinese who spoke not a word, not even "yes" or "no." Canada has a great and amazing future ahead of it. We put our money where our multi-cultural mouth is.

One tiny detail I found interesting: I've said that we either swore or affirmed allegiance to Queen Elizabeth. The judge did mention in his speech that we could do whichever we chose, but did not feel it necessary to explain the difference to any who might not already know. I intended to affirm since I'm an agnostic. Then when it came to it, and we were all repeating after the judge, he loudly used the word "...affirm ..." —and nearly everyone obediently parroted it. I heard one maverick say "...swear...." Apparently in Canada even the judges don't push belief in God on others these days. It made me think of the Liverpool City Council, who recently renamed their airport John Lennon Field and put a big sign at the entrance saying, "Above us only sky"—a line which, as all fans of Moondog Johnny know, means, "There is no God."

Anyway, I'm Canadian now, eh?

(And still an American citizen. These days you can be both, as long as you're willing to eat both back and front bacon. Something to do with free trade....)

Thanks for All the Fish

FIRST PRINTED JANUARY 2002

MY SISTER-IN-LAW persuaded an operator to crash my Internet connection to tell me my wife's maternal grandfather had died in New Bedford. It's a day later and I feel like my system is still crashed. I expected, and to some extent have accepted, the death of the century, the millennium, even George Harrison—but *Vovo*? It's nothing less than the end of an era, of a way of life older than the concept of cities. He was one of the very last men to leave home in wooden ships and pull up fish from the sea with his hands.

God must have loved Frank Parsons. He died in his sleep, at home, at age 100.5. He'd outlived two wives, lived to hear great-great-grandchildren giggle uncontrollably at the faces their Vovo made. He was once a major force in the Massachusetts fishing industry; his descendants still own the best pier in New Bedford, plus a superb seafood market there and another in Florida, both called Captain Frank's. Until his final year, he danced 'em into the ground every week at the senior center. I heard him invent and tell a joke—a good one—at his centennial last summer.

He was born, like his father, in Fuseta, Portugal. The family name was Paixao, then, which means "passion," but became Parsons at Ellis Island. Henrique Paixao was a doryman: a lunatic who deliberately leaves a perfectly good ship in a two-man cockleshell and rows into the fog in search of enough fish to founder him. Happily, the *second* time Henrique and his mate tried getting lost in the fog on the Grand Banks, it worked: instead of being caught and sent home to Fuseta, or drowning, this time they reached Newfoundland, and eventually made their way down to Cape Cod without troubling anybody at the border.

Henrique lived happily, some say a bit more happily than he had a right to, in Provincetown for a year or two. Then one afternoon a knock on the door turned out, most unexpectedly, to be his wife. With the kids. Not unreasonably, she wondered why Captain Passion hadn't sent for her...or at least sent word he was alive, and maybe a few *escudos*. He explained how busy things had been, and how you couldn't seem to get *escudos* here, and they say he was so slick he might have pulled it off...if a soprano voice from the kitchen had not picked that moment to call out the Portuguese for "Dinner's ready, sweetcakes!" There was trouble, then.

Senhora Paixao's ire is understandable: things had not gone well at Ellis Island. Somehow, she'd bullied an Immigration official into letting her enter the US to join an illegal alien whose address she did not know—whose *name* she did not know—and who wasn't expecting her. Persuasive woman. The problem was, her babe in arms had pink-eye. Very common: smoke-stack cinders often blew into steerage. But this official decided it might portend disease, wrote "DEPORT" on the baby's forehead with grease pencil and told its mother she could certainly enter America...as soon as she shipped her infant back to Portugal.

Weeping with frustration, her Herculean effort wasted, she stumbled away into the milling crowd, became aware that on top of everything else the baby was wet—

—stopped short. Glanced around. Put her hand into the diaper. Used the urine to wipe away the mark on her son's forehead. And walked boldly through the gate into America, carrying the baby who would from that day on be called Frank Parsons, and who would live a hundred years.

He owned his own boat by eighteen, competing with his father and eventually eclipsing him. He made the shift from sail to powered vessels more smoothly than most, wisely got into the processing end of the business early, moved to New Bedford and bought a key pier, owned pieces of plants as far away as New Brunswick and Labrador and put fish on tables from Bangor to Miami.

On his ninety-fifth birthday, Vovo drew me a detailed map to the secret spot no other captain knew, where the finest cod could always be found in quantity. Later, I showed it to one of his great-grandsons, the last fishing captain in the family. He sighed. "I know the spot. There's no goddam cod there now—or anywhere else on the Grank Banks. Vovo's living in the past." A year later he quit fishing, sold the boat and is now a whale-watch skipper.

The fish are *gone*. Next summer, for the first time in living memory, there'll be no Blessing of the Fleet held in Provincetown. Once a hundred boats and more sailed out every July to hear a bishop beseech God's mercy on the brave fisherman. Someone did, at the last minute, manage a final, fiftieth annual Blessing, a whopping four boats...by bringing in three ringers from Gloucester. There's no fleet left to bless in P-town. Captain Frank lived to see every Blessing there ever was or will be. The cod may come back one day, they say—though they don't say when—but even if they do, it won't be men stalking them any more, just software and machines. Oh, there'll be men aboard to service the machines, and since they'll be afloat

I suppose it's proper to call them sailors. But they won't be fishermen. Not like Frank Parsons.

It was a noble occupation. Probably as old as hunting—now also extinct—and certainly older than farming, which is circling the drain. Hemingway based a pretty good book on a fisherman, Cuban rather than Portuguese, who coincidentally also died this week with three figures on his odometer. Jesus apparently recruited a lot of his posse down at the pier, and served only fish sandwiches and red wine at parties. Captain Frank would have approved that menu.

He weighed anchor and set sail at the traditional hour: with the tide, sometime between four and six in the morning. I'm violently allergic to fish, myself—but he was a tough, smart, funny old man, and I'll miss him. If we have the wit, we all will.

All things must pass, George Harrison sang. All things must pass away. Isn't it a pity.

Phone-y Manners

FIRST PRINTED FEBRUARY 1997

I N ROBERT A. HEINLEIN'S science fiction novel *Friday*, an encyclopedic synthesist with eidetic memory (read: a genius among geniuses) is assigned to analyze all of human history and prepare a report on how, specifically, to spot a dying culture. She identifies several telltale indicators—inflation, violent crime, dominance of one gender over another, ratio of productive versus nonproductive citizens, of enforceable versus unenforceable laws—but only one surefire sign:

"Sick cultures show a complex of symptoms... but a *dying* culture invariably exhibits personal rudeness. Bad manners. Lack of consideration for others in minor matters. A loss of politeness, of gentle manners, is more significant than a riot. This symptom is especially serious in that an individual displaying it never thinks of it as a sign of ill health, but as proof of his/her strength."

As I type this, they're re-running the pilot for *Due South*. The script (like the splendid TV series it foreshadows) makes, remakes and then underlines the point that the single identifiable characteristic Americans associate with Canadians is our almost eerie politeness.

But I find myself wondering if it isn't a slightly pathetic thing for us to pride ourselves on: *compared to Americans, we seem polite*. Sort of praising with faint damns, isn't it?

Addressing a topic as vast as Canadian manners here would be silly: allow me a paradigm. I suggest that an excellent clue to overall manners is how Canadians behave *when they believe themselves anonymous*, when they see little chance of being held responsible for rude behavior. How polite are we "in the dark," as it were? Road manners and cyberspace manners suggest themselves in this connection, but let me pick an approach for which I have hard data I've collected and verified personally: telephone manners.

My phone machine, constantly in circuit, explains that my wife and I concentrate for a living, and invites all callers to leave a message. If it's someone we recognize or want to talk to, we interrupt our work and take the call. For reasons too silly and complex to explain, we're stuck with a phone number that looks institutional. About half the calls we get are wrong numbers. In the last decade, exactly *one* caller who reached us in error—out of roughly 10,000—took the trouble to say, "Excuse me, wrong number," before hanging up. The other 9,900-odd barged into our home by mistake, seized our attention with an imperious alarm bell and then exited without apology, slamming the door behind them. Before we got our new digital answering machine, we then had a (*squeak!*) *beeeeeeeep* (*squeak!*) to fast-forward through on playback, wasting even more time. (Not counting the occasional nit who cursed us for being the wrong number.)

God bless Call Identify. I customarily write until dawn, and am often in the mood for some diversion at around four A.M. "I'm sorry to disturb you," I now say, as politely as I can, "but I just got your hang-up message, and had to be sure whether you were my aged aunt having a stroke in a phone booth or simply a lout." About one in five apologizes; all, I think, learn something.

In the fullness of time, as more people do this sort of thing, phone manners will improve somewhat. But we'll deserve little credit. As suggested above, they're only manners if you still have them when you're masked. Phone manners will improve only for the reason LA drivers now signal their lane-changes more often than Vancouver drivers: because someone's liable to shoot at them if they don't. Not good enough.

Attention is energy. Who seizes my attention by clumsiness, stumbling like a drunk into my living room, owes me an apology. Our society is a huge underdesigned machine composed of over 30 million cranky, creaky gears meshing together. Moving parts in contact require lubrication. The only social lubrication we have is good manners. A good deal of that meshing now takes place under conditions of relative anonymity: behind the wheel of a car; on the phone; in cyberspace. If we fail to keep the machine oiled, *even where it doesn't show*, even where no mechanic can be found liable for failing to do so, it will seize up . . . and we will all die. Badly.

————

My number contains several repeated digits adjacent to each other on the keypad. An infant, allowed to use a phone as a toy, is almost guaranteed to reach me. I then get to listen to *boop beep boop* until the machine switches off—two full minutes, unless I get up and quell it. I used to think it was one kid, until I got Call Identify. Then I learned to my surprise that it was *hundreds* of kids. But that's not the weird part.

I've called back about eighty of them by now. *Every single time*, the adult who answers is, unmistakably, recently arrived from the Indian subcontinent. (I can't nail it down any finer than that: I am not qualified to distin-

guish an Indian from a Pakistani from a Bangladeshi by accent or displayed name.) I have absolutely no explanation for this and do not claim it says anything comprehensible about that notoriously polite racial subgroup—but I feel obliged to report it, in hopes that some wiser mind may be able to explain it.

For what it's worth, nine out of ten apologize—and none repeat.

Night of the Impolite Canadian

FIRST PRINTED FEBRUARY 2001

'M GUESSING IT WAS 1968. In those days there briefly existed on this planet a phenomenon I despair of explaining to the modern consumer called "folk music." Before it all blew over, it offered sporadic employment to people like Tom Rush, Tim Buckley, Phil Ochs, Fred Neil, Judy Collins, John Koerner, James Taylor and Bob Dylan, some of whom went on to become legitimate musicians.

One of the best songwriters in folk was Tim Hardin, an American. His biggest commercial success was a song called "If I Were a Carpenter," a hit for Bobby Darin. He wrote the folk classic "Reason to Believe" and a haunting jazz ballad called "Misty Roses." He was one of the best performers of his songs, with a smoky, fragile voice and guitar-playing as crisp as breadsticks. He seemed poised to become one of those rare folksingers to earn a living. Then someone gave him some heroin.

By the time of which I speak, Mr. Hardin had already flamed out at least once—he'd actually fallen asleep onstage at the Royal Albert Hall. Now, chastened and fresh out of rehab, he was ready to try a career-reviving comeback. A tour was booked. A humble, low-key folkie tour: no smoke-bombs and lasers, just Mr. Hardin and an unknown for a warmup act, another solo singer-guitarist-songwriter like him.

Why his management booked this acoustic double-bill into my university's main stage, I'll never understand. It was a large state university, with a concert venue—a quadruple gymnasium—so humungous that a more typical bill was The Who. I didn't care. I may as well confess this like a man: I was a folksinger myself, in those days. I've been completely rehabilitated through a twelve-step program—swear to God—but back then, I was one of the first in line for Tim Hardin tickets.

Then, in the few months before the concert actually happened, everything changed....

Not for Mr. Hardin, but for his warm-up act. Lightning struck, and set her ablaze. A shy folkie with the obligatory long blonde hair, hailing from some place so nowhere it wasn't even in America, she unexpectedly became a pop star, overnight. So when Tim Hardin's big evening finally arrived,

the house was packed...but nearly everyone had come to hear this Joni Mitchell chick.

She was wonderful of course, held the huge crowd spellbound in the palm of her hand, and when she was through, the standing ovation seemed to go on forever. Then Tim Hardin came out on stage, and Ms. Mitchell left....

...and so did a good quarter of the audience.

The doors of this dark gymnasium, enormous ones, were located on either side of the stage, and the lobby outside was brightly lit. So the policy was to keep those doors shut while someone was actually performing onstage. Otherwise you were shining a big light into the audience's face, wrecking the ambience. Those wishing to enter or leave were required by ushers to wait until the song-in-progress was over. This is good policy when only a few people want to go through the doors. When *many* people try to leave at once, however, the result is large milling crowds on either side of the stage....

As far as they were concerned, the show was over. The star had already performed, and this blockage at the door was just some temporary screwup. They made no attempt to keep silent—didn't even bother keeping their voices down. Some shouted, the better to be heard over that guy up onstage nattering on about carpenters and tinkers. Cigarettes were lit, some containing tobacco; raucous laughter rose above the general hubbub.

Tim soldiered on. He finished his first song, to a smattering of applause, watched the doors open and a flood of people *race* to escape his music. He began another song, watched *more* chattering crowds form at his left and right as he sang and then flee the moment they were allowed to. He started a third tune; same result...

He stopped in mid-song, unslung his guitar, leaned closer to the mike said, very softly, "How would you like it if somebody pissed in *your* canteen?" and left. Some folks didn't even notice.

But they sure noticed when an avenging angel swept down from the bleachers, trailing blonde hair like fire. Ms. Mitchell *sprang* onstage, grabbed the mike and for the next five solid minutes she cursed that crowd. We were barbarians, pigs, reptile excrement; she profoundly regretted having performed for us, and would tell every act she knew not to come here because we didn't deserve to hear music; she maligned us and our relatives and ancestors until she ran out of breath and stormed offstage. Leaving behind hundreds of baffled people...and a handful like me, cheering even louder than they had for her songs.

Mr. Hardin cut that tour short and went back to heroin. His performance at Woodstock the following year was cut from the movie. It took him another ten horrid years to die, at thirty-nine. At his final gig in 1979, they say he played one song—Hoagy Carmichael's "Georgia"—over and over, until he cleared the place. I mourn his loss still and urge you to hunt his work on the Net.

But I've been waiting ever since for a chance to thank the first Canadian I ever met for her magnificent rudeness—not to mention her astonishing command of invective—and now I've finally got it done. If there's ever anything I can do for you, Ms. Mitchell, I am yours to command.

Pull Up a Soapbox

Hail on the Chief

FIRST PRINTED APRIL 1998

THE LATE JOHN BRUNNER'S classic non-novel *Stand on Zanzibar* depicts a near-future world driven mad by a combination of overpopulation and runaway technology. One memorable recurring character is a drug burnout named Bennie Noakes, permanently skulled on powerful psychedelics, who spends his life in front of the tube watching the news channel, shaking his head and murmuring over and over, "Christ, what an imagination I've got!" I've often felt like Bennie as I watched my own TV news. Surely I must have been hallucinating what I saw and heard.

Could OJ Simpson really have told an interviewer he's getting more sex now than he did when he was married, and then pretended to knife her with a banana on-camera? Can it possibly be true that the state of Texas—Texas!—now forbids condemned prisoners a cigarette before their execution, to protect their health? Did the Belgians really let Dutroux escape?

And did the entire American population really all simultaneously develop a psychotic fascination with their president's penis?

At the time I emigrated from the US, many Americans believed the president to be a crook and held him responsible for the protraction of a bloody and unjust war—and to be sure, I occasionally heard private ribald speculations about his sex life. But the *New York Times* did not print them. Walter Cronkite did not quote them. It would have been inconceivable. Unpopular as that man was, when he spoke unexpectedly to antiwar protesters at the

Lincoln Memorial one night, every one of them addressed him as "Mr. President"—nobody called him Tricky Dick to his face. Americans may disrespect the man...but they respect the office. Things couldn't have changed that much in a mere twenty-five years: somehow I've been dosed with powerful drugs, and that whole Zippergate thing was a lunatic fantasy I had. Christ, what an imagination I've got!

Well, wait a minute. A memory has just surfaced. Once again I am broiling in the Florida sun...

It was during the first Bush administration. Having been Toastmaster for the fiftieth World Science Fiction Convention in Orlando, I'd had the great good fortune to meet a NASA official who kindly gifted me with a VIP pass to attend a space shuttle launch—a childhood dream come true. When the big day dawned, thousands of stationary vehicles full of sightseers blocked the highway leading to the spaceport—but thanks to our magic piece of paper, my friends and wife and I passed them all on the shoulder, cleared the checkpoint, drove over the causeway and joined the elite line of perhaps a hundred cars full of citizens privileged to watch the launch a mere mile or so away from the pad. We were not surprised that the line moved slowly—official vehicles had urgent use for the same road—but we were somewhat dismayed when it stopped altogether. And *stayed* stopped.

The sun beat down. Air-conditioners overheated their engines. People stepped out into murderous heat to ask each other the obvious question, to which no answer was forthcoming. Fifteen minutes passed, very slowly. Up the road in the opposite direction came a motorcycle cop with a bullhorn; he drove past us very slowly, ignoring all pleas and gestures, braying, "REMAIN IN YOUR VEHICLES" over and over. Our vehicles were by now solar ovens. A million years went by...mosquitoes gorged...sunblock ran down our necks...children cried...tempers began to climb...the damn launch was only fifteen minutes away, now—and suddenly, all became clear.

Coming toward us on the opposite side of the road at twenty kilometers an hour, shimmering in the heat, a vision: a flotilla of black stretch limousines. A phalanx of motorcycle cops with automatic weapons. Chase-cars full of shooters in suits and black shades fore and aft. The truth began to dawn. Sure enough, as the second limo came even with us, five meters away, its tinted rear windows powered down, and there they were. Identical robotic waves, identical ghastly smiles, like terrible twin parodies of the Queen. Danforth and Marilyn Quayle.

Mr. Quayle's duties as vice president had included direct responsibility for America's space program. Three months away from leaving office, he had decided to pay his first visit ever to NASA turf while they still had to let him in. We all realized we'd been kept broiling in the sun so the Secret

Service could make absolutely sure there wasn't an alligator with an Uzi in one of the drainage ditches beside the road.

And as the motorcade crawled past, and Mr. Quayle waved and smiled—I swear to you—all of us in that lineup gave him the Trudeau Salute.

(The Secret Service did not shoot us. The cops did not pistolwhip us. I didn't see anybody photograph us or our license plates. Nobody seemed to notice. Least of all the Quayles: their smiles never faltered, their waving hands never trembled.)

The motorcade passed, traffic started up and we were in time to see the *Endeavour* lift, the fiftieth shuttle launch ever, an experience too profoundly moving and awesome to convey in words. If anyone had told me, back in the 1950s when I started reading science fiction, that one day I would see a spaceship take off with my own eyes...well, I'd have found it hard to imagine. But if they'd told me that on the same day I would see hundreds of Americans loyal enough to have VIP access to government property all publicly give the vice president of the United States the finger, I'd have flatly refused to believe it.

Plot a curve. Start with the Johnson administration, when it became acceptable to publicly call the president a baby killer. Place another data point at Watergate. Another for the years during which the president was clearly senile. Enter a fourth point representing the event I just described. Extend the curve....

I take it back. Maybe I haven't been dosed with drugs: perhaps the whole Zippergate thing actually did happen, and Ken Starr is a real person. In that case, maybe I'm not taking enough drugs.

There Are No Good Bushwhackers

FIRST PRINTED MARCH 1999

I LONG AGO LOST THE LAST SHRED of hope that I will ever in my life be offered anyone or anything in politics to root *for*. But I have clung to the idea that it might be possible to sort out which, of the two or three bands of brigands seeking my consent to be mugged at any given time, I most urgently needed to be *against*.

But these are the Crazy Years. All bets are off. Lately, every time I think I've identified who it is I'm most against...his enemies do something so spectacularly sleazy that I feel forced to defend the son of a bitch.

There is a memorable moment in the film *Butch Cassidy and the Sundance Kid* in which Butch, about to battle to the death with a mastodon named Harvey Logan, suggests they define the rules. Logan stares at him in awe and contempt. "Rules?" he bellows. "In a *knife-fight*? No rules! Peep." The last syllable, of course, is occasioned by the unexpected impact of Butch's boot into his crotch. The most stupid and homicidal thug soon learns that it is good to have rules—even in a knife-fight. Politicians and pundits used to be that smart...but not anymore.

The most egregious example was the carnival to the south a few years ago, where Mr. Clinton's enemies insisted on keeping their fangs sunk in his flesh with the mindless tenacity of the pitbulls so many of them chanced to resemble, and without even a plausible surface appearance of any interest in the truth. Consider, for instance, a column by Jeff Jacoby of the *Boston Globe* entitled "Rape? Sounds like our guy." Taking his headline from that fount of thoughtful analysis, *Newsweek*'s "Conventional Wisdom" box (a short feature of satirical one-liners), Mr. Jacoby reprised every allegation of Clintonian sexual misconduct that years of effort and hundreds of thousands of dollars have failed to substantiate, as if they were facts; he ignored the only existing hard evidence of the president's sexual behavior; and he concluded that Juanita Broaddrick's recent utterly unsupported and highly suspicious allegation of a twenty-one-year-old rape by Mr. Clinton must be true. "Sounds like our guy." Other commentators have made the same point, in just those astounding words.

Forget the fundamental unfairness of condemning someone because he "sounds like our guy." (Black? In a white neighborhood? With money in his pockets? Sounds like our guy.) What about common sense? Mr. Jacoby quotes Mrs. Broaddrick's explanation for why she came forward now, of all times—"I didn't want my granddaughters and nieces when they're twenty-one years old to turn to me and say, 'Why didn't you tell what this man did to you?'"—and apparently he fails to notice that it makes absolutely no sense: they now *will* have to ask her just that question, and could not possibly have done so if she'd kept silent.

Forget that too. Think instead about what we actually know: the Bill that Monica described to Baba Wawa. That man may be a fool, may be a simp...but could he conceivably be a predatory rapist, who uses sex to establish power? He was fifteen months into their affair before he had an orgasm, for God's sake—long after she'd had several. By her vivid account, she had to more or less drag him into things, and did so eagerly. The kind of man described by Mrs. Broaddrick, Paula Jones and Kathleen Willey, who gets his jollies from coercion, from resistance, from force, could not plausibly have been interested in, or vulnerable to, a compliant and dangerously uncontrollable little volunteer like Ms. Lewinsky. He just doesn't fit the profile. It doesn't sound remotely *like* our guy.

Yes, he's an admitted liar. But many Christians are unaware that the Bible nowhere forbids lying. What the Ten Commandments *do* forbid, specifically, is only a carefully limited *kind* of lying—the very kind Mr. Clinton's enemies appear to excel at: bearing false witness against others.

It drives me crazy to be forced to defend Mr. Clinton, as I am not one of his fans. His positions on space, the Internet and Free Trade, among others, strike me as particularly wrongheaded and dangerous. But his enemies leave me little choice.

Similarly, and closer to home, I have strong reasons to dislike BC Premier Glen Clark. His administration's spectacular mishandling of the Fast Ferry project may yet have me commuting via water-wings. Yet I am so appalled by the sleaziness of recent actions by his enemies that I may feel forced to support him in the next election.

The recent pointless raid on Mr. Clark's home, which just happened to end up on TV by (it says here) incredible chance and astute reporting, stinketh like a mackerel in the moonlight. Mrs. Clark says when she opened the door and saw Mounties and cameras, she assumed her husband was dead; for that alone, someone should be horsewhipped. After they left, Mr. Clark himself noticed they'd somehow overlooked the documents they had nominally come to seize and delivered them himself. (Sounds like a crook to me!) Those who were frightened by the film *Wag the Dog* can relax: politicians just aren't that slick. Their frame-ups are much clumsier than Hollywood's.

I have doubts as to Mr. Clark's wisdom and competence—but I will take an incompetent idiot over a bushwhacker any day. If his enemies are unwilling to fight fair, they *must* be wrong.

Partisan politics has become so psychotic an arena as to effectively disenfranchise all voters, leaving a thoughtful citizen with absolutely no sensible way to influence his country's destiny. At this point, I almost don't care *who* wins: I just want them all to put away the knives. Once we all accept knife-fighting as legitimate political discourse, the next step is gunfights. Ask someone from El Salvador or Bosnia or Rwanda what that's like.

The Opposite of a Great Lie

FIRST PRINTED NOVEMBER 2000

THE GREAT PHYSICIST Niels Bohr said that there exist what he called Great Truths. How you know them, he said, is that the opposite of an ordinary truth is a falsehood—but paradoxically, the opposite of a Great Truth is *another great truth.*

An easily-grasped example might be the classic metaphilosophical observation, "Love stinks." Few will argue, yet the flipside is equally self-evident: sometimes love smells quite intoxicating. "Life sucks." Sure. And rather well, if you're lucky.

Other Great Truths that spring readily to mind include "Civilization is a good thing," "You can't live with 'em," "Music is universal" (how many raga, samisen, klemmer, oud or didgeridu CDs do you listen to regularly?), "Life is hilarious" or Mr. Spock's famous, "The needs of the one outweigh the needs of the many."

Being a scientist, Dr. Bohr had an eye for Truth. It may never have occurred to him—who had survived World War II—that just as there are Great Truths, there also exist Great Lies.

I would like to talk about one particular recent Great Lie, even though it's both a comparatively trivial one and a pathetic failure—because I think it illumines something more dangerous to civilization than bullets or bombs.

On September 2, 2000, I received an e-mail from Claire O'Leary, wife of the excellent sf writer Patrick O'Leary. She'd just gotten one of those multiply-reforwarded e-mail jokes that now infest the Internet and thought I would find it of interest. It consisted of a long list of incredibly stupid things said by Vice President Al Gore, with dates and attributions—and there's no denying they were hilarious. Anyone with a sense of humor who saw them would hit the "forward" button and spam her entire address list almost by reflex. Here are just a few examples, personal favorites:

"If we don't succeed, we run the risk of failure." "We're going to have the best-educated American people in the world."

"We are ready for any unforeseen event that may or may not occur."

"One word sums up probably the responsibility of any vice president, and that one word is 'to be prepared.'"

"I stand by all the misstatements that I've made."

Well, sir, I did indeed find all those funny quotes fascinating, and Claire and I exchanged several letters about them.

Now we jump ahead over two months, to November. An e-mail arrived from a Toronto friend, ace wordsmith Eric Posner—and almost at once an identical message from Linda Richards, co-creator of the outstanding book review website www.januarymagazine.com. They were both forwarding another of those viruslike e-mail joke collections, which they thought I'd enjoy, and indeed I found it as hilarious as the one Claire had sent.

Precisely as hilarious.

That's because it was—almost—precisely the same message. The only small change was that in this version, all those magnificently mindless quotes were attributed to Governor George W. Bush.

"It's time for the human race to enter the solar system."

"Republicans understand the importance of bondage between a mother and child."

"Verbosity leads to unclear, inarticulate things."

"I was recently on a tour of Latin America, and the only regret I have was that I didn't study Latin harder in school so I could converse with those people."

———

And we're not even up to the punchline, yet.

The reason Claire, Eric and Linda all knew I'd love what they were sending me is that they'd all just read my novel *Callahan's Key* one month before Claire received the first dumb-quotes e-mail. Every one of my book's nineteen chapters happens to begin with a quote. Each is marked by outstanding stupidity tempered with invincible ignorance. I personally researched the authenticity, provenance and date of each quote, with some care, and I promise you that *every damn one of them first entered history through the mouth of J. Danforth Quayle.*

You guessed it: every one of the new disputed Gore/Bush quotes is actually a recycled Quayle quote.

The irony gets thick on the ground, here. Mr. Quayle, for those who've succeeded in forgetting him, was vice president during the administration of a Republican named Bush. Now partisans of a different, scrubbier Bush seek to palm off Big Dan's legendary malapropisms and misstatements as those of their Democratic opponent, also a vice president.

Whose own partisans turn out to be precisely as dishonest. And just as stupidly so, to think they could fence such well-known stolen goods and get away with it.

Remember the scene early in *Butch Cassidy and the Sundance Kid*, where Butch is about to fight for his life with knives against a mastodon named Logan? "First we got to settle the rules," Butch says, and Logan, enraged, straightens from his fighting crouch and says, "Rules? In a *knife fight*? No rules!" and as those last words leave his lips, Butch kicks him so hard in the groin that Logan's boots leave the ground. That's American politics today.

It became clear during the whole pointless Whitewater/Zippergate affair, as we all slowly realized that no matter what, the Republicans simply *would not* play fair and let the man who won the election govern. Obviously the Democrats feel it's now Payback Time, and I fear we have all only begun to hate hearing about Florida electoral politics. Nobody seems to care anymore about fair, or right, or true. It's a knife fight. At such times, truth is only the first casualty, and fast disappears beneath the other corpses. *Without civility, there is no civilization.*

Free Speech Is Worth Paying For

FIRST PRINTED MAY 1997

'M PREJUDICED. Who isn't? Some acquire prejudices by experience or analysis; some accept them prepackaged from some authoritative-seeming source. None of us could function without them. But Robert Heinlein taught me the *price* of prejudices: regular maintenance. I must constantly reevaluate mine, check them against new data and discard any, however cherished, which yield bad results.

Wake me in the night and ask if I believe in free speech. Yes; absolutely. Nothing should ever be censored by any group for any reason. The only conceivable alternative is to concede that any bully with enough muscle should be allowed to censor anything they want, and I'm not aware of any instance when that cure did not prove far more dangerous than any disease it was allegedly meant to fight.

But let's check this prejudice again—three times.

Check one: a columnist for a tiny British Columbia newspaper was publicly pilloried by something calling itself a Human Rights Tribunal. Media accounts were vague on just what sanctions this tribunal is empowered to impose, but the issue seemed clear: complainants alleged that this man, hereinafter known as DC, was a hate-monger. The tribunal sought to censor or at least censure him. DC monged hate by writing that a) 6 million weren't killed in the Holocaust; it was half a million, tops; b) Jews control the media (except his); and c) *Schindler's List* maligns innocent Germans and oughta be called *Swindler's List*.

The stated theory is that this palpable nonsense damages all Jews by somehow making them fear the Holocaust might return. The right to express unpopular beliefs threatens those who were once legally persecuted for holding unpopular beliefs. We can forestall Nazism by acting like Nazis. To counter nonsense, shine a spotlight on it, give it an international forum, gang up on it and give it underdog appeal.

Crackpots seek attention; to give them *any* is to reward them. The hearing so far has been a swell party and media opportunity for several pickuploads of DC's supporters, catered by their enemies at public expense. The sensible way to handle them is to try to forget they exist. Let them blather like the Internet goofs who can prove that Bill Clinton has personally ordered fifteen hits or the gummint is hiding a dead ET at Roswell: harmless background static.

Check two: the citizens of BC almost unanimously condemned the local RCMP's abortive attempted censorship of *Women on Top*, Nancy Friday's eight-year-old third book of women's sexual fantasies—which *was* censored in Manitoba.

I own a copy. Guess what? Those fantasies often explicitly and graphically depict activities including incest, child sex, rape, torture, bondage, domination, bestiality and homosexuality—all specifically prohibited by Canadian law. The RCMP were simply trying to enforce the code we hired and required them to. Dozens if not hundreds of Canadians are presently serving prison time for possessing materials much less raunchy. What do most of those perverts have in common? Testicles.

Should the book then be censored? No. *A fantasy is not a wish.* I often fantasize strangling the yahoos who saddled us with obscenity laws, but I'm no more likely to actually *do* so than when I began. Heterosexual women should be permitted to fantasize about anything they please. But so should straight and gay men, and gay women.

("What about *real* porn? Photos or films of actual child-abuse, videotaped rapes, snuff films?" But censorship does not apply here. No one in North America has *ever* attempted to commercially publish or market such material, so far as I can determine after years of inquiry and many false alarms. Pedophiles and other rapists may indeed sometimes swap or sell souvenirs, but that's covered by existing statutes pertaining to evidence of crime and/or complicity therein.)

It's check three that gives me the most pause.

A friend once forwarded some spam: a broadcast e-mail, a deliberate attempt to tug the coat-tail of everyone online. A joker whom I'll call "Wart" is selling revenge, retail. He offers ten ingeniously diabolical ways to shaft someone from ambush—and for fifteen bucks, he'll send you the *really* nasty ones. He specifically promises to teach you how to destroy any marriage, affair or friendship, shatter any reputation, ruin any livelihood, get any cop in trouble with IAD...and how to guarantee no one will ever suspect you or obtain justice if they do. First-strike capability. Stealth sadism.

Losing faith in the justice system? Let Wart make you a more effective vigilante. Hotheads weren't dangerous enough behind the wheel; Wart can make them as invulnerable and mighty as they are cowardly. It's an escalating arms race of hate and well-poisoning. My friend—a wise, educated and honorable man—prefaces his forward with, "My God! This man is *sick*! He's *horrible*!...and I'm going to keep this list, because there's a few here I might use. You never can tell when you might have a burning need to *get even*!!!"

Surely, if anyone should be censored, it's Wart. What he does is on the same moral level as selling discount AK-47s to fist-fighting school kids. This is not gibberish about Jewish conspiracies or steamy thoughts about a poodle. Wart peddles an intrinsic evil that is almost irresistibly fascinating to even good people, by which I mean myself. I'll be a long time forgetting some of the wickedly brilliant suggestions he made. Shouldn't we pass a law?

No. I see Wart as the man who yells "Fire!" in a crowded theatre. I will defend his right to speak, without legal hindrance...and if any of his victims should want to form an informal group to beat him senseless, I'll do my best to urge that his injuries be kept nonlethal and offer sympathy to any dependents if I fail. I'll support civil action by any victim of any prank he suggests, or applaud his prosecution for criminal conspiracy. To me, Wart is more deserving of being treated as an unlicensed arms dealer than guys who write encryption software. But I won't censor him. He has the right to publish his offer...and anyone who receives it has the right to send him a hundred blank replies. A day.

Prejudice intact. I still find no pressing reason for any honest citizen to tolerate censorship. Even in the Crazy Years....

I Want a Really Interactive Newspaper

FIRST PRINTED JUNE 2001

THERE'S ALREADY AN INTERACTIVE VERSION of most newspapers. Well... more interactive than the paper one, anyway. There are spots on it which, once poked, produce a tangible response. If you haven't tried it, set the choke, advance the spark, crank up your browser and steer for your local paper.

Progress on this interactivity thing has been slow, though. Most stories in digital newspapers contain "hotlinks," little cybersurfboards which, taken at the flood, will bring you to additional facts or references. If you want such data from a more traditional paper—a *paper* paper, if you will—all you can do is try tracking the reporter through voicemail, which is designed to enrage you. Cybernews is a step in the right direction.

But they haven't got it down yet. Somehow they never seem to provide a hotlink to the information I *really* want. And judging by the long faces on the artificial intelligence crowd, it may be awhile before that improves. Random examples:

Remember Mafiaboy, the sixteen-year-old hacker who in 2000 briefly disrupted the serenity of the gods? (CNN, Amazon, Yahoo, eBay—those gods.) His "attack" was utterly harmless, analogous to a vandal gluing the mall doors shut for an hour. His show-trial has happened, and Sidhartha Banarjee's article (meet me under the bodhi tree, Sid; we'll have a sitdown) in the *Globe and Mail* said this: a social services representative recommended to the court that the kid be made one of the first underage hackers ever to actually do hard time. Why? "Because he's unrepentant."

I want a hotlink explaining what secular law requires him—or anyone—to repent. Or why any reasonable person would expect him to, since his actions caused no one but himself any measurable harm and generated an international notoriety most teenagers can only dream of.

The social worker also recommended they revoke Mafiaboy's passport, because the boy allegedly told him that "if the authorities forbade him to use computers, he'd move to a place where websites are much less secure, such as Italy." Forget that Mafiaboy could never have said anything so hilariously cyberclueless: no authority has the right to forbid computer use, any more than it can forbid a boy to read…and in any case, no noise a minor can make with his mouth justifies abrogating his freedom to travel. So I'd like a hotlink to investigate just how contemptuous of civil liberties one can be and still find work in child social services.

Here in Vancouver a man named Stumpo, responsible for a transit strike that crippled the city, somehow managed to get his name in the papers nearly every one of the days it went on. Yet not once did he say or do anything to bring relief one day closer for his helpless victims. Where's the button that will let us administer a nonlethal electrical shock to him, hourly?

Vancouver had a great police chief, once. How great? Bruce Chambers' first official action was to march in the 1996 Gay Pride Parade—and he's straight. (Not that there's anything *wrong* with that…) Class plus courage. He held the heretical opinion that the police should serve the needs of citizens, even at the cost of inconvenience. Vancouver also had a famous criminology pioneer, once. Dr. Kim Rossmo *invented* geographic profiling, an ingenious forensic tool that catches serial killers. Chief Chambers hired him: a coup. Then an "old boy's club" of senior officers succeeded in getting the Chief turfed for being a shit disturber and admitted non-redneck. Shortly after that they decided Vancouver had no use for any internationally famous lifesavers Chambers had hired either, whatever that silly contract said.

Dr. Rossmo is suing for wrongful dismissal. Several former senior officers testified that they too were forced out or demoted for supporting Chambers. Wait, I'm almost to the punchline: the inspector who used to oversee the force's needs for facilities and officers is now in charge of—are you ready?—organizing the Gay Pride Parade. Cop humor.

Where's the hot button to demand compensation and/or reinstatement for Chief Chambers, Dr. Rossmo and their colleagues? Where's the URL for a mayor with the courage to clean house, and turn the Vancouver police department from a private club controlled by a secret cabal into the world-class force a city with property taxes this high should have?

I lived in an upscale district of Vancouver for a decade. (Renting.) Very late one night I surprised two thieves breaking into my ancient Accord, and moronically chased them two blocks bellowing "CALL 911!" before it dawned on me that if I caught those fellows, they would kill me. Trudging back, oxygen-starved and adrenalin-poisoned, I saw enough houselights on to be sure several people had phoned the police, but phoned them anyway when I got home. (For a hippie, I'm fond of cops: my favorite uncle was a New York homicide detective.)

Thirty-five minutes later—half an hour past disgraceful—units responded. By then many of my neighbors and I had discovered dozens of cracked

cars along our block alone, cameras, laptops, CD players and other pawn-ables missing. The cops took down (some of) our information and ignored (nearly all) our questions. I respectfully raised two points I thought urgent: a ton of stuff was missing... but the two I'd chased had been empty-handed. I felt this implied a staging area within walking distance, difficult to conceal from even casual search, or else a heavily-loaded, easily spotted vehicle. I kept explaining this until I realized the officers agreed... but didn't care. My neighbors and I watched them stand by their cars chatting for an hour, hellbright lights left spinning to assure the formerly asleep they were safe, before they deigned to give us the report number they'd assigned the moment they'd arrived, so we could go to bed. None of us ever heard another word from the police, despite repeated inquiries. Several of us sent lists of missing property with descriptions and serial numbers. Nobody ever got back an acknowledgment, much less a single stolen item. Maybe not one got pawned. Maybe I'm Sir Paul McCartney.

Where's the hotlink to a real cop? I bet Bruce Chambers would have known.

Lead Us Not Into Temptation

FIRST PRINTED OCTOBER 1998

Y OU'VE HAD A LONG HARD DAY, and you're sitting at a bus stop waiting for the bus to come take you home. A stranger sits down beside you—not a bum or a weirdo, just a guy—and leans over and murmurs, "You look like you could use a little pick-me-up, friend." You look at him suspiciously, and with a furtive glance to either side he produces and surreptitiously shows you a baggie full of fat marijuana joints. Even through the plastic, the pungent smell reaches you. "Finest BC hydro," he says. "Dollar a joint."

Perhaps you smoked pot in your youth, but it's been years since you even knew anyone who had any—and now all of a sudden you find yourself feeling nostalgic for the sixties. Perhaps you've never smoked pot in your life, and this is the first time you've ever been offered any—and all of a sudden you find you're curious. Perhaps you know someone else who you think will be pleased by a surprise gift. For whatever reasons, you decide to accept the man's offer and slip him a loonie.

And he puts the cuffs on you.

Spider, your science fiction background is showing again. That's a ridiculous scenario. Law enforcement officers aren't allowed to *solicit* drug purchase offers, to break the law—everybody knows that.

Wrong. In Canada they are.

But surely a cop can't *tempt* you into committing a crime, and then arrest you if you succumb? That's entrapment, isn't it?

Yes, it is. And it's perfectly legal...in Canada. As of May 1997, police in this country are specifically permitted to grow, manufacture, traffic and/or sell illegal drugs in the course of conducting a criminal investigation...of a crime that would not have existed without them. In (undefined) "extreme cases," they need not even ask their senior officers for permission first.

But surely you would have noticed the passage of such a startling law. There would have been intense controversy, long and vigorous parliamentary and public debate, international publicity, threatened court challenges.... Such a fundamental reversal of the most basic principles of legal ethics and human rights simply couldn't have been accomplished in a free country without anyone noticing, could it?

Not if it had been done fair and square, no. But it wasn't. It was done covertly, surreptitiously—not by law, but by regulation.

As Chad Skelton reported in the October 6, 1998, *Vancouver Sun*, "Regulations are a necessary but poorly understood part of the legislative process.... Laws usually set out the broad explanation of what is and is not permitted...and delegate the fine-tuning of those rules—by means of regulations—to government departments....While new laws are usually the subject of fierce parliamentary debate and press coverage, regulations are passed quietly every day in Ottawa with few taking notice."

You *were* informed of the new regulation permitting police to break the law at will. It was "published for public comment"—twice!—in the *Canada Gazette*, a government publication with only 9,000 subscribers. Few members of the public have ever seen a copy, and Mr. Skelton quotes John McIntyre, the director of the BC Civil Liberties Association, as saying, "Lawyers wouldn't even read it on a regular basis." The first time the regulation was published there, in May 1994, it was written in legalese, incomprehensible to the average layman. The second time it ran, accompanied by a "plain English" explanation (no mention is made of a "plain French" version), was the month it went into effect, May 1997. Even Mr. McIntyre had never heard of it, until the Vancouver RCMP offered fifty kilos of cocaine for sale, busted three men who agreed to buy it and confiscated the $1.2 million they had offered. (A similar "reverse sting" in Montreal also went unremarked, perhaps because the cops only grossed $140,000 then.)

Nor is the power to break the law afforded only to the RCMP: it can be given to any police force a provincial attorney-general designates. It is presently held by twelve different police forces in BC and sixty-five nationwide—with more doubtless to come. The Montreal sting was done by local police.

The solicitor-general's office did not, of course, promulgate this stunning new "regulation" without consultation. No sir. They solicited input from the Canadian Association of Chiefs of Police, provincial governments and Crown prosecutors. Somehow they did *not* get around to seeking the opinions of civil liberties groups, defense lawyers or the public during the three-year approval process. As Robert Anton Wilson said of the current controversy over medical marijuana use in California, "The people cannot be allowed to meddle in their own affairs."

Mr. Skelton quotes a spokesman for the BC Trial Lawyers' Association, Ian Donaldson: "The idea that police are now above the law...is something

I would have thought would be public debate, as opposed to being snuck through by regulation."

Mr. Skelton also spoke with Michel Perron, a senior adviser to the federal solicitor-general and the bureaucrat who shepherded the new regulation through the approval process. Mr. Perron "said fears of entrapment are exaggerated... However, asked if the new rules could be used to investigate an individual suspected of using marijuana, Perron said, 'There is no distinction in the regulation [of] the amount or the type of drug.'"

Will the regulation stand up under court challenge? Opinions differ sharply; we won't know for sure until some years after the first cases work their slow way through the legal system.

Meanwhile, Canada—a country where people care so much about human rights that many of them will risk pepper-spray in the eyes merely to protest the presence of a visiting politician from a land without such rights—is now the only nominally civilized nation on earth in which the police are allowed to tempt people into criminal activity and then arrest them for it.

The Process

FIRST PRINTED OCTOBER 1997

YOU HARDLY EVER HEAR of judges committing suicide.

A guy gets caught promoting bogus stock, cheating people who agreed to gamble. He faces the admiration of strangers, the contempt of his friends and an extended vacation in a place where they won't give him a special phone line for his modem and it can take days to get a hooker sent in. Instead, he sky-dives without equipment. A kid gets caught with a ten-millionth of a lethal dose of cannabis—a vanload—and hangs himself in his cell rather than face his parents. A betrayed spouse makes the ultimate complaint. These we hear about all the time.

And then there are the people who must deal with such doomed bent souls all day long. How frustrating it must be to try and straighten out all those derailed lives when you're forbidden to use common sense or compassion or any tool but a single unwieldy blunt instrument called The System. It must be like being a combat surgeon before anesthesia, when all they had was a knife and a saw. You always hear about cops eating their guns—see? there's even a special expression for it—and you think, who can blame them, with what they have to see and be unable to resolve? Somewhat less often, you hear of social workers who either simply burn out, or find themselves guilty of some monstrous life-destroying error at work and decide to handle it the way Jehovah would have.

Considerably less often, you hear of lawyers committing suicide—and that is odd, since they are the ones who always seem to be faced with all the most weighty and poignant ethical dilemmas on all the TV shows. The TV defense lawyers agonize over their obligation to knowingly help criminals and psychos return to work and cringe at their own shameful pride in their skill; the TV prosecutors suffer over their inability to outwit the defense lawyers and occasionally question their own integrity as they offer plea-bargains to monsters. And when prosecutors and defense lawyers argue in chambers, the TV judge always frowns as he listens and ultimately renders his decision with the air of a man who knows he will be haunted by it for many sleepless nights to come.

But they all always find a rationalization and are prepared to carry on by the time the closing credits roll. And so it is in real life, where you hardly ever hear of a big shot defense lawyer who commits suicide, because in a moment of clarity it suddenly came to him that he is evil scum, or a prosecutor whose rigid sense of justice continues to operate after a DNA test conclusively proves that one of his past triumphs was the execution of an innocent man, or a judge whose self-respect finally breaks under the weight of all those dreadful deadly mistakes he made or allowed The System to *require* him to make. Perhaps the money consoles them when they wake in the night. They can afford Prozac and melatonin: maybe they don't wake in the night.

Or perhaps when they do, they tell themselves that they did about the best anybody could have done with the clumsy instrument of the law—that, considering their massive caseload backup and limited resources and frozen budget, they removed from the streets and processed and warehoused about as many genuinely dangerous individuals as society was willing to pay for...along with, to be sure, an inevitable percentage of poor bastards who wandered into the gears, generally owing to defects of complexion...and that nobody bats a thousand. I hope they do have some such comforting thought, for we cannot spare any of them, even the incompetent ones.

But I can't agree with that kind of thinking. That can't be good enough. They may have to settle for that—but I'm a taxpayer, and I don't. More than I want a balanced budget, I want a world in which the helpless can get protection from the beasts.

Arlene May of Craigleith, Ontario, sobbing, handed her twenty-two-year-old daughter a document one day: her own will. She was sure Randy Iles was working up to killing her. She was sick of subjecting her other four children to the turmoil and trauma of shelters and safe-houses, and she refused to be run out of her own home any more. The daughter offered to move back home and defend her mother, at knifepoint if necessary. Arlene said it wouldn't make any difference. She was right. Randy Iles did everything the daughter could have done himself: immediately after he put two bullets through Arlene's chest, he put one through the place where his own parents had tried unsuccessfully to grow a brain and fell dead beside her on the bed.

The daughter told all this to a coroner's jury in Toronto last week, and the Canadian Press account implies that she was a little irked. At the time he murdered her mother, you see, Iles was out on bail. *Three times* out on bail. On *three prior charges of assaulting Arlene May.* He was under at least one court order to have no contact with her.

Think about how bad a "domestic disturbance" has to be for the cops to actually cuff someone. How aggravated the assault must be before a prosecutor will file charges. The judge has to know that the creature standing before him is probably not some politically incorrect *Honeymooners* fan who picked the wrong moment to quote Ralph's famous, "One of these days, Alice—bang, zoom, right to the moon!" line to his wife. And if he doesn't, the *second* judge sure does. Now tell me what was going through the mind of that *third* judge who looked at Randy Iles and read his file and set a bail within his means.

Maybe he was so overworked his eyes glazed over. Maybe he knew he didn't have a cell to *put* the bastard in, or the funds to feed and clothe and entertain him there. Maybe he simply calculated, with cold practicality, that he and the state couldn't afford the *time*—that the endless hours of droning rituals necessary to remove this particular loose cannon from the street would be better spent on the fellow in line after him, who looked even more toxic.

I would like, badly, to think it was one of those. Not only are they all fairly honorable explanations, *but we can throw money at all of them.*

Where I grew up, in the Bronx in the early fifties, a Randy Iles would have come to the attention of the beat cop. We had beat cops, then, who knew every family on their beat. The first time Randy gave Arlene more than a black eye, the beat cop would have taken him into the parlor and explained that a man has pressures and women can drive you nuts, but from now on Randy should follow his wife around and make sure she didn't bang into anything, because henceforth, every bruise discovered on her body was going to become a greenstick fracture somewhere on his. If his behavior had persisted despite negative feedback control, there's a good chance Randy might have fallen down some stairs, as often as necessary.

Give me back a world like that and I don't care how big a deficit you run. If you do, fine: I'm willing to ante up. Double the taxes I presently pay for prosecutors and courts and prisons and police manpower; I won't squawk.

But perhaps more money would not have helped Arlene May at all. It's hard to imagine a system with jaws strong enough to stop a determined lunatic that will not unreasonably infringe on rights of all the rest of us, or that could not be misused by an angry wife as easily as muscles can be misused by an angry husband. To stop Randy Iles, someone would have had to point a gun at him and use it. I'd hate to be married to a beat-cop's girlfriend.

The thing is, it's hard to tell whether the Randy Ileses are freaks or a growing trend. You seem to hear about them more often these days than you did thirty years ago—but is that a genuine increase, or just a combination of changing perceptions of domestic violence, growing media lust for sensationalism and a population growth so robust that today if someone is a one-in-a-million freak, that means there are at least three hundred of them in North America alone?

Maybe there is *nothing* that can be done about the occasional Randy Ileses, except to wish we knew what makes them and how to fix it. But if that's true, you'd think you'd hear of judges committing suicide more often.

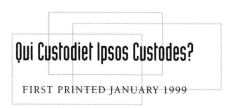

Qui Custodiet Ipsos Custodes?

FIRST PRINTED JANUARY 1999

I N THE VERNACULAR it means, "Who will police the cops?" It has been a good question for a long time—as evidenced by the fact that it's proverbial in Latin. The Romans were probably paraphrasing earlier epigrams in Hyksos. There may even be an expression for it in Great Ape.

Humans are inherently disorderly, yet crave order—every blessed one of us wants to be the *only* one allowed to break taboos. The only solution ever found is to separate out the biggest, meanest mothas, give them the best weapons and exclusive right to commit deadly violence and let them enforce whatever taboos the old men and women can dream up. What prevents them from running wild? Innate moral integrity...plus the fear that *other* big men with weapons will come for them if they do.

And they will...if the king has half a brain. Nothing—*nothing*—can more quickly or surely shatter a social contract than the general realization that the police have gone rogue. Any hope of a civilized society immediately becomes a doomed joke.

So we have to have cop-cops. But, oddly, we don't want them to be too good at it. An entire generation of movies, TV shows and novels about cops, a relentless onslaught of propaganda, has persuaded us that IAD officers are the *villains*: the handicap the noble hero must bear in his struggle with Evil. Internal Affairs officers are always depicted as heartless swine, who live to destroy a good cop's career just because he committed some trivial technical mistake while Doin' What He Hadda Do. The Rat Squad, they're generally called. Nothing could be lower than a cop who would look to hurt another cop (merely because he disgraces the badge), right? Ask any cop.

Can there be any clearer proof that deep down, most cops think of themselves as at least potential criminals?

Requiring cops to adhere to the laws they enforce hobbles them, we're told. After all, the other side gets to cheat. Andy Sipowicz on *NYPD Blue* has been perhaps the most eloquent exponent (at least since Eastwood quit playing Dirty Harry) of the proposition that sometimes an officer just has to "tune up" a suspect—that is, beat a confession out of, or kill him. Ah,

"…but only when you know you're right." That's who I want arbitrating the complex moral dichotomies of our time, someone sure to be infallible: an uneducated overweight civil servant with a jaundiced world-view and a nine millimeter.

In Abbotsford, BC, in 1999, a bunch of these secular Popes surrounded a house where they had reason to believe marijuana existed. Naturally they were armed to the teeth and keyed up: everyone knows pot-sellers love a shoot-out with overwhelming forces. This house, which they put under surveillance for two hours, had a gigantic banner in the front window reading, *"Happy Birthday!"* and was surrounded by children playing street-hockey, who all cheered and went inside when a grownup yelled "Cake and presents!" Imagine the astonishment of the officers when, kicking the door in and brandishing cocked firearms, they found a birthday in progress and the house full of children.

It must have been during those two seconds it would have taken a reasonably considerate moron to safety and holster his weapon that they received their second stunning shock: the dog they knew was there *was there*. The one they'd had to pepper-spray the last time they'd busted this suspect in this house, five weeks earlier. Who could have expected such a thing? Furthermore, the dog had apparently spent the time practicing Transcendental Meditation, for he now evinced an ability to levitate and, it says here, "bit one of the officers on the upper arm." (He was also a disguise expert: although the police swear he was a "pit bull," his photo looks nothing whatsoever like one—even his owner was fooled.) But much had changed in those five weeks: pepper-spray was now out of the question, even for a dog, so the officer's partner did what his bosses maintain was the correct, reasonable thing: he blew the dog away.

Say that again: a policeman popped two caps in a room full of children to save his partner from the bite of a flying dog, and his superiors have no problem with that.

They refuse to say what kind of gun was used, so one must presume it was non-reg, a hand-cannon. Children as young as six months old were spattered with blood. So were their parents. As I write this, the TV news just reported that police response to their loud complaints has been to arrest one for assaulting an officer (if true, good man!) and criticize the rest for allowing their kids to attend a party at a "drug house." One sees the sad truth of this: they should indeed have known smoking pot is an activity known to attract trigger-happy idiots. It was in this part of the world, only a few years ago, that a boy was shot dead for making the fatal mistake of having a TV remote in his hand when officers kicked *his* door in. (They were looking for a pot-dealer who'd once lived in another part of the building.)

Nor has BC any monopoly on this sort of thing. In Sunderland, Ontario, a cop busted a twenty-year-old for pot possession, and the foolish young man utters a threat against him. A few weeks later, the officer and three other cops decide to discuss it with him at his home at eight P.M. They end up gut-shooting his father and kid brother. One cop has a black eye, and another "barely escaped death when a bullet passed centimeters from his nose," even though none of the civilians had guns. The cops don't want to talk about it; there's a publication ban.

The hell with Andy Sipowicz and Dirty Harry! I want *more* Internal Affairs-type cops—with bigger budgets and broader powers. What a good policeman does is a holy chore, and the power he is given is sacred: he *must* be worthy of it. Otherwise good people start to fear the cops more than the crooks. . . .

KAY, AS USUAL, we had an election and little or nothing important has changed. How could it? Nobody was *offering* any change. So I guess I can't duck the responsibility any more. I am founding my own political party.

The Sentient Party, I will call it. What follows are some of the planks of my platform. Or, putting it another way, these are the minimum conditions under which I'll agree to rejoin the human race:

—NGWOT. This stands for "No Grieving Widow(er)s On Television." If elected, I will introduce legislation to mandate vicious public horsewhipping for any alleged journalist who ever again sticks a microphone in a stricken survivor's face and asks how it feels. But this is merely emblematic: in fact, no journalist will ever again be allowed to film or tape anyone, for any reason, without their express prior consent. If you camp on some victim's lawn, you go to jail. It is long past time we tamed the arrogant bastards who think of other people's misery as a career opportunity. They shame us with their assumption that we *want* strangers ambushed for our entertainment. The people have a right to know *diddly*, until a judge tells them—and decent sentients prefer it so.

—CCA. Criminalize Car Alarms. They have not prevented the theft of a single vehicle, serve no rational purpose and always make me want to go offer the thief my help so the ordeal will end sooner. For a first offense, death. If offenders persist, we'll try and get them help. But I suspect anyone dumb and pretentious enough to believe that even a possible danger to his precious car is worth disturbing everyone for six blocks is beyond help. (*Silent* alarms will be encouraged.)

—DDMAF. Don't Do Me Any Favors. This is a catch-all plank, inspired by anti-tobacco bullies like BC's Glen Clark and Joy McPhail, but aimed at *any* self-righteous fascist who wants to take away my freedom For My Own Good. Even if it did not lead to transparent idiocies like trying to extort (even *more*) money from tobacco companies on the pretext that their product costs society money, it would still be evil.

Even if Clark and McPhail were capable of doing kitchen arithmetic (that is, were not politicians) and could grasp the obvious point that the younger a citizen dies, the *less* money he or she costs society for health care, it would make no difference: what they and their ilk really want is *not* to save us money but to have the warm pleasure of *forcing* benighted addicts to quit. This has been tried for decades with alcohol, heroin, morphine, cocaine, methedrine, PCP, LSD, mescaline, marijuana and hashish, and has never once proved to be anything but a doomed, costly, ineffective, life-shattering and disgraceful fiasco; I suggest it will not work any better with a substance used by somewhere between a quarter and a third of us.

Also under this plank, anyone making derogatory remarks about Dr. Kevorkian would be beaten senseless; anyone interfering with a physician's right to dispense mercy, in Halifax or anywhere, would be forcibly intubated and put on a respirator; Greenpeace would be sent to live with the seals (on whatever rations they can devise for themselves there, building shelters without wood); and anyone seeking to "protect" me against certain forms of entertainment would be forced to watch Mr. Rogers reruns and read Nancy Drew until they agree to sodomize a goat (a volunteer goat, I hasten to add.)

—MSR. This is the *radical* plank: Make Stockholders Responsible. At present, any fool may buy stock in any company *and unload it five minutes later.* The directors must court his goodwill and seek to fulfill his wishes— but since he could well be gone in five minutes, they *must* assume that his primary (indeed his sole) wish is to maximize immediate short-term profit at any cost. Often enough this *is* his wish: we have all heard of companies purchased for the express purpose of dismantling them. Net effect: no major business on this continent is presently being run intelligently. Control is in the hands of strangers who happened to pass by, and will leave when they've finished looting.

Solution: a single law. Henceforth, no one may sell any stock that he or she has not owned for at least one year. You want to buy a piece of control of a business, you gotta commit to stick with it for awhile. People's livelihoods are not game pieces. When the screaming finally begins to die down from that one, hike it up to two years...and keep hiking it. Presently the outraged stockholders will start to notice that *they're making more money.* And that it's sounder money, since it exists in a healthier economy. And that fewer people want to mug them for it. Even the rich can be made rational, with patience and a big stick.

—CDEW. This one is, admittedly, a pet cause of mine: Canonize Donald E. Westlake. As the *Washington Post's* cover blurb for his newest novel *The Ax* wisely says, "If there were a different set of values at work in our glum society, Westlake would have won National Book Awards and Pulitzers...there would be statues of him in every municipal park." I suggest only that this does not go far enough. If elected I would arrange, as a gesture of American/Canadian amity, to give Mr. Westlake a perpetual lifetime blank cheque on our treasury, to draw from as he sees fit for any purpose that pleases him—and I would require all Canadians to possess at least one copy of every book he has published (except *Two Much*, an inexplicable failure), and *two* copies of every novel involving John Dortmunder. Regrettably, I do not believe I could expand this program to include *pseudonymous* Westlake works, the "Stark"s and "Holt"s and so on; I'd like to, but even British Columbia does not have that many trees. This single plank could make Canada—indeed, the world—a noticeably better place.

—CGC. Canonize George Carlin. This one speaks for itself.

This is not meant to be a complete list of goals, by any means, but rather a first effort toward a position paper. And I think it gives you the general tenor of the party I hope to create. If enough of you rally behind me, I promise I'll follow this through all the way. As long as I don't have to know what the hell a "husting" is or wear a tie.

Present Imperative,
or Social Mahooha

Burning the Sambuca

FIRST PRINTED AUGUST 1997

ONALD WESTLAKE WRITES hilarious novels about a thief named Dortmunder and his criminal associates. None of them is a mental giant; each is sophisticated only in the minutiae of his own professional specialty. But they all have a basic common sense that serves them far better than intelligence or education seem to serve the rest of us. In *Nobody's Perfect*, for instance, Andy Kelp is bribing a cop by buying him dinner. The cop, to demonstrate how suave he is, orders a Sambuca liqeur and does the hip ritual of lighting it to roast the floating coffee bean. He glances at Kelp for his reaction. "What's that burning?" Kelp asks. Puzzled, the cop says, "The alcohol." Kelp looks at him. "Then why do it?" he asks. The cop blinks... and hastily blows out the Sambuca.

For me, this resonates. One of the funniest things humans can do is voluntarily cooperate in their own mugging—and lately we seem to be doing so in epidemic proportions. Conventional wisdom says the world has steadily grown more cynical and suspicious in the last half century... but the evidence I see does not support the claim. I think the more sophisticated we think we've become, the easier we are to fool.

I first noticed this in the seventies. At that time the most popular recreational drug had four pluses and one big minus. It was non-addictive, dirt cheap, made its users pleasant company and had zero undesirable side effects. Unfortunately, it also smelled nice—which made it too easy to bust.

The drug dealers' solution startled me. "We have a new product we think you're going to like even better." Tell us about it. "It's almost as addictive as tobacco, it makes you so obnoxious even other users can't stand you, it's easy to counterfeit, the high lasts less than half an hour, there's a fair chance it could kill you with normal use and it's guaranteed to leave you uptight, impotent, constipated and bleeding from the nose." Gee, that *does* sound pretty good...but I don't know, I'm kind of attached to my stash.... "Wait, you haven't heard the best part: *it costs a fortune.*" Whoa, cried a generation, why didn't you *say* so?

It worked, for over a decade, because no one heard Andy Kelp asking, "Then why do it?"

Soon it happened again. A man came before the nation and said, "I have an unbelievable deal. Just because you're a special person and I like your face, you know what I'm going to do for you? *I'm going to let you wear my name on your ass. In big letters.* Isn't that *great?*" Confused, but unwilling to appear unhip, the nation said, uh, what *is* your name again? "What's the difference? It's the name of a Michael J. Fox character in a trilogy they'll be making in a few years—who cares? The point is, I'm willing to let you be a walking sandwich sign for me—I'm going to let you make me a star!" But, uh, what's in it for us? "Not a damn thing—*plus*, you get to pay twice as much for the pants! It's called a 'lifestyle statement.'"

Kelpless, we reached for our plastic. In a few years, we were paying heavily for the right to wear alligators on our tits, for no reason anyone has ever explained. Now all the young men seem to wear the same clown suit—excuse me, clone suit—and it's impossible to find a private-eye novel which doesn't compulsively list the brand names of every item of the hero's wardrobe, and there are no cheap clothes.

Computer nerds, monitoring reports from the plague zone, realized their hour had finally come. They tested the waters with the PC: it did the jobs of typewriter and a calculator very well, and almost nothing else; required a learning curve that compared unfavorably with reactor maintenance, and typically cost, when all necessary peripherals were in hand, at least $5,000. (An early prototype, the Macintosh, failed—despite a completely unnecessary twenty percent price hike—because it did many things very well and could be mastered by a child.) UnKelped North America fell in love. Naturally most of the people who bought one rarely used either typewriter or calculator. Along came stunted parodies of 25¢ arcade games for hundreds of dollars—up front. Another bonanza. So they decided maybe we were dumb enough for the Big One....

...and trotted out the Internet.

Consider the selling points. You'll need twice as much gear, it'll be even harder to hook up, and no matter *how* diligently you study it, you'll never get it to work consistently—it's fundamentally buggy. You'll need to pay a service provider more than you probably do for cable TV, and service won't be half as reliable. Best of all, you'll give up the last shreds of privacy you have left, deliberately laying open your most intimate secrets and your credit to anyone on earth. And what do you get for that effort, expense and risk?

An infinite heap of suspect data in total disorder.

That's right: it's been deliberately set up as an anarchy. You know, that system of organization that's failed catastrophically and tragically every time it's ever been tried? They used to say an infinite number of monkeys at an infinite number of typewriters would eventually produce the works of Shakespeare, and we're determined to disprove that. We're going to build the biggest graffitti wall the world has ever seen, and irretrievably commit all the painfully acquired wisdom of our culture to it.

And wait'll you see how *tedious* it is. Turning every single page takes at least a minute—because they *all* contain superfluous graphics—so you can spend an hour at the simplest tasks. At three dollars an hour. (They can fix that. You can access the suspect data almost instantly—just lay out a few thousand bucks for a new computer and pay another small fortune for a direct Internet connection. To any complaint, there's always an answer, and the answer is *always*, "Give me more money.")

The scam was so successful, it blew the secret: now everybody's doing it. A man in Seattle has convinced millions a cup of coffee so incompetently roasted it isn't worth a quarter can, with a dime's worth of other ingredients and the labor of a sullen teenager, become *five* cups of something with a foreign name (that you can't even light) worth $3.50 a crack. People who *know* their lives are stunted and impoverished by the telephone now pay for the right to be pestered anywhere, anytime, in high-speed traffic or at the beach. They're lining up to buy DVD players, since the word is out that they cost a bundle, they don't record, the special features don't really work, movies cost twice as much and a single scratch can ruin one forever.

Perhaps it all began when, somehow, a whole generation agreed to think of their houses—their actual *houses*—not as homes, but as disposable poker chips in a high-stakes game...and kept on doing it, even after they realized no sum will ever compensate them for being permanently rootless gypsies, miles from everyone they love. When it seems sensible to set fire to perfectly good alcohol, you know you're living in the Crazy Years.

The Fall-Guy Shortage

FIRST PRINTED JANUARY 1997

I DON'T KNOW WHETHER civilians have begun to consciously notice the problem yet—but I can tell you that we writers are in a state approaching panic. It is our function to be the canaries in society's coal mine, identifying problems before they affect anyone important—and what we are beginning to sense in the air is not just the end of civilization, or even the end of fiction, but the potential end of the only thing that could possibly compensate us for either: humour itself.

See if you can work it out for yourself. It's right under your nose, really. What do civilization, fiction and humour all require to exist?

That's right: a fall-guy.

There can be no civilization without scapegoats. Unspeakable things must be done to make a civilization flourish, unforgivable things—and somebody has to carry the can. In fiction the need is even more pressing: no matter how endearing you make your characters or settings, in every single story someone must be punished—the protagonist, if it's Serious Literature, or the villain, if it's Trash. And as for humour—well, it is not exaggeration to say that humour is the fall-guy, and vice-versa.

Picture that most enduring evergreen of the field: a man slipping on a banana peel. Funny? Eternally so. But now imagine the slippee is your favorite grandmother. Still funny, to be sure—but noticeably less so. Imagine it's you. Hmmm—not very funny at all, is it? Now imagine the victim is your boss. See what I mean? Now it's twice as funny. The more deserving the fall-guy, the riper the joke.

For us to endure as a society, we desperately need people that we all agree it is alright to hate. And these days the cupboard is damn near bare.

In a vain and reckless attempt to make ourselves more likeable, we no longer permit ourselves to hate people who speak a different tongue—or those with a different complexion, or politics, or superstitions, or habits, or any of the old stand-bys. Hell, half of us have even stopped insulting the other gender (in public)! The only large groups still fair game are fat people and white males. (Oh, bosses are still good, and politicians—but both of those tend to come under the heading of "white males," don't they? Besides, it's not so much fun laughing at someone you know is probably going to have the last laugh.)

Society requires fall-guys—untouchables, on whom we can all unload our own random rage and contempt. These days witches and Jews and cripples and Gypsies and native people and people of colour all have apologists—and good attorneys. We need whores (how dare they sell what is most desperately sought, at a fair price?) and queers (how dare they offer to give it away?) and welfare mothers (how dare they get stiffed for it?) and junkies (how dare they avoid the problem?) and the homeless (how dare they not die when their credit fell to zero?). This civil rights nonsense has to end somewhere.

In fiction, the problem is even worse—since so many of us writers have at one time or another *been* whores, queers, supported by the Canada Council, junkies or homeless. Screenwriters, teleplay writers, novelists, dramatists, political speech-writers—all of us are crying out for acceptable villains. It's worst in the adventure field, where they need someone so universally agreed to be vile that any conceivable brutality inflicted on him by the hero will elicit applause—people we want to see now-Governor Arnold blow into chopped meat. And the supply is dwindling. Gooks won't do anymore.

It began back in the fifties, when the TV show *The Untouchables* was forced to stop giving its mafiosi Italian names—and that opened the floodgates. We're almost down to terrorists, serial killers and drug dealers, these days. And sadly, they're all beginning to wear a little thin as literary devices. Despite our best efforts at publicizing them, there just aren't many actual terrorists or serial killers—since both gigs require so much effort and risk, and pay so poorly. And drug dealers tend to turn up on many writers' own Rolodexes, so it has to be crack or heroin.

But society, as always, has shown us artists the way and brought us the ideal villains just as we needed them most:

Thank God for child molesters.

Seduction of the Innocent

FIRST PRINTED JANUARY 1997

PAUL SIMON ONCE SAID, "the words of the prophets are written on the subway walls and tenement halls." I have myself seen the future writ large upon my own sidewalk.

A few years ago, that sidewalk became so damaged as to require repair. The freshly poured concrete naturally attracted graffittisti with popsicle sticks, determined to immortalize themselves. How few opportunities there are these days for a writer to have his or her work literally graven in stone! Inevitably, one of these was a young swain who wished to proclaim his undying love to the ages. His chilling masterpiece of . . . er . . . concrete poetry is located right at the foot of my walkway, where I must look at it every time I leave my home. It reads:

Now, I don't know about you, but I decline to believe that even in this day and age, any set of parents elected to name their son "Tood." I am forced to conclude that young Todd is unable to spell his own flippin' name . . . despite having reached an age sufficiently advanced for him to find Janey intriguing. (Assuming her name is not, in fact, Jeannie or Joanie.) As I make my living from literacy, I find this sign of the times demoralizing.

I was going to argue the case that illiteracy is on the increase—but on reflection, I don't think that's necessary. I don't suppose there's a literate human alive who doubts it. Let's move on to the more pressing questions: why is this happening, and what, if anything, can be done about it?

The late great John D. MacDonald, in an essay he wrote for the Library of Congress, put his finger on the problem: the complex code-system we call literacy—indeed, the very neural wiring that allows it—has existed for only the latest few heartbeats in the long history of human evolution.

Literacy is a very hard skill to acquire, and once acquired it brings endless heartache—for the more one reads, the more one learns of life's intimidating complexity and confusion. But anyone who can learn to grunt is bright enough to watch TV...which teaches that life is simple, and happy endings come, at thirty- and sixty-minute intervals to those whose hearts are in the right place.

Literacy made its greatest inroads when it was the best escape possible from a world defined by the narrow parameters of a family farm or a small village, the only opening onto a larger and more interesting world. But the "mind's eye" has only been evolving for thousands of years, whereas the body's eye has been perfected for millions of them. The mind's eye can show you things that no Hollywood special effects department can simulate—but only at the cost of years of effort spent learning to decode ink-stains on paper. Writing still remains the unchallenged best way—indeed, nearly the only way except for mathematics—to express a complicated thought...and it seems clear that this is precisely one of its *disadvantages* from the consumers' point of view. Modern humans have begun to declare, voting with their eyes, that literacy is not worth the bother.

It is tempting to blame the whole thing on the educational system. But that answer is too easy, and the only solution it suggests—shoot all the English teachers—is perhaps hasty. By and large they are probably doing the best they can with the budgets we give them.

Nor can we look to government for help. Even if a more literate electorate were something politicians wanted, they are simply not up to the job. I've given up trying to get anyone to believe this, but I swear I once saw a U.S. government subway ad that read, "Illiterate? Write for help . . ." and gave a box number.

Those of us who are parents, however, can do some useful work. We can con our children into reading.

I offer two stratagems.

My mother's was, I think, artistically superior in that it required diabolical cleverness and fundamental dishonesty; it was however time- and labor-intensive. She would begin reading me a comic book—then, *just* as the Lone Ranger was hanging by his fingertips from the cliff, endangered-species stampede approaching, angry native peoples below...Mom would suddenly remember that she had to go sew the dishes or vacuum the cat.

By the age of six, I had taught myself to read out of pure frustration. So Mom sent me to the library with instructions to bring home a book. The librarian, God bless her, gave me a copy of Robert A. Heinlein's novel for children, *Rocket Ship Galileo*...and from that day on there was never any serious danger that I would be forced to work for a living. Mr. Heinlein wrote stories so intrinsically interesting that it was worth the trouble to stop and look up the odd word I didn't know. By age seven, I was tested as reading at the level of a college junior.

The only problem is, you cannot simply hand the child the comic book: you must read eighty percent of it to her, and then stop reading with pin-point timing. With the best of intentions, you may not have that much time or energy to devote to the task of seducing your child.

If not, try the scheme my wife and I devised. From the day our daughter was old enough to have a defined "bed-time," we made it our firm policy that bed-time was bed-time, no excuses or exceptions—unless she were reading, in which case she could stay up as late as she pleased. The most precious prize any child can attain is a few minutes' awareness past bed-time. She went for the bait like a hungry trout . . . and was invariably chosen as the Narrator in school plays because of her fluency in reading. Today she works for the largest advertising agency in the world.

Doubtless there are other schemes. But one thing I promise: if we leave the problem to government, or the educational system, or a mythical animal called society—if we leave the problem to anyone but ourselves—we will effectively be surrendering the battle and giving our children over into the hands of Geraldo Rivera. As Mr. Heinlein said in his immortal *Stranger in a Strange Land*, "Thou art God—and cannot decline the nomination." Our only options are to do a good job, or not.

You Never Forget the First Time

FIRST PRINTED NOVEMBER 2001

NEUROSCIENTIST LAWRENCE FARWELL, a former faculty member at Harvard Medical School, runs a company in Fairfield, Iowa, called Brain Wave Science. Drew Richardson, once chief of the FBI's chemical and biological counterterrorism team, quit his job to join this company. Its funding comes from private investors, but David Akin, who authored the November 2001 *Globe and Mail* article "Brain Wave," writes that one is the CIA, which has already kicked in over a megabuck. What does it make? Deja vudoo.

Dr. Farwell says—and offers impressive hard evidence to prove—that the human brain reacts differently if it is seeing something *for the first time* than if it has ever seen it before. He says he can accurately detect the difference, which he calls the P300 Effect...with something approaching 100 percent reliability. No one except my wife is perfect, of course, but in repeated double blind tests, Dr. Farwell has yet to rack up a single failure.

Think that through. You are a Muslim foreign national who seeks to enter the United States. An FBI agent or Immigration official wires you up with Dr. Farwell's gear. He shows you an al-Qaeda training manual. It's not the first time you've seen it? You're going *love* the climate at Guantanamo....

That's as far as Mr. Akin's article took matters: immediate implications for the War on Terrorism. Fair enough, that was his assignment. But I'm a science fiction writer: I can't stop thinking about the social implications of a new technology.

I'm your wife, and you suspect I'm cheating on you with my secretary Joe. So you ask me to visit Dr. Farwell with you. He hooks me up, and shows me a photo of Joe's bedroom, from inside. Oops: P300 Effect proves I've seen it before. But you want to be sure about something like this. So we use a digital graphics program to put Joe's face on a generic male body of the right proportions—nude and rampant—and behold, it turns out I've seen *that* before, too. I can now probably forget alimony. Unless we get the same results with you and *your* secretary....

You say you didn't rob that bank—but it turns out you've seen the inside of the vault before. You swear you've never sold drugs—but you seem to have seen a pound of raw cocaine somewhere. You insist you were nowhere near that mugging, never laid eyes on the victim—but we can prove you've seen him, bleeding on the ground. Oops....

Now turn it around. You're my drug-running buddy...but when I have a defrocked disciple of Dr. Farwell hook you up, I find that you have seen every page of the Police Training Manual before. Bang....

You're my publisher, and it seems you've seen, somewhere, royalty figures for my last book *in black ink*, meaning that the book *has* earned out its advance...contrary to the royalty statements you sent *me*. Judgment for plaintiff....

Naturally there are already critics. We all *want* to believe accurate lie detection is impossible. Well, perhaps it is. This is just a strictly limited kind of *truth* detection. The machine doesn't care what you *say* about the al-Qaeda manual...it merely reports whether in fact you've seen it before or not. So far, nobody's caught Dr. Farwell in an error. The FBI once sent him twenty-one people, telling him some were agents and some were not, period. He told them which seventeen were and which five weren't, correctly. One man has already been proven innocent of a felony by this technique...after serving twenty-two years. (Tragically, he's still in prison. The law is always baffled by new technology and frequently baffled by the truth.)

Much remains unclear, of course. Ben Bova, during the years he edited *Analog Magazine*, famously read at least the first and last two pages of every single submission. Call it a gazillion manuscripts in round numbers. If I pick the least memorable page of the least memorable story, and show it to him again...will his brain really realize it's the second time?

Suppose you show me a picture of something I've frequently *fantasized* seeing before. Couldn't that produce a false positive? You show me a picture of the Taj Mahal, and P300 Effect says it's not the first time I've seen it. But...have I seen the Taj itself before, or just other *pictures* of it? Are you certain?

Show me a photo of my own home...taken from an angle I've never seen it from before. What does my brain report, P300-wise?

Okay, I've seen the al-Qaeda manual. Can you prove I didn't see it on CNN? Or in a Schwarzenegger movie? Are you *sure* it was a pound of cocaine I saw, not a box of laundry detergent? Suppose I'm simply *mistaken* about whether I've seen a given place or face before. Is the P300 area of my brain mistaken, too? Or does it have a better memory than I do? (If so, is there any way I can tap into it?)

Another point to ponder: you can only show me that al-Qaeda manual *once*. No retakes, no do-overs. Of course, if there's still any ambiguity afterward, you can show me photos of known terrorists, or devise other traps...but the point is, no trap can be tried more than once.

Finally: if you want The Man to be able to catch terrorists this way...then be prepared for him to hook *you* up to Dr. Farwell's gadget, too, should you ever be suspected of a crime. Under what circumstances should which authorities be allowed to candle your head? If your lawyer arrives before they hook you up, is it moral for him to show you a photo array of incriminating objects and places, to spoil the test?

Deja vudoo, indeed.

Lay Off the Lady

FIRST PRINTER JUNE 2003

WORDS CANNOT EXPRESS my contempt and disgust for the pack of weasels currently snarling at the heels of Martha Stewart. All of them deserve to be pantsed, painted blue and sent back to kindergarten to start learning all over again, from the top, how decent people are supposed to behave. For it was back in the schoolyard that they went fundamentally wrong, and their entire lives since have been warped by what someone failed to teach them there. You remember them from that age: the sniggering little snots who gathered at recess to make up vicious lies about whichever girl was clearly prettier, smarter, sweeter, better bred and raised and—most unforgivable of all—more confident than the rest. The ones who had to tear down anyone taller than them, so that they could endure being pygmies. The rotten part, the part that hurts to remember, is that we let them get away with it and even laughed at some of the vile slurs they disguised as jokes, merely because the jokes were funny.

We should stop now. Martha Stewart has done nothing wrong that anyone can prove. What she is accused of having done is so obscenely trivial, so monumentally inconsequential, it's simply not conceivable that any prosecutor could honestly believe she belongs anywhere on the Top 500 White Collar Criminals list, much less at the head. Every one of the trough-swilling headline-hunting swine currently hounding her is a disgrace to their office, and I sincerely hope a day comes when Ms. Stewart is able to sue each of the slimy bastards into a poverty approximating that of their souls. I've only slightly less contempt for the media jackals who've aided and abetted them, and for the mob of cackling yahoos who've joined the parade with torches. Shame on all of them. In a land overflowing with thieves in suits, Enron end-runners, really evil snakes who've routinely robbed and raped the helpless all their lives, sick bastards who've gutted entire industries for profit or simple amusement, toads who've conspired to start wars or support terrorists, the brave defenders of justice have all managed to saddle up and ride down on a woman whose basic offence is to be a successful businesswoman with superb taste. They haven't the time or resources to run down the guys who stole billions, let alone mere millions—but a whole platoon of the chair-warming civil serpents are available to hound a woman they claim ripped off $45,000. Even if that were true this would be a bogus bust, a major hummer.

And they know it isn't true. If it were true, they would try to prove it in a court of law. They know damn well they can't. So the Pharisees have pulled a Reverse OJ, and gone after her, not in criminal court, where you have to prove your case beyond a reasonable doubt, but in civil court, where the persecutors—pardon me, prosecutors—need only "a preponderance of evidence" implicating the accursed—excuse me, the accused.

But that wasn't enough. Just to make absolutely sure even semiliterate yak herders in Lo Monthang know them as Orwellian masters of hypocrisy so monstrous it would gag a maggot, they announced that Ms. Stewart had committed another crime...by protesting her innocence. This, they say, had the effect of unfairly manipulating her company's stock price. She should have allowed them to reduce it to zero without protest. She did not have the legal right to say, "But that's not true!," even though it wasn't. I take the failure of these whited sepulchres to be destroyed by bolts of lightning from a cloudless sky as conclusive proof of the nonexistence, or at best malfeasance, of God.

Until recently I held no strong opinion about Martha Stewart one way or the other. I never really grokked either MarthaMania or the immediate backlash. As I understood it from her infrequent appearances on my radar screen, what she stood for and packaged for sale amounted to Not Sleep-walking Through Life: trying to put a little style into what you were going to have to do anyway. I can see where someone who's proud of being an oaf could find that wearing. So could the desperately overworked, of course, but where would they find the time to come across Ms. Stewart?

Of my own experience I can report only one thing: Ms. Stewart's employees like her. They're not afraid of her. I know this because my daughter Terri spent a couple of years as Print Production Coordinator for *Martha Stewart Living* magazine in New York, and one day when my wife and I were in town we visited her at work. She gave us a tour of that amazing building—the kitchens alone are worth a column—and at one point as we strolled a corridor she suddenly gestured with her eyes, and there was Martha, talking to a dozen or so employees. I noticed their body language—both the ones she could see and the ones out of her field of vision. None of them was terrified of making a mistake, saying the wrong thing, not having an answer ready. They were attentive—but from interest, not terror. I know when my kid's afraid, and she wasn't. She was not in a hurry to get her weird parents out of the boss's sight.

Terri hasn't worked there for several years. But last week she was present in the green room of a TV show I was taping, and when people began telling Martha jokes—because it's not possible to be in the media and not hear Martha jokes today—my daughter spoke up and defended her. Both as a boss, and as a businesswoman of integrity. She mentioned that Ms. Stewart makes a point of taking every department of her empire out to brunch at regular intervals, getting to know each employee. This happened to be Mary Walsh's crew, so they were familiar with that sort of thing, and that sort of loyalty. But you could tell they'd never expected it from Martha Stewart.

School Will Be Ending, Next Month

FIRST PRINTED AUGUST 2003

I N AUGUST, school is at the very bottom of the list of things any healthy child wants to think about, well below Hmong poetry, hemorrhoids and the heat death of the universe. Why? Society's default answer is: because modern children are lazy irresponsible hedonists, and school represents hard work and serious (i.e., difficult) thought.

These would indeed be excellent reasons to hate school. But they miss the point. As summer rounds the clubhouse turn, every teenager in the land is working as hard as hell, learning things hand over fist—useful, important, practical, fascinating things about life as she is actually lived—and in another month, they'll once again be reined in and locked away for nine months in a place where almost nothing they're compelled to learn will be of any perceptible use.

For a North American liberal arts education, I think mine was fairly broad and deep; it was certainly varied. Catholic school (nuns) until first grade, Catholic high school (brothers) with Junior year spent in a seminary, two years of Catholic college (priests) and five more years of secular university—all resulting, barely, in a B.A. In addition to extensive studies in English literature and composition, I was taught physics, chemistry, biology, astronomy, six kinds of mathematics, history, geography, geology, sociology, French, philosophy, psychology, economics, linguistics and probably half a dozen other things I've omitted. Of all these, the only course I have used often, and expect to use often in the future, is a biology course I took in my last year of university. It was taught by the department chairman, Dr. Elof Axel Carlson, and titled Biology for Liberal Arts Majors Who Need A Science Credit. In it he told us about the startling big developments in biology that were going to come along and change our lives in the next twenty or thirty years and invited us to plan how we'd handle them when they arrived. I've thought of him every year since; I named the villain of my first novel after him. That, and cockiness, are all I have to show for nineteen years of—trust me—expensive education.

Here's a (very) partial list of the utterly essential life skills school did not

teach me, would not have dreamed of teaching me, which I had to learn myself by trial and painful error:

- How to cook. Yes, we made muffins in Home Ec; that has nothing to do with how to cook. Nobody ever taught me, for instance, that the secret of perfect bacon is to cook it in the nude...so you won't set the heat too high.
- How to do simple household plumbing and carpentry. I don't mean making an ashtray in Shop, I mean how to make the damn tap stop dripping.
- How to build a fire
- How a ninety-year-old man splits firewood
- How to balance a checkbook—and what to do when it cannot be balanced
- How to fill out a tax form—with particular attention to red flags that commonly trigger an audit
- How to start a business
- How to operate a business
- How to fold a business
- How to buy a car or house without getting burned
- How to drive—not as a short, extracurricular offering, but as a serious, in-depth, yearlong study, with simulators, intensive training in proper emergency reflexes, tours of morgues and burn wards, etc.
- Basic, and advanced, first aid for common emergencies
- When to kowtow to a bureaucrat, and when to bully him
- How to bully a bureaucrat (one of the most underappreciated skills in the western world)
- How, and when, to offer someone a bribe
- What to do if you're arrested. What not to do.
- How to lie effectively and elegantly. Useful in every profession and occupation.
- How to spot the lies in a commercial, ad, speech, newscast or newspaper column
- How to spot the traps, cons and loopholes in a legal contract. Perhaps these last four items could be bundled together under the heading of Bullshit Detection.
- How to find the third harmony in a song
- How to apologize
- How to give a good backrub and footrub
- How to drink. For God's sake, how hypocritical can we *be*? We all know they're going to do it; why must they fumble their way to responsible drinking? Why must their experiments be utterly unsupervised?

- Which drugs are really dangerous, and which are really harmless. Really.
- How to cool conflict, calm rage, defuse tension, keep a crowd from becoming a mob. How to handle a drunk.
- When and how to demonstrate. The rights, and obligations, of a demonstrator.
- When and how to meditate. Anything whatsoever to do with spirituality (as distinct from religion), really.
- How to deal with a racist, religionist or sexist joke
- How to make a difference in local politics. How to organize, generally.
- How to type! And how to use a computer effectively. Again, not as a brief summer elective, but as a serious subject.
- How to research. How to use the library, newspaper, morgue, museum, county courthouse, people. And oh yeah, the Internet.
- Some of the important universal truths of the universe, that are not self-evident and don't seem to fall into any particular subject's jurisdiction. Here's one, for instance, that for some ridiculous reason can take a man decades to figure out on his own: anger always—*always*—turns out to be fear disguised. If you're enraged, you're terrified. Or here's another, that actively contradicts some of what they taught you in physics: *shared pain is lessened, and shared joy is increased.* If I'm hurting, and I share it with you, somehow we end up with less than half a hurt apiece. If you share your joy with me, somehow it more than doubles. Awesome. And another, so counterintuitive you might never stumble across it without help: when you're at rock bottom, at the very end of your rope...the thing to do is find somebody worse off, and help him.

Let teachers teach stuff like this, and I guarantee kids will come to school early and stay after class voluntarily.

What Is It With Bankers?

FIRST PRINTED SEPTEMBER 2000

I S IT SOME SORT OF fundamental sociomathematical principle? "Wealth times sense of humor equals a constant," perhaps? That would help explain why writers of humor so often die broke....

Bankers handle vast amounts of our money every day. Let's presume they must be very smart, to be in that position, and God knows they can afford to dress better than the rest of us. So why are "banker" and "cool" antithetical concepts? Something about the profession seems to require, or perhaps merely causes, total atrophy of the sense of humor gland. If I really strain, I can come up with maybe two bankers I can picture grinning...and neither is expected to get out of the joint any sooner than 2015. If a banker appears in a joke, it's a safe bet he'll be the butt of it—and it will get a big laugh.

Wouldn't you think bankers, of all people, could afford to spin themselves a better public image? On the contrary, they don't seem to care what we think of them. Remember: these are the people who have traditionally provided, for the use of their customers, the cheapest, shoddiest pens it is possible to buy...and chained them in place to prevent their theft. Deaf to all irony, they must be....

I normally treat the business section of any newspaper as something impeding access to the comics, but my humorist's eye was caught a while back by an account of a six-year David-and-Goliath legal struggle that ended in victory for the little guy. In this case the "little guy" has assets of just under $2 billion, so you might want to pause just a moment here and adjust your own sense of humor. Nevertheless the term is apt—because the big bullies who got their comeuppance are worth, literally, more than a hundred times as much: the kind of fellas who might well say "A billion here, a billion there, pretty soon you're talking about real money"...but without intending it as a joke.

Six years ago, Richmond Savings Credit Union of British Columbia, the little guy, launched a witty ad campaign known as the "Humungous Bank" campaign. It centered around the slogan, "We're not a bank. We're better." Sadly, I missed it, but Mr. Constantineau says it "portrays Canada's big banks as gigantic, uncaring institutions staffed by robotic employees." One can only imagine the shock and consternation this controversial allegation must have provoked in Richmond.

Well, sir, major executives of some of Canada's truly humungous banks decided to make it absolutely clear to the whole world that they are, in fact, *exactly* the sort of pompous, humorless bullying dweebs they were being called out there in Richmond. So the mighty Canadian Bankers Association, representing *over two hundred billion dollars*, dropped heavy lawyers on the tiny Richmond Savings Credit Union from a great height, seeking to prevent it from trademarking the offensive slogan, "We're not a bank. We're better." They spent *six years* and God knows how much of their depositors' money arguing, absurdly, to the federal Trademarks Opposition Board that the credit union had "used the word 'bank' to describe its services." (If I say I'm smarter than a banker, I have *not* used the word "banker" to describe my own intelligence. Nor flattered myself much.)

The CBA had to do this, says a spokesman, because "Humungous Bank was a negative campaign, and banks were concerned about the effect it had on their staff." He did not describe this effect, but one can easily imagine the brutal trauma that must have been experienced by employees of very large banks when they were accused, doubtless for the first time in their lives, of being "robotic" servants of "uncaring institutions." Except, perhaps, for the tellers, who in recent years have by and large been *replaced* by their caring employers with ATM robots and Internet software....

I empathize with alien creatures for a living. I can picture myself, at least momentarily, in the shoes of a CBA bigwig—doing as they did, saying what they said. But here's where my empathy, or perhaps merely my imagination, fails: I cannot, even for an instant, see myself doing it without giggling. Uncontrollably.

That's why they're never gonna let me run a really big bank. Nothing to do with that bunco thing at all....

In any case, after all that time and effort, the bigshot bankers failed: the Trademarks Board recently ruled against the CBA and in favor of RCSU—which, vindicated, now plans to relaunch the Humungous Bank Campaign this fall. Good for them, I say: may it bring them many new customers. Smiling ones.

Don't big bankers realize their very humorlessness makes them an irresistible target for mockery? Thirty-five years ago, my anarchist friend Slinky John (who wore at all times a button that read, "Go, lemmings, go!") became annoyed with an officious official at his bank. So one day he presented the man with a cheque for $100.17. Firmly ignoring the frivolity of the odd amount, the banker soberly counted out five twenties, a dime, a nickel and two pennies. Slinky John picked up the twenties, tipped his hat, and headed for the door.

"Sir?" the banker called. "Sir!"

"Keep the change," Slinky John said grandly, and left.

(Kids, don't try this at home! For one thing, the rules have changed since those days. For another, bankers nowadays are more likely to have studied martial arts than they were back then....)

I've been reading humor for forty-five years and writing it professionally for twenty-five, and if there *is* anything funnier than tipping a banker, I can't think of it at the moment. I heard it was more than forty-eight hours before someone higher up the chain figured out a way for that guy to account for the seventeen cents, close out his drawer and go home to his family. I imagine he remembers the incident to this day...and *still* doesn't understand that if he had only laughed, Slinky John would probably have come back and retrieved his change.

I believe there's even some sort of proverbial expression regarding what should happen to people if they can't take a joke, isn't there?

"More than enough is–a too much..."

FIRST PRINTED MAY 2000

ENOUGH IS ENOUGH. Isn't it?

Commenting recently on a friend's manuscript about six characters pursuing a public billion-dollar prize, I expressed the opinion that only a fool would think a sixth of a billion dollars is a good thing to have. I think I startled him. "Are you seriously saying you'd turn down $167,000,000?" he e-mailed back. "*Really*?" Here's an edited version of my reply:

In a hot second. No question in my mind. I'd go as far as murder, if that's what it took.

$167,000.00, I'd accept. Eagerly. I would *consider* $1,670,000—if there were a strong nondisclosure agreement. But a public award of 167 million? In US dollars?

I've never met, seen or heard of anyone with that kind of money who looked or sounded happy to me...and I'm certain I wouldn't be. I have few friends, but good ones, and I cherish my privacy. Why would I want a guarantee that most people I'll meet henceforth will be vampires or freeloaders, that they'll keep coming out of the woodwork until years after I die and that from now on the only folks I'll ever spend time with who *don't* envy and resent me will be, by and large, either predators or compulsives...who'll mistake me for one of them?

That kind of money destroyed one of the great friendships of this century, and the greatest songwriting team of all time. Lucre, not Yoko, broke up the Beatles. Having money on that scale is not merely a fulltime 24-7-365 job, it's one that calls for someone who enjoys the work.

Hiring other people to do it for you won't serve. Ask the surviving Fab Two. How can you trust your employees? It's hiring junkies to guard your smack. Nearly everybody has a jones for money.

I'm not romanticizing poverty. It sucks. People who are dirt poor aren't necessarily any better company than the rich. But I think EXTREME wealth is as bad as extreme poverty. In the last century I can think offhand of only a single human who, given hundreds of millions, continued to produce exceptional creative work. Chap named McCartney. (A rule-proving exception in many ways: he also never spent a single night apart from his late wife, except when in jail.)

Picture your character A, handed all that money. Suddenly she is fat, juicy prey for a thousand predators—people who've not only been screwing others all their lives, but were born with a taste for it and would probably do it for free. In what fantasy universe could she possibly cope? How would she tell a champion from a viper? Her only hope would be to give it all away so fast she was tapped out before they could gear up to come after her. And she wouldn't know how. . . .

So far I've never once worried that someone might kidnap my daughter to get leverage on me. One single minute of such worry. . . . No, 167 mill doesn't come *near* being compensation enough for that. Never mind worrying about my wife's security, or my own. . . .

. . . which brings me back to the Beatles. Specifically George Harrison. Safe in his own bed in his own mansion on his own estate, a few years before his death, protected by the best security system and guards he can buy. At four A.M. he hears glass breaking and sits bolt upright in bed. Twenty goddamn *years* since his old comrade was murdered in New York, and he still wakes instantly at a noise in the night. And behold, it turns out *he's right to do so*: at that, he's just barely alert enough to save his own life, with his wife Olivia's courageous help. How much do you suppose The Quiet Beatle would have paid for one really sound night's sleep?

These are all practical considerations. Morally and ethically. . . I have a fairly large ego, like any artist, but I just can't persuade myself that in ten standard lifetimes I could produce work worth 167 megabucks. That much money would be like a Hugo Award for a book I didn't write—to keep it would inevitably erode my self respect. Yet the dispersal of that much raw energy back into the eco(nomic)system would be a task fraught with moral and practical ramifications, one I don't hanker for and am certain I would bungle.

Money's only fun in medium to medium-large denominations. Name a multibillionaire you'd really like to trade places with. . . or even be trapped in a long conversation with. Do you really think Bill Gates is having more fun than you are? *Look* at him. He obviously can't stand to look in a mirror, or he'd get a damn haircut. There can't be many people on the planet who love him, or ever will, and he knows it. Nearly everything he sells, he took from its actual creators; all one can really admire him for is good judgment and ruthlessness. No wonder he gives historic sums to charity.

The philosopher Marx astutely observed, "More than enough is-a too much." (I speak here of Chico.) I'd certainly like to be richer than I am now. But the *most* I want, the upper limit, is Enough. I haven't worked out the

exact sum…not in years, anyway…but if some hypothetical benefactor gave me sufficient funds to

- cover existing mortgage, taxes, fuel, food, drink and recreational substances costs,
- buy my choreographer wife half a dozen trained dancers and a studio,
- buy myself one CD and four books per week,
- take one trip a year to somewhere,
- upgrade my computer platform every third year and
- anonymously bail one friend per year out of, say, a $10,000 hole,

then that, for me, would be Enough. I'd be done, then. (I have free medical here in Canada, remember.) I don't know what that number is, in today's dollars, but I'll bet it's not much more than a megabuck, invested prudently.

That's "My Wildest Dreams," right there. Any more would be a nuisance, like more ice cream than you can eat before it'll spoil. A less sedentary person than myself might well be able to burn up, say, three or four times as much money. But 167 *times* as much?

I don't want, never did want, As Much As Possible. I don't even need More Than Any Other Kid On The Playground. All I want is Enough. I've been baffled every day of my adult life that anyone would ever want anything more. But apparently most folks do.

As the narrator of my latest novel says at one point, in a different context, "I'll never understand people. Even being one doesn't seem to help."

Please Don't Talk About Him 'Til He's Gone

FIRST PRINTED OCTOBER 2000

O CTOBER 9, 1981. My wife Jeanne had been invited to perform with Beverly Brown Dancensemble in New York that autumn, so I was there rather than home in Halifax. There had been no publicity anywhere about the date, but I didn't need any. I told my six-year-old she was playing hooky today, and we took a bus to Central Park West.

To the Dakota. Where we found several hundred other people milling about who also had not needed anyone to tell them whose forty-first birthday it was that day.

There was no organization of any kind to the group, no common denominator except a palpable sadness. Many were silent. Many wept aloud. Some sang his songs together, fighting not to cry and failing. Some held banners. Some held candles. Some held babies. This was New York, of course: dozens of busy pedestrians passed through the crowd without noticing its existence. But there was enough commotion to slow traffic. I took my child across the street and lifted her up so she could get a better sense of it.

She naturally wanted to know why these people were all here and why they were all so sad—why *we* were here and why I was so sad. A man had been murdered on this spot ten months before, I said, a man who had written many songs that changed the lives of everyone, and we'd all come to pay our respects on his birthday. Just then a stretch limousine glided to a halt before us. Its tinted rear window powered down to reveal a woman about whom two things were instantly clear: she was at least ninety, and she had always been wealthy enough to buy Donald Trump for cash.

Her puzzlement was clear and understandable. Central Park West is not a neighborhood where they tend to get a lot of spontaneous gatherings of…well…not-rich people. Especially with guitars. She wasn't annoyed, but she was curious. "Excuse me, what is the occasion, please?" she asked us.

I went blank. I couldn't think how to explain it to her—the gulf seemed too great. I gestured helplessly at the building across the street, and a man standing next to me pointed there too and said simply, "It's his birthday."

She glanced where we were pointing, and I saw her recognize the Dakota, and then a split second later I saw her get it, saw her face change as realization dawned. It hit her like a slap—this woman who had almost certainly never been slapped in her life. Suddenly and explosively, she burst into tears. "Drive on," she sobbed.

That universally loved, Johnny was.

"Who killed him, Daddy?" my daughter asked a little later. And as I began to answer, the man standing next to us, the same guy who had said, "It's his birthday," leaned over and said to her, very softly and very kindly, "We do not say his name."

"Why not?" she asked.

"He says he did it because he wanted to be as famous as John," the man told her. He shook his head and turned his gaze the Dakota. His voice was still soft, still kindly, but with a steely undertone now then that made my daughter cling tightly to me as he finished, "*We cannot permit that.*"

I agree. John Lennon was murdered by He Whose Name We Must Never Mention. That's HWNWMNM for short, and it's *supposed* to be unpronounceable. The enormity of what was done can never be diminished...but the utter insignificance of the twerp who did it can never be overstated. Or that of the horse he rode in on.

I don't want to ever know any more about HWNWMNM than I do right now. I don't need to understand his incomprehensible motives; I don't care to be privy to his unthinkable thoughts; I don't wonder what was failing to go through his mind at the moment he backshot his better; I'm not at all curious what his life is like in prison or what his family think of him now or what friends remember about him or his thoughts on the nature of violence. If he has a biographer, someone please offer that person honorable work instead.

Lawrence Block, in his most controversial (and arguably his best) novel, *Random Walk*, dares suggest that perhaps killer and victim *find each other*, that in some sense the prey needs the predator too and in some mystical way seeks out its own death. It's easy to be infuriated by this theory...but in the case of John Lennon, believing it is tempting. Everyone knows the irony of his song on the White Album, "Happiness is a Warm Gun." But how many know the eerily prophetic lyrics of "I'm Scared" (from *Walls and Bridges*, his penultimate post-Beatles solo album), in which he flat-out predicted that hatred and jealousy, "the green-eyed, goddamn, straight from the heart," would kill him? Consider the very last album the Beatles ever recorded together, *Abbey Road*: most people think the first sound they hear when they play it is John saying, "Shoop—" But listen carefully on good headphones, or check the outtake on the *Anthology* CD package: what he actually whispered over and over, and what the whole world heard in the manner Dubya calls "subliminable," were the retroactively blood-chilling words, "Shoot me...."

So it is just conceivable that, given twenty years, he might have forgiven HWNWMNM—as the little bastard had the audacity to suggest before his recent parole hearing. But I have not. Nor has anyone else: a Compuserve poll asking whether he should be granted parole drew a flood of responses, *every one* negative...and unsurprisingly the parole board agreed. All the publicity about his parole hearing, in other words, has been worse than pointless, playing right into his hands, giving him just what he wanted: delusions of worth.

If history must record who did the awful deed...let it use no name, but only what George called him: "one who offended all." Let him not even have an obit when he finally dies. What he did, any bacterium could have done...and for cleaner motives.

"There are not many places to go once you've killed John Lennon," *Time* quotes him as saying on the twentieth anniversary of Johnny's death.

Just one. Oblivion.

A God Too Old to Change, or Pope Sinks Hope

FIRST PRINTED JULY 1998

NOW THAT THE FUTURE is just around the corner, different groups are reacting in different ways—usually predictable ones.

The Catholic Church, for instance, ain't going.

(Fair disclosure: as George Carlin once said, "I was born Irish Catholic; now I'm a human being." I left the Church thirty-five years ago, following a year in the seminary. Those who enjoy sausage should not see it being made.)

On June 30, 1998, Pope John Paul II declared any deviation from Roman Catholicism's "definitive truths" to be a violation of church law. John Paul did not name these truths, but his chief of doctrine quickly supplied specifics, which suggest the Pope has drastically extended the doctrine of papal infallibility.

This is a doctrine the Church has historically been most careful to limit, and for obvious reasons: it is hard to imagine a doctrine more offensive to other religious groups. It says: the differences between my sect and yours are *not* merely a matter of mistranslation, or accumulated copying errors over centuries, or God speaking differently to different cultures in different conditions. I'm right and you're wrong: God told me so, personally—and not millennia ago, but just now.

Even someone who believes that must notice how arrogant it sounds. Hey Jack, if you're infallible, how come you didn't warn us about Brian Mulroney? So when I was in Catholic school, we were taught that if those of other faiths criticized papal infallibility, we should correct the misconception: the Pope was infallible *only* when he spoke "ex cathedra," which he did solely in matters of faith and morals.

Problem is, the phrase "matters of faith and morals" means anything the Pontiff says it does. The wholesale butchery and rape of innocent Muslims by Christians practically next door to him over the past decade, for instance, is not a matter of faith or morals—or were there mass excommunications in Serbia I didn't read about?

What then *are* the important faith-and-morals issues of the day, the points God chose to stress in his last conversation with the Pope, the things a Catholic now *must* believe if she is to call herself a Catholic?

God dislikes women: forget female priests, for all time. God finds women too repulsive to deal with directly. Nor is He comfortable with men, if they have recently been sexually intimate with a woman: forget married priests, too. The Church's principal miracle, Transubstantiation, is reserved not merely to males, but to celibate males.

God dislikes gays: as with women, even celibacy isn't enough to excuse a homosexual: forget gay priests. In fact, forget gays: they remind God of women.

God likes overpopulation: the miracle that *can't* be taken away from women is actually a duty, which they must perform relentlessly: effective birth-control is prohibited, and procreation remains the only valid excuse for sexual pleasure. God cannot do arithmetic, so Catholics must multiply.

God hates singles: the fourth most powerful compulsion He hardwired into us (after the compulsions to eat, excrete and tell other people what to do) is forbidden outside matrimony. God feels sexual ignorance makes for a good marriage. Widow(er)s lose the right to a healthy sex life until they correct their defect.

God is a sadist: terminal patients in agony are forbidden to seek premature relief; He sent that agony deliberately and requires them to experience every pointless drop, or be damned.

God is a bigot: in a bizarre footnote which may stir more controversy here and in England than in America, Catholics are now specifically forbidden to believe in "the legitimacy of Anglican ordinations." Rejecting the literal interpretation (the Pope just called the Archbishop of Canterbury a bastard) we are left with two possibilities: the Pope simply stated a tautology (Anglican clerics are not Catholic clerics) or he issued fighting words (Anglican clerics are not men of God at all).

God likes to fool us: Catholics are forbidden to doubt "the legitimacy of papal elections"—in which fallible mortals infallibly choose an infallible Pope. The copious historical evidence that the chain of Apostolic succession was broken more than once during the Middle Ages is just one of those tricks, like fossil evidence of evolution, that God sometimes uses to tempt evil people—the rational ones—into revealing themselves.

God isn't perfect: Catholics are forbidden to doubt "the canonization of the saints." What then of Saint Josaphat? Don't bother looking him up: he isn't in the roster any more. But he was for centuries—until someone finally got around to closely examining the original field reports—and realized the man they described was better, and rather more widely, known as the Buddha. He is by no means the only deletion from the "undoubtable" list over the years, but certainly the most embarrassing.

God hates dissent: the above beliefs are required of all Catholic prelates, priests, theology teachers and religious superiors (I've always found that last an oxymoron), without argument, on pain of sanctions including excommunication and eternal hellfire. (Parishioners may argue, as long as they lose.)

Faced with the twenty-first century, Catholicism has opted to lunge headlong into the seventeenth. Its conception of God now closely resembles Chairman Mao. Like him, and like the Anti-Drug Empire, the Church has decided that if something isn't working, you just shut your eyes and do it twice as hard. (Same slogan as the drug war, too: "Just say 'no.'") It has opted for authority over reason, stasis over change, death over life, and so it will continue its steady dwindle. A pity, for during its first two millennia it accomplished enormous good—perhaps even as much good as harm. Who knows what it might have accomplished if it had been willing to grow? I'm glad there are other, less intransigent Christian sects extant—for the third millennium will belong to the rational, and they simply aren't going to swallow such sexist authoritarian nonsense. Not even in the Crazy Years.

You Just Can't Kill for Jesus/Allah/Jahweh/Rama/Elvis....

FIRST PRINTED APRIL 2002

God is omniscient, omnipotent and omnibenevolent—it says so right here on the label. If you have a mind capable of believing all three of these divine attributes simultaneously, I have a wonderful bargain for you. No checks please. Cash, and in small bills.
—ROBERT ANSON HEINLEIN

A FEW YEARS AGO we finally persuaded psychiatrists to remove homosexuality from the list of recognized mental disorders. Maybe it's time we started lobbying them to *add* belief in God to the list. Belief in an angry, intolerant one, anyway.

I'm told 81 percent of Canadians believe in God, or at least claim to when asked by a pollster whose expression makes it clear the only other possible stance is satanism. I believe what that statistic actually means is that most of my fellow Canadians realize the universe is larger than themselves, sense there is something higher and better to aspire to, yearn for a deeper understanding of suffering and mortality, have difficulty accepting that 12 billion years of blindly bumping particles just happened to produce their love's left eyelash and Lennon and McCartney and/or are capable of awe and wonder. I refuse to accept that four out of five of my neighbors believe in a bearded paranoid in the sky who enjoys having His feet regularly washed in the blood of heathens and licked clean, and plans to torture most humans for eternity.

It seems to me that if a religion decides, with an entire planet to pick from, to select as its most sacred spot one already in use by another religion and to kill for possession of it...then and there, that religion is disqualified. Revealed to be bogus, whatever else it professes or does, until the day it recants. It cannot be a genuine, bonafide religion if it permits (much less requires) spilling human blood for God—it *must* be either a fraud or a severe mental disorder. If the religion already in possession of the sacred spot spills civilian blood to keep the place...they're disqualified too. Any shaman who believes God wants children orphaned or maimed over the zip code of His temple is by definition out of touch with God, incompetent to preach.

I'm calling for minimal standards of shamanic competence. Physicians must swear to "First, do no harm," before we let them use a scalpel on so much as a dead frog; it's time we started requiring that much of our soul-doctors. "*First, kill no unbelievers....*" Any faith that won't go at least that far should forfeit tax exempt status.

All four of the world's major religions are presently in disgrace, and all are hip-deep in denial. How many Arab imams have publicly denounced Arafat or suicide-bombing? How many Israeli rabbis have loudly repudiated Sharon or provocative settlement? How many Hindu or Muslim leaders in India have spoken out against the madness there? How many Catholic cardinals have condemned abortionist-murderers, bishops covering for pedophile priests or Pius X's quiet complicity in the Holocaust? I'm sick of all four allegedly godly gangs: I don't even use their product and I'm disgusted by the shoddy merchandise they peddle. I demand assurances that a given religion will *not* cause or potentiate mass homicidal psychosis or priestly pedophilia before we let it indoctrinate helpless children and vulnerable adults. Bloodthirsty, authoritarian theology threatens Canada as much as tobacco, obesity and booze put together, and endangers our planet more than global warming, nuclear winter or rogue asteroids.

I have not been what most would call religious since I left a Catholic seminary at fifteen. (Still a virgin, oddly.) But I get along very well with people who are religious, even profoundly so. I'm prepared to prove it: I've been happily married to a monk for twenty-seven years now.

I'm not a Buddhist myself—I use Irish whiskey—but I respect my lay-ordained wife's Soto Zen faith highly. As far as I can tell Buddhists don't seem to go in for holy war, though there are as many flavors of Buddhism as there are sects of Christianity. Get a Buddhist totally outraged, and he tends to set *himself* on fire... taking care for bystanders downwind. Siddhartha Gautama's message has spread across the planet, not by blood and conquest, but by example and adaptation—altering to fit the local culture as it passed from India through Tibet to China, thence to Japan, and most recently to North America. Most Buddhists seem far more interested in achieving the *real* state than in acquiring real estate.

I note too that Buddhism is one of the rare religions that does not have a central god. (Though Tibetan, Korean and Burmese varieties did incorporate preexisting pantheons of gods and demons.) Buddha is not divine; the name means only "Awakened One." The historical Buddha was the seventh in a series of twenty-one buddhas. There's no UberDaddy, no paradise to bribe with, no hellfire to threaten with, no Satan Great or small. There are hells...but they're states of mind. Tolerance appears built into Buddhism's very bones; it seeks only freedom from delusion. Buddhists may belong to other religions—that sort of says it all.

I don't object to people believing silly things; I believe some silly things myself. Where I draw the line, where I suggest all civilized residents of this crowded starship *must* soon draw the line, is the point at which someone's God tells him to go kill those unbelievers in the next valley. That's the basic litmus test I'm proposing. A God who says He wants you so much as *arguing theology* with your neighbor, much less trading punches (let alone bullets), is not God at all, but 1) a damnable hypocrisy invented to excuse villainy, or 2) the same voice all the *other* schizophrenics hear if they stop taking their medication.

My friend Stephen Gaskin once said, "Religions only look different if you get 'em retail. But if you go to a wholesaler, you'll find it all comes from the same distributor anyway." Fine with me. But I want minimal consumer safety standards instituted in the metaphysical marketplace. Caveat emptor just isn't working.

Biting the Hand That Leads Us

FIRST PRINTED FEBRUARY 1999

UILD A BETTER MOUSETRAP, and the world will probably mug you and forget you.

We do not treat our genius inventors well. We take their creations, and often give them little or nothing in return—not even the cold consolation of credit for their achievements.

Consider the archetypal case: the man who created the twentieth century, single-handed. I'll bet you don't know his name. All technology which exists in this century, and could not have existed in the last, derives directly from his extraordinary work—yet when *Globe and Mail* readers (an educated crowd) voted for the "most influential people of the century," his name was obscenely conspicuous by its absence, even as a runner-up. I'll give you a hint: he made electricity practical.

If you guessed Edison, you've proved my point. Edison championed the virtually-useless DC (direct current). If your city were powered by DC, there would have to be a power plant every two blocks. Instead we use the more practical AC (alternating current)—which Edison lied, lobbied and tortured animals to try and suppress. I'm talking here about the chap who invented radio.

No, not Marconi. Guglielmo ripped off radio from the same man I'm speaking of—the US Supreme Court ruled it so, after lengthy consideration. In addition to radio and alternating current, this man invented and patented the electric motor, transformer, condenser, the robot, the remote control, five different propulsion systems, all the essential components of the transistor and half of the basic circuits needed to build a computer. If you know his name at all, it is probably as the inventor of a coil used as a special-effect in the 1931 *Frankenstein* film. He was called Nikola Tesla, and he died broke in 1943—eight months before the Supreme Court proclaimed him the true inventor of radio. Shamefully, he was not even inducted into the Inventors Hall of Fame until 1975.

Tesla is merely the template, the first- and worst-screwed genius of this century. Few of his successors have had better luck. Consider the man who wrote the most successful computer operating system in history: DOS, precursor of Windows.

Now you're sure I'm crazy. Has there ever been a luckier man than Bill Gates? An interesting question—but moot, because Mr. Gates didn't write DOS. Nobody at Microsoft did. Actually, depending on how you look at it, *two* men did—and neither one ever saw a penny from it.

Last year's splendid PBS documentary *Triumph of the Nerds*, a history of the personal computer, unraveled the saga. When IBM decided to enter (and conquer) the PC market, they needed two crucial pieces of software: a version of BASIC, and an operating system to run it on. Microsoft had the former, now a potential goldmine. But it ran on Gary Kildall's CP/M operating system—and Mr. Kildall, inexplicably, declined to deal with IBM! But there was a freeware rip-off of CP/M floating around called *QDOS* (for Quick and Dirty Operating System), and it was functionally indistinguishable from the real thing. Its author, Tim Patterson, had a day-job whose rotten contract gave his employers ownership of any intellectual property he produced, even if he did it at home on "his own" time. Bill Gates found this out, fast-talked Mr. Patterson's bosses out of all of the rights to QDOS, forever, for US$50,000 and soon became the richest computer geek in the world.

Mr. Kildall died soon thereafter, probably never suspecting the extent of his blunder. What about Mr. Patterson? I don't know. The documentary featured extensive interviews, both archival and recent, with the pioneers of that industry. All they had for Mr. Patterson was a photograph and a few seconds of an old appearance on his local community cable channel from *before* his program became famous: apparently PBS could not persuade him to be interviewed today.

Forget the money. Assume there is a certain inner satisfaction in changing the world for the better that's worth more than money. It's a pretty thought, anyway. But what about the *credit?* Anyone who's eaten at a McDonald's knows conceiving an idea worth billions is a way to make thousands—but at least it's still the McDonald brothers' *name* up there above the arches. Tesla deserved more than wealth, he deserved immortality—and thanks to Edison, Marconi and his friend George Westinghouse, got neither.

When I first saw *Triumph of the Nerds*, I made a conscious effort to fix both Mr. Kildall's and Mr. Patterson's names in my memory. Weeks later, I noticed I'd forgotten both. But PBS re-ran the documentary, and this time I taped it. A good thing: I ultimately viewed that tape twice more before I succeeded in committing both names to memory.

This year a sequel to that documentary examined the history of the Internet. We met, in succession, the inventors of such things as the personal computer, mouse, modem, Internet, World Wide Web, e-mail…and they pretty much all had two things in common. If you didn't catch the documentary you've almost certainly never heard of them—and none made a dime. I'd like to tell you all their names—but I accidentally wiped that tape, so the only name I can remember now is Douglas Englebart, father of the mouse.

It's *hard* to remember a name nowadays. A hundred thousand hype machines churn nonstop, insistently repeating Important Names of nitwits. Attempting in self-defense to filter them out, we reach a point where any name we've not heard fifty times is not really heard. And when we do hear one, sometimes what we hear is wrong. The retraction never quite catches up with the original error. (After thirty years and endless corrections, one still sees news stories inaccurately alleging that Sir Paul McCartney's late wife Linda was related to the Eastman Kodak family.) The odds are good that within weeks of reading this essay, you'll be unable to recall Nikola Tesla's name.

Sometimes I worry. In this Age of Information, even geniuses are better-informed than they used to be. They may start noticing the same pattern I have—*before* they start their careers—and say the hell with it. If they do, it will be our fault. As long as we permit improving the world to be a thankless task, we deserve whatever we get.

Whatever

FIRST PRINTED MAY 2003

IT'S A TURNKEY OPERATION. One size fits all. Plug and play. Who am I this week? Whatever.

The computer salesman knows nothing about computers, any more than the bookseller reads—they were both selling shoes last week, next week they'll be selling timeshares. Whatever.

The company is totally controlled by stockholders who will never pass through the town the factory is located in and have not the vaguest idea of what product the factory makes. For that matter, few of the people at the factory care whether the product they're making is any damn good; they're thinking ahead to their next job, because they *know* their real employers are a pack of passing looters they'll never meet. Whatever.

Call your insurance company and the phone will be answered by someone in Atlanta; call the same number the next day, and you'll speak to someone in Seattle who has no record of, or interest in, your previous call. The Minister of Health will be the Minister of Forestry next year, and Minister of Defense the year after that; nobody even thinks this is weird. The marketing department could care less what the product is. Whatever.

All the cars look identical to one another, probably because they're all identical to one another. "You want to go where anybody knows your name." Before you know it, you're in a mind space where you start to get a warm fuzzy feeling from dialing up Amazon.com because, no matter how long you've been away, the Amazon robot will always remember your tastes in music and can remind you. Whatever.

Disconnect.

We all crave freedom, avoid entanglement, strive to evade definition— and thus know less and less about what we're doing. Nobody would be caught dead actually *caring* about something. We're coming to be like bits in a computer chip: not much caring whether we're zeroes or ones—much less whether the pattern of zeroes and ones we're part of represents a spreadsheet or a love letter. There is more beauty, and dignity, in a hoe. Even a chamber pot has a purpose.

My former brother-in-law Clark Spangler designs synthesizers. The first time he went to Japan, to inspect the Yamaha factory that was producing his famous CS model, he was considerably startled by how incredibly *proud* everybody he met there was—proud of their job, their product and their company. On the assembly line he met a man who, he still maintains, was unmistakably the happiest man on the face of the planet.

"This little guy's entire job consisted of standing beside a conveyor belt and, as widgets came endlessly by, picking them up and tightening the third screw from the top," he told me. "He did this all day long, every day, had done this all his life—and he was just so serenely, self-evidently, transcendently happy that when other workers had problems they used to like to stand around near him, just to take a hit."

Fascinated, Clark spent time with the man, curious to understand the source of this unfailing joy. "It turned out to be so simple," he says. "This fellow *knew*—knew for a fact, right down to his soles—that he was the very best third-screw-from-the-top-of-a-widget tightener there was."

How many of us sophisticates can even comprehend that kind of pride? What do *we* have to be proud of? "Not much is needed to destroy a man; merely persuade him that his labors are useless." How many of us do anything actually useful anymore? And what of those who do?

The nurses are useful and deserve to be proud. But they must spend a large and growing portion of every day explaining to helpless people in pain that they will not be getting what they deserve, because it simply isn't there to be gotten, because the tax money intended to pay for it was stolen. Hard to be proud of that, even though they know it's not their fault.

The same with the teachers: they're past masters at making bricks without straw, and nonetheless every day they must shortchange the students they love, because they've been given no choice; donating massively of their own time and money isn't always enough to restore the pride they deserve to enjoy.

The police have every right to be proud...but along with all the good they do, they're also required to help force prostitutes into the control of pimps, enforce hideously absurd drug laws that generate most of the crime in the first place, wave drunken drivers through the system and back out onto the highway and sometimes mace crowds of protesting citizens at the behest of creeps in expensive suits. Such things erode pride.

The social workers ought to be proudest of all, the proudest people in our whole society—for they do the work of nurses, teachers and police combined, and more, for wages an assistant manager at MacDonald's would scorn. Nobody is more overworked or underpaid. *Everybody* else's failures—the mistakes and omissions of parents, schools, churches, cops, mental health professionals, lawmakers, politicians—all end up on the social workers' plates. All they see all day are the terrified and the doomed, whom they can't help—and nobody ever sees them at all. Until, inevitably, they drop one of the fifty eggs we've demanded they juggle at a time, whereupon we flay them alive on the front page and cut their budget a little further.

No wonder each new generation disconnects just a little more. They're getting smarter, that's all. They see how our society treats those who do give a damn. Pretty soon a day will come when we're *all* too smart to care, and everyone is tragically hip. Shortly after that, we'll join the auk, the passenger pigeon and the dodo in the evolutionary Trash Folder.

Or, we could start learning to value and reward those who care.

Environmental Floss

Loathe Yourself, Fine—But Leave Me Out of It.

FIRST PRINTED JUNE 2001

THE FIRST STORY I EVER WROTE, "The Dreaming Dervish," concerned a beautiful dancer in a trance, endlessly spinning in a transport of ecstasy, whose concentration is disturbed when she notices she has contracted fleas. She takes steps to change her blood chemistry; the fleas are exterminated; the dance goes on. Tomato surprise: the dancer is Mother Gaea; the blood is her fresh water, the fleas were us. Ta-dom!

In my defense, I was twenty. The year was 1969. The story was written for free...and worth every cent.

I evolved. My first novel *Telempath*, a few years later, involved a genius who found a way to make nasty industrial civilization vanish overnight—by simply enhancing everyone's sense of smell a thousand fold. He soon learned that civilization at its worst never smelled as bad as 6 billion rotting corpses...and that when the few starving survivors redefine you as "dinner," industry—at least the part that used to produce .44 caliber firesticks—can come to have retroactive charms.

I'd decided by then, in other words, that for me, if it ever comes down to a choice between noble Mother Gaea and my filthy quarrelsome fellow monkeys—and it does, all the time—I vote for us. We can get *more* planets, build 'em from scratch if we must—but the universe can never get another human race.

And would be poorer for the loss. That's the key, right there. The single most important question we have to face if we're to survive this new millennium is: *do we deserve to?* Or are we, when you come right down to it, just too disgusting to live?

I don't care how healthy Gaea is if there are no humans left aboard to appreciate her splendor. I have difficulty believing any rational person could feel otherwise. But over the years since I wrote *Telempath*, I've watched with astonished dismay as more and more of my contemporaries—not ignorant peasants but expensively educated aristocrats—have come to feel this planet would be a far nicer place if only there weren't any damn people on it. God forbid we go to space and despoil Mars too.

I believe this attitude to be insane, profoundly sick, a brain-virus that may turn out to be the most deadly of all the psychic cancers we've created for ourselves. It bespeaks a deep species-wide self-loathing which I suspect may result from deep personal self-loathing given too much free time to fester. Perhaps it made a kind of sense during the period when two loud-mouthed governments deemed it in their own best interest to repeatedly warn the world that the End of Everything was, in Mr. Jagger's words, just a shot away. If you believed total doom was inevitable, then loathing your own species was a way of saying hey, those grapes were sour anyway. But that period *ended*.

And still we have endless articles like Alanna Mitchell's recent four-part series, "Are we on the road to extinction?," whose clear subtext is that we deserve to be. Or conferences like the one held at UBC a few years ago, "Remaining Human in the Face of Our Growing Dependence on Technology," in which 250 visibly well-nourished philosophers, psychologists, spiritual seekers, alternative health practitioners, entertainers and even a slumming scientist or two came by jet plane from around the planet to agree with each other that technology is toxic, consumerism is unnatural, computers cause alienation and loneliness, civilization pollutes and we're stressing the ecosystem to the point of collapse. Oddly, none of them volunteered to kill or sterilize themselves.

"Consume" means "eat." There is a technical term for lifeforms which do not consume: we call them "dead." Consumerism is utterly natural; everything alive is a consumer. Only humans have learned (or ever tried) to occasionally accomplish it without bloodshed. Everything alive pollutes: excretion is part of the definition of life. Only humans make any effort to regulate or recycle their wastes. Every life-form grows until it stresses its environment and is slapped back down again. Humans are the only ones who even attempt to live in harmony with their environment. For *damn* sure they're the only ones who think they should be better at it and keep trying to learn how.

Computers cause alienation and loneliness? Only in those too afraid to use them. Everyone else is busily forming an astonishing multitude of new planet-wide communities based on shared interests—communities stronger and more tolerant and generous than any ever seen before in history.

Technology is toxic? But for technology I'd have died at fifteen when I had my first lung collapse. Without trifocal technology I'd be too blind to read, write or drive safely. In my twenties I spent several years in the woods, deliberately trying to live without technology, in order to minimize the "footprint" I was leaving on the ecology. Finally I realized I was enlarging it. A woodstove is *more* polluting and energy-wasteful than electric heat— and offers constant risk of serious injury, from saw to chopping block to firebox. Kerosene is *more* polluting, dangerous and energy-expensive than electric light—and stinks. I never did learn how to make my own axe-head, knife, stove, horseshoes, plow or even typewriter.

Even with such aids, I spent every waking minute trying to survive. Today I fritter away most of my time thinking deep thoughts, writing trenchant essays, reading good books and writing better ones—on a computer nobody even dreamed of back when I wrote "The Dreaming Dervish" in longhand. If you want to believe my life in the woods was somehow nobler, purer, I urge you to try it yourself. People without technology tend to bury most of their children and to die before thirty themselves...often with relief.

The problem with technology is the large number of people who haven't got it yet. There's nothing wrong with this planet that couldn't be cured by making everyone on it rich. We may never conquer envy, but we can unquestionably abolish need if we put our minds to it. The way to do that is the method that's been working steadily for the last three centuries now: more, better, more efficient, cleaner, smarter, more humane technology.

Some Cats Know

FIRST PRINTED JUNE 2001

L ET ME EXPLAIN WHY I grind my teeth hard enough to generate sparks whenever someone—invariably a person with something to sell—speaks sonorously of "what science now knows about global warming."

I have a deep and abiding respect for science. It *earned* that respect, with several trillion man-hours of tedious, painstaking work. Science is basically The Facts. The Anti-Crap. For millennia, the only definitive way to settle any argument was with force. Most beliefs were religious beliefs, matters of opinion, subject to error, endless debate or monarch's whim. Finally came science, which simply means knowing. (Latin *scio*="to know") Really knowing, for certain—even if someone bigger and stronger disagrees.

"Look," said one early scientist, "there are countless things I don't know and never will. But this thing I *know*: if you drop a coin and a cannonball from the same height at the same time, they'll hit the ground together. Look: I can prove it." And by golly he did—and anyone else who tried got the same result unless they cheated.

How'd you figure that out? one bystander asked. "Well," he said, "there's this method I use. I wonder why something is so, and I think up a theory, *and then I test the theory*." By the sword? "By experiment. I make a prediction based on my theory, and test it. A test so clear that even someone with a different theory has to admit I'm right." That's it? "Well, I keep really good records, so I don't have to keep repeating the test every time a skeptic shows up." That basically is science. Clever folks frowning at each other and saying, "Oh yeah? Prove it," until finally they know a few things for sure.

Well, once you actually know a few things, you can finally start *getting* somewhere, and after awhile people were living past thirty, and more than half their babies lived to grow up, and a lot of them had cable and high speed Internet access and time to worry about the fate of Mother Gaia or even read a Spider Robinson novel. Pretty cool. So I have great respect, not only for the traditional sciences, but even for those newer fields, like psychology or sociology or nutrition, that are still striving earnestly to achieve that noble status—and there are a lot these days.

Planetary ecology is one of the feeblest.

It has only just begun the long difficult process that elevates an area of intellectual interest to the level of a science—not surprising when you reflect that only fifty years ago, nobody had ever heard of it. Today it is—at its best, when it isn't just a way to be heroic without actually doing anything brave—largely good intentions, wishful thinking and pious hopes in search of significant data and meaningful experiments. Acupuncture has a far better-established claim to be called science.

Here is what ecologists *know*, so far, that they didn't basically cop from some preexisting science: the whole biosphere is interconnected, such that a butterfly flapping its wings in Borneo may cause a tornado in Calgary. An admirable insight. But as to exactly how the butterfly does this, or what Calgary might one day do to locate and dissuade it, we are nearly as clueless today as we were in 1950, or in the Stone Age.

Theories we got. Boy, have ecologists got theories. So do handicappers and other theologians. Predictions they have aplenty, too. It sometimes seems they produce little else—all, interestingly, long-term: the predictors will be safely dead before the results come in.

And isn't it a funny coincidence that not one single ecoprediction ever seems to be a cheerful one? Almost as if they'd noticed that "We're doomed!" is a grabbier headline than "We're hangin' in there...."

What they don't have, and won't anytime soon, are many *experiments*. We only have the one planet. (So far.) To make perceptible changes to something so vast requires forces as powerful, and hard to control, as a meteorite or an industrial civilization. No matter what scale you work on, results take decades or centuries to show up. And the people who live on the planet may object to your tinkering.

So what do ecologists actually study and base most of their apocalyptic predictions on? What is the fundamental basis of their "science," as presently constituted?

Computer models.

Computer models are *caca*. Forget facts, or even theories: they don't deserve the status of a guess. Computer models are games one plays with oneself, as meaningful as throwing knucklebones or fashioning a voodoo doll—oracles only slightly more sophisticated than a magic eight-ball. The greatest programmer who ever lived cannot construct a computer model that accurately and fully describes a single cell...much less a stem cell. The most powerful computer ever constructed cannot reliably predict the behavior of a single five-year-old...let alone an electorate of adults. Nortel's model of the telecommunications business—a single industry—turned out to have major predictive shortcomings. Nineteen billions worth.

All computer models fail to factor in the (inevitable) invention of newer, better technologies, changing social customs and the discovery of new resources. The notion that a system as complex as a single storm can be meaningfully modeled with a Pentium chip, or even a bank of Crays, is absurd; to claim to have modeled the biosphere is to declare oneself a fool, one short step above someone who thinks Myst is a real world.

A great many such fools currently claim—*demand*, actually—the moral right to direct and constrain the actions of every government, industry and society on earth, to micromanage the entire atmosphere, on the basis of their computer-game scenarios. Fair enough; everybody has a right to his hustle. They may even turn out to be right in the end, for all I—or they, or anybody—know. It just makes me crazy when they or their fans call them "scientists," that's all. That ain't right. It's a term that shouldn't be debased, like "veteran." In the immortal words of Leiber and Stoller, "If a cat don't *know*...he just don't know."

Voluntary Poverty Threatens Real Poor People

FIRST PRINTED JUNE 2001

Others say the human population level is okay and can continue to increase because science will meet our needs with new sources of energy and things like that. But even if we can sustain 10 billion people, then as time goes it will become 15 billion then 20 billion. Impossible!
—THE DALAI LAMA

SHOCKINGLY SLOPPY THINKING for one both so educated and so wise. It's very simple, Your Holiness:

- Every society that ever got rich promptly lowered its birthrate toward Zero Population Growth level. (And started to fill with starving immigrants.) Without exception in recorded history. No society that was *not* rich *ever* did so.
- Every society that ever got rich stopped having civil wars, and then wars period. No society that was not rich ever has.
- Every society that ever got rich developed and adopted the concepts of personal freedom and representative government. No society that was not rich ever did.
- Every society that ever got rich emancipated its women, minorities and other untouchables. No society that was not rich ever has.
- Every society that ever got rich soon began legislating religious freedom. No society that was not rich ever has.

What is it the Dalai Lama doesn't get?

Humans *always* overpopulate, then kill each other fighting over scraps...unless they manage to build (or stumble into) a society *so* wealthy it can afford the luxury of people who've decided to limit their birthrate for the sake of Mother Gaia. You'll rarely find anyone not rich who gives a *damn* about her: a starving man hasn't the luxury. Loving the whole biosphere would be utterly incomprehensible to the average human throughout history: a hungry terrified diseased savage whose only hope of an endurable old age (one's forties, that is) is to have fifteen kids, of whom, if he/she is lucky, as many as two males may survive to adulthood.

If we keep industrial civilization going, and growing, until we're *all* rich, then at that point, whatever it is, the population will level off. Or even decrease. And not one member of it will go to bed hungry.

On that day I won't give a flying fart what's gone extinct in the process, or whether there are fewer pristine parklands for environmentalists (only) to hike through. At that point, we will disassemble every bit of pollution on this planet, atom by atom, and make it into anything we think we'd rather have instead. We will *make* as many trees as it pleases us to look at. We will *recreate* every extinct species we had the goddamn brains to preserve a DNA sample from. (Now there's a practical task for ecowarriors…who *aren't* parlor poseurs.) We'll invent *new* species Mother Gaia never dreamed of: really cool, fun ones.

Can we crank industrial civilization that high? Is it really possible to make everybody that rich? Yep. It's called nanotechnology, and it's less than a century away. Maybe way less. Your grandchildren will be able to literally do anything they can imagine, and have anything they desire that they can describe. *Their* children's hardest feat of imagination will be trying to picture a world in which people used to *need* stuff. And sometimes didn't get it. For details see *The Engines of Creation* by C. Eric Drexler.

The human race *must* pursue that glorious vision: die trying if necessary. We dare not throttle back the machine at this point. It's a cranky old machine, jerry-built, run by committee and *very* low on fuel. If we permit it to so much as stall, we'll never get it running again: there just aren't enough metals and fossil fuels left in the ground to start over. All we can do is pray the furshlugginer machine will run on fumes long enough to get us to nanotech, the Ultimate Gas Station.

If it doesn't—and it may not—billions may die. But if we don't try, those billions will certainly die. The die was cast centuries ago, when we committed, irrevocably, to the Industrial Revolution. It's *way* too late to change our minds.

Until nanotech arrives, people will shit and machines will produce exhaust, and that's not sufficient reason to either shut off all the machines or kill even one of the people. Instead we must learn how to turn shit into fertilizer, and waste into assets. ("nuclear waste product" = popular nonsense term for a priceless irreplaceable resource for which no practical commercial use presently exists, i.e. something that won't *need* to be stored for ten thousand years . . .) And you don't do that with less technology, but with more and better technology.

The ultimate fate of mankind will depend on the outcome of a contest between two incompossible mindsets. Here's the antinomy: suppose you *must* choose between one of two imaginary futures.

2100 A.D., VERSION A: Mankind, cats, dogs, horses and dolphins are the only creatures still alive on earth. They're all thriving, well fed on synthetics, and there's copious cheap energy around...but every single other species that lived 100 years ago is now extinct. (*Really* extinct: all the preserved DNA got accidentally defrosted.) There isn't a blade of grass anywhere that isn't a Disney fake; all the songbirds are robots; there are no germs, because there's nothing they could eat that they're allowed to. Grim, eh?

2100 A.D., VERSION B: Every species of life that was alive in 2001 is not only alive but thriving, every species that vanished since the Industrial Revolution has been restored and fascinating new ones are appearing daily. Gaia is blooming. But: there are no human beings, anywhere. Nor ever will be again. They all died.

That's not the choice, but imagine it were. *Which do you pick?*

That's a question like "are you for or against slavery?" One which can— and I believe should—divide households and set brother against brother.

I say anybody who picks Future B is profoundly ill. In mind, or soul, or both. I'm a human. In a crunch, I vote for humans. Sure, some are jerks...but some are Dalai Lamas. Any animal too sick or ashamed of itself to stick up for its own kind is not only a fool, it must be a human being. No other species produces members that dumb.

Ain't That a Shame

FIRST PRINTED AUGUST 2001

STAND CLEAR, PLEASE; I feel a rant coming on. I've just heard for the *n*th time, and once too often, some smug Pharisee on a TV talk show use the word "consumer" as a term of opprobrium. We ought to be ashamed of ourselves, was his point, because we deliberately permit a "consumer society" to exist even though everyone knows that it is an evil thing.

But I'm grateful to him for leading me to an interesting insight. Even subtracting the ten pounds they say the camera adds, I could see that he himself had not missed any meals recently...and musing on that, I suddenly reached a better understanding of why there's so much psychotic pressure placed on us all to be scrawny these days.

There's nothing intrinsically sexually undesirable about a normally fleshy person of either sex: if there were, the human race could hardly exist. An afternoon in any museum should demonstrate the proposition even to the logically-challenged. This generation of this society has *chosen* to find anorexia attractive and a normal body repulsive. But *why*? Why would any male pick a feminine ideal with hips unlikely to survive childbirth, undeveloped breasts and insufficient body fat to survive even the most transitory hard times? Why would a woman yearn for a mate whose status is so low that he needs to be in as good shape as a common laborer or warrior? Why would anybody seek sensual pleasure with someone who evidently has either no appetites or inhuman restraint?

The point, I now suspect, is that body fat is visible proof of having...whisper it...eaten.

Somewhere deep in all humans lies a powerful, perhaps irresistible need to be ashamed. In every culture or clime we *always* find or invent something to be mortally embarrassed about—ideally, something we absolutely cannot help. We need, God knows why, a good reason to second-guess the supposedly infallible God who made us in His image, an excuse to cringe every time we look in the mirror.

In contemporary Western society we recently gave up the ancient right to be ashamed of having genitalia and a need to use them. This lets us have lots more fun than our forebears, and since we've developed effective birth control we can (finally!) afford the indulgence. Unfortunately, it leaves us with little to really despise ourselves for except our equally disgusting digestive system: our unforgivable—and just incidentally, quite unavoidable—need to eat and excrete. This, if you've been wondering, is why sex comedies aren't working anymore lately, and poo-poo wee-wee comedies are. So today we, the educated elite, are ashamed that we "consume," and we are mortified that we "pollute our environment." The way every other living thing does, happily and heedlessly.

We can, of course, always take shame in the fact that no matter what we do or how hard we police ourselves, in all times and cultures men and women seem to assay out at about five to ten percent homosexual. Finding the genitalia and sexual needs of the opposite sex to be acceptable doesn't mean your own can't be stomach-churningly disgusting. And we can also be somewhat ashamed that we're racist. Far less so than any other known species, to be sure, and North Americans are probably the *least* racist humans that ever walked this planet. (Disagree? Ask a Carthaginian. Or a Korean...in Japan. Or a Chinese in Uganda, or an Indian untouchable at home.) But still, distrust of the strange *is* an inborn instinct we have not yet tamed utterly, so it'll do for a proof that we don't deserve to live.

We're accustomed to lament the fact that we're so bellicose. But a half century comparatively free of bloodshed—by historical standards—has begun to spoil that particular form of self-flagellation. We still have local skirmishes and civil wars, but with the end of the Cold War and the minting of the Euro, warfare is beginning to look like a game we're finally learning to outgrow.

No, our best present excuse for frissons of horror at our own awfulness is consumption and its despicable result: this unforgivably comfortable technological civilization we've built for ourselves. Somehow—more or less by accident, as a result of billions of random selfish decisions interacting—we've cobbled together a truly astonishing machine: one which makes it possible for six billion people to survive, with an historically unprecedented minimum of warfare, famine and plague, to an average age exceeding sixty years; one which produces so much loot, most of us can get at least some without having to kill or die for it.

But this remarkable machine is imperfect. It does not share its wealth evenly. Instead it tends to discriminate in favor of those who thought it up, built it and keep it running. Worse, it produces exhaust, emits soot. Therefore it does not deserve to exist. It is...oh most damning of words, most withering of indictments...*dirty*. It should be throttled back sharply at once, if not shut down altogether, so that we may return to a superior state of harmony with nature which history has somehow neglected to record.

We know, for fact, that wind, water and sunpower are simply not enough to keep six billion people alive and happy—not even close. So our plan is to wish they were, very hard. Perhaps after a century or two of restored harmony with Mother Gaia, living like other animals—I mean Disney animals, of course—we'll be able to live down the shame of having once tried to live longer or better than Mother intended.

Then we'll have having-once-had-greatness-and-blown-it to be ashamed of, of course. But on the bright side: boy, will we all be thin.

Extreme Forms
of Argument

Mass Destruction Isn't Rocket Science

FIRST PRINTED JANUARY 2001

I'VE KEPT SILENT UNTIL RECENTLY on the subject of NMD—the controversial Nuclear Missile Defense shield that President Bush and Defense Secretary Powell intend to deploy over the United States by 2005. The subject is so complex I've had trouble making up my own mind.

An excellent, albeit greatly condensed, synopsis of the antinomy was given in an episode of *The West Wing*...and while fictional President Bartlet, predictably opposed to NMD, also predictably won the debate, I found it noteworthy that the opposing side was argued *not* by one of the callow youths around him, but by his most trusted adviser Leo, the character who's always been presented as sane, wise and practical. Leo argued so passionately and intelligently for NMD that it seems even a flaming liberal like Aaron Sorkin, then still writer/producer, considers this a topic on which reasonable people may differ.

As I said, his synopsis necessarily suffered from the compression required in TV drama. But it helped clarify my own thinking enough that I now have an opinion. Let's begin with the main arguments *against* NMD:

1. It doesn't work. This is the mantra President Bartlet kept chanting to Leo, and he's right: of three attempted missile interceptions to date, two have failed—badly—falling well short of the Pentagon's own minimum criteria for deployment. The *best* test so far missed its

target by *miles*. And they've been working on this since the Reagan Administration.

2. Even if they get it working, there are simple, effective counters—radar chaff composed of cheap mylar balloons, for example.

3. Its proponents say it'll cost US$60 billion. In other words, it cannot possibly cost less than US$150 billion. Even for the US government, that's...a bit pricey.

4. It's illegal. It breaks America's word, flagrantly violating the 1972 ABM treaty.

5. It's *vigorously* opposed by Russia, China, Germany, France and several other nations, since it would theoretically permit a US first-strike attack. Some say NMD would "allow the US to militarize space."

6. So far, the US has never asked for use of Canada's radars, on which NMD utterly depends; they simply assume our obedience. Pardon me, I meant "our cooperation."

Now the NMD camp's rebuttal:

1. It *will* work. And soon. If we can pace a hurtling comet at 100 meters, or thread an orbital needle out by Jupiter—and we have—we can certainly manage to swat flies; it's simply a matter of beating the engineers hard enough. We already know how to defeat far more sophisticated countermeasures than radar chaff.

2. It'll give the US economy an infusion of (at least) $60 billion, creating jobs, profits, tax revenue down the line—*plus* plenty of new spin-off technologies. To date, every penny the US federal government ever spent on space technology has been repaid, *in hard cash*, thirteen times over.

3. The ABM Treaty is irrelevant in today's world; it was signed twenty-nine years ago in a Cold War world with no Internet, where nuclear material was tightly controlled.

4. NMD opponents seem unaware that Russia *already has* a missile-shield of its own in place over Moscow. As for China, it opposes NMD but supports Pakistan's ICBM (intercontinental ballistic missile) program; meanwhile it's quietly building up its own nuclear capacity *and* a new antisatellite (ASAT) system which is vastly more destabilizing than NMD, since it's clearly aggressive in purpose. "Militarize space"? Space has *been* militarized for decades, folks—do try and keep up. At least seven nations presently have or claim to have a nuclear ICBM program underway. There may be others that are simply more discreet.

5. NMD will provide work for the next generation of talented aerospace engineers and technicians—the ones who were forgotten when the voters got bored with space, after Apollo. It will help preserve skills, knowledge and hardware that cost billions to acquire and today are being lost or forgotten. This is my own favorite "pro" argument: I like anything that furthers space travel.

But now I'd like to raise two points I haven't seen mentioned elsewhere yet, though they seem to me glaringly self-evident.

Assume you want to nuke Manhattan. You're obviously crazy—but no matter how crazy you are, why in God's name would you choose a *rocketship* for your delivery vehicle? It's immensely expensive, hard to build in secret, intrinsically unreliable, easy to see coming and everyone knows where it originated.

What's wrong with a cigarette boat? Or a Cessna, or a truck?

In John McPhee's book *The Curve of Binding Energy*, former H-bomb designer Theodore Taylor stated that a serious nuclear weapon requires only a few hundred pounds of uranium. Drug smugglers run that much dope across the US border every day with no apparent difficulty. (And uranium's a much smaller package than an equal weight of heroin.) Once it's in, who can say where it came from? And everything else you'll need to make an atom bomb is freely available in the States. In my 1992 novel *Lady Slings the Booze*, I described how a moderately clever terrorist (or government) could kill nearly everyone in a large city with a single concealed nuke, triggered by radio signal...and still leave most of the city intact.

But forget all that. Everything I've said above may be beside the point. As usual, the generals are earnestly planning to win not the next world war, but the *previous* one.

Hiroshima and Nagasaki are ancient history. If there's ever a military assault on the US, it probably won't be nuclear...but biological.

You can't fight measles with missiles. Biowar is far more efficient than rockets, immensely more cost-effective, leaves all the treasure and real estate intact...and who's to say whether those bugs are manmade, and if so by whom?

I fear that NMD may be simply irrelevant. As my colleague John Varley says, the world may well end—if we are all stupid enough to permit it to—not with a bang, but with a sniffle.

What Does It Mean to be Human?

FIRST PRINTED SEPTEMBER 2001

A S A SCIENCE FICTION WRITER, I'm probably best known for a series that began with the first story I ever published and twenty-eight years later has metastasized into nine books, all involving a fabulous tavern called Callahan's Place. If I were forced to condense the entire million-word saga into a single word—and I can't tell you how many journalists have asked me to do just that, over the years—the word would be *tolerance*. Specifically, tolerance of the weird. Mike Callahan ran the kind of bar where, if a pink gorilla walked in and ordered a beer, he'd be allowed to drink it in peace. Customers included a talking dog, a cyborg starkiller, the man who accidentally created AIDS and the Internet itself come alive. Callahan often said he didn't insist his customers be human, as long as they had good manners.

Okay, science fiction boy: define "human" for us, in light of the World Trade Center Massacre.

Robert A. Heinlein's classic *Stranger in a Strange Land* concerns a Martian named Valentine Michael Smith. The only survivor of the first human expedition to Mars, Mike is raised from infancy entirely by Martians...then, in his twenties, he is returned to Earth where he spends the bulk of the book being baffled by human beings and trying desperately to learn to become one.

There comes a point when Mike has learned to *imitate* a human quite well, to speak fluently and obey even the most confusing human customs. But he just doesn't *get* humans—can't understand, for instance, why if there is hunger, nobody volunteers to become soup. In particular, he does not get humor. Mike cannot laugh, cannot fathom why humans sometimes bark like that...and it bothers him.

Then one day at the zoo, he tosses a peanut to a monkey. A bigger monkey comes along, beats the little monkey up and steals his peanut. Mike watches. The little monkey gets up, looks around...spots an even smaller monkey and suckerpunches it. And suddenly, for the first time in his life, Mike begins to laugh. And laugh, until he falls to his knees and they have to carry him away, gasping for breath. At last, he understands humans...and thus finally is one himself.

A few days ago I e-mailed several friends a Salon.com essay by Afghanian-American Tamim Ansary, urging us not to blame the starving people of Afghanistan for the actions of the Taliban that crushes them or the terrorists it shelters among them. One respondent agreed, but said the terrorists themselves and their supporters should be "stamped out like cockroaches." I emphatically agreed.

Today Jef Raskin, the man who thought up the Macintosh, responded. "Stamp them out like cockroaches? No. Capture suspects and try them like humans. We have had too much treating humans like cockroaches."

I sent a hasty reply I now regret, saying I was comfortable with a definition of "human" which excluded the Nineteen Nitwits, and anyone who helped them.

I was dead wrong. That's *exactly* the way those Nineteen Nincompoops thought. They were able to butcher thousands of innocent strangers because they had redefined "human" so as to exclude them. Just like Milosevic or Pol Pot or Amin or Hitler or Stalin in *their* turn. If we do the same to them, they win. As Walt Kelly said during the Vietnam War, "We have met the enemy, and he is us."

That's the very essence of human civilization: the sense to realize that revenge *is not possible*, that the generational feuders of Belfast and Jerusalem and other such places are wasting not only their blood, their substance and their lives, but their time. It's a game that can never end, unless and until one side simply makes up its mind to stop. Maybe not to forgive—maybe that's too much to ask—but just to *stop*. For the sake of the children, who don't *care* whether their ancestors slew or were cruelly slain, and shouldn't have to.

Like everyone else in the civilized world, I am too heartsick to stand it, and like everyone else, I would like to transmute my pain into anger. It's slightly easier to carry, and *much* easier to unload. This tragedy also offers me license to unleash some of that free-floating rage and bitterness I carry around, the accumulated residue of a lifetime of petty indignities, frustrations and humiliations. The murderous anger that must have led the Nineteen Numbskulls to bushwhack nearly 3,000 strangers somehow sanctifies my own anger, makes it righteous. In the very words the Blues Brothers used to justify killing or crippling dozens of policemen doing their jobs, "We're on a mission from God."

Well, the Nineteen Knuckleheads thought they were too.

Back in 1976 my wife Jeanne and I wrote, in a novella called "Stardance," these words:

"This is what it is to be human: to see the essential existential futility of all action, all striving—and to act, to strive.... This is what it is to be human: to reach forever beyond your grasp.... This is what it is to be human: to live forever or die trying.... This is what it is to be human: to perpetually ask the unanswerable questions, in the hope that the asking of them will somehow hasten the day when they will be answered.... This is what it is to be human: to strive in the face of the certainty of failure. This is what it is to be human: to persist."

I imagine the Nineteen Nimrods felt the same way, as they saw their unsuspecting targets grow larger in their windshields. They were human, all right. Sick, but human. I apologize, Jef: you were quite right. Let us accord them the same humane treatment we gave Eichmann. Sure, it's more than they deserve. But hey—I want more than *I* deserve. Who doesn't?

Let's not demonize them. Let's just bring them in, try them, offer them a bit of a lie-down...at Tim McVeigh's table...and then, as quickly as possible, do the one thing in our power that might make them squirm even more in the flames of Hell. Forget them.

The Only Thing We Have to Fear

FIRST PRINTED DECEMBER 2001

A S USUAL, THE TRUTH turned out to be both stranger and (thank God) duller than fiction.

Media accounts of the videotape of Osama bin Laden discovered shortly after the World Trade Center Massacre all seem to focus on the same aspect: at last, proof he was behind it! I had thought that case was proved long ago, and even if I hadn't, that was still the least interesting thing about the tape as far as I'm concerned. Assuming it to have been reported accurately, here's what I find most fascinating:

1. Mr. bin Laden was stunned when the towers came down.

He volunteers this information. He says he had presumed the destruction would be limited to those floors above the points of impact. That's right: the fiendishly brilliant criminal genius we've all been so terrified of for months now, the millionaire mastermind whose intellect was so vast it wasn't safe to show him on TV lest he somehow send his minions coded instructions right under our noses, is an idiot. He did absolutely no homework. He knew *nothing* about the construction of those towers, never troubled himself to study the blueprints. He who made his billions largely in construction is utterly ignorant of engineering, architecture or even basic physics. He didn't even assign an underling to bone up on such matters and brief him at any point during his planning process. The man just plain got lucky.

What we all thought was the ingenious coordination of the WTC attacks and the anthrax assault was an illusion too, purest serendipity. Mr. bin Laden seems to have had exactly the same secret weapon the cartoon character George of the Jungle famously depended on: Dumb Luck. And he doesn't even have the sense to be embarrassed about that. As George's colleague Bugs Bunny would say, what a mo-*roon*.

2. He casually admits betraying his own men.

An unspecified number—perhaps most—of the Nineteen Nitwits apparently thought they were on a suicide mission; they believed they were engaged in a simple generic hijacking. They were not martyrs: the correct technical term would be "suckers." They probably died screaming, just like their victims. Since they did not knowingly, willingly, give their lives for jihad, they might well be roasting in Islamic hell right now for all Mr. bin Laden knows.

Or cares. He reportedly expresses no shame or even sorrow for their deaths, and makes no apology for, or even defense of, his appalling treachery. It does not occur to him to reassure his surviving followers worldwide that he will sacrifice *them* only if it should ever prove absolutely, positively useful.

He seems to believe the same thing we all mistakenly thought for awhile just after September 11: that somewhere, he has a large force of eager kamikaze fanatics at his disposal. We believed at least Six Hundred were ready to ride into the Valley of Death at his command. It now appears he may have been able to come up with as few as eight...supported by eleven other trusting chumps who probably expected at worst to get tear-gassed and handcuffed, face a few tough questions from Geraldo and a bad headshot on CNN before getting exchanged for some American or Israeli hostage or another.

The Einstein of Evil—Fu Manchu, Rayt Marius, Lex Luthor, Dr. Moriarity, the Dark Lord of Mordor and You-Know-Who all rolled into one—is an ignorant fathead and doesn't care who knows it. The most sophisticated technological artifacts he seems familiar with are fax machines, cheap camcorders and box-cutters. And jeeps, in which to run away. He cheerfully admits bushwhacking his own troops as policy. His notorious success at mass murder, he admits, was at least two-thirds an accident. His entire escape plan was to go hide behind a big bunch of starving people. We're talking about a mental midget and a moral microbe. His best friend has to have noticed by now he has a heart the size of a raisin.

For fear of this thumbfingered hamhanded braindead stumblebum, we should all swallow Bill C-36? He isn't worth swallowing a Tylenol-2.

Mr. bin Laden isn't worth an extra half hour of wasted time at the airport and a twenty-four dollar ticket surcharge, forever—much less a heart-stopping momentary lurch in the planetary economy—and he *certainly* isn't cause for Canada to abandon such useful concepts as the right to open due process, the right to counsel of choice, the right to remain silent, the right to be presumed innocent until proven guilty, freedom from arbitrary search, seizure or arrest or any of the other minor alterations of the present social contract contained in that bill. Terrorism is a terrible disease, yes...but personally, I'm far more terrified of the self-appointed surgeons of Parliament who propose to cure the disease with radical amputation of essential parts of our country's brain and heart.

Even the so-called "sunset clause" recommended by the Canadian Bar Association—basically, an expiry date—is nowhere near enough protection or reassurance to suit me. Would *you* care to sit in jail without counsel until sunset...if sunset were five years away? Suppose the next diabolically lucky terrorist happens to be of *your* ethnic background? As Silver Donald Cameron pointed out recently, one man's terrorist is another man's freedom fighter: Nelson Mandela would be considered a terrorist, if he hadn't won. Just about every friend I had in the sixties would easily have qualified as a potential threat to national security under the vaguely defined parameters of C-36; today they are, without exception, assets to their community, society and culture. The ones who aren't in jail, anyway.

I'm not willing to sacrifice the kind of people governments usually keep thick dossiers on—you know, undesirables like Harlow Shapley, Nikola Tesla, Mahatma Ghandi, Robert Oppenheimer, Lenny Bruce, Farley Mowat, John Lennon, Ken Kesey, Judith Merril—to try and guard against an occasional Keystone Konspirator with the devil's luck.

Strapped for Takeoff

FIRST PRINTED SEPTEMBER 2001

COULD WE ALL PLEASE take a deep breath—take an Ativan, if necessary—and just *chill* for a minute? I'm much more afraid of panic than I am of terrorists, and when we reach the point where American airline pilots—of all people—start behaving irrationally, it's past time for a reality check.

Okay, Captain Rambo: there you are in the securely locked cockpit of your 757, packing the loaded sidearm you say will make you feel safer. Here comes a bad guy. A guy who, in order to become your target, has to have killed or neutralized every flight attendant, controlled all the passengers and then come through a locked pressure-sealed bulkhead in a big hurry. My question is this: how worried is this guy going to be about a middle-aged man in a sedentary profession with a .22 pistol? (Surely you weren't even dreaming of using some more authoritative caliber?)

Whatever the caliber of your weapon, consider your tactical situation. The enemy can stand beside the hatch, reach in with just his gun hand and spray bullets randomly: anything he hits is good for him and bad for you. Your return fire is *most* unlikely to shoot the gun out of his hand; far more likely it will hit—

—*me*. See me, back there in coach, in seat 27C? Trying desperately to duck, only it's physically impossible for a six-foot-one man to crouch in one of those tiny damned seats? I'm the one who's probably going to take that round you just fired—

—*if* everyone else on the plane is lucky, that is. Because you know better than I do what's probably going to happen if the slug misses me. There are no wasted cubic inches in an airliner: if that slug doesn't hit somebody, odds are it'll either wreck something crucial or depressurize the cabin...or both.

The enemy isn't that dumb: instead of potting away at you with a handgun, he has almost certainly announced his arrival in your life with something more sensible, like gas or smoke or pepper spray. Are you sure there's no place outside your sealed cockpit from which someone knowledgeable enough could add, say, nitrous oxide to your cockpit air supply, Captain? Or cyanide to your water?

Let's grant you some of the quibbles I hear you muttering. Let's say you spend your whole transatlantic flight breathing and drinking exclusively from bottles. You carry a newly invented zero-cost gun that fires high-velocity low-impact needles of a magic new drug that makes people instantly unconscious with no long-term health risks, and you are an expert in its care and use. Suddenly your cell phone rings. Answering it, you hear an unearthly shriek, and then a heavily-accented voice says, "Your child still has one eye left, are you going to do exactly as I tell you?"

Face it: there is no security this side of the grave. Spending a fortune upgrading airport security is much worse than useless: it's exactly what Osama bin Laden would like to see us do. Raise the price of air travel and he has won, as though he'd damaged every single plane in the world.

Surely if there's any lesson we should have learned from the WTC Massacre, it is that security precautions are mostly irrelevant. For the last several decades we have spent countless millions of dollars, irradiated trillions of bags and hard drives, impeded, inconvenienced and insulted millions of honest travelers and wasted enough paper to give every living human three copies of each of my thirty-one books. It accomplished *nothing*. When the enemy was good and ready, he took and held three out of five target planes using box-cutters.

If we demand a security system good enough to keep out every box-cutter, the price of an airline ticket must at least double, and probably worse. And then the enemy will use the con's old standby: a sharpened toothbrush handle. Forbid passengers to carry any utensil whatsoever, and he will garrote the armed sky marshal with his necktie, or she will with her pantyhose. Require all passengers to submit to anal probe and board naked: how will you cope with two or three martial arts experts? Do you know how many planes fly each day? We don't *have* enough martial artists to cover them all.

There is no security measure, however expensive, that the enemy cannot circumvent dirt cheap. So why throw away barrels of good money that could be used to buy better intelligence and catch the bastards before they ever get to the airport?

A lot of American airline pilots are of my generation. I think I know a little of how they feel now. We spent the first three or four decades of our lives at least half-expecting Ragnarok to come at any time, fearing that any day now world war might break out and bring the end of everything. It seemed inconceivable that the Soviet Union could ever just quit. Then it did...and in the dozen plus years since, we've slowly allowed ourselves to relax, to hope, finally to believe that we might yet live out our days without seeing another planetary bloodbath. No wonder we're so angry and frightened now. It's always confusing and infuriating when your alarm clock goes off.

Perhaps we should try and remember that: remember how well it turned out the *last* time disaster seemed inevitable, and calm down a little. As my wife, a Soto Zen Buddhist monk, often tells me: don't just do something, sit there. Molasses border crossings, fascist national ID cards, gunmen on planes, biowar panic—these things will affect *only* honest citizens, and won't impede terrorism in the slightest.

Frank Herbert wrote, "Fear is the Mindkiller. Fear is the little-death that brings total obliteration. I must face my fear. I must permit it to pass over me and through me." Sounds to me like a wonderful way to annoy a terrorist. Not to mention save a few megabucks with which to buy and equip better spies.

The Beam Up Mine Own

FIRST PRINTED APRIL 2003

COMPARED TO THE AVERAGE IRAQI, I've suffered nothing from this war. I have not spent one minute at risk, or in fear. Well, maybe a minute or two last week, when I walked through midtown Manhattan and noticed that every street corner had a minimum of eight cops. But nothing actually happened. Unlike some, I do understand the difference between a virtual war and a real one, between an imagined threat and one that turns your niece into hamburger and rags.

Nonetheless, for a while there I was starting to *feel* invaded—by war fever.

Every morning, the Iraq war was on nearly every page of my paper. First in the news, which alternated between telling me things I have no business knowing and things I wish I could avoid learning, both in excruciating detail. Then in the comment pages, in which a brigade of blind men and women explained the elephant: the war is good; the war is bad; the war is really about oil—no, it's a secret struggle between the dollar and the euro—no, it's a vendetta by the Bush family—no, it's a parting prank by the Clinton administration....

Nearly every TV channel insisted on telling me about the war. The news channels would barely consent to mention anything else. The worst part was realizing that, compared to what I have come to accept as a reasonable evening's entertainment, real butchery is unbelievably boring. So I couldn't even bring myself to switch to some channel where people had the courtesy to die properly lit and in frame. Okay, forget television. I'd go to the office and—

—find fifty e-mails about the war. It's like the comment section of this newspaper, but without the rigor, wit or credentials. The war's really about the Christian fundamentalists trying to exterminate Muslim fundamentalists...no, it's arms dealers repossessing the weapons of mass destruction Saddam failed to pay for...no no, the war is really about sand. (What do you think computer chips are made of? Do you have any idea what percentage of the world's silicon is currently found in Iraq?) Just add your name to this virtual petition, here, and surely it will then acquire enough manna to break America's will to fight—

Enough. In the first place, I never found a single e-mail commentator who had any more right to an opinion than I did, which was none. None of us had access to accurate information, nor the training, experience or skills to analyze it if we did. We were simply blowing smoke. As I age, sometimes the things I said as a callow youth return to embarrass me—and particularly anything I had to say about a war while it was going on. I always find, ten or twenty years afterward, that everything I thought I knew was wrong, my premises were mistaken and my logic was flawed.

In the second place, if some savant had in fact uncovered the secret key to what went wrong in Iraq...what good would it have done either of us? Say we'd shouted it from the hilltops and convinced all reasonable men and women. That's one to five percent of the population, none of them in positions of power. The people in positions of power don't much care what reasonable people think, say or do.

In the third place, if we 'd had the power to shorten the war...would we have wanted to? Isn't that exactly what America did wrong the last time it tried to oust Saddam? Stop too soon, to placate civilians who thought war with actual bleeding in it was just too awful? Let's say this conflict really was about the US ensuring its survival—securing its oil supply, or supporting the dollar, or whatever. Did we really want it to lose? Some may believe that America dominates the world economy unfairly, and that this has been bad for the world...but do they seriously think European domination would be in some way better? Don't they know any history? America is like capitalism itself: just awful...and miles better than the second choice.

Even then, it was way too late to do anything. We had no idea what the right thing might be, and we still don't. All the things we could do, just to be doing something, seem certain to make things worse. We have way too much information, none of it reliable. We have way too much theory, none of it experimentally checkable. We have way too many opinions, all of value zero. The noise level is starting to frighten the children. Let's all shut up now, and pray to God that America hasn't screwed things up too badly.

Then maybe someone will notice how, even though Air Canada went broke the very same week we privatized it, fifteen years ago, the BC government has just sagely decided to do the same thing with not just the power company, but also the only road that goes to my home, the BC Ferries system. Essential public service monopolies are now owned—owned—by people I didn't choose, over whom I cannot ever have any influence or regulatory control, who serve for twice as long as George Bush and can't be impeached, whose whims are unappealable, unrepealable law, and who freely admit they care only about money and will scrap my ferry, my only lifeline, unless it turns a profit. Suddenly my longtime prospects don't seem a whole lot better than if I lived in a suburb of Baghdad. Mr. Campbell's government now guarantees me precious few more services than Saddam provides the Kurds—BC's medical care, social assistance, legal aid, human rights, police protection...even its power, water and road systems are all plummeting toward Third World standards. Yet everyone around me is talking loudly about events we can't influence on the other side of the planet.

Where are the UN peacekeepers to keep the hospitals open, the lights lit and essential ferry service running for the thousands of island dwellers, here in BC? What human shields will deter the inexorable Olympics invasion? Where are the humanitarians who'll protect me from my local tyrants?

"It claims to be fully automatic— but actually, you have to push this little button, here . . ."

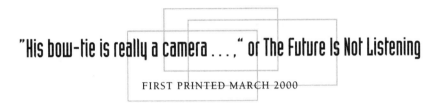

"His bow-tie is really a camera . . . ," or The Future Is Not Listening

FIRST PRINTED MARCH 2000

'VE ALWAYS BEEN INTERESTED in the future, and I've spent a considerable portion of my life—certainly the overwhelming majority of my professional life—trying to get *other* people to pay attention to it, too. I became a science fiction writer in part because I thought if I made speculating about tomorrow seem entertaining enough, I could persuade large numbers of my fellow citizens to think about it, for a change. I thought that would be a good thing.

Now, since the Millennium's come, everybody and his sister's dog is not merely thinking about the future, but talking about it at the top of his lungs. Worse, he's starting to *do* something about it. And I'm beginning to wonder if I made a dreadful mistake.

It might have been better to leave the design of tomorrow to random chance and nerds like me who enjoy that sort of thing. Getting people who don't read science fiction involved in building the future may prove in hindsight to have been disastrous. Because in our enthusiasm to recruit ordinary civilians to our cause, we told them the designers of tomorrow will make a classic buck. Inevitably, here comes the flood of fools.

The new Gold Rush is obviously underway—and in its opening stampede, common sense is being trampled under thundering hooves. Instead of being thoughtfully designed and elegantly built by sensible people like thee and me, the future is being slapped together by idiots out of mismatched parts and put on the market before the glue has set.

Consider a magazine I encountered in my optometrist's waiting room: a *Scientific American Presents* special edition called *Your Bionic Future*. It contains an article headed "Smart Stuff." No sense naming the author; it's not her fault. She just wrote what they wanted her to write: progress-pimping. Look at the wonders tomorrow may bring!

Let's.

"At Columbia University, a computer scientist is crafting eyeglasses that do more than just help you see. Want to try a restaurant in a foreign city? Glance above the restaurant's door and your glasses will immediately become windows to the Internet, offering you a review of the kung pao chicken or coq au vin served inside. Need some help during a presentation? Look to the right, and your glasses will flash your notes....

"...repair workers who fix airplanes or cars while wearing the glasses could do without notebooks full of instructions. And down the line, when the glasses have finer resolution and tracking devices, doctors might even use them during surgery."

Do you really need me to create a satirical little science fiction vignette demonstrating that this is one of the dumbest ideas ever? Isn't it a case of ducks in a barrel?

Surely you can imagine just as well as I the surgeon who, bending over your incision and squinting to the right, is actually checking his stock portfolio...or looking to see if any hot new videos have been posted at www.sensuoussheep.com. I'm certain you don't need my help to imagine yourself walking the streets with your terrified gaze fixed straight ahead at all times, lest you accidentally invoke the spray of hype that issues like ghostly radar chaff from every object you walk past. When hundreds of strangers are staring at *you* in expectation, waiting to hear your speech, which would you rather depend on: a stack of index cards...or something as reliable as, say, your web browser? "Moving on to the Fall line, we find...uh, 404, file not found...just a minute...shit. Excuse me—I seem to have crashed. There'll be a three-minute delay while I reboot my glasses...."

This "Smart Stuff" article appears to have been written by Q. You know, the old bird who was always supplying 007 with pens that turned into death rays, watches that could translate ecclesiastical Fukienese into conversational Urdu and shoe-heels with a fully-stocked bar. Apparently most people feel, subconsciously, that there's something profoundly futuristic about multifunction devices—especially if the functions have as little as possible to do with one another. And so we're offered:

- a "false fingernail that can direct robots"
  (Interesting. Lose one of those, and a single hair, and you've given up both your ID data and your DNA. Any competent wizard can now cast evil spells on you! The ancients were right: guard your nail and hair clippings.)
- "earrings that 'check stress' by monitoring your blood volume pulse"
- a "sports bra that measures your respiration and muscle tension"
  (I predict a huge spin-off market: software that hacks into her earrings and bra and lets you know exactly how you're doing at seducing her.)
- a "shoe that tracks skin conductivity, another sign of stress"

I don't *want* my clothes to nag me. "You're too tense. Listen to me, I'm your bra: you need to relax. If you won't listen to me, ask your shoe." I don't *want* to go around wearing a ring that will instruct my coffee machine to brew a cup of Tanzanian Peaberry every time my blood-to-caffeine ratio exceeds a certain value. I want to notice that I feel like a cup of coffee, and choose to make one, and maybe this time I want the chicory-mix from the Cafe du Monde. I don't *want* eyeglasses I can check e-mail on—as it is, I already get idiots complaining that I've allowed a whole eight hours to elapse before responding to their latest electronic summons. I don't *want* the refrigerator to order eggs for me when I run low—maybe I'm just sick of eggs, did you ever think of that, Dr. Einstein?

Consider a 1999 *Newsweek* cover story, "Technology: What You'll Want Next," which makes it terrifyingly clear that the people responsible for creating—and selling us—our future haven't the slightest clue what we want it to look like, and are happily preparing to force-feed us yet another endless shopping-list of horrors *they* think sound really keen (and lucrative). None of the stuff they've conned us into buying before actually *works* very well...but we bought it nonetheless and have not demanded our money back loudly (enough), so they're planning to repeat the scam indefinitely until stopped by force of arms. Thus *Newsweek* now breathlessly hypes the Home of the Future, "A Really Smart House"—by which they mean...

(pause for drum-roll, during which I advise you to sit down, place a stick between your teeth, and take a firm grip on your underwear)

(Are you ready?)

(You really think so, eh?)

...a house in which every single system and utensil is connected to the Internet.

Swear to God: the technoweenies honestly believe what you want, and will pay a fortune to acquire, is a home in which every single thing you own behaves as reliably as your Web browser does now.

The coffeemaker, fridge, microwave and toaster "will all be privy to your schedule"...so they'll function automatically whether you happen to keep that schedule or not; you'll have to advise them all if you decide to sleep in. The dishwasher "will note you've changed detergents and e-mail the manufacturer so it can revise and optimize its own internal software"—translation: every single load of dishes will be an adventure! Your computer, says *Newsweek*, will be "woven into your sports jacket"—making every spilled drink a potential kilobuck disaster and dry-cleaning dangerous, as well as apprising any hacker of your every move. The very fish in your aquarium will be dependent on the kindness—and programming competence—of strangers. Even your junk will be getting junk e-mail.

Everything in your life, in short, will depend utterly on that group of humans who've generally proved themselves sloppy, irresponsible and short-sighted: computer programmers and software designers. (Can you say "Y2K?") Folks who have in fifteen years made absolutely zero progress toward learning, let alone anticipating (and much less meeting), the routine daily needs of society's most easily-served customers—professional writers (there is not one good word processing program in existence, and it's hard to imagine an easier challenge)—are about to take on *everyone's every* need.

Soon, your stereo will be e-mailing your TV to request uploads of interesting soundtrack music, and the TV will have to check with your lawyer's FAQ program about copyrights before complying. Your closet will be exchanging devastating bon mots about your taste in clothing with your dresser, while the hamper and washing machine snicker over the latest stains in your underwear. I dare not even hint about the incestuous horrors that will occur in the dark inside your refrigerator. The VCR will tell any hacker who's interested just which porn movies you watch, and the video camera in every room will report just what you do while you watch them.

A netspamming virus written by a mischievous twelve-year-old will corrupt the microprocessor in your pants, causing them to change size at random, and your toilet may never stop flushing. Nor will that "smart" toilet ever stop sending detailed analyses of your stool and urine samples to your doctor...*and* that curious twelve-year-old...or your competitors, or your employers, or the government.

In short, there will be absolutely no object in your life which will *not* bite you on a tender spot at least three times a day, the way your computer does now. And they will all incur charges without consulting you first. Every one of the pre-sets on your telephone's speed-dialer will be reserved for assorted Help Lines, on which you'll spend the bulk of every day, on hold. Assuming you ever get through, there'll be even less help there than ever before—for the whole system will be so unimaginably complex that it won't be even theoretically possible for even a computer program to understand it well enough to debug it, much less a human.

Mars ain't far enough; I'm moving to Pluto.

The Internet should do what it's good for—e-mail, data exchange and pornography—and stay out of my face otherwise. I'll let computers run my home the day I find one that never crashes, hangs or misunderstands my intentions. Or accepts cookies from strangers.

But being a relentless optimist, I still believe good can come of technology as easily as bad. Here are some of the simple everyday miracles of tomorrow I'd actually pay serious money for—and as far as I can tell, nobody is working on any of them:

- a CD player that *remembers*, after being told once, the order in which I usually prefer the tracks of a given CD to be played. And can also command my amplifier to advance the treble for jazz, retard the bass for hip-hop or reset tone controls to flat for classical. (It'd be nice if the sound of a ringing phone put it into pause mode.)
- a computer that boots *instantly*. Doesn't anybody but me think insane that my car, stove, stereo, TV, printer, furnace and water heater all start instantaneously...but the most expensive and high-tech piece of gear I own needs three full minutes' notice before it can let me jot down a thought?
- a VCR (and/or TV) that *doesn't* require total reprogramming after every furshlugginer power outage. Ever hear of PRAM, fellas?
- a mass return to shoelaces that *aren't made of slippery material*, so I don't have to do twice as much tying to keep them from slipping as I used to twenty years ago.

Like many writers, I am—as you know—a *serious* coffee drinker. The only secret of good coffee (besides avoiding Starbuck's beans) is fanatic cleanliness: I clean my trusty Black & Decker drip coffeemaker with a damp paper towel at least twice a day. Still, brown mung inevitably builds up on the underside of the drizzler (pardon these technical terms), and also in those ribbed channels on the floor of the filter basket. I usually buy a new machine every year or so.

It's the damnedest thing, but apparently you can't buy a good one any more. All the ones I've seen, even the current Black & Decker model, now seem to have that damn "drip-stop" feature.

This feature is, always, a catastrophic malfunction waiting to happen: a flimsy five-cent bit of plastic and spring whose inevitable failure will necessitate replacing the whole furshlugginer machine. Meanwhile it collects brown mung, concentrates it at the worst possible place and cannot be cleaned effectively. Above all, it's unnecessary: if you absolutely *must* have coffee before the cycle finishes, why not just replace the carafe with your cup, then swap back again when it's full?

They solved a problem I didn't have...poorly...and now it appears they've forced the flawed solution on me.

Isn't there some way for us to communicate with the people who're inventing our future: designers and the industries who pay them? Wouldn't they welcome a little help in identifying our real desires, the better to pander to them? Wouldn't it be more efficient to sell us things we actually want to buy, and thus be able to fire half the advertising and marketing weasels? Present market research techniques simply aren't working—again and again techno-wizards solve problems we didn't have and fail to guess our actual needs or desires.

I fantasize a huge website, with a page for every consumer industry and links galore—a sort of perpetual town meeting. Someplace where innovators can run proposed new technologies past interested consumers...and we can protest them before it's too late. Where we can tell companies what we hate about their present products and suggest improvements we'd actually like —or even propose new products altogether. I wish someone would offer to sell me a continuously self-tuning acoustic guitar, for instance. Or a word processing program that does *not* force me to pay for (and waste disk space on) elaborate and powerful page layout, graphics, table, sound, video, outlining, voice annotation and mail merge functions I'll never use.

Or a self-cleaning coffeepot. Without those mung-collecting little ribs on the floor of the filter basket....

Sting of the Cyber Trifles, or How I spent my winter worktime

FIRST PRINTED NOVEMBER 2002

IT BECAME CLEAR that I needed a new(er) Powerbook. Even with cable access, Amazon.com took two and a half minutes to load. The computer matching my needs was hard to find. So I went to eBay. It was even slower than Amazon, but I persisted. In only an evening I located an auction for the machine I wanted. I checked the seller's User Feedback, and it was pretty good, so I posted a bid.

Next day eBay canceled that auction: the seller was a fraud. Whoa, I thought, it's good to see eBay has sharp security procedures in place. Those words would come back to taunt me. I found another Powerbook being auctioned by someone screen-named "Mypaltoo," and made damn sure this one was praised by all eight previous customers. I entered that auction—and won!

The seller then identified herself by e-mail as Aleksandra Rubleva of Auburn, Washington, and insisted in very broken English that I make payment through a service called MoneyGram, which only takes cash. I didn't want to wait for a cheque to clear, most private individuals aren't equipped to take Visa and for all I knew Russian emigrés don't believe in money orders. So I sent Gosphazha Rubleva over a thousand dollars. Never heard from her again.

After increasingly urgent e-mails went unanswered, I went to eBay. In mere hours, I was able to obtain Confidential Member Information on Mypaltoo—who in reality is a nice woman in Ohio named Gail. I phoned, and she was shocked and sympathetic: she hasn't visited eBay in over two years. Someone hacked into eBay's password records and pirated her identity...and God knows how many others.

You'd think that—receiving input from a member inactive for two years, from a different state, using a different e-mail and IP address on a different computer containing *none* of the "cookie" files eBay insists on placing on computers as a condition of membership—eBay might smell a rat. You'd be wrong. If they've taken *any* steps to detect identity theft, I can't imagine what they might be. What *would* trip their alarms?

In fairness, I myself missed a clear sign—*one*—that something was rotten in the state of Bookmark. If I'd happened to open all eight of Mypaltoo's feedback comments at once, I might have noticed none bore a date less than two years old. And if I'd started with the presumption that eBay's security is a joke and every member's identity is open to question, this might—or might not—have made me suspicious.

In only a day, I managed to notify eBay of the fraud—*despite* the procedures it provides for that purpose, which make voicemail look like fun. Finally eBay said a) it would launch an internal investigation, the results of which would not be shared with me, b) reporting the matter to the authorities was my problem and c) I could ask for a token partial refund of $175 maximum—*much* less than I lost—but my claim must be filed no less than thirty and no more than sixty days after the fraudulent sale. And might be unsuccessful.

Guess what law enforcement authority has jurisdiction in this? The two-man RCMP detachment out here on my remote island (pop. 3,000). I swear to God. Corporal Greg Louis, an outstanding officer but no Internet maven, took my complaint and has been diligent in updating me on progress…but we both know there won't be any.

On my own initiative, I posted feedback about Mypaltoo. For days I received urgent e-mails from members confused because I said she was bogus, and eBay still listed her as legit. I was able to save *them* thousands. Apparently it took eBay almost a week to deregister Mypaltoo.

When the statutory thirty days had passed, I'd already bought—without eBay—a new Powerbook. That two and a half minute homepage then loaded in *six seconds*. So I only spent twelve hours of the four days afterwards trying to file my Fraud "Protection" Claim.

The Fraud Protection Program is a dribble-glass joke, visual voicemail, designed to send you in circles forever no matter *how* fast your computer is. To apply you *must use* the proper Fraud Protection Claim Form. It took me three determined attempts to secure one. The first two requests—hours apiece—produced auto-response e-mails telling me I needed the form I'd just requested, and directing me to a place I'd already been where it didn't exist. It may be coincidental that I mentioned my position as newspaper columnist on my third, successful attempt.

Then I submitted my claim…and since I faxed it, was promised a decision in only three weeks. Two days later eBay e-mailed me: my claim might—isn't that cute? *might*—be denied unless I supply the original auction page. EBay knows that's impossible: it took that page down after the auction—thirty days ago. I faxed them that news.

Then I left home for two days. I returned to find the last straw, a two-day-old e-mail from eBay: it would cancel my claim within seventy-two hours unless I reconfirmed that it hadn't been resolved! Barely making the deadline, I assured them "Aleksandra" had not spontaneously repented and made restitution.

EBay uses utterly ineffective security measures to protect its customers—and a *brilliantly* effective system for covering its own ass after the inevitable thefts occur, making even their inadequate token refund exquisitely difficult to obtain. EBay not only enables crooks, it competes with them in sleaziness after the fact. As if I'd go through all this crap to take eBay for their miserable $175.

If by some miracle my claim is granted I'll only have spent nine hundred bucks for an amusing e-mail—and wasted enough writing time to have earned five times that much money. If I were an investor thinking of putting money into online commerce, I'd be too stupid to have any money. Cyberspace is chockfull of crooks—InfoHighwaymen—and the cyberauthorities clearly either can't or won't stop them.

Compared to What?

FIRST PRINTED JULY 2002

These days a cop with any decency at all looks like a hero
The millionaire knows billionaires who think that he's a
zero
The shoes a lord rejected are a godsend to the churl
And an immie in the shower looketh mighty like a pearl

So remember on those days when in your bed you shoulda
stood
That somewhere there is someone who makes even you
look good
It's only your perspective that has got you in a muddle
You ain't too small a frog: you just been in too big a pud-
dle....

—FROM "PERSPECTIVE," BY JACOB STONEBENDER

IT USED TO BE, you could be weird if you needed to. I suspect we're all going to miss that, by and by.

I was a weird kid. I read books. Without pictures. I laughed at things nobody else did. At eleven I was six foot one and weighed 125 pounds. I got beat up a lot. I didn't like it, but couldn't help noticing how much they enjoyed doing it. One day a short stranger picked a quarrel, insisted on a fight and halfway into my usual beating I had a sudden cosmic epiphany: it came to me that I could take this chump. At last I was going to experience the *fun* part of the transaction! So I settled in, went to work and beat the stew out of him, just as I'd fantasized doing for so long—

I *hated* it. It was less fun than being beat up. Much less: it added embarrassment. Here was this poor bleeding sobbing fool, shamed by his own bad judgment, and I had done it. Being punched had never been my fault: this was. Cracked knuckles turned out to hurt more, and longer, than black eyes or fat lips.

So okay, now I knew I was not and would never be normal. I was weird.

That was something useful to know. A place to stand, an identity to grope toward. I'm a weirdo...what is it they do, exactly? Fine, give me some of that. Science fiction novels? Love 'em. Long hair, beards, guitars, peace, theogens, poetry? Bring it—the weirder the better.

Forty years later, I find I've had a perfect marriage for more years than my own parents were lucky enough to get; our daughter is a peach; I live in the only civilized nation in this hemisphere, in a part so beautiful tourists pay to come here and gape at us; most of my thirty books are still in print; and my rolodex includes private numbers for Donald Westlake, Lawrence Block, John Varley, Mikhail Gorbachev, Amos Garrett, Jef Raskin, Janis Ian, Stephen Gaskin, Paul Krassner and Henry Kissinger. (I fantasize a conference call.) Weirdness has worked out well for me. Please note: I am *not* recommending it, it's not for everyone; I'm merely asserting that it was a viable choice. It taught me that when I'm alone, I am in good company. Even before it started paying off, it was always a refuge, a way to go, an accepted category for those who fit no other. An option.

But I grew up in a smaller world. Just try and be weird today!

How would you go about it? In a world with a Karla Homolka fanclub on Usenet, what would you have to do to qualify as weird? Fly a tall building into an airplane? Worship a god who commands his children to *heal* the heathen? Respect all those who love truly, however they express it? Buy stock in a company because you share its beliefs, support its long-term goals and wish its employees well? Decline to bid for the Olympics? Resign high office with dignity?

You want to be weird today, you got two big problems. First: *there are six billion of us.* Since all people are at least a little flaky, that many of us overwhelms the very concept of weirdness. Say you're so kinky, you're a one-in-a-million freak. Well, that means there are three dozen of you in Canada alone! And three hundred more just below the border. Enough of you to hold annual meetings at Harbourfront—apply for a grant—lobby for tax breaks. Just think how many counterparts you have in China and India.

The second problem, and the death knell for weirdness, is *the Internet.* In what some experts believe may have been the single greatest irony of the last irony-packed millennium, this was invented by—of all possible people in human history—the US Department of Defense, as a hedge against nuclear attack. One of the many unplanned side effects (Ted Sturgeon used to say there are no side effects, only effects, some of which you wish not to think about just now) has been the destruction of weirdness as a refuge.

Once I was a teenager crazy about science fiction novels...with no clue that some of the greatest sf fans of all time, and two of my favorite authors, lived mere miles from me. Unless they were unusually diligent, there was no easy way for even the mildly weird to *find* each other back then. New York's a lonely town when you're the only surfer boy around.

Today, it doesn't matter if you're a left-handed transexual skydiving albino dwarf with a hammer toe, more than two HIV-positive parents and a taste for goats in leather chaps: a few minutes with Google, and you'll find enough likeminded souls to start your own branch of the Anglican church.

Well, that's good, isn't it? If this goes on, in a few more years, *everybody* will be Out, and the bigots will be too busy masturbating each other over at www.bigot.com to organize any pogroms. Surely to God that has to be good, not to mention ten thousand years overdue, right?

But what are the strange kids—the underbodied, overminded *different* ones—going to do without weirdness to fall back on? When nothing is weird, what will teach them that they are not at all like anyone else, that nobody is, that we're all aliens, and that that's just fine? Something, I hope. Science fiction novels, perhaps.

Don't Go Toward the Light...

FIRST PRINTED DECEMBER 1999

WHEN I WAS A KID we had dark rooms. Only when we chose to—I'm not that old! But what I mean is, if you simply shut off the light, you had darkness. Real darkness: if the room had curtains or lacked windows there wasn't even starlight. Whole rooms of total utter blackness, space enough for any number of fantasies or fears, canvas for infinite imaginings. Minefields of adventure, in which all you risked was a bruised shin.

I think it began to change in the 70s, with those little glowing digital clocks. Before I noticed it happening, suddenly every single room in my home seemed to contain something with a clock, or a pilot light, or a stand-by light, or a status light, or a power-on light, or a glowing reset switch. Invariably in Christmas colours, for some reason: red or green. (Why? Traffic light resonance? Then why are so many of the lights indicating "go" status red?) Even photographers seldom truly have darkrooms anymore.

Do we really need that much constant reassurance that everything's okay?

Sometimes I miss dark rooms. Even the smallest morsel of light takes most of the unknown out of a room. A totally dark room might be the airlock of a starship...or a time machine...or the throne room of the Galactic Empire after the Emperor has gone to bed—

—but one tiny orange "ready" light, and it's only your living room...and you're once again confined to a world that has no starships, time machines or galactic empires.

And if you close your eyes, sooner or later you fall asleep. And *miss* all that dreaming....

Off the Road

FIRST PRINTED OCTOBER 1997

MY DAUGHTER TERRI graduated from college, and—to my delight—chose to revive the splendid old European tradition of *wanderjahr*. She simply hopped into her car and headed off across the continent for an indeterminate time, with the loosest of plans and no deadlines. She'd been a student all her conscious life and was determined to see what it was like to be "a live human, free on the earth," for a change.

My wife and I did more or less the same thing in our own early twenties, before we met. So we helped her prepare, fed her superfluous advice, then hugged her and waved goodbye. And ever since, I've been thinking about Terri's journey and contrasting it with the ones Jeanne and I each took at about the same age.

For a start, we hitchhiked. If that word is unfamiliar to younger readers, I mean we stood beside a road heading the way we wanted to go, held up a thumb and got into any vehicle that stopped for us. Everyone we knew traveled that way, and nearly all of us got away with it. We seldom carried—or needed—weapons more authoritative than a jackknife. With rare exceptions, the greatest hazard we faced was a boring conversationalist or a horny drunk.

To be sure, females (and males, too) sometimes had to fend off unwelcome propositions—they weren't a felony, back then. But it was quite rare to meet someone who wouldn't take a firm no for an answer. In especially rough regions, the American Deep South for instance, hitching in pairs was almost always adequate protection for women.

Serial killers? I can recall only one back then—a strangler in Boston.

What we did often have (on long-haul hitches, at least) were long searching meaning-of-life-type conversations with people whose minds worked so differently from our own or anyone we knew that they might as well have been a different species, sometimes. I think this was an education at least as crucial as the kind we'd gotten in school.

One of the important things I'd never previously suspected, for instance, was just how much kindness is out there in the world. Again and again, total strangers stopped for us, went miles out of their way for us, bought us meals or coffee, offered us crash-space or part-time work, showed us sights we'd have missed, got us medical help...without asking anything in return but our company and the warm pleasure of having helped another monkey.

And I think my journeys gained something because I was autonomous, with no possessions save what I could carry. It was liberating. And broadening: somebody else chose what station to play on the car radio, and as you moved across the continent, the music changed.

All unthinkable now, of course. Terri traveled surrounded by over a ton of metal, kept it locked at all times and carried a cell-phone in case she needed 911 in a hurry. She had few conversations with anyone but waitresses and gas-jockeys—except on that cell-phone, with people she already knew, at umpty dollars a minute. Everywhere she went, she heard the same music: the CDs she brought with her. Every minute she wasn't actually in the car and moving, she had to worry that someone would try to steal it. Perhaps there is still just as much kindness in the world as I found...but Terri dares not take the risk of finding out.

She has no choice. Even if she were not—intelligently—too afraid to hitch-hike, most of the drivers out there these days are—intelligently—too afraid to pick up hitchers. The world has changed.

My generation truly believed, back in the sixties, that we were going to save the world...or at the very least, hand it over to our kids in better shape than we got it from *our* parents. Thirty years later, it seems we have done a rather shoddy job.

Don't trust my memories. Have you seen *Cape Fear*—the original, mid-sixties version? There's a scene where the mother arrives to pick her daughter up after school, but the kid doesn't come out. So Mom goes inside to look for her...leaving her car not only unattended and unlocked, but with the door wide open! In Miami! It's still there when she gets back. No moviegoer saw anything odd about this at the time. The world has changed...and not always in the way we hopeful invincible flower-children thought it would.

I take what comfort I can in small improvements. The car Terri drove is much safer, for example, and vastly more mechanically reliable. (Are you old enough to remember how crummy cars used to be before the Japanese came along?) It was cheaper to run and much less polluting. The cell-phone *is* a nifty gadget. She heard those CDs—in a moving car!—with better fidelity than anyone but a serious audiophile had ever heard in my day. And there are other, more subtle improvements in the world, too. When the Honda dealership in Madison, Wisconsin, charged her over three hundred bucks to *not* repair her power steering, she simply repudiated the Visa charge. Each time she stopped for a few days with a friend or relative, she could use their computer to get her mail and research the next stage of her journey. And so on. But these are all meager consolations for what has been lost.

And perhaps it will be even more disconcerting for Terri when her kids reach their twenties. Her cohort is right on the cresting spine of The Great Digital Divide; those who come after will see everything differently. They may not even make many actual meat-journeys. Why go to all that expense and risk when it's so easy to visit anywhere on earth for mere pennies? Of course, anywhere on earth will look remarkably like a computer screen....

But who knows? Perhaps, in time, a small, cynical, practical generation will be able to reverse some of the grosser mistakes of a large, naive, idealist generation. Humans solve problems, sometimes faster than we can create new ones. Perhaps by the time Terri's children are old enough to develop itchy feet, the Wheel will have turned again...and they'll be able to ride their thumbs once more, just the way Grandpa and Grandma did in the Olden Days.

Got to Admit It's Gotten Better

FIRST PRINTED DECEMBER 1999

When I become was, and now is back when,
Will someone have moments like this;
Moments of unspoken bliss?
And will there be heroes and saints
...or just a dark new age of complaints?
                              —MOSE ALLISON, "WAS"

I'M SUPPOSED TO BE JEREMIAH, HERE.

Not the inarticulate oenophile bullfrog who was a good friend of the late Hoyt Axton. I'm speaking of the cranky curmudgeon they named the jeremiad after. I've spent years writing columns where the basic mandate was to be my readers' surly seer and pessimist prophet, casting a jaundiced eye on the future and muttering of impending dooms.

And seldom was that mandate so timely as at the turn of the millennium. Normally science fiction writers are almost the only citizens who pay any attention at all to the future—beyond the next fiscal quarter—and we customarily spend our professional hours trying to con and cajole readers into joining us. (We perceive an urgent need for smarter voters.) But in December of 1999, thanks to the imminent approach of an utterly meaningless non-event—some fuss about the date; perhaps you've heard of it—suddenly everybody and his chatgroup were talking obsessively about the future, for a change. Big surprise: most of us are paranoid. We can't help it; it's hardwired into us.

So suddenly I was unusually popular. Commissions and assignments abounded, invitations to appear on panels, participate in colloquia, write essays, play talking head. "What will things be like in the next twenty/fifty/hundred/thousand years?" asked the editors, producers and webmasters. They all had the same deadline, and I got the sense most of them hoped I would hint darkly of dread disasters on the horizon, futuristic fiascoes we'd be lucky to survive.

Unfortunately, they all wrote valid cheques, so I did my best to accomodate as many of them as I could. Which meant that for a while there I was heartily sick of scrying and decrying—if I'm lying, I'm dying. I propose a conceptual one-eighty. I'd like to glance *backward*, at the twentieth century's latter half and some of the unexpectedly wonderful technology it has been my fortune and privilege to come to take for granted in that time.

I was born in 1948, so let's say I'd basically finished booting up by about 1955. By then I'd already been innoculated against ghastly things called smallpox and polio. Music came on big fragile vinyl plates and you paid extra for "high fidelity" (mono), which today would be considered unacceptably poor for a taxicab radio. And they only sounded *that* good the very first time you played them, no matter how careful you were. Even at seven I sensed how fiercely proud my father was that we could afford a color television. Its screen was smaller and had much poorer resolution than the monitor I'm typing this on, and its audio made low-fi records sound good. It had rabbit-ears on top, which you configured by hand for each channel—all six of them. Nobody had FM, or a portable AM. If you got a phone call from more than fifty miles away you knew someone had died. Dad's company gave him a new car every year—and on winter mornings he routinely budgeted half an hour to get it started. The furnace in the basement wasn't much more reliable. We knew people who'd flown on airplanes, but didn't expect to ever get that rich ourselves. Computers existed—men raced around inside them, replacing blown vacuum tubes. They could perform thousands of operations in a single second! *If* you spoke Computer. I expected nuclear war in my lifetime. Everyone did.

You've read all this before, seen a documentary on A&E or the History Channel. But I don't know if they've conveyed just how unexpected and astonishing every one of the technological wonders of my time were when they came. I read my first sf novel when I was six, and it described a landing on the moon, and I must ask you to believe me when I tell you that an attempt to discuss the subject seriously with my teacher got me sent to the school shrink. I've seen correspondence in which he warned my parents that continued exposure to such fanciful nonsense could "damage the boy's psyche by over-stimulating his imagination." (Thank God my mother knew mahooha when she heard it!) A mere fifteen years later, Armstrong told that teacher and shrink to take a flying leap for all mankind. And even I, a lifelong space-travel buff, was stunned that we'd really pulled it off.

Positive change always takes us by surprise. Sf writers often look for hopeful futures, but not one of us predicted that the Soviet Union, the Berlin Wall, apartheid, the Cold War or Nuclear Winter could not only go away, but do so without bloodshed. Yet every one of those godsent miracles was a direct and (in retrospect) inevitable result of technological change.

Lasting peace in the Middle East or Ireland or Serbo-Croatia will probably seem impossible right up until a week after they've come. Then—at last, thank God!—they'll be old news, as boring as space travel.

I can hang from my belt a recording of Louis Armstrong playing "Old Man Mose" thirteen years before I was born, with better sound quality than Pops heard when they played back the master that day. My Honda *always* starts on the coldest morning, is much less likely to kill me than a '55 Ford and the dashboard clock keeps time. After thirty years' fruitless search for a copy of William Gresham's *Nightmare Alley*, I can now click a mouse, locate a dozen copies, order one with another click and be reading it tomorrow. I've watched a Space Shuttle take off from two miles away. Nobody ever has to get lost again, unless they choose to switch off their GPS and cellphone. It's been a *great* century, and I belong to the luckiest generation of monkeys that ever griped.

And I'm sorry to disappoint the paranoid, but the next generation might actually abolish hunger, poverty, racism, death, taxes and even loneliness. No foolin'. Half the geniuses who ever lived are alive and working now. Who says living in interesting times is a curse?

The New Idiot Box

Be Less Than You Can Be, or
The most important component is the off switch

FIRST PRINTED APRIL 2000

WHY, THE OLD JOKE ASKS, does a dog lick his testicles? Answer: because he can. Perhaps it's time to ask whether that's a good enough reason.

Classic military doctrine says you must plan not for what you think the enemy will do, but for the worst he *can* do. If he can, he probably will. Humans like to push the envelope, to operate near the redline: we tend to do about as much as we possibly can (get away with) in any given area. Given half a chance we'll eat ourselves into obesity. Given very mild stimulus to a certain spot in the medial forebrain bundle, and the means to keep the current flowing, we'll sit and starve to death with big grins. As I drive along cursing the slow traffic, I'm traveling twice as fast as the fastest horse my grandfather could have ridden...and once traffic opens up, I'll reach speeds twice again as fast, speeds he could only have achieved by falling off a very tall cliff or being shot out of a cannon.

But why I'm in four times as much of a hurry as Grandfather was, I don't know. Maybe just because I *can* be?

E-mail is a wonderful thing. Yes sir, wonderful. A powerful tool, they keep saying. An enormously powerful tool. At sixteen, I was hired as a nightshift janitor at a hospital, my first legal job. The first night, my boss,

Reverend Willie Brown (who was moonlighting on his day-gig as pastor of, I swear I'm not making this up, the First Church of the Ugly Death) introduced me to a machine called a buffer. Before letting me touch it, Reverend Willie gave me a lecture/demo on the philosophy and parameters of its user interface—though I'm not sure he used those precise terms—and tried to impress on me that it was an enormously powerful tool. He did in fact use *those* exact words, which is why I'm remembering this now. I assured him I understood.

Then he stood aside, and I put that sucker right through a wall. Only by a miracle were there *not* sleeping patients on the other side of it, in whom I could have induced cardiac arrest.

For the rest of that summer, Reverend Willie ran the buffer, and I pushed an idiot stick. That buffer didn't *look* all that powerful—but it was. And it gave you positive feedback, which makes a system tend to oscillate wildly out of control, fast—as when a microphone is placed too close to its speaker, for instance.

So it is with e-mail. What seemed to me at first a miracle of convenience has come to feel like a cybernetic Sorcerer's Apprentice, mindlessly flinging bucket after bucket of information at me, heedless that I'm drowning.

It's wonderful that I can send a letter to someone on the other side of the globe within ten minutes. The problem arises when some fool on the other side of the globe sends me *his* manuscript, knowing I'll have it in ten minutes . . . *and therefore expects response within fifteen minutes and becomes shirty if it's late.* Simply because I now *can* spend every waking hour harking attentively to the peremptory summonses of strangers and friends alike, it's assumed, for some reason, that I *will.*

I've searched my hard drive carefully, and can't find any contract in which I agreed to answer e-mail *at all,* much less promptly. I never even promised to *read* any.

I concentrate for a living . . . so I take great care to keep a low profile in cyberspace. I don't join forums, visit chat rooms or give out my e-address indiscriminately. I try not to even *think* about *alt.callahans,* the metauniverse created over a decade ago by some folks inspired by my Callahan's Place books—said to be the largest non-pornographic newsgroup on USENET. (Its core membership far exceeds the population of the town I live in, and each month they upload more words than I've written about Callahan's Place in a quarter-century of doing so for my living.) My browser is configured to reject all cookies. I don't buy anything online unless I'm sure the vendor safeguards its mailing list.

And yet every day, at least the first two hours at my desk are spent dealing with e-mail.

In the Olden Days, I'd get a handful of letters a day, five days a week. Maybe two would require an answer; at the end of the week I'd write a dozen replies or so and mail them next time I passed a postbox. Now, I get at least fifteen letters a day—and that's seven days a week. A hundred tugs at my lapel, however brief, every week. Each knows I felt the tug nearly instantaneously, and is liable to yank again, harder, if I don't respond promptly enough to suit their sense of their own importance.

Two hours a day for seven days is 35 percent of a forty-hour week. Answering mail, which once took an hour or two a week, now eats up a third of my time. A powerful tool indeed. As Pyrrhus said, one more victory like this and I am screwed.

Naturally there are even more stupendous victories looming ominously on the horizon....

I'll hold out as long as I can...but sooner or later the bastards will find some way to force me to accept one of those damned palmtops, you watch. Then it's game over: I'll never be free again, not in a rowboat, a hang-glider or halfway up a cliff. My attention will be perpetual hostage to any idiot who wants it; no matter how far back up into the forest primeval I trek, the dread words "You've got mail" will e'er haunt me.

Quoth the PalmPilot, "*Evermore*...."

Thanks to digital technology, our bosses can follow us anywhere, summon us from bed or bath. Our jobs can take over our waking lives. Much as science has given our government the theoretical power to destroy human life on earth, it's given each of us the power to pester everybody else until then, 24-7. We can become the generation that went from the forty-hour week to the 112-hour week—excuse me: from *one* spouse working a forty-hour week to *two* spouses working 224 hours total—without any significant increase in real income. We have that power now...if we are boneheaded enough to use it.

To paraphrase *Cool Hand Luke*, what we could use around here lately is a failure to communicate.

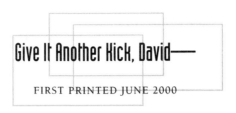

Give It Another Kick, David—

FIRST PRINTED JUNE 2000

WHEN GALAXY ONLINE decided to remake their site in June of 2000, the result was a completely redesigned, impressively beautiful, and far more powerful and flexible than ever home page...on which almost nothing worked. I tried using the recommended browser-iteration and plug-in, on an accelerated PowerPC with oodles of RAM, over the fastest connection Compuserve Canada will sell me, and it took me nearly half an hour to load and inspect the new home page. From there it took me another half hour of desperate thrashing about to find a functioning path that led to *any* of the splendid nonfiction, fiction or streaming video content that had been available on this site as recently as two days earlier

When a regular website doesn't work, that's business as usual. No big deal. But when the Galaxy Online website doesn't work, it's a sign of the times, isn't it?

Galaxy Online is highly interested in cybertechnology, their technical staff is among the best and most creative in the world, they have visionary leadership, access to the very best state of the art tools and lore, some serious funding and the finest minds in the field available for consultation...and even *they* are lucky when the damn thing works at all.

We science fiction authors believe in the future. We are inclined by nature, training and mandate to be optimistic about tomorrow.

But with each passing year my computer gets just a little slower and less reliable. And that, I fear, is the *good* news from cyberspace. The rest of the house, all the stuff that used to be as reliably dumb as a bag of hammers, seems to be getting entirely too smart to suit me.

After that abortive attempt to log in to the Galaxy Online site, I mentioned it in correspondence with interface expert Jef Raskin. He replied in part:

"Sadly, even the best-intentioned web designer, without understanding even the little that is known about cognition, is in over his or her head today. And when you do understand, then it is clear that you can't do a good job given the existing browsers and computer environment. There's just no way to build a really good web interface on present day software systems."

It is to this intrinsically unstable platform that our culture proposes to entrust nearly everything of any value to us. It will probably be just after the very last actual physical retail sales outlet ("store," they used to call them) has gone out of business that we will all suddenly realize the system we scrapped them for simply doesn't work reliably.

And bookmark my words: in a few years it will be almost impossible to buy any household appliance or device that is *not* "Internet-ready," "wirelessly online" and empowered to take autonomous action in your name. And forgive a crusty old cynic (I used to cut off the crusts, but it's hard to dunk without them) for suspecting that their default setting will most often be: "spend the customer's money as lavishly as can be justified, and tell us all her most intimate secrets." That's when they're working *right*, I mean....

Hang on to all your present appliances. Cherish them. Nurse them along just as long as you can, replace only what you absolutely must. Every smallest aspect of your life, from your toaster to your toothbrush, is being relentlessly "wired" as we speak, by clueless greed-dazzled cybercarpetbaggers who don't seem to understand the fabled information superhighway is just barely an improvement over two empty Campbell's tomato soup cans connected by a taut string.

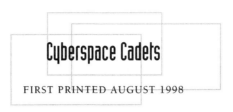

Cyberspace Cadets

FIRST PRINTED AUGUST 1998

Y OU SAY YOU'VE NEVER HEARD of Tulip Mania, your library doesn't
stock *Extraordinary Popular Delusions and the Madness of Crowds* and
you want to know just how bad could this Internet Goldrush business
really be? You think it's merely another fad, like the hula hoop or the Spice
Girls?

I wave my magic wand. Zap! You are now Bikenibeu Paeinu. But don't
worry: spelling it is everyone *else's* problem, for you are the Prime Minister. Of Tuvalu—a collection of nine small atolls (small even as atolls go, I
mean) hard by the International Dateline, so remote that the nearest land-
mass of consequence, Australia, lies 2,600 kilometers distant. You govern
some 9,200 souls whose principle export is copra and average income is
under $500 (Canadian!). In a good year they might get to milk as many as
1,000 tourists, making Tuvalu a destination roughly as popular as Passaic,
New Jersey. There may not be fifty computers in your whole nation. How
could Internet Fever possibly affect you or yours?

Surprise, Prime Minister! About five years ago, some geeks in suits on the
other side of the planet devised the "domain-name" system for Internet addresses. Assignment of the most popular domain names—.com, .edu, .org,
and .net—is, by fiat of the US government, a monopoly of the Virginia firm
Network Solutions, Inc., which has registered over 2 million .com addresses
alone since 1993. But as an afterthought, possibly born of the subconscious
awareness that the US government has little claim to any authority in this
matter, it was also decided to assign a domain name to each of the 159 nations on earth, to do with as they pleased. The planners went so far as to pick
the names for them—to save them the bother, you see—and when they got
down as far as Tuvalu, it turned out .tu was already taken (I presume by Tu-
nis or Turkey), so without another thought they awarded Tuvalu the domain
name....

You've already spotted the significance, haven't you? (So why didn't
they?) Tiny Tuvalu has the exclusive worldwide right to assign Internet addresses ending in .tv.

How many networks or cable stations would like to have such an address? *All* of them. How much is it worth to them? Well, what it's actually *worth* is the square root of minus one—I confidently predict not one station will ever induce one viewer to watch one additional minute because its Website address is cute—but the important question is, what are broadcasters (not to mention the vast transvestite market) willing to *pay* for the worthless privilege in the present hysterical climate?

Plenty, says Toronto-based Information.ca Infotouch Corp., and it's ready to put its money where its mouth is. It is now offering to give you (you're Prime Minister Paeinu, remember?) somewhere between sixty and one hundred *megabucks—per year, forever*—for the right to sell your domain name abroad. If you divide it among your constituents, each will make *twenty-two times his usual income* this year, and every year hereafter. And even if you steal the whole score, most of it *has* to trickle down, eventually, if only because there is nowhere else on Tuvalu for it to *go*. This could be a bigger cash cow than Liberian ship registry. And what are you *trading* for all this manna?

Absolutely nothing. Hot air.

Even in Tuvalu, they can sense that the Crazy Years have come.

About as Reliable as a Computer . . . .

FIRST PRINTED SEPTEMBER 1999

MY WIFE ONCE ASKED ME to print out 200 programmes for a play she was starring in. The document already existed, from a previous run, and needed only a couple of lines updated. I figured five minutes' actual work and an hour's laser printer time, tops. A day later, not a single new programme existed yet, and I'd ruined almost 300 sheets of paper. Software problems, then hardware problems, then failure of a new toner cartridge.

I bring this up because, as I was cursing, Jeanne mentioned something interesting. She said in the fifteen years I've been printing out programmes for her dance concerts and plays, and manuscripts for my novels, *not once* has an important print job gone smoothly—they *always* require at least an extra day of frustration, rage and heartache. And you know something? She wasn't exaggerating.

So I called some friends, with widely different cyber platforms and levels of expertise . . . and none of *them* had ever had an important print job go smoothly either.

We're in denial. Intelligence doesn't help: the brighter we are, it seems, the more determined we are to stick our heads in the sand. That's exactly the problem: somehow we've become enthralled by sand. We've become silicon-worshippers.

Don't get me wrong: I love my Mac. I was a professional writer for eleven years before I got one, and I occasionally have actual nightmares about being forced to use a typewriter again. No one who has not spent a decade wrestling one of those mechanical monstrosities for a (precarious) living can possibly imagine how odious they were. The error-correction process in particular was a horror. Hours of tedium and constantly interrupted concentration. On computer, I fix mistakes without thinking about it. I pick up copy *here*, and put it down over *there*—magic! Lots of cute font and size options. If I get bored, I can go sink imaginary battleships. I'm addicted, now, and can never go back.

But I used to spend fewer unpleasant hours with Correctype than I now spend trying to get my computer to work right. And I've got one of the good ones.

I fantasize about using a time machine to visit my 1984 self. He's just contemplating purchase of his first computer, and asks my advice.

Well, I say slowly, it's not the price; it's the upkeep. In buying that Fat Mac, you're also committing to all the ones after it, each bigger and faster—and more expensive. Fifteen years from now you'll be on your fifth, with 160 times more RAM and a hard drive 300 times roomier than anything you can buy today, running programs so huge they couldn't possibly be loaded onto any 1984 personal computer. And for its intended purpose—as a typewriter-replacement—it will be not quite as good as the one you're about to buy.

That's right, I tell my bemused younger self: as a writer's tool, a modern Powerbook PowerPC with 80 megs running Microsoft Word from a CD-ROM is inferior in several important respects to a 1984 512K Mac running MacWrite 4.5 from a 400K floppy.

Then why upgrade? he asks.

Because everyone else will. By 1999 MacWrite will be a fond memory; Fat Mac parts and repairmen will be long extinct. Everyone will use Microsoft Word. It will force on you many unwanted capabilities—page layout, outlining, graphics, charts, sound, "spell checking" (an exciting opportunity to spend hours teaching a machine how to spell common words), grammar advice (expletive deleted), a thesaurus (easily one fifth as good as the worst in print), voice annotation, even *video* annotation... but as a word processor it will be just barely useable: slow, clunky, unstable and (sigh) the unchallenged universal standard.

So what's this gonna cost? 1984 Spider asks.

By the millennium, I reply, between hardware, software and this and that, you'll be in for something like twenty-five large.

He pales. Wait, I say. To be fair, by the time you're in that deep, you'll have a genuine miracle you didn't expect: the Internet! And I riff awhile, explaining that.

Let's see if I've got this, he says. It's like, back in the sixties when Ken Kesey and the Pranksters were outfitting the Magic Bus, and Neal Cassidy wired up speakers and mikes at every seat, all live at once—and there was so much noisy chaos that within twenty-four hours all the speakers got ripped out—like that, only on a planetary scale?

I explain further. He frowns. So basically, he says, we're talking about a stupendous heap of suspect data? With no index or table of contents or editor or peer review?

And none possible, I admit. In essence, it's an immense encyclopedia that any moron may contribute to and nobody can edit... and for some reason the whole world will decide to behave as though it were a source of reliable information. They'll let their hard drives be colonized by parasite programs given the deceptively friendly name "cookies" and share the most intimate details of their lives with invisible strangers. They won't even *notice* their browser crashes at least twice a day. Everything will run unbelievably slowly, and there'll be several competing access systems, *none* delivering more than half of claimed speed at best.

Then I tell him how much fun large print jobs will be.

As I say, I'm committed to my Mac now. But I think the 1984 Spider, given honest projections, might just have kept his typewriter. Ask any programmer: if it runs successfully once, it's considered ready to market; if it runs twice in ten tries, it's ready to ship. But whatever you type on a typewriter is what comes out on the page, at once, every time, with 100 percent reliability.

WYSIWYG, they call it.

Nuking Themselves in the Foot or, Look out, tech's press!

FIRST PRINTED MAY 2000

ROBERT A. HEINLEIN said the way to assess the intelligence of a committee is to divide the IQ of its stupidest member by the number of members. There's a rather large software concern whose recent corporate behavior has been so transcendently stupid as to suggest that an IQ no higher than that of its own rather notorious operating system has been divided by the number of installed copies worldwide, then given a negative exponent equal to its founders' personal wealth expressed in Canadian pennies. If a corporation is an imaginary person, this one makes Homer Simpson look like Freeman Dyson.

Unfortunately, I can't name it here. *D'oh!*

I dare not. Its lawyers—as if they don't have enough to do—have censored people who said critical things about it in what amounts to a techies' coffeehouse in cyberspace. Imagine what they might do to me!

But to get the full beauty of this, you need a bit of historical/technical context. This corporation—we have to call it something for discussion; let's arbitrarily honour comic Phil Silvers and call it BillCo, shall we?—BillCo had a spot of legal trouble a few years back in one of the larger nations adjacent to Canada. Less said the better, of course, but in essence a large-ish number of folks there felt BillCo was (a) too big, (b) less than competent and (c) a bit of a bully. There had even been loose talk, at the higher levels of that nation's justice system, about crippling or dismantling BillCo by government fiat.

It was at this cusp in BillCo's corporate history that an unfortunate occurrence unfortunately occurred. One of the most popular of its many products contained an innovative feature—ironically, one of the few genuinely original features ever offered by BillCo—called "scripting," which unfortunately was really not a feature but a bug. A gaping security flaw, in fact, *begging* to be exploited: a backdoor big enough to admit a Visigoth horde in full kit without waking the watchdog.

Get this: BillCo's e-mail agent—let's call it LookOut! for convenience— was *deliberately designed* to let strangers easily send you e-mail that can issue commands to your computer without consulting you. No, really! If you use BillCo's operating system—let's call it OpenWindow—and run LookOut!, your computer's no longer merely user-friendly: it's now a user-slut. One too dumb to carry condoms...or even take names.

Perhaps the thinking—if any—was that somehow only corporations as big and respectable as BillCo would ever take advantage of this wide open back window. But then the worldwide Peabrained Vandal community, after months of inexplicable restraint, finally decided the time had come to party, and things got ugly real quick. Dismayed LookOut! users soon found their promiscuous program had given them not just viruses, but worms, which is exactly as horrid as it sounds.

Turns out quite a few people use LookOut! and some version of Open-Window. Collectively they lost a fair amount of time and data—and money—and it's safe to say many were unhappy and some outright peeved. It was only a matter of time before they all wised up and figured out how the vandals got in. If I had been a BillCo attorney, already sweating a momentous verdict, I'd have spent my time preparing to go to the mattresses again, restocking the bunker with supplies against yet another long siege. And if I were (*shudder!*) a BillCo PR flack, I'd have spent that time racking my brains for some way to make BillCo skew positive—come across warm and likeable and beleaguered by bureaucrats.

Hearken to what they did instead.

There's another operating system I *can* call by its right name here, because nobody owns it. Linux is open-source: anybody can get under the hood and suggest or demonstrate improvements, and good ones get adopted by the community. This makes for superb, cutting-edge software—free! A number of years ago, for instance, volunteers developed Kerberos: an open-standard security system that authenticates the identity of users who log into Unix networks. Theodore Ts'o and others worked on it together until it was Way Cool, inviting others to use and/or improve it.

Then BillCo showed up at the barn-raising, eager to help.

Next thing you knew, OpenWindow 2K had a version of Kerberos built in. Only theirs was copyrighed. Proprietary rather than free. And funny thing: it didn't interact effectively with Unix or Linux computers....

A few programmers discussed this at a website called Slashdot. It bills itself as "news for nerds," and that's exactly what it is: a big public bulletin board on which nerds rap with each other. No matter how heated the discussion might have become, there was no possibility of any tangible consequence in the real world. Until BillCo decided to try and censor it.

I'm not joking: BillCo asked Slashdot to delete the Kerberos discussion-thread. No specific "or-else" was named...but it was lawyers did the ask-

ing. It's alleged that some miscreant revealed secrets of BillCo's proprietary software. . . .

Say again? The sergeants of BillCo—which was seriously threatened with the corporate equivalent of lobotomy and castration, and which only the week before damaged millions of its customers through apparent gross Internet-security incompetence—decided in their corporate wisdom that that was the moment to make sure not only Linux weenies, but everyone literate, thinks of them as creeps and bullies. That'll make the federal judges feel merciful. . . .

Wish I could help. But so far my attorney and I have never met, and I like it that way. So please don't e-mail and ask which OS I'm talking about. Apropos of nothing, by the way, my neighbor Homer hates black birds—so my crows oft win *d'oh!*'s.

Devil's Advocate

FIRST PRINTED NOVEMBER 1999

SOME OF US HATE MICROSOFT. But nearly all of us hate Bill Gates. His features are available on dartboards, "Wanted" posters and squares of toilet paper. I know several terrific and savage jokes about him, and so do you. Every professional comedian has at least a dozen. If you want your photography to appear in every single print medium in the world, just lurk in ambush until you catch a candid shot of Mr. Gates with an unflattering expression on his face. Any day now, handgun shooting ranges will start replacing their generic silhouette targets with just such pictures. He may not be the antiChrist, but he seems to be the antiSaraLee: nobody doesn't hate him.

Why? His massive wealth obviously must have a lot to do with it...but that can't be the whole story.

Try this experiment: buttonhole average citizens on the sidewalk, and ask them to identify a photo of Bill Gates. I predict a *very* high success rate. Next ask what he is famous for—and again, a very high percentage will have at least a vague idea, although they may be hazy on the details. ("The guy that, like, invented computers," "The richest son of a bitch on earth" and "Doesn't he own the Internet?" will be commonly-heard answers.)

Now repeat the experiment—using a photo of Warren Buffett, a man richer than Mr. Gates.

I predict the number of correct identifications will be roughly zero. If you reveal his name, you'll get a bit more response: several people will give you the same wrong answer—some variant of, "Isn't he that guy that sings about Margaritaville and cheeseburgers in paradise?"

What is it that makes Mr. Gates a uniquely excellent focus for society's free-floating hatred? After all, we didn't *have* to buy his kludge of an operating system or his bloated buggy applications. That was *our* fault, for failing to do our consumer homework. A few hours' research would have showed us that a better operating system existed, and that it made sense to pay 10 percent more up front to get a machine in which installing—or *deinstalling*—an application was effortless, connecting up peripheral equipment was utterly painless, graphics and sound functions did not require elaborate and buggy workarounds, and so on. If we had, *that* system might now be the de facto world standard instead of Windows. We did not, in short, *have* to settle for what we now have.

Why did we do it, then? For the same reason we used to give our first-grade teacher for silly behavior: everybody else was doing it. The great and powerful Oz—almighty IBM—had given DOS and its descendants-to-come the Seal of Approval, and that was all anyone wanted to hear.

So it's not Bill Gates's fault that he's rich. That's *our* money he has, and he has it because we gave it to him. We were not absolutely required to buy the cheapest and dumbest operating system available; we chose to.

Is that it? Do we loathe Mr. Gates so much because he symbolizes, and thus reminds us of, a series of bad decisions that *we* made, and of which we now repent? For those bad decisions certainly impact on our personal daily lives. If Warren Buffett decides to corner some market or raid some industry, his decision may affect me...but I'll probably never notice the effect. Whereas even I, a confirmed Mac guy, must use—and curse—Microsoft Word every working day of my life. (I have to. Everybody else is doing it.)

But I remind myself that there might not *be* a Macintosh today if it hadn't been for Mr. Gates. I got one of the first Macs sold—and for a *long* time, its survival was in doubt, because there was almost no software for it. Just about the only non-Apple application available was...Microsoft Word! Mr. Gates, an early Mac enthusiast, had ordered Word ported over to the new platform. Others slo-o-owly followed his lead, and the Mac began acquiring the third-party software that saved it from oblivion.

Last week I took a notion to reread a document I wrote back in 1984. Problem: it was created with MacWrite, the Apple word processor then bundled with the Mac, and now extinct. I still have that version of MacWrite here in my office—on a 400K floppy!—but it's useless to me. Apple did not maintain backward-compatibility with its own products, so if I try launching MacWrite 2.2 or 4.5 or even MacWrite II on my present PowerPC desktop, it crashes the system.

But my present version of Microsoft Word (v5.1a) can read a vintage-1984 Word document. In fact, it can read a 1984 MacWrite document!

Civilians seldom realize how *rare* backward-compatibility is and always has been in the computer industry. The only company to provide it routinely has been Microsoft. So I have Mr. Gates to thank for the fact that I *was* able to reread that old 1984 file after all.

It bears repeating that Mr. Gates has given more money to charity—real money, not hot air—than just about anyone else in history. ("More" both in dollars and as a percentage of his net worth.) And if he's done anything uniquely awful with the residue, I haven't heard about it. He married for love. He did *not* get contact lenses or shoe lifts or plastic surgery to look more like Diana Ross. As multibillionaires go, he seems a pretty decent guy. Okay, he made those billions by exploiting the creative work of others, and paying them beans for it—but what billionaire didn't?

There were some excellent arguments for breaking up Microsoft's monopoly. (You remember how much cheaper and easier making a phone call became right after they broke up Ma Bell, right?) But if we go that route, let it not be simply because we want to see old Bill get one in the eye. I'm not sure the man has it coming.

"Fool, fool, back to the beginning is the rule—"

FIRST PRINTED JANUARY 2000

IME WAS, A SCIENCE FICTION WRITER could be presumed not to be a Luddite. But times have changed. I could probably name six—successful ones!—who openly despise science and its whole ethos, loathe sf and its entire pantheon; several seem to have entered the field for the specific purpose of sassing Robert A. Heinlein. (Now that it's safe.). I myself am obviously an unreconstructed hippie, and I majored in English. So first let me summarize my anti-Luddite credentials:

Not one of my seventeen science fiction novels (and no more than a handful of my very earliest short stories) is set in a depressing future. The bulk of my short fiction, beginning with my very first sale to Ben Bova, originally appeared in *Analog Science Fiction/Science Fact*, fondly known in the field then and now as The One With Rivets—or Ben's next magazine, *OMNI*. I owned a 512K Macintosh (a "Fat" Mac!) before they hit the street, having wheedled one out of Apple Canada as a Celebrity Endorsement. I think anyone who says phonograph records sound better than CDs is kidding himself, I'd rather we burned uranium than oil or coal or gas and I think within this century nanotechnology will make everyone immortal and ultimately rich. (Or destroy the race. No third choice. But I'm very optimistic.) I'm alive today because of surgical procedures that were sf when I was born. I'm as far from being a Luddite as I think it makes sense to get. I *like* good technology...what little of it there is.

That said, I think we need to scrap nearly every single piece of software in the world and start over.

Even Linux may not be radical enough rethinking—though it is clearly far superior to anything else presently extant in the noosphere.

Early in 2000, the US National Weather Service unveiled a new IBM supercomputer capable of 2,500 billion calculations a second that would give them warning of impending weather problems up to ten days in advance. They booted it up, fed it oceans of data from around and above the planet, and that afternoon at 3:30 they announced with uncommon confidence that there was a 40 percent chance of light snow next day totaling less than one inch.

You're way ahead of me. That night, the white hammer fell on the entire eastern seaboard. *North Carolina* got 51 cm (20 inches), for Chrissake. The nation's capital took 46 cm (18 in), enough to shut down the federal government and give a quarter of a million workers two days off with pay—120 megabucks down the drain right there. "One expert," the *Times of London* reported, "said the forecasters had been deceived by the computer rather than believing their own radar, which told them that heavy snow was already falling...." At least seven deaths were attributed to the unexpected storm.

Now think about this: that story was awarded half a column on page twenty-two of my local paper.

It isn't even considered news anymore if a supercomputer screws up and paralyzes the government and half the country. By now we all *know* computers screw up all the time. Y2K, eh? Yet again and again we sit there staring at them, mesmerized, while just outside our window the blizzard is plainly visible on the horizon.

I was perhaps one of the first civilians to "get" that computers screw up all the time. That's right, I'm so ancient I can actually recall a time when men in white coats said, with a straight face, "Computers don't *make* mistakes." And were believed. I'm going back a quarter-century or so, now. After seven years at three different universities (don't ask), I'd finally completed the requirements for a degree. A week before graduation, I noticed I hadn't received any of the standard bumpf everyone else had—invitations to order cap and gown, sit for photos, select a class ring, etc—so I wandered down to the registrar's office and inquired.

That university, I learned, had recently become one of the first in the country to acquire a supercomputer. It cost a fortune, filled a building the size of a small high school and Did Not Make Mistakes. So they had loaded all the university's records into it...and then trashed the obsolete hard copies.

You know what comes next. The computer contained no record of my existence. Garbage *out*....

To graduate, I had to obtain affidavits from every professor I'd had there. Two were dead. One was catatonic: bad STP. Another was underground, hiding somewhere in Algeria with Eldridge Cleaver and Timothy Leary. Imagine the fun. The following October, I finally received my sheepskin in a moving ceremony in the Dean of Men's office, attended by him, his secretary and myself. I wept, with relief, and the secretary had the grace to sniffle.

The truth? I've always kind of *liked* that computers screw up often. Tell the editor your computer crashed, just as you were about to save the changes, and she will groan in genuine empathy and extend your deadline. Computer-savvy since 1984, I was nonetheless one of the last kids on my block to get e-mail...and only surrendered when I finally grokked that *it was at LEAST as unreliable as the post office*, that you could always claim not to have received a message, and be believed. A certain amount of inefficiency and screw-up in life affords a level of comfort and deniability I find agreeable...even if it did bite me on a tender spot once in college. And as I say, nowadays we all *know* computers are unreliable: at least we're warned.

But when things are so bad that hundreds of thousands of commuters get stranded on snowbound highways without warning, and we have to (and we *did* have to) spend many gigabucks warding off potential Y2K disaster, and we all take it for granted that our own computer will freeze or crash regularly, and I don't have a single friend with whom I can reliably exchange formatted documents by e-mail without *tsimmis*...maybe it's time to go back to the beginning and start over.

Windows is a shell built on a shell grafted onto QDOS—"Quick and Dirty Operating System," itself a ripoff of CPM, written at a time when nobody'd ever heard of mouse, GUI, Internet, streaming video or plastic coasters that hold sixty gigabytes. It was turned into the de facto world standard by a man who honestly believed "64K should be enough for anybody." Gates may have renamed the system he stole MS-DOS, for Microsoft Disk Operating System, but it still remained, at bottom, a quick and dirty operating system, meant to run on the most primitive hardware imaginable. And for generations now they've been simply piling code on top of it, trying to mask, muffle or circumvent the profound flaws built into it.

The only reason it survives is that very soon after it appeared, this ripoff OS was itself able to rip off at least some of the "look and feel" of yet another operating system. That one was originally dreamed up by a truly extraordinary man called Jef Raskin, who named it after his favorite apple: Macintosh.

Then Steve Jobs heard how cool it was, and came and took the project over, and it became the legendary Macintosh Marathon Race To Destiny. You've probably read about it: Big Steve bullying a team of eccentric geniuses into outdoing themselves, working twenty-six-hour days and nine-day weeks while chanting, "Artists ship!" Perhaps you've heard how they got the very first Mac demo program to run correctly without crashing for the first time *ever* only a few hours before the Mac was to be publicly unveiled with maximum fanfare. That first Macintosh was a 128K joke, a $2000 etch-a-sketch, and the OS and all the existing programs that ran on it (both of them) were badly flawed. The romantic mystique of Jolt Cola Programming had gotten the machine out the door on deadline, all right, and it really was insanely great—at least potentially.

It just didn't work very well.

Ever since, they've been applying increasingly more sophisticated and complicated band-aids. The OS that once fit onto a 400K floppy, along with a word processor and a novelette-length document, now has to be loaded from a CD-ROM because it's so grotesquely bloated that using 1.4MB floppies would take too much time. And today it takes me three times as long to open a blank word-processing document as it used to take me in 1984 on a Fat Mac—three times as long to boot up in the first place, too.

And this is the *intelligent* operating system. Its imitators are worse, just barely usable. The most commonly used word processor on earth, Word, is a grotesque kludge, the Jabba the Hutt of software, and, as of this year, can no longer open and read Word v1.0 files.

This ain't workin'—time we started over.

Like I said, I'm not a Luddite. I'd rather run Word 9 on the worst Windows machine ever built, driving a dot matrix printer with fanfold paper, than be forced to earn my living with the best electric typewriter IBM ever made.

But even more, I'd like to have a *good* computer, with a sensibly-designed and well-written operating system, that does *not* keep constantly pulling my attention away from my work. If only I could find one....

Friends tell me—quite emphatically, some of them—that the system I want is here, and it is called Linux. It never crashes, they say. And Any Day Now, there will be just dozens of applications available to run on it. And the best part, they say, is that Linux *will not stop getting better until it is perfect*...because nobody owns it, anybody can get at the innards and tinker with them until they're bug-free and there's no pressure to ship by deadline ready or not. There is a persuasive logic to all this....

And yet, I wonder if even Linux goes back far *enough*.

I am massively ignorant here—but it's my understanding that Linux shares the same basic paradigm as the Mac or Windows systems. One boots up a Linux machine, and it loads software which eventually produces onscreen some sort of "desktop" (even if it doesn't actually employ that specific visual metaphor): a conceptual environment of some sort, a "place" containing menus of individual task-specific programs called "applications" and the archived documents produced by them. The user may then "launch" one or more applications, switch among them, use them to view, edit or create documents, and ultimately return to the desktop to launch new applications, copy documents, perform file hygiene or shut down the machine.

Is it written somewhere by the finger of God that this is necessarily the only or even the best way to design an operating system? Granted, it's vastly superior to its immediate predecessors, systems employing the dreaded "modes" metaphor. But is it really the perfect paradigm, beyond improvement?

Since 1984 I'd believed as an article of faith that the Macintosh Metaphor, the graphical-user-interface Apple developed from concepts pioneered by Xerox, was the best possible interface. Microsoft clearly agrees, for they've done their level best to imitate it, given the limitations of their OS. Everyone agrees: whether Apple original or Windows knockoff, long live desktops, icons in folders, applications and documents. It must be the perfect system, since there is no other. There are a few die-hard adherents of the dreaded command line interface (just as there are guys who'll never abandon their 8-track) but all reasonable people know the perfect conceptual paradigm has been found.

Okay, there *are* still people who find even GUI computers counterintuitive, *unfriendly* in the extreme...but those people are just stupid, or stubborn, or superstitious, or they're just not trying...and in a few generations they'll have been mercifully selected out of the gene pool anyway. (Never mind that these throwbacks constitute 85 percent of the population of North America and more than 95 percent of humans worldwide.)

So I believed for years. And then I seemed to hear a voice, saying, "Friend Zebadiah—are you *sure?*"

Just because the Mac/Windows scheme is the best in sight, is it necessarily the best possible? Does your mind naturally store data in folder-trees? What's so inherently great about little icons? Deeper: what's so unimprovably wonderful about the metaphor of an imaginary desktop, from which one launches task-specific applications that create mutually incompatible files? Before you got a computer, did you ever have a desktop that *remotely* resembled the one onscreen?

Wait, now: everyone knows graphic icons are superior to mere text-based—

In all cases? Imagine you're a newbie, sitting down at your first computer, contemplating a button that depicts a rectangle with an isoscele trapezoid contiguous above. Say you grew up in an apartment building. Or a mansion, or an igloo, or a grass hut, or a geodesic dome, or underground in Coober Pedy, Australia. Which would you decipher quicker? That baffling graphic? Or the simple word 'home'?

I use Microsoft Word every day of my working life. Over on the left margin is a toolbar: twenty buttons with graphical labels. What do they all mean? Well...I can tell you instantly the three I use regularly. Another three or four are fairly obvious. A diagonally slanting tube with a cap at the lower end, for example, is clearly a lit cigarette: the icon means "No smoking."

Ah, no—I was mistaken: that's not a cigarette, it's a pencil, with its eraser downward, so the icon must mean "delete." You select some text and then click that icon and it goes away, right?

Sorry, squire: in fact that eraser-head icon means "Undo."

Most of the other icons aren't even that self-explanatory...and some just beat the hell out of me. And I've been doing this a long time. What would a new user make, for instance, of the icon that depicts something she's unlikely ever to see or use: a floppy disk?

All these heretical thoughts were put in my head by a correspondent who asked, "Do you know why every time you boot up you have to wait nearly three minutes before you can *do* anything? And then two more to reopen the document you were working on, find your place and resume working? It's because the original Mac designer screwed up."

Hey, has Microsoft got anything better, wise-guy?

"No. But I do."

Right, I thought.

"My computer boots instantly. Flip the power switch, and you're looking at the last screen you saw. The stuff you'll need to resume working on it loads invisibly in the background, in the order you're liable to need it, during the four or five seconds it's going to take you to find your place on-screen, set your fingers on home row and decide on your first keystrokes. Everything else, the stuff you *might* need later on, loads whenever it gets a chance."

That *is* neat. Do all the applications—

"My computer doesn't use applications."

Huh?

"Or you could say all the applications are active, all the time. But the user never has to think about such things. He just sits down and works. Like a surgeon, whatever tools he calls for are put in his hand as he needs them."

I tried to picture that. Right now I have on my Mac: 1) a word processor with lousy graphics, page layout and movie modules, 2) a paint/draw program with a lousy text-processing module, 3) a photo program with lousy text processing and paint/draw powers, 4) a page layout program with lousy text-processing and graphics capability and 5) an e-mail program incorporating a rotten text-processor, lousy graphics and little else. Endless duplication of effort. And none of those programs can read the files of any of the others without conversion rituals.

"In my interface, all the applications are always open, and totally compatible: together they *are* the operating system. The user never has to think about *anything* but what he or she wants to do next."

At this point you're probably wondering why I was still listening to this crackpot.

One word: rep. Turns out this was the *second* interface this fellow'd dreamed up, and the previous one hadn't turned out badly at all, however critical of it he may be now. He named that one after his favorite apple: Macintosh.

Yes, that man behind the curtain, to whom you definitely *should* pay attention, a peer of The Great and Wonderful Woz himself, is the original head of the Macintosh project, Jef Raskin. He is as close to a Renaissance Man as it is possible to be anymore, an intellectual omnivore of frightening appetite: even a partial list of his accomplishments would fill an essay this size, and a list of his hobbies would overflow this website. An outline of his *interests* might well occupy enough bandwidth to perceptibly slow the Net. Also he's modest. He recently wrote me: "It is gross exaggeration to say, as you do, that I am the only living human who's ever thought seriously about interface design. I may have been one of the earlier ones, but there are thousands. Most of whom are doing really dumb work."

As an antidote to which, he has written a splendid book called *The Humane Interface*, which was published in 2000. I can count on the fingers of one foot the number of books about software design I've ever loved—or for that matter, seen—but this one I found as riveting and mind-expanding as a good science fiction novel. (Full disclosure: I'm quoted, briefly, in a chapter heading.) He even did his own cover illo.

The book reminded me of the late Victor Papanek's classic *Design for the Real World*. Both mercilessly, often hilariously, flay existing examples of stupid design, then contrast them with intelligent design, and thus begin to derive therefrom some clear, basic, fundamental principles of what a good design should and should not do. (The products Mr. Papanek designed were physical rather than virtual.) I put Mr. Raskin's book down understanding much better why most of the software I have to use pisses me off. I almost want to propose a law that henceforward all software designers be required to read *The Humane Interface*.

That system, by the way—the applicationless, instant-boot computer— actually exists. Or did. Mr. Raskin not only dreamed it up, he designed it, sold it to the money, got it built and even got the sumbitch shipped. Not by some under-financed startup, either, but by a major player, Canon. The Canon Cat, it was called. Sure, its desktopless-dancer paradigm sounds a little weird to indoctrinated Mac or Windows zombies like you and me...but they say people who'd never *touched* a computer before sat down in front of a Cat and just...well, *started working*, without knowing the hierarchical file system from the patriarchal legal system. It was a computer aimed at the *other* 85 percent of the population, who don't think yours is fun. Major buzz began building....

...and within weeks, Canon was bought by a larger corporation with its own new computer, and the Cat was put in a sack and tossed in the river.

Next time you get in your car, look down. Observe the layout of the accelerator and brake pedals, and take just a moment to contemplate it skeptically, as though it were *not* handed down by God. At once, you notice the design—absolutely standard across the planet—is fundamentally brain-damaged. Clearly it requires more time and work to get one's foot from accelerator to brake (lift foot *high*, move it to the left a measured amount, lower it again) than to get it from brake to accelerator (slide foot to right until it falls off pedal)—which is exactly backwards. If your foot should slip, you won't accidentally brake, inviting possible minor damage to you from behind...you'll accidentally accelerate, causing likely fatality to someone else in front of you. Henry Ford just wasn't thinking that day, that's all.

But don't bother designing an intelligent layout. *It's too late.* Billions of people already do it the stupid way, by habit. If you introduced a smarter design—somehow miraculously destroyed every single existing car and replaced them with improved versions overnight—hundreds of thousands would still kill themselves unlearning their bad habits. The present scheme is like the Chinese alphabet or the QWERTY keyboard: a disaster it's way too late to undo.

But at this point in history, despite what all the hype may have caused you to gather, *hardly anyone on Earth owns a computer.*

It is not yet too late. There's still time to rethink operating systems and the software that runs on them from the ground up, with long-term goals and capabilities in mind for once, and get it right this time.

Character Defects

FIRST PRINTED MARCH 2000

YOU KNOW HOW I FEEL about software. But I don't just want to scrap Windows—and Mac, and BEOS, and Linux, and Unix—I don't merely propose we rethink the whole "desktop and applications" metaphor, as I suggested in the last essay. No, I want to go back even further, back to fundamentals, and reform ASCII itself.

ASCII, the American Standard Code for Information Interchange, is or should be something to be grateful for. Almost *nothing* about computers is standardized—but ASCII is, which is why it is (barely) possible for all of us here on the Tower of Babel to exchange data at all. It's the set of characters that *every* computer recognizes, the ones you're limited to in a text-only document or message, the ones sent to your computer's printer if you select Fastest output, the ones most e-mails are made of.

It's wonderful that ASCII exists. It would be even better if it didn't suck.

As it is presently constituted, ASCII makes it enormously difficult for me to do my job. Thanks to ASCII, every time I write something my attention is *constantly* yanked away from what I'm writing, and forced onto how I'm writing it—sometimes two or three times in a single sentence...or even more.

It just happened. In the last sentence of the previous paragraph, it happened three times. Did you notice?

First I wanted to italicize the word "constantly." If I were writing copy intended to be printed out on paper, such as a story manuscript, I would simply have italicized the word and kept on writing. But I'm writing copy that will be submitted electronically, as e-mail, a text-only document, so I'm restricted to the ASCII character set.

And ASCII has no way to indicate italic characters. (Or boldface characters either, for that matter.)

Sure, there are workarounds. That's the problem: there are several.

One of my editors likes italic text rendered in CAPITAL LETTERS, because that stands out and catches his eye. But another insists I denote italics in lowercase, but _with underlines before and after_—because that way she can convert my copy back into actual italics by simple global-replace, *without* having to retype all the italicized copy to get rid of the uppercase letters. Yet another editor prefers that I indicate italics with, of all things, *asterisks*.

I could solve the problem just by developing a more phlegmatic style. Or, all the damn editors could get together and hammer out a standard method of indicating italics, and I could just learn it and stop thinking about it. (Until I switch back to working on my novel again....)

But forget italics: ASCII doesn't even have a complete set of a writer's most basic tools: punctuation marks, for example. We don't have many, and they're crucial: our only way of giving the reader stage directions. ASCII—apparently created by people who'd never written anything more stylistically sophisticated than a user's manual—lacks a couple of absolutely fundamental punctuation marks: the em-dash...and the ellipsis.

When I'm writing a book, to be printed out and mailed to New York, I indicate an em-dash with an em-dash. (The term means literally, "a dash as wide as a letter m.") But when I'm writing newspaper copy to be submitted by e-mail, thanks to ASCII I must indicate an em-dash with a pair of hyphens. If a linebreak happens to occur between those two hyphens, the intended em-dash is easily overlooked.

(Some editors therefore ask that I put a space on either side of the double-hyphen -- like this -- quadrupling the number of keystrokes required. I plan to ignore these editors as long as possible.)

When I'm writing a book, an ellipsis takes a single keystroke...and my word processor is smart enough not to break a line in the middle of the ellipsis. When writing e-mail or news copy, I must use three periods to indicate an ellipsis, tripling the number of keystrokes, and inevitably a line break will come just there.

(One editor actually requested spaces around all the periods—*sextupling* the number of required keystrokes. I let her live....)

Worst of all, I have to remember *which convention to use.* That means I can *never* put my full attention on what I'm writing: I must constantly remind myself what format I'm using at the moment.

Imagine that a small change has been made in the driving laws. From now on, you must use *only* your right hand to drive—on streets whose names begin with A, C, E, G, I, K, M, O, Q, S, U, W and Y. On all other streets, you must drive with only your left hand. But during the last quarter of every hour, the rules reverse. Make a mistake and a policeman will stop you and lecture you, wasting your time.

Now imagine that you spend all day on the road, every day....

Accents? Don't even think about accents. In the same sense that one might argue that a power structure is racist or sexist or classist, ASCII is clearly linguist. Its creators made no provision or accommodation whatsoever for speakers of any language but English. No French accents *grave* or *vergule*, no Hispanic inverted-question-mark or tailed-n, no Germanic umlaut, no Cyrillic "zh" character, no circumflex, not so much as a dipthong. I live in a bilingual country, where accents can be—have been!—important enough to start a riot. But I bet they won't be in twenty years. Even the most rabidly separatist Québecois will probably have abandoned them, because they can't be e-mailed: there just is no convenient way to render accents in ASCII.

And can somebody explain to me why there are ASCII characters for "plus," "minus" and "multipled by"...but *not* for "divided by" or "the square root of"?

For that matter, how can it be that in the universal world standard character set, there is no provision for either superscript or subscript? Could ASCII possibly have been standardized so geologically long ago that its creators had never heard of math or chemistry, exponents or isotopes, never envisioned anyone wanting to say "two to the fourth power" or "two hydrogen atoms and one oxygen atom" without having to switch to a graphics program? Without subscripts, how can you know whether by "U-235," I mean an isotope of uranium or a Nazi submarine? ASCII can't even directly express Robert A. Heinlein's version of The Number of the Beast; it must be paraphrased as something like "six to the sixth-to-the-sixth power," robbing it of its beauty.

And as long as we're going back to basics—I know this point is now moot, since floppy disks seemed to have joined eight-track tapes and pagers on the trash heap of technological history, but doesn't it tell you something that *every single blank 3.5" floppy disk ever sold was manufactured upside down*?

Take a look at one. The blank label will almost certainly have text printed on it somewhere—the word "index" if nothing else. So will the little metal sliding door that protects the naked disk within: it'll have the manufacturer's name in big letters. But if you orient things so all that text is right-side up, you will find that the label itself is now down at the *bottom* end of the disk. Where, if you file your disks vertically like everyone else on the planet, you won't be able to read it. And now *all* your disks will have that metal slide—the part that if a careless sleeve happened to accidentally swipe it open, all your data would be at risk—sticking up.

Not being an idiot, you probably store your floppies in the caddy upside down so you can protect your data and actually read the furshluginer labels. So the manufacturer's logo on the slide is down at the bottom, both hard to see and upside-down: it can't do much subliminal good as advertising unless you customarily shop standing on your head.

How much faith would you have in a car that said ɐpuoH on the trunk? The first time I ever so much as *approached* a computer, even before I was ready to switch it on, I contemplated that startup floppy...and wondered about the caliber of the minds to whom I was about to entrust my professional livelihood for the next few decades.

Let's start over and approach this business as though doing it intelligently were a good thing.

Space

Headline

FIRST PRINTED APRIL 2001

O N APRIL 12, 1961, Yuri Gagarin climbed into a deathtrap called Vostok, yelled "Poyekali!"—"Let's go!"—and was blasted into orbit. Vostok's hatch blew off on the way down, and Major Gagarin had to eject. Having flown 200 miles high, he came down the last 23,000 feet by parachute. This was kept a state secret until recently, because under international rules, "a pilot must stay with his craft from takeoff to landing before any record is ratified," and the Soviets feared technical disqualification. Ridiculous, of course: landing literally on his own two feet made his accomplishment *more* heroic. But one wonders if carrying that secret affected his foolish decision, seven years later, to become a test-pilot, like America's astronauts. His plane augured in just months before Apollo 11 fulfilled the promise his historic flight had made.

Fifty years ago the first animals were fired into space and recovered alive: one monkey and eleven mice. Forty years ago, the first human orbited Earth and returned alive, setting an altitude record of 200 miles. Apollo 8 raised that record by 240,000 miles; Bill Anders took the first photograph of the whole Earth from space and days later, in lunar orbit, also shot the first Earthrise ever seen—changing the perspective of the human race forever. Right after that, Neil Armstrong and Buzz Aldrin became the first to walk on another planet. Altogether, twenty-seven people, all American males, have made the half million mile roundtrip to the moon. They're the only people since the dawn of time to actually *know*—from the evidence of their personal eyeballs—just how incredibly tiny, lonely and fragile our planet is.

The moon has been lonely now forty years.

There've been a hundred Shuttle flights. Mir became the first Soviet product in history to *exceed* its warrantee, bless its scattered shards. But none of these went much higher than Gagarin did forty years ago: about two hundred miles. The crew of Apollo 17 were the last people ever to see the entire Earth at once...and by then, hardly anyone on it cared anymore.

The one future that no science fiction writer of my generation ever dreamed came to pass: man actually *did* go to space, brushed his very fingertips against incalculable wealth, endless adventure and the first truly infinite frontier...then yawned and quit. The Apollo Program is one of very few things the US has ever spent money on that returned its investment, in hard cash—thirteen times over, so far. NASA will be happy to show you the figures. So much for "throwing money away in space when we have so many problems here at home." Space is a better investment than real estate and oil combined.

The smart money's beginning to figure that out, and the tide has finally started to turn. In 1997, for the first time ever, there were more commercial launches than government ones. They generated revenues of $85 billion. Two thousand satellites will go up in the next ten years. NASA's finally found an identity it can sell to Congress and is energetically exploring the solar system with unmanned probes, simpler and cheaper than spaceships. Priceless data is pouring in. We're finally beginning to get a handle on how planets form.

And how they're destroyed. The current best theory for how the Moon got there is that it's a chunk of Earth, blasted clear by some unimaginably violent collision. Think about that a moment. If we saw something coming *today*, all we could do about it is go two hundred miles up and shake our fists at it.

My personal hopes rest not on governments or corporations, but on individuals: crackpots and dreamers. Right now a dozen small outfits are competing diligently to design cheap earth-to-orbit vehicles. And once you're in orbit, you're halfway to *anywhere*.

NASA today represents adventure for robots; private space development is adventure for stockholders. I want adventure for ordinary people. As far as I know, except for a few amateur guitarists, no *artists* have ever been sent to space.

But a new window of opportunity is about to open. Launch costs are dropping and will plummet shortly. Russia sold a slot in their space sta-

tion crew for $20 million. Humanity can send up a dancer/poet/painter/ composer—or for that matter a priest/rabbi/mullah/imam—any time it wants to badly enough. Maybe government and industry can do without a new frontier, but art needs one desperately, and so does the human spirit.

I propose that the next contribution to space exploration should be the arts. So far only jocks, geeks, congressmen and construction workers have been to space. Every one came back profoundly spiritually affected. Let us develop and launch a new generation of dancers, writers, composers and other Muse-chasers...and pray that through their creations they'll be able to convey to the rest of the race that our mutual salvation, our destiny, free energy, unimaginable beauty and infinite possibility all hang just over our heads, waiting for us to evolve the wit to make ladders.

And we're running out of fossil fuels fast....

"...still I persist in wondering"

FIRST PRINTED JULY 2004

"And still I persist in wondering, whether folly must always be our Nemesis ..."
—EDGAR PANGBORN, "MY BROTHER LEOPOLD"

WHAT'S THAT WORD FOR AN ORGANISM too dumb to evolve any further, that engages in suicidally stupid behavior even in the face of irrefutable evidence that it won't work, has never worked and never will work? Oh yeah: "human," that's the word I'm looking for.

No matter how sophisticated, enlightened or even kind a society may painstakingly make itself—no matter how clever, fair or even wise the systems it may devise for the correct assignment and smooth transfer of power—it always seems to work out that sooner or later, leadership of the land somehow falls into the hands of a Major Bonehead. Doom follows.

His exact nature can vary, but some characteristics are invariant. The Major Bonehead—well, that's one right there: he's always a belligerent militarist, so General Bonehead would seem more correct...except that he's always totally ignorant of military matters, so Major is in fact more appropriate. He's always a rabid isolationist who claims to be responding to his people's demands for his full attention; they soon realize how much better off they were when his attention was elsewhere. He's always convinced that everything bad is the fault of people who are smart and know things; naturally he drives them from the land.

An excellent example of what I mean is discussed in Deputy Comment Editor Val Ross's book *The Road to There*. In 1402 the brilliant eunuch Chen Ho conned the Ming Emperor Zhu Di into underwriting the most amazing fleet the world had ever seen—not just a lot of ships (300), and not just big ones (nine-masters, 120 meters long), but ships vastly superior to anything Europe would produce for centuries. They basically conquered the western Pacific as far as Australia and Vietnam, and brought home unimaginable wealth in the form of knowledge: new ideas, insights, technologies. Then Zhu Di died, and his successor, Major Bonehead...excuse me,

Zhu Zhanji…declared, "I do not care for foreign things." The construction of sea-going ships was forbidden on pain of death. Going to sea in a boat with more than one mast was deemed espionage. Most of Chen Ho's priceless documents were burned, as "obvious exaggerations." The government focused its efforts on helping the starving people, and China entered a Dark Age it has struggled cyclically to leave ever since.

A similar phenomenon has occurred recently in the United States of America. For the past half century, with only brief and ineffective exceptions, its leaders have tended to be reactionary, isolationist, cheap and profoundly proud of their admittedly remarkable ignorance. The most recent avatar has pulled off the astounding feat of personally pissing away, in only two years, more international good will than the United States has had to waste since the period immediately following the end of World War II, disgracing and betraying the dead of the Twin Towers by beating, bombing and bullying utterly innocent people in their name—sublimely oblivious of the historical irony in the British Empire being the only major nation on earth to stand by them against the wicked freedom-hating French! I think it's fairly clear—no, pellucidly clear—that the omphaloskeptic spirit of Zhu Zhanji has fallen over America like a funeral shroud in recent decades. Seal the borders, paint over the windows, suspend the civil rights of all non-citizens and quit wasting money on that scientific research crap—it only causes problems anyway. 9/11 could not have suited the present administration better if they'd invented it (he said subjunctively).

Historians will spend centuries debating the exact point at which America began to lose it. For my money, the fateful moment came when Richard Nixon—*as he spoke* to Armstrong and Aldrin on the moon by phone, congratulating them for their magnificent achievement—used his other hand to gut NASA's budget, for the unforgivable sin of having been thought up by a Democrat. It took years for the word to get out, but it was on that day that any hope of a meaningful American space program began to die a slow horrid death. Today, after thirty years in which even an accidental Democratic administration gave its space portfolio to Dan Quayle, America has—let's face it—a space shuttle that doesn't go anywhere useful, a space station that won't do anything useful even if ever they finish it and a lot of blather about a Mars mission that we all know will happen shortly after biogeneticists produce a winged pig. Plus a bunch of spy satellites, which they basically inherited from the Eisenhower and Kennedy administrations, and robot probes.

When China—clueless, backward China—successfully sent up its own first astronaut, only thirty years late, the general American reaction was, how quaint. Next, they'll invent the electric guitar. Even more amusement was provoked by China's straightforward admission that it has a most ambitious long-term space program. Not only does it envision a real, high-orbit space station, it openly plans a permanent settlement on the moon. As far as I can tell, not a single civilian flinched when that statement was made, and not a single commentator frowned.

And now with all those other responsibilities on his plate, George W. Bush has suddenly remembered to mention that he, too, always meant to establish a permanent lunar base, a Bridge Between Worlds (he just forgot to mention it before), and by golly, what's wrong with now? It isn't as though he were running a half-trillion-dollar deficit or something....

The great Jef Raskin e-mailed me: "Yeah, and you can keep your bridge, too, Mr. Bush. I am all for space exploration. We should have a habitat on the moon and telescopes on the far side where earthlight and radio noise are not a problem. And we must go to Mars, and even farther. But I don't believe you have any real interest in space. You are just trying to pick up some PR points from the successful (so far) Mars shot, act friendly with the voting geeks and offer the promise of rich contracts to the firms (so many in Texas!) that are into aerospace. After the election, you will, as usual, renege on your interest in space. No money. Of course."

Great as is my respect for Mr. Raskin—I'm typing this on one of his brainchildren, the Macintosh—I'm afraid, terrified really, that for once he's missing the incoming knifepoint. A radio telescope is about the only practical thing a lunar base is really good for—it doesn't help us get to Mars at all, and earthlight doesn't bother the Hubble. But how many billions do you think Mr. Bush would spare from his military budget to obtain even God's own radio telescope? As many as one? How profound do you suppose is his curiosity regarding the origins and destiny of the macrocosmic universe, based on past intellectual performance? Remember how hard he fought for stem cell research?

This is far worse than pork-barreling for aerospace firms. I think Mr. Bush heard the Chinese announcement, and—*mirabile dictu*—remembered something he'd been told, once. I first heard it from Robert A. Heinlein, half a century ago, and it will never change. This may sound like melodrama, but it happens to be cold fact: the first party to establish a permanent lunar base owns the world, forever. Whether or not it chooses to exercise that power depends entirely on its own sense of moral restraint. Oof.

It is not even theoretically possible to defend against or withstand an attack from the moon. The aggressor does not need a single missile or even a bomb, nuclear or otherwise. Just a catapult. Anything that throws rocks. It doesn't even have to throw them very hard: lunar escape velocity is not high. What Star Wars shield can even detect an incoming rock falling from Luna, let alone stop it? It has no flare, no heat signature, no electromagnetic output, no albedo to spot. It has no guidance system to fool, no electronics to fry. And by the time it reaches earth, it carries enough energy to do as much damage as a medium-sized nuke...without all that pesky radiation.

Nor is it possible to fight back. If you're at the bottom of a well, having a rock fight with a guy up on ground level, it doesn't matter how many rocks you have, or how hard or accurately you can throw, or even how many gods are on your side: you lose. (For extended discussion, see Robert A. Heinlein's 1966 novel *The Moon is a Harsh Mistress*, still in print.)

I think Flightsuit Boy has decided America should own Terra. It seems something he'd find more appealing than having the keenest radio telescope in town. And here's the kicker: Given a choice, who would you really rather see get the gig? Bush Nation...or the People's Republic? Think thrice. (Can you say "Cultural Revolution"?) America may no longer be the Camelot JFK made us believe in, but it does still concede that (many of) its serfs (of the right ancestry) have (some) rights (while on American soil).

Who'll get the gig is unclear. Mr. Heinlein said once: "Beyond doubt, humanity is going to space. But the working language may not necessarily be English." I wish I spoke Mandarin. Or even Fukienese.

The Day It Hailed Columbia

FIRST PRINTED FEBRUARY 2003

I WAS AWAKE WHEN IT HAPPENED. I write all night, and retired at a typical seven in the morning. All seven of them were dead by then, ashes scattered across East Texas. But who listens to the news as they go to bed? When I finally woke, I knew something was terribly wrong the moment I saw my wife's face. "It's not family or friends," Jeanne said quickly, "but it's bad." And she told me, and then we held each other, hard.

It has a special meaning for us: she was once supposed to ride one of those suckers.

In the late seventies and early eighties, NASA had a Civilian In Space Program. The idea was that fading public interest in space travel might improve if taxpayers got to see somebody other than jocks and scientists go up. If they heard a poet or composer sing to them of the stunning majesty of space, or saw a trained dancer in free fall, or even just an ordinary person gaping out a porthole at the naked stars, then perhaps more of them might finally Get It and realize that going to space is going to be like leaving the womb for our species and will make us at least that much more beautiful and happy and productive and wise.

Jeanne and I won the 1977 Hugo and Nebula Awards for "Stardance," a novella we co-wrote about the first zero gravity dancers. She's a modern dancer and choreographer, and was then the founder/artistic director of Halifax's Nova Dance Theatre. At the 1980 World Science Fiction Convention, in the Boston Sheraton's Grand Ballroom, she premiered a dance called "Higher Ground," about the mental and spiritual evolution she had undergone in the course of inventing zero gee dance for our story. It depicted space travel as the natural end result of the first monkey that ever stood upright—as a dancer's highest leap, the one from which (as they used to say of Nijinski) you don't come down again until you feel like it. The dance incorporated some zero gee special effects by technomedia wizard Bob Atkinson toward the end, so that Jeanne seemed to actually go weightless on stage, while a film backdrop put the starry universe behind her.

Her performance elicited an eight-minute standing ovation. Backstage, Ben Bova, then editor of *OMNI* and well-connected at NASA, asked her if she would be interested in dancing in zero gee for real? Jeanne became a Civilian In Space candidate...along with singer John Denver and a number of others.

Then they sent up the first one, great-hearted teacher Christa McAuliffe, on the *Challenger*.

When that O-ring let go, seven remarkable lives ended, and so did the Civilian in Space Program—at least for our lifetimes. It was very nearly the end of the entire US space effort.

Our phone rang off the hook that day, and for days thereafter. Reporters all around the globe had found Jeanne's name in the list of finalists for a shuttle seat. That could have been you, each one pointed out, in case she'd missed it. Now what do you think of all this rocket nonsense, Ms. Robinson?

Jeanne spent days saying, over and over, "I'd take the next flight." When they expressed disbelief—and they all did, politely or otherwise—she cited figures for number of fatalities per billion passenger miles, proving that space travel is the safest form of transportation ever devised, hundreds of times safer than riding a tricycle in a living room. Not one journalist quoted that part.

It's easy to spin a new disaster to support your political agenda. Within minutes of the shuttle's destruction, a CBC newstwit was asking my colleague Rob Sawyer on the air if he didn't agree that the tragedy was caused by American arrogance in the Middle East? He was so stunned by the question he answered it.

As Richard Nixon chatted with Armstrong and Aldrin across a quarter of a million miles, he was cutting NASA's budget with his other hand. Nobody since has ever raised it. After the *Challenger* tragedy, NASA was ordered to become safer, but given no more money to do it with. Remarkably, they succeeded far beyond any reasonable hope. Numerous missions have flown safely since *Challenger*. A space station is well begun, and as of yet not one construction worker has had a fatal accident.

Ask any engineer: you can't throw a two-lane bridge over a fifty-cent river without planning for at least a few deaths. There are always accidents when something big is built. The tunnels from Manhattan Island each had a sandhog casualty rate comparable with combat, in a holy war...and all those utensils accomplished was to get you to Brooklyn, or worse, New Jersey. The space station may one day get us to the stars.

There are only three buses left in North America that go to that stop, now. Columbia was the oldest. There are way fewer spare parts around than there used to be, and fewer technicians trained in their installation. Just to stand still, to maintain its present bare-bones agenda, NASA is going to need a huge whack of money. Right away. Just as America is preparing to spend every spare dollar building the kind of rockets that are *supposed* to explode and kill people—and to aim them down instead of up.

Columbia needs replacing. We need to put people on Mars, and in orbit, and keep them there. As the world simmers and stews in its own madness, the one thing we cannot afford to cut is our only means to rise above it. Robert Heinlein said *this planet is too fragile a basket for humanity to keep all its eggs in*. We're easily dumb and quarrelsome enough to drop it, one of these days. If that happens, it would be nice if there were grandchildren somewhere to whom the cautionary tale might be told.

We all looked up the night Columbia went down. It was a good time to look up. Maybe the universe was trying to get our attention.

The Virgin Next Door Is Wet

FIRST PRINTED MAY 2002

GET OUT THE GOOD STUFF and a shot glass, friend: we're blowing this pop stand! Earth, I mean. Not in some distant rosy future, but in my lifetime! It looks like the human race is finally going to get a second basket to keep its eggs in...not a moment too soon...and, by God, maybe even *neighbors*. Who says we never get good news?

I'm neither joking nor exaggerating. Hearken to the simple, incredible fact: NASA's Mars Odyssey probe has positively confirmed the presence of water ice on Mars. Not just some, but enough to cover the Red Planet to an average depth of about 500 meters (1,640 feet) if melted. Swear to God; if I'm lyin' I'm dyin'. This inconceivable treasure is located around the Martian south pole, just about *everywhere* below sixty degrees latitude, and—I feel like Scrooge on Christmas morning, I can *not* stop grinning—it's approximately one meter down. You could dig a well with a Garden Weasel.

The first major implication is stunning enough: we can go there anytime we want now—not as a stunt, but to stay, to live. And not "hopefully sometime before the end of the century," as the most optimistic Mars-hounds were saying right up until the Odyssey probe sent back the glorious news— but within the next twenty years.

Because we can do far more than just drink that water. We can crack it with free solar electricity, producing oxygen to breathe and hydrogen to burn for power. And we can grow things in the water—not just food, clothing and medicine, but plants that will build a Martian atmosphere for us over time, looking pretty all the while. Free food, free water, free power and one third gravity—anybody who can't build and sustain a civilization with advantages like that is a disgrace to his immigrant ancestors. (And with the possible exception of some folks in Olduvai Gorge, *everybody's* ancestors are immigrants.)

The BBC says the trip is psychologically impractical because Mars lies at least 300 claustrophobic days away, and anyway after that long in weightlessness, return to gravity might be devastating for the crew's health. Get a clue, can't you, Beeb? First, the correct figure is seventy-two days, using proven technology we knew how to build in 1980: solar sails with a constant acceleration of one thousandth of a gee. Constant boost builds up like compound interest. (For proof, and discussion of several nontrivial details I've neglected here, see *Expanded Universe* by the late Robert A. Heinlein.) These gossamer fairy-wings can be built in orbit for a tiny fraction of the trillion dollars the BBC estimates a Mars mission would cost...and there's no reason the ship they tow can't be spun, providing at least Martian gravity (one third gee) for the crew the whole way. One beauty of solar sails is you don't waste energy hauling an engine or fuel: it's all payload. So your ship can be *roomier* than the nuclear subs in which men live for a year without difficulty.

Ten weeks to Mars! Roundtrip, 145 days. Does that seem a long time, in this instant-results world? The Pilgrims in the *Mayflower* took nine weeks and three days to cross the Atlantic and reach Provincetown. England, Holland, Portugal, Spain and France all managed to create and maintain worldwide empires that far away—what matters in economics or politics is not distance but *time*.

Astonishingly, so far nobody seems to have noticed the *second* major implication of striking ice on Mars, and it's worth an essay of its own. I'll thumbnail it here in the form of a question: does totally sterile water exist in nature, anywhere on earth? We've found life here that survives in conditions more extreme than those on Mars. I'm now expecting at *least* Martian microbes: short on conversation perhaps, but a biological bonanza. We lonely Terran lifeforms may have finally found some cousins...right next door.

Starsong on My Desktop

FIRST PRINTED JULY 1999

SOMETIMES, LIFE TURNS OUT *better* than you ever anticipated. Even if you're a science fiction writer who fancies himself an optimist.

Classic example: about thirty years ago in a sunny field in Nova Scotia, I married my wife Jeanne in an outdoor triple-wedding. Hippies came from hundreds of miles around...and so did a vacationing video crew from New York. More or less for the hell of it, they set up their gear—golf-cart sized battery packs, massive cameras, trunks of peripherals, a whole truckload of stuff—and taped all three weddings. Afterwards they showed us all an instant replay. And then we thanked them kindly and bid them farewell. It never occurred to any of the six of us—and especially not to me, the professional futurist—to ask them for a copy of the tape, or even get their names and addresses. *This was 1975.* What could you do with videotape? Bring it to your local television station and ask to use their equipment after signoff? Home VCRs were beyond imagining...a whole two years away. (And a lot further than that from affordability.) How I wish I'd been more prescient!

I've been a science and technology buff since I read that first Robert A. Heinlein novel at age six. But if I could go back in a time machine and tell my six-year-old self that one day he will see, with his personal eyeballs, a spaceship taking off a mile away...that before he dies the innermost secrets of genetics will be understood and the entire human genome mapped...that in his lifetime, *perfect* music reproduction will become trivially cheap and small enough to clip to his belt...I suspect he'd flatly refuse to believe me.

And if I got my younger self to swallow those whoppers, he'd surely choke on the preposterous notion that he will one day own—carry like a purse—a computer *over a thousand times* more powerful than the one that will carry three men to the Moon and bring them back alive (another prophecy he'd find too good to be true).

And this sort of thing is accelerating...for if you had told me, even as recently as *ten* years ago, that one day I would use that selfsame computer, the one I'm typing on now, to search for intelligent life in space—seriously, usefully—I'd have said you were crazy. If you'd persuaded me you were both sane and correct...I believe I'd have gone mad with joy.

Well, now I have—for today I have honest-to-God starsong on my desktop. It crossed countless lightyears and reached Earth last March 5, just over an hour before midnight. I'm combing it for signs of sentience, right now. Really. WHEEEE!

If finding other sentient races out there in the Big Dark doesn't thrill you, you may as well stop reading now, for we'll never understand each other. Still here? Prepare to be thrilled. If you own any reasonably modern computer, you can now be a meaningful part of the Search for Extraterrestrial Intelligence...and it won't cost you a *dime*, or a lick of effort.

Simply surf to http://setiathome.ssl.berkeley.edu/ Downloading the Seti@home software takes five minutes with a 28.8 modem; installation is utterly painless. With it comes a chunk of raw data from the SETI radio observatory at Arecibo—the actual sound of the stars. Over the next week or two, whenever you're not using your computer it will quietly chew away on that data, doing Fourier transforms, hunting for signal (the right *kind* of signal: a "chirped pulse") amid the noise. You can watch it working, if you wish. When it's done, in a week or so, it'll ask permission to log on, upload its results to the University of California at Berkeley and download new data. You get credit for each chunk you process. If an information-bearing signal is detected in a chunk you handled, you go down on record as one of the co-discoverers of mankind's First Neighbors. Think of it as the biggest Lotto in human history...for although your odds are terrible, how many names will be more immortal than yours if you succeed?

Be advised: the competition is exceedingly industrious! Only two months after the Macintosh version of the software came out, Mac users had already logged nearly 2,500 *years* of CPU time. Pentium/Windows users, with a considerable head start, had put in over 30,000 years.

But what does it cost you to try? Nothing...except processor cycles you were already paying for, and wasting, anyway. If you're a real enthusiast, you can let Seti@home operate constantly, in the background—which on my Powerbook 540c slows overall performance roughly as much as a spooled print job—but it can also be configured as a screensaver, using your CPU only when you're not.

Windows users will need 32 MB of RAM, the ability to display 8-bit graphics in 800X600 resolution, 10 MB of disk space and an Internet connection. Mac users will need the above plus a PowerPC processor and OS 7.5.5 or later. Many versions of UNIX and Linux are supported, with **/2 and BeOS (but *not* WebTV) soon to come. And it's available in twenty other languages.

Since Hitler ranted at the Munich Olympics, our species has been braying electromagnetic signals at the stars as if we were sure we're the only carnivores in the jungle—and it cannot be denied that most of what we've broadcast to the universe has been blather. Might it not be an excellent use of our powerful new cybertechnology, our mighty Internet, to *shut the hell up and listen together*, once in awhile? Governments are too dumb: it's up to us.

If You Can Fry an Egg in Space, Hilton Wants to Talk to You

FIRST PRINTED OCTOBER 1999

'VE HAD A DREAM since earliest childhood. I want to go to space.

I've wanted it ever since I read Robert A. Heinlein's science fiction novel *Rocketship Galileo* at age six. Mr. Heinlein clearly yearned to go to the moon—and considering the world he'd been born into in 1907, he came astonishingly close. At one point during the Apollo 11 mission, NASA staff and press were clustered around President Johnson at Mission Control. Then Robert Heinlein entered the room...and LBJ found himself alone. Everyone present knew which man had done more to put Armstrong and Aldrin on the moon.

I'm less ambitious. It doesn't have to be the moon; even Low Earth Orbit would suit me fine. I just want to view my home planet from the box seats. Each year the bonds of earth seem a little surlier; I yearn to slip them. I want to lounge in comfortable free fall, free from backaches, neck-aches, swivel-chair spread and sore feet. I want to get from *here* to way over *there* by merely flexing a toe. I want to hang out where brawn is a disadvantage and physical strength a nuisance, where nobody is taller than anybody else. I want it so badly I collaborated with my wife Jeanne on three novels set in space, just so I could have the warm pleasure of imagining myself there for months at a time...and get paid for it.

So I was inexpressibly delighted to hear Hilton Hotels Inc. announce they're looking into the feasibility of a space hotel.

This is *not* the first serious proposal for an orbital hotel—but the Hilton name lends considerable credibility to the idea. A 1997 study indicated that space tourism is a multibillion dollar market "if economic and technical barriers can be overcome."

They already have competition for those gigabucks. Robert Bigelow, owner of the Budgets Suites of America chain, has formed a new company called Bigelow Aerospace, and committed *half a billion dollars* to building an LEO-to-Luna "cruise ship." Notice this presupposes the passengers can get to Low Earth Orbit.

Hilton, by contrast, is only cautiously optimistic. "Is this only for young, healthy people," a spokeswoman wondered, "or can the John Glenns of the

world go up there and have a good experience? If you want your New York steak or pasta primavera, is it going to be in pill or freeze-dried form?"

Of course, she answered the first question herself: Senator Glenn proved that even the present put-a-big-bomb-under-their-butts method of reaching orbit is accessible to seniors—and better methods are coming. A decade ago hardly anyone but Bob Truax was working on LEO passenger vehicles; today there are dozens of firms competing for large prizes.

But that second question is interesting. How does *cooking* change—especially luxury hotel cooking—in zero gravity? Heat won't rise; eggs won't stay on a pan; nothing will stay in or on anything; most existing utensils are useless. Somebody is going to get rich solving these problems—for Hilton or some other outfit. Any designers out there with flexible minds?

Consider music. Jeanne and I spent hundreds of hours deriving and refining the fundamental principles and basic vocabulary of zero-gee dance together—we even took a crack at designing an orbital luxury hotel in the third of our three novels. But the physics and logistics of mounting an orchestra in zero-gee—or even a simple jazz band—defeated us: we had our free fall dancers working to canned music. Humans *always* bring live music with them wherever they go, and they won't all want to play a keyboard strapped to their thighs. Someone is going to invent musical instruments for space conditions... and it would be nice, it seems to me, if that someone were Canadian.

America brought the world crew-cut jocks in space, mumbling arcane jargon and doing incomprehensible things. Canada, in addition to the worthy Canadarm, has already given the world dance in space, at least in theory. Good music would make a nice companion gift. So would good food.

Mind you, these are not the points that will sell space tourism to the rich. Civilians have no idea how difficult it is to bring them dance or live music under *earthly* conditions, so they won't be impressed just because it's three times as hard. Tourists *expect* good food and good live music.

I hope I've inspired someone out there to design a zero-gee kitchen, or to begin creating the new cuisine it makes possible, or to dream up zero-gee musical instruments. And I hope the first dancer in space is a Canadian—or at least someone who's read our books and doesn't have to reinvent the wheel. But that stuff isn't what will sell space tourism. Nor will the comfort of zero gee for aching limbs, or long-sought liberation for paraplegics and arthritics, or lightened cardiac load, or even the view.

No, the flood of bookings for the High Hilton will come when the vain rich finally get through their heads one basic fact of space physiology that NASA's always been too bureaucratically hidebound to mention. In the absence of gravity, the fluids of the body totally redistribute themselves.

The legs get slimmer, the chest gets bigger....

Senator Socksdryer and the Two Million Dollar Boondoggle

FIRST PRINTED JULY 1999

T HIS IS, HONEST TO GOD, a true story. As you'll see, it's not one NASA is especially anxious to discuss—but I had the good fortune to spend some time in conversation with Buzz Aldrin when we were co-Guests of Honour at a science fiction convention a few years back, and he graciously confirmed the central facts for me.

It's difficult to remember now, and almost impossible to believe, but back in the late 1960s NASA enjoyed a fairly lavish budget. The US government was either intelligent enough then to know basic research *always* pays off in the long run—or, more likely, so desperate to Beat Russia to the Moon that money was no object. Even then, however, there were noisy critics of this "blank-cheque" approach.

One now-forgotten congressional ignoramus-and-proud-of-it whose name rhymed with "foxfire," then notorious for the cheapshot "Golden Fleece Awards," which made fun of any scientific project he didn't understand (that is, any scientific project), was particularly caustic about the $2 million NASA wasted developing a zero-gravity pen for the Apollo astronauts: an ingenious nitrogen-pressurized ballpoint capable of writing smoothly in free fall. What, Senator Poxliar wanted to know, was wrong with a Number 2 pencil? It seemed a reasonable question to some. Indeed, the Soviets issued pencils to their cosmonauts…albeit for reasons which have only become fully clear in retrospect: they (the nation, not the pencils) were broke.

Hearken now to what happened to Apollo 11. Fast-forward through the launch, the trip, separation from Collins in lunar orbit, the descent, Eagle's truly hair-raising landing, the bungling of the "…one small step…" line—fast-forward through almost the entire historic mission, in fact, and cut directly to its final moments on the lunar surface. Armstrong and Aldrin are done, now. Time to go home, and the only task left before liftoff is to remove those big (and now useless) backpacks and toss them out the airlock to save launch-weight.

But the interior of the LEM compares unfavorably for size with a phone booth. As Commander Armstrong is removing his backpack, he brushes

against a wall...and accidentally destroys the ignition switch for the ascent engine. Just snaps it off clean, flush with the wall. He and Aldrin have zero tools, not so much as a screwdriver: all left up in orbit with Collins, to save weight. There is no backup switch, no alternate way to launch the LEM.

It dawns on Armstrong and Aldrin that they are now dead men walking...a *really* long way from home....

...and then, God be thanked, Armstrong remembers what Senator Jocksfire called the Two Million Dollar Boondoggle. That egregious tax-payer-ripoff frippery: his zero gravity pen. He retrieves it, roots around in the ruins of the switch...and becomes, among his other distinctions, the first man ever to hotwire a vehicle on another planet.

Had he and Aldrin been issued Number 2 pencils, they'd still be on Luna today, slowly turning to leather. (I picture them in their final pose, each raising to Senator Mocksflyer a gesture which might be construed as resembling a Number 2 pencil.) The rest of the Apollo Program might never have happened, and today humanity's presence in space might be even more unforgivably feeble than it already is.

You can buy a descendant of that Space Pen in most stationery stores today for under ten dollars. I carry one, to remind me of the importance of budgeting the luxuries. (And to write refrigerator notes. And just in case I ever need a spaceship ignition key.) Had NASA then been run like most high-tech companies are today—had it been legally *required* to maximize immediate stockholder profit at all times, and overseen by gimlet-eyed bean-counters unwilling to "waste money" on "fripperies" like blue-sky R&D—the history of our species might have been a sadder and far less proud thing.

If there's one thing the Apollo Program proved, it's that it is *impossible* to waste money on pure research: Apollo is in fact the *only* thing the US government has ever spent money on that returned its initial investment, in hard cash, within ten years. Naturally, this unmistakable, inarguable lesson has been ignored or forgotten—by the very government that benefited directly from the Apollo program's returns and by the entire English-speaking community of high-tech investors and entrepreneurs. In these vaunted economic Good Times, budgets for research in general and space in particular are everywhere at historic lows, and even NASA has been forced to learn to run "lean and mean" like the CBC—kept, that is, on a starvation diet in the hope that it will starve. We here in North America have raised up the dumbest group of aristocrats in the history of man, too stupid to make hay while the sun is shining, too shortsighted to lay in firewood against the coming winter. Thirty years from now, what will there be to spin off *from*?

Time for us to take the long view and invest lavishly in the future. While we still can. You never know when a frippery will turn out to be crucial.

Nostalgia for Tomorrow

2001, by God!, or Looking back at the future

FIRST PRINTED JANUARY 2001

'M SOMEWHAT AMAZED to discover just how amazed I am to have made it to the new millenium.

I was born a few years after Hiroshima, so I'm of the generation for whom Arthur C. Clarke and Stanley Kubrick's 1968 film *2001: A Space Odyssey* proverbially represented the distant future. "Boomers," we're called. I first saw the movie at twenty. I remember working the math in my head as I left the theatre, and realizing I'd have to live past fifty in order to see the real 2001.

And I recall concluding that would probably never happen.

Not because I anticipated poor health. I was myself so flush with youth and strength that for me their inevitable decay was still only an abstract intellectual concept, as hypothetical as 2001 itself. As things have turned out, I am now older than my mother ever got to be...but I knew nothing of that in 1968. And yet I more than half expected to be gone before 2001 rolled around. Why?

Well, because I expected that almost *everybody* would be gone by then.

And so did most of my contemporaries, whether they still remember it or not. We confidently expected atomic Armageddon. And nothing less, either. I'm not talking about exchange of a few ICBMs, casualties in the hundreds of millions, a few cities uninhabitable for a century or so—long before Carl Sagan and others gave it a name, we expected Nuclear Winter

227

itself. The end of humanity, for sure, and possibly even the sterilization of Terra.

Everyone felt that way. Everyone sophisticated enough to give the future any thought, at least. It's hard to remember now, perhaps because it's not something we like remembering. Deep down, a whole generation expected the End of Everything to arrive, and soon. If you didn't understand that much, you weren't bright enough to be worth talking to; you probably still believed in Santa Claus.

Some of us actually *yearned* for apocalypse. And not just the religious zealots who welcomed nuclear firestorm as God's punishment on the wicked and the heathen, a long-overdue Second Flood. Even the rational started to think that maybe we might as well get it over with. There was a strain of what was then called "post-holocaust" science fiction (Nazi-survivors had not yet claimed exclusive use of the word "Holocaust"), and one branch of it suggested the horror ahead might turn out to be a blessing in disguise, a necessary pruning, a culling of the flock. It would certainly teach technological civilization the error of its ways, in no uncertain terms, and at the same time conveniently remove the enormous mass of people that made technological civilization an utter necessity. Those lucky enough to live through it and competent enough in Darwinian terms to survive its aftermath might then build a new Eden together, powered by windmills and waterwheels and ruled only by nice people.

We did not, quite, all despair—thank God. We clung to hope, some of us anyway; we cherished its embers and fanned them into flame when we could. I became a science fiction writer four years after I first saw *2001: A Space Odyssey*, in part because I hoped that if I could only imagine enough happy futures, loudly enough, maybe someone would get confused and build one for me. But nearly every SF story about the future written during that period—that is, most of the SF ever written, including my own—contained, somewhere within it, some equivalent of the phrase, "…assuming we don't blow ourselves up, first." Rare was the fictional universe without at least one burned-out planet bearing mute evidence of a technological civilization which had failed the nuclear test and destroyed itself.

The only thing as obvious as the Armageddon problem itself was that it was utterly intractable. The Cold War was permanent, eternal. Capitalism and communism could never ever coexist. The Evil Empire's commissars would never yield as long as there was a single peasant left to sacrifice. Neither would the equally evil swine who protected us from them, the bloodthirsty baby-killing military-industrial complex. Mutual Assured Destruction was inherently unstable, an accident waiting to happen. Hope was all very well, denial was a perfectly workable strategy for living. But to actually believe you'd see the next millennium was as crazy as...oh, I don't know, as crazy as believing South Africa might ever give up apartheid. Or dreaming that smallpox, still the all-time champion slayer of human beings then, could somehow be eradicated forever. Or expecting equal rights for women anytime soon. Or anticipating a meaningful European Union. Pie in the sky stuff.

And so we mostly ignored *2001*'s story—the silly idea that technology might actually bring us closer to our creators, that perhaps gods *do* live in the sky after all—and we focused on its most memorable feature: the mind-bending plunge through a space warp at the end. That sequence has been quoted, or stolen if you prefer, by at least a dozen movies since, and nobody who's seen it ever forgets it. It's a magnificent metaphor for the way the future comes at us: much too fast, way too bright and gaudy, a confusing flood of images that race by too fast to comprehend.

The real future has turned out to be somewhat less wonderful than Clarke's fictional one. We do *not* have a meaningful presence on the Moon yet, and there are no manned expeditions to Jupiter planned. On the other hand, the laborious and expensive phone call Heywood Floyd makes to Kubrick's daughter would today be direct-dialed and dirt cheap. Modern mainframes can deal with contradiction without going insane. And the Cold War ended peacefully—perhaps the first war in history to do so.

2001 was once the far future for us Boomers—and now, after the real thing has arrived, I hope history will remember us, despite our name, as the generation that could have made very big booms indeed, had many excuses to and did not do so once. It was a great millennium: we got out of it alive.

The Future Ain't What It Used to Be

FIRST PRINTED MARCH 2003

WANT MY MONEY BACK. This millennium sucks.

Remember the last one? Only a few years past, and already it feels like a lifetime ago. I'm a science fiction writer: I look forward by training and inclination. Future equals good. Or at least better. I spent the closing half of the twentieth century yearning for the arrival of the twenty-first, because it was my conviction that things could only get better, and therefore they would.

It seemed a reasonable assumption. All my life, each year things seemed to get—on average—just a little bit better than they'd been the year before. Sure, there were exceptions, setbacks, rude shocks. The year they got Martin and Bobby certainly stands out in my mind as a dark period. It got ugly in what used to be called Croatia, and in Rwanda, and other places. Hell, I still can't believe some imbecile backshot John Lennon.

But overall, things tended to improve slowly but steadily, at least in my experience. The Berlin Wall suddenly dropped, one day, as though it were no more than a pile of bricks and stones. The Soviet Union itself, *the* dark monolithic menace that had overshadowed the first half century of my life, folded its cards without firing a shot. Nelson Mandela walked free, apartheid ended. The abominations in Bosnia, and then in Africa and in other places, *finally* began to start the world thinking halfway seriously that something like a Terran Federation might be a good idea. Somebody punched out Geraldo Rivera on camera. There seemed every reason to believe we were finally getting somewhere.

Consider: at the turn of the millennium . . .

- the economy was booming. The Age of Deficits was finally over for good; we'd learned our lesson. Unemployment and inflation were down, budgets trending toward balance. It still seemed remotely possible that at least some of the promises on which Free Trade was sold to Canada might not be total mahooha. Hard to remember, I know.
- peace in the Middle East seemed *just* around the corner, thanks to the patient diplomatic efforts of a well-informed, articulate and creative

American president. It took time to realize that poor taste in mistress-
es was a sensible reason to replace him with a man who's proud to tell
you that foreign affairs are something he himself is never ever going
to have, swear to God, and whose idea of diplomacy is smiling while
delivering an ultimatum.

- a bunch of Arab terrorists tried to—get this—blow up the World Trade
  Center. Of course they failed ludicrously. Terrorists usually did, except
  in very far away places. They were figures of fun: the bearded buffoons
  who jabber and squabble and shoot ineffectually in all directions in
  Back to the Future and a dozen other films. They couldn't even take out
  a satirist: Salman Rushdie toured at will. The only modern terrorists to
  have effected serious damage and taken a significant number of lives on
  American soil, at that time, were all white male Americans. Specifically,
  Tim McVeigh in Oklahoma City and the FBI in Waco. (Forget the over-
  hyped Unabomber: OJ had a higher body count.)
- musicians and writers were optimistic. Recording music had just
  stopped requiring hundreds of thousands of dollars worth of machin-
  ery and expertise; the sound quality of consumer playback had just
  reached perfect. Publishing books suddenly no longer absolutely ne-
  cessitated printing twenty-five paper copies in the hope of selling one,
  and writing them no longer required a (shudder) typewriter. Now, by
  God, writers and musicians were finally going to make a few bucks.
- the Internet was going to make us all filthy rich. 'Nuff said.
- just about everyone on earth knew, in his or her bones, that the United
  States of America would *never*, under any circumstances, first-strike a
  weaker opponent. It had just proven it, by allowing the Soviet Union
  to surrender. Everyone knew John Wayne doesn't hit first. Or if they
  didn't know it, America damn well did.
- the province of British Columbia still believed it had some sort of obligation to spend perfectly good money on hospitals, health care, nurs-
  ing care, education, special ed, social services, family services, legal
  aid, police protection, infrastructure, public housing and a publicly
  accountable ferry system. It had not yet come to understand that the
  only proper uses of tax dollars are encouraging international sporting
  competitions and paying fines in Hawaii.
- the Beatles had two new singles out, both terrific. More were possible.
- the US seemed poised to legalize medical marijuana. Or more accurately, the individual states still entertained the delusion that they had
  the power to do so, merely because the Constitution said they did and
  their citizens voted for it.

- you could board an airplane in under two hours, carrying a nail clipper.
- there was, or at least seemed to be, so little that was *real* to worry about, we all had endless time to waste worrying about nothing at all. A millionaire murderer's glove size. An ex-princess's stupid death. Y2K. Anybody remember when our biggest fear was that at the stroke of midnight on January 1, 2000, our term papers would be lost, planes would fly into skyscrapers, Revenue Canada would forget how much money we owed it and, through an error on the part of his computer dating service, Michael Jackson would accidentally bring home an octogenarian?

We were living in the Golden Years, for a while there, and were too dumb to know it. Instead of appreciating it, savoring it, making sure that half a century of that kind of forward progress would continue, we took our finger off the number for a minute. We decided it was safe to coast. We yammered about the End of History and invented "reality TV." We decided we could afford to let dimwits take the reins of power for a moment, just to shut them up. How much damage could they do?

I choose to believe that the true Golden Age lies always ahead of us, never behind. But some years it's harder than others.

Futures We Never Dreamed

FIRST PRINTED AUGUST 1996

FUTURES THAT SCIENCE FICTION never dreamed of have come to pass.

Sf has never claimed to predict the future, mind you. That's not its job. What most sf writers do is try to create plausible futures that will generate compelling stories. Even our implausible futures are plausible, sometimes. That is, even when we create a satirical future, one we don't expect you to really believe—say, a world in which politicians are selected for intelligence—once we've set the original, wild-card ground rules, we tend to proceed with rigorous logic and internal consistency. We can't help it; that's our training.

Part of the theory is that a reader comfortable at adapting to unlikely-but-possible futures—for recreation—will be less disoriented by Future Shock in real life, and thus be a more intelligent voter and a happier citizen. But this only works if the imaginary futures make sense. Spending time in a cartoon universe, with rules that change as the author finds convenient, accomplishes little of use. So sf writers generally expend immense (and almost completely invisible) effort on making even our most improbable future worlds work logically.

One would think that after a century or so of this we would—quite incidentally—have produced quite a few startlingly accurate predictions by now. This turns out to be the case—and the case has been made elsewhere, and I do not propose to make it again here. Successful "prediction" by throwing darts is a trivial aspect of sf, one which can easily get in the way of understanding its true strengths and virtues.

What I'd like to talk about instead are some of the futures we sf writers could never have imagined—but that have come true.

The recent fuss about evidences of life on ancient Mars brings up the most obvious and appalling: in eighty-some years of commercial sf, not one writer ever predicted, even as a joke, that humanity would achieve the means to conquer space—and then throw it away. None of us guessed there might be raised up a generation so dull and dreamless they would not realize (or listen when they were told) that incalculable wealth, inexhaustible energy and unlimited adventure are hanging in the sky right over their heads, a mere two hundred miles away. We could never have conceived of a society that, faced with an imminent rain of soup, would throw away its pails.

A few years ago in Florida I saw and photographed perhaps the most transcendently sad, baffling, infuriating sight I have ever seen: an Apollo Program booster, one of two or three left in the world, one of the most stupendous devices ever built by free men...lying on its side on the ground, rusting in the rain. I wept along with the sky.

It is as if Ferdinand, informed of the discovery of the New World, were to have forbidden any more of his ships to sail beyond sight of land—"We've got urgent problems right here in Spain: we can't go throwing money away in the ocean"—and no more sensible monarch could be found anywhere in Europe.

The next most obvious example: I don't think one sf writer predicted the quiet collapse of the Soviet Union. Even the most liberal of us accepted without question the seeming truism that a slave state could never collapse until the last kulak was expended. Apparently with all our vaunted exploration of the behavior of alien cultures, we failed to do enough homework on one of the most prominent ones available for study on our own planet. In our defense, nearly every scrap of data permitted to leave the USSR was as suspect as they could make it—and even the spooks, privy to much more and better data than we were (and paid to specialize in it), were caught just as much by surprise. But it's still embarrassing.

Many sf writers have hopefully predicted the eventual conquest of all diseases. But none of us could have dreamed that one day mankind's oldest and deadliest scourge, the taker of more human lives than any other single cause—smallpox—would be eradicated from the planet, utterly and forever...and that the event would arouse no notice at all. Did they have a party on your block when the last smallpox vaccines were destroyed awhile back? Was there a parade in your town, honouring the heroes and heroines who avenged millions of our tortured, disfigured and slain ancestors? Are you familiar with their current efforts to do the same for polio, chickenpox, diphtheria and other diseases?

Several sf writers foresaw the VCR. Not one of us ever guessed that by the time it arrived, a sizable fraction of the populace would feel incompetent to operate one. We still have trouble grasping that there are people with shoes on who find it a challenge to set a watch, twice, and specify a channel number. Even harder is understanding why some of them seem *proud* of it.

I haven't checked, but I'm sure at least some sf writer predicted the disposable lighter—and that none ever envisioned a feature mandated by law which would make them virtually useless for senior citizens, musicians and invalids, while perfectly accessible to toddlers.

Nor could any of the thousands of us who foresaw computers, or even the dozens who foresaw personal computers, have guessed that in the end an operating system that Spoke Human would be supplanted by one that required you to learn to Speak Computer.

Being logical folks, perhaps we tend to be interested in and think about and write about other logical folks—so all of us, save Robert Heinlein himself, failed to see the Crazy Years coming.

Evil's Rootkiller, or Brother, can you spare a paradigm?

FIRST PRINTED NOVEMBER 2000

ONCE THIS PLANET WAS OWNED jointly by Portugal and Spain. Most Terrans did not *know* that at the time—but it was true, nonetheless. My source is literally infallible. In 1494, Pope Alexander VI drew a line across a map, and declared with the authority of God that this side belonged to Spain and that side to Portugal. No, really.

And Alexander's ruling was effective. If you've ever wondered why Brazilians speak Portuguese, that's why: Brazil happened to lie on that side of the Papal Perimeter. Spain had Columbus and *conquistadores*, Portugal had great navigators, and together they divvied up the incalculable wealth of the New World. So today Spain and Portugal are the two most powerful nations on earth, their mighty economies the bedrock of western commerce, their languages spoken by all civ—

Oops.

What happened? Half a millennium later, the former co-rulers of Earth are second rate powers, at best. What ruined them? War? Plague? Intrigue?

Money.

Specifically, all those shiploads of treasure you've read about in a hundred books, seen in a dozen movies. Gold. Silver. Emeralds. Sure, lots ended up on the bottom of the ocean—but all too much made it home. Spain and Portugal were suddenly *rich*....

Unfortunately, they were rich in *money*, not *wealth*.

Gold is not wealth. Gold is what you use to *buy* wealth. Wealth is desired consumables. Corn. Wheat. Iron ore. Potable water. Arable land convenient to a market. Stuff you couldn't ship across the Atlantic, at least in the sixteenth century.

The two Iberian superpowers got tons of new money, but almost no real new wealth. Economics 101: too many *pesetas* and *escudos* chasing too few potatoes is a recipe for disaster. Massive inflation, balance of trade collapse, currency devaluation: both economies went to hell and stayed there. Too much money can actually destroy wealth.

So turn it around. *What happens to money ... if the supply of wealth should suddenly become infinite?*

Time to start thinking about it. There is a new and utterly astounding prospect on the horizon called nanotechnology. It involves Very Tiny Machines which move individual atoms around in order to build things the same way nature does: molecule by molecule. At viral speeds. If nanotechnology works even half as well as its advocates hope—and so far, all the signs are good—we may have near-infinite wealth sometime within the coming century. And if it comes, it will come all at once.

I know: early nuclear power enthusiasts once promised "energy too cheap to meter." This is fundamentally different—by many orders of magnitude. Nanotechnology hopes to produce objects that basically grow themselves, out of free parts.

If it works, the day I finish programming a "stem cell" nanoassembler to make, say, yachts on command, the effective cost of such a yacht plunges to *zero—everywhere.*

I can send that assembler seed's instruction-set to Tasmania instantly and cheaply, the same way I filed this column: over the Internet. Load that set into an invisibly tiny, self-replicating assembler there, and it will make free yachts from random Tasmanian atoms just as easily as mine does from Canadian atoms. *All* God's chillun got atoms....

Sooner or later, the same will apply to absolutely any commodity which can be made from molecules. Everything humans buy or sell except original art, sex and other personal services, in other words.

We'll all be Totally Rich. There will simply be *too much wealth to steal.* Want it to literally rain soup? No problem—how about a whiskey shower for dessert? If all those Porsches are cluttering your lawn, tell them to disassemble themselves. As for real estate, by God we *will* make more—as much as we want!

Money is basically a scheme for keeping score in a presumed zero-sum game. We collect it to protect ourselves from famine or other scarcity. It exists only because scarcity exists. Once we're all infinitely rich, there will be be no real use for the stuff. We'll have to quit the habit of trading work for what we want: there simply won't be enough work to go around. (For awhile, programming various skills into nanoassemblers, or designing new products, will constitute useful work...but these are clearly finite tasks, and ones which people capable of them will probably do for the fun and prestige of it.)

If you think the dawn of the Information Age has been disorienting, wait'll you see the Age of Plenty. In the last century, humanity has slowly and painfully begun weaning itself from imperialism, genocide, racism, slavery, religious tyranny...hell, we've even begun trying to stop abusing our own spouses and children. But wait until we have to give up *money.*

And all those funky things that grow in the damp shadows beneath it. Class structure. Snobbery. Poverty as social control. Income as proof of character. Wealth as license to misbehave. Many of the truly hateful things about the world-as-it-presently-is, if not most of them, derive from scarcity. And before the end of the century, we might just run plumb out of the stuff.

I suspect we'll find the conquest of Death far less traumatic than the death of Money. Science fiction has often imagined long life, but seldom universal wealth. And as with any profound change, it's the transition period that'll be the worst. Some of the most profoundly sick people our species ever produced—those addicted to pushing other people around—will be forced into mental health for want of victims...and they'll go kicking and screaming. It'll be worse than all the junkies in history going into withdrawal at once. How will the Donald Trumps of tomorrow prove their superior worth, majesty and importance without cash for a codpiece? What if ruthlessness and avarice themselves became obsolete, pointless?

Closer to home, how will we persuade other people to perform services (like making up interesting stories) for us—if not by simply waving money, universal irresistible catnip, under their noses? Well...I think we're just going to have to try asking them nicely. Or devoting a little thought to what *they* might want or need, and performing some service for *them*.

The Golden Rule, they called that...way back in the twentieth century, when anyone but electrical engineers still cared about gold.

Plus ça Change

FIRST PRINTED MAY 1997

FOR SOME TIME NOW, it has been getting harder to dream a dream that isn't apt to up and come true on you—forcing you to live with all its new complications and implications, which once could have been safely left for your grandchildren to worry about.

Isaac Asimov used to say that when his father was born, man had not yet left the surface of the Earth in powered flight; when Isaac's father died there were footprints on the Moon and color video cameras halfway to Saturn. Progress has certainly been progressing, and perhaps you agree with the cat who, after making love to a skunk, said, "I reckon I've enjoyed about as much of this as I can stand."

But oddly, the picture becomes brighter the further ahead you look. Focus past the immediate future, the next administration—gaze from the science fiction writer's stance at the *near* future, the next generation or so—and things improve somewhat.

If you worry that accelerating future shock may make you a Stranger in a Strange Land, allow me to reassure you. Let me tell you about the familiar, bedrock universals that will carry over into any world of tomorrow, reminding you of the world you know now. Every so-called "law of nature" is vulnerable to new and better observations, save one.

I'll bet cash on it: Murphy's Law will outlive thee and me.

For instance:

- If tickets become available in your lifetime for regular passenger service to Luna, or Mars, or Titan, you can reliably expect that the seats will be too cramped for a scarecrow, the in-trajectory movie will be one you have already seen and hated, the food will be tasteless and toxic and the coffee will qualify as an industrial solvent. The flight you wanted will be overbooked, and you'll never see your luggage again. And parking anywhere near the spaceport will cost more than the trip.
- Similarly, if vacation paradises are built in orbit during your lifetime, you will find them full of the *wrong kind of people*, infested with *tour-*

ists rather than thoughtful travelers like yourself. Everything will be mercilessly overpriced, including air. If your hotel is in "luxurious free fall," you will need bellhops not only to handle your luggage, but to handle you; they and all resort employees will customarily be found floating a few feet distant, one hand drifting your way, palm upward (relative to you). Be *certain* to tip the air steward adequately. The plumbing will be indescribably barbaric and give you at least one disease unknown to your doctor at home. The promised "romantic spacewalk" will consist of fifteen minutes in something very like a coffin with arms, with plumbing that makes the stuff inboard look good. Half the photos you snap will be spoiled when you forget to keep the Sun out of frame; the rest will be ruined by cosmic rays. The entertainment *will* probably be truly spectacular, but the drinks will cost two weeks' pay apiece, and their essential recipe will be two parts hydrogen to one part oxygen. Upon re-entry, you will sprain something, and when you land a horde of sadistic customs inspectors will gleefully insult you, confiscate your souvenirs, subject you to something like a full-body CAT scan with unshielded equipment, stick a hundred needles into you and fog any surviving film. Then you'll get home to find out that (as Tom Waits said) everything in your refrigerator has turned into a science project, the water was left running in the bathroom and your next-door neighbors had a *much* better time at the Luna City Hilton for half the money.

- When it becomes possible for you to buy an antigravity flight belt, you will find that fresh out of the showroom it requires expensive repair; that the warrantee is worthless; that the resale value plummets with every passing second; that the device wastes immense amounts of precious resources, has inadequate safety features and requires expensive licensing, registration, insurance and inspection rituals every year; that parts are unobtainable; that the roofs are full and there's no place to park; and that some little pipsqueak Third World country makes a much better one for cheaper. Presently you'll notice that the sky is full of idiots. The wise will tend to stay indoors.

- When fusion power finally starts to come on-line, its implementation will be delayed, and its costs exponentially multiplied, by a vocal environmental lobby angrily demanding a return to something safe, clean and natural, like fission.

- When you can afford a TV linkup that offers you 245 channels in 3-D with digital stereo surround sound, there won't be a damn thing worth watching on any of them.

- About the time they complete a Unified Field Theory, someone will identify a fifth, incompossible force. You'll never be able to understand it. Your teenager will grasp it at once.

- When they perfect a method for keeping people sexually vigorous into their nineties, they will simultaneously extend the lifespan to a hundred and fifty. (And you won't be allowed to retire much before a hundred.)
- If intelligence-enhancing drugs are ever perfected, they will for some reason fail to work within the city limits of Ottawa or Washington. (Note: the same may not be true in Tokyo . . . or Beijing . . . or . . . .)
- When the whole world is linked together by computer network, and you have a billion petabytes of information available to you, you will not be able to find the little piece of matchbook cover on which you jotted down that essential access code.
- Finally—perhaps most ominously—as computers become smarter, as they reach the threshold of human intelligence, it will become possible . . . and soon after that, *necessary* . . . to *bribe* them.

Myself, I take a peculiar comfort from one final rock-certainty: no matter how weird the world of the future may get, laughter will always be—just barely—enough to get you through it.

Intellectual Property

St. George, We Need You Now!

FIRST PRINTED APRIL 2000

I T'S SOMEWHAT LIKE MENSTRUATION: once a month, I bleed a little and grow melancholy for a few days.

Every month *LOCUS* arrives in my mailbox. You simply can't function as a science fiction professional without a subscription to *LOCUS*. Twelve times a year it tells you just how much better than you most of your colleagues are doing, lets you know which of your editors have just been fired, reveals what your agent has been indicted for, fails to review your new hardcover and features a glowing cover story/interview with some punk who got in the business fifteen years after you did. And none of that is the bleeding and melancholy part I mean.

No, I'm talking about the sick sinking feeling that comes when, having delayed it as long as possible, you finally flip to the stats in the back. The monthly bestseller lists.

Yes: lists, plural. *Seven* of them. My flip remarks a couple of paragraphs ago notwithstanding, *LOCUS* really is an unparalleled cornucopia of priceless data, and legendary publisher/editor Charles N. Brown takes his job seriously. Each month he brings you *four* genre bestseller lists, *plus* three separate overviews of genre titles that showed up on mainstream lists.

In the issue I'm looking at right now, for instance, the biggest and to my mind most useful chart is the *LOCUS* Bestseller List. Compiled with data from twenty-six different sf and fantasy bookstores in the US and

Canada, it gives the month's top ten hardcovers and paperbacks and the top five trade paperbacks, media-related titles and gaming titles. Below all that is a large and insightful New & Notable list compiled by the *LOCUS* staff. On the facing page are three more genre bestseller lists: from Barnes & Noble/B. Dalton, Waldenbooks and Amazon.com. Finally below those are notations of genre titles that appeared that month in the Bestseller lists of the *New York Times*, *Publishers Weekly*, *Washington Post*, *Wall Street Journal* and *USA Today*, plus *PW*'s Children's Fiction list.

Guess what all these lists have in common?

Almost nothing. Agreement between them is oddly uncommon. This month, for example, the four main lists of top ten paperbacks (*LOCUS*, B&N/Dalton, Waldenbooks and Amazon.com) contain a total of almost thirty different titles between them, and no title appears on all four lists. This puzzling disparity of consumer behavior is typical.

One thing, however, the lists *always* have in common (and now at last we come to the bleeding and melancholy part):

Month after month, fantasy kicks science fiction's ass.

And has for so long I can no longer recall the halcyon days of yore when it was otherwise. In three of the four lists I'm looking at now, seven of the top ten paperbacks and six of the top ten hardcovers are fantasy. And that makes it an unusually good month for sf.

It's the same in film and television: sci fi has faded badly of late. R2-who? Last year's *Star Wars* prequel feels conflicted in retrospect, *Lord of the Rings* with WWII dogfights grafted on: aerial combat, in an airless environment. Even the venerable *Star Trek* franchise is starting to show signs of boldly going where Buck Rogers and Flash Gordon went long before. As with *Star Wars*, its latest incarnation seems to be a retro look back at what happened before all the interesting stuff. This is the storytelling equivalent of Cheyne-Stokes breathing.

Science fiction as a genre has spent most of the last century trying to cajole people into thinking seriously about the future, to teach them how to cope with technological change. And now that the new millennium is finally here, and the pace of change has increased to the point that even the dullest citizens realize they *must* think seriously about the future at regular intervals or else go under, now that they actually have *Star Trek* communicators hanging from their belts and take for granted that they will live forty years longer than their grandparents…people seem to have decided en masse that they'd much rather think about wizards, elves and enchanted swords. The Potter and Baggins empires battle for dominance of movies and merchandising; the question seems to be whether you prefer your cartoon battle of Good Versus Evil performed by plucky individuals or by great stupid armies with pointed sticks.

We apparently want to be transported back to an earlier, simpler, more magical age. You know: back when those few ignorant peasants who didn't die in childbirth, starve, succumb to an infected cut, catch smallpox, become bear-dung or disembowel one another over some obscure point of theology could reasonably hope to die of old age, toothless and terrified, in their thirties. Phooey. Where I come from, the Mightiest Wizard in the Whole World is always a pissant, for his world is an insignificant backwater in a third-rate galaxy. In my universe, *everyone* can be immortal, rich and beautiful, and the stars are their stepping stones.

It's a new millennium, and what dies must be replaced, renewed. Paul Krassner just ceased publication of his legendary counterculture journal *The Realist* after fifty years, and *The Onion* is simply an inadequate substitute. The last hope for one more Beatles song died with George, and this generation's Beatles has yet to emerge. Well-meaning nitwits are trying to brick all us Canadians up inside Fortress Canada, with a cask of Amontillado perhaps but with only the most provisional rights or freedoms. And I am disturbed by the growing realization that today's bright teenagers—always science fiction's bread and butter—no longer want to know what the future is going to really be like; they are willing to imagine no more, no better, no further, than their great-grandparents did.

"The worm on the skyhook"

FIRST PRINTED OCTOBER 2003

FUTURIST IS SOMEONE who ponders exciting future developments…twenty years after the science fiction writers have exhaustively discussed them and definitively settled most of the major questions they raise. Since he is unaware of their work and knows nothing whatsoever about human behavior, he always gets the story wildly wrong. He brings you either terrifying warnings of horrors that are never going to happen, or breathless hype for wonders that are never going to happen. Soon, you conclude that anyone who thinks about the future loses IQ points for some reason, and go back to reading about trolls, Orcs and wizards. And we sf writers sigh and go back to what we were doing: examining the problems you'll be facing in twenty-five years, solving them and placing the solutions into thoughtful, wildly entertaining stories you will never read even if someone puts a gun to your head.

It happened recently with cloning. Suddenly you all woke up and noticed something called cloning had existed for a quarter of a century. Rather than go to the library and learn the solutions long since found for all the problems it creates, you consulted a futurist. He assured you the sky was falling, the race was doomed and the biosphere was toast. Naturally you shrieked for your lawmakers to protect you. Since there was no actual doom to protect you from, and thus no special interest group outbidding you, they were delighted to take your money, and now iron laws prevent you from realizing any benefits whatsoever from cloning technology while providing multiple avenues for abuse.

Sf writers want to explore how humans interact with the technology they now require to survive, so they range far ahead and study—study both technology and people. Futurists know little about either: they just want to make you say either "Wow!" or "Yow!" They're like lookouts on the prow of a ship, yelling either "Iceberg!" or "Open water!" back to the crew on a bullhorn, quite unaware that the boys up on the bridge with the radar have already done a far better job of plotting course. Problem is, the crew would rather listen to the lookouts.

The most recent example I've seen is the skyhook: what the Led Zep generation calls the stairway to heaven.

To give you an idea what a fresh new story this is, bear in mind that the trigger incident for it is *the second annual international conference on the subject*, co-hosted by *the Los Alamos National Laboratory*...which was held over a month ago. If the idea of a space elevator were any more novel, it would be forgotten. And I don't just mean that Jack's Beanstalk is one of our oldest myths. It was first proposed as a serious technological possibility in 1979 (remarkably, simultaneously but quite independently) by two different sf greats, Sir Arthur C. Clarke and the late Charles Sheffield, in their respective novels *The Fountains of Paradise* and *The Web Between the Worlds*, and has since featured in at least seventeen other novels (see http: //jolomo.net/sf/beanstalk.html).

It's certainly easy to see why we were excited twenty-four years ago: for the life of us we could never figure out why you weren't. An elevator to space can mean literally better-than-free access to orbit: in theory, for every ton of payload you want to lift, you can simply send down the cable as counterbalance a ton of raw ore from the asteroid belt, so it won't even cost anything to run the elevator. Think of it! Instead of spending $670 a pound to lift something to Low Earth Orbit, barely over your head, in a space shuttle, you could take your whole family and a covered wagon to High Earth Orbit for free. And HEO is literally "Halfway to Anywhere"—from there, the same rocket blast that takes you to the Moon will take you to Pluto, or Arcturus—it'll take longer to arrive, is all. For the fuel required to fly from Toronto to Boston, you could put yourself in orbit around Jupiter and start terraforming Ganymede.

Then, of course, we sf writers all thought the matter through...and quietly put the concept of a beanstalk away with other childish dreams that can't work in the real world.

I'm not talking about the technical difficulties its new proponents keep glossing over, like nobody having a clue how to produce, let alone cheaply, the incredibly strong, thin, lightweight "carbon nanotube" fibers needed to keep a beanstalk from snapping like string. Never mind that if such strong, thin, lightweight substances existed, cost of launch to orbit would instantly plummet to a fraction of its present value anyway. Let's also ignore the million nontrivial engineering problems...because they're irrelevant. No beanstalk can or will ever be built. Believe me, I wish with all my heart that it could, and the reason it can't makes me so sad and ashamed for my race I want to cry. But in this post-9/11 world there's simply getting around two adamantine facts.

One, it is not even theoretically possible to protect a beanstalk, with

100 percent certainty, forever, against terrorism. (Or, for that matter, design failure.)

And, two, if one were ever brought down, it could be a whiplash of fire laid on the earth, a scourge of Biblical proportions wrapped round the globe, a thirty-five-kilometer-wide swath of total destruction with no hope of escape for anyone in its path. Even Hollywood has never dared contemplate a nightmare of such magnitude. It would leave a mark on the planet that would still be clearly visible from space by the time our sun goes red giant.

If, implausibly, you were both rich enough *and* dumb enough to build a beanstalk, your neighbors would stop you.

So can we put this charming fantasy away with antigravity belts and food pills now, and talk about some of the really interesting stuff ahead—nanotechnology, gene hygiene, brain/machine interface, immortality, SETI—before some damned futurist gets hold of them? It's all waiting for you down at your local sf bookstore, or library.

They Don't Make Unreality Like They Used To

FIRST PRINTED JUNE 1998

I'VE NEVER SEEN *The Truman Show*, but, as with so many big budget films nowadays, I feel as though I have. Part of this is because since the film was so successful, the contest began immediately to identify what earlier work it was ripped off from. In a letter to the *Globe and Mail*, reader Martin Bott noted that the film's premise is strikingly similar to that of an episode of *The New Twilight Zone* which ran "about ten years ago." A CBC radio commentator whose name I missed found a considerably earlier antecedent: *The Peeping Tom*, a 1960 movie so controversial he claimed it destroyed the career of Michael Powell (who'd previously directed *The Red Shoes*).

Longtime readers of mine will be unsurprised to hear that I trace the source of *Truman's* premise to the dean of science fiction, Robert A. Heinlein. In 1941, Mr. Heinlein published a science fiction classic, "They." I can quote large sections from memory; I think it safe to say that no one who's read it has ever forgotten it. It shares the underlying notion of *The Truman Show*—an over-literal reading of Shakespeare's "All the world's a stage, and all the men and women merely players."

"They" follows the thoughts of an unnamed mental patient as a succession of people try to argue him out of the delusion for which he's been committed. He's a paranoid solipsist: he believes that the whole world genuinely revolves around him, for some unknown and presumably evil purpose. He feels his entire life has been an elaborate plot, carefully choreographed to keep him too busy and distracted to ever get any serious thinking done about the many obvious and blatant internal contradictions in what he's been told about reality. A shrink tries to reason with him...but of course part of the joke of the story is that solipsism is invulnerable to assault by logic. Then his wife is allowed to visit him, and tearfully begs him to give up his silly fantasy and come back to her...and the emotional approach nearly works. But he cannot erase the memory of that day they were both leaving the house in a driving rain, and over her protests he went back inside for something, and glancing out a window, happened to see...a bright sunny day. A glaring continuity-error, like Jim Carrey's Truman nearly getting creamed by a falling stage-light. So he rejects her, too, and, "The creature he knew as Alice went to the place of assembly without stopping to change form. 'It is necessary to adjourn this sequence. I am no longer able to influence his decisions,' she reported."

In June of that same year Mr. Heinlein's only peer, Theodore Sturgeon, published another classic, "Yesterday Was Monday," with a different and much lighter spin on the world as elaborate fake. Harry goes to sleep Monday night, and wakes up in Wednesday. The problem is, Wednesday hasn't started yet. It's still being built: an army of workers is in the process of assembling it, making it look just like Monday did, only one day older—trimming the grass to the correct height, for instance, putting just the right increment of grime on all the buildings, getting everything ready for the cast. Harry spends the story trying to find the producer, so he can get back to Tuesday—currently in progress—and resume his life.

The notion that reality is a vast con-game probably predates both Heinlein and Sturgeon. I won't be remotely surprised if someone can name much earlier antecedents for the premise: what makes great literature is generally not original ideas but original treatment of ideas a thousand years old. But it is instructive to observe how two different eras treat the same idea.

Positing that the world is faked raises two obvious questions: who could pull off so elaborate and difficult a hoax, and why would they bother? In "They," the nameless protagonist has no answer to either question, and the reader is given only elliptical hints that his tormentors are incomprehensibly alien creatures with unimaginable motives. In "Yesterday Was Monday," Harry ignores both questions: he doesn't *care* who's writing the script, or who the audience might be; all Harry wants is to get back into character and slip back into his comfortable life as a garage mechanic.

Half a century later, Mr. Sturgeon's story was adapted into...the same *New Twilight Zone* episode cited in Mr. Bott's letter to the editor! I regret that I haven't seen it, but if Mr. Bott's synopsis is accurate, the adaptor took the same odd approach *The Truman Show* does. To explain how and why a person's entire lifetime could be a fraud, both modern writers posited not unknowable aliens with inconceivable technology, nor God Himself as a playwright/producer...but that other universal symbol of absolute power and mysterious motives: a cable channel.

To the TV generation, raised on the Loud family, confessional talk shows and fishbowl scrutiny of anyone who dares achieve prominence of any kind, this must seem a more hip explanation than either aliens or God. It is certainly much less plausible. Forget mere practical implausibilities, like a cable station with a budget bigger than Canada's. Accept for the sake of the story the absurdity of a whole nation transfixed by a boring man going about his business; there actually *are* two women who've placed cameras in their homes and live their whole lives in public view on the Internet—for an audience of dozens, yes, but that's enough of a trend to satirize, these days—and reality TV is, for some ungodly reason, getting more popular every day.

What I boggle on is the *emotional* implausibility. Hapless Truman is being raped—repeatedly, profoundly and most publicly—and his movie requires me to believe that throughout his entire life, there hasn't been one moral or compassionate person in all of North America.

I seem to be the only one who has a problem swallowing this. Could these be the Crazy Years?

Recutting the Crown Jewels

FIRST PRINTED NOVEMBER 1997

'D LIKE TO EXAMINE the recent film ostensibly based on one of my mentor Robert A. Heinlein's immortal science fiction novels.

There: I couldn't even get through one line without allowing my bias to show. The "ostensibly" gives me away. But I cannot remove it—for the film assays out to no more than 10 percent Heinlein content, net...and, in my opinion, perverts or subverts nearly every one of the few elements it does reluctantly take from its source. I don't think any true friend of the book (and there are millions) could possibly leave the theater other than enraged and dismayed.

Starship Troopers is one of Robert's most challenging works. Published in 1959, it's perhaps the most difficult of his forty-six books for a child of the sixties to come to terms with, since it strongly champions two things that fell into grave disrepute around then: the military and the concept of personal responsibility for one's actions. It was *so* controversial that it was rejected by the entire editorial board of Scribner's, ending a decade-long association. But Putnam's snapped it up at once, and wisely so: it won Robert the second of his five Hugo Awards and became one of his bestselling titles, continuously in print for forty-five years. Its absorbing surface story of how Basic Training turns a callow young man into a competent combat officer during a time of interstellar war is underlaid with profound and trenchant discussion of (forgive the use of these obsolete terms) morality, duty and social justice, based on the provocative speculation that we might one day develop a *scientifically verifiable code of morals*. And eye-popping visual special effects are built into the book's very core.

It would, in short, make a *wonderful* movie. Instead, its name was contemptuously placed on a lame and pointless cartoon.

A modestly successful cartoon, to be sure. I saw it in a theater totally full of eighteen-year-old boys having a wonderful time, and I'm sure those few who can get a date will come back with one to see it again. (It's a gross out flick, featuring blow-dried young models to whom things happen that are so terrifying and disgusting that a guy's girl might just, for a moment, find him less terrifying than the film and cling to him.) During the first week nearly 3 million people bought a ticket; doubtless its makers were pleased.

But they *could* have sold at least another *ten* million tickets. That's a fraction of the known—proved—Robert Heinlein fans in North America alone...all of whom have been waiting more than half a century for Hollywood to give him some respectful attention. A competent team could have made a *faithful* adaptation of that novel for the same money or less—and still pleased the testosterone brigade.

But nobody wanted to. Director Paul Verhoeven and screenwriter Ed Neumeier don't try to conceal their contempt for a book that praises the military even as they exploit it for gore. For example, Sergeant Zim, though tough, is wise, compassionate and decent in the book; in the film he's a grinning sadist who enjoys crippling and maiming his own cadets. The book, while it's entertaining the reader, also provides fascinating instruction on principles of tactics, strategy and command, as adapted to interstellar interspecies warfare; the film's "army" is an armed mob, milling about with no battle plan and no leadership, firing aimlessly. (A *co-ed* mob. They all shower together, and there is no sex.)

Even in terms of sheer action-spectacle, the filmmakers ignored one of the best parts: the powered suits. In the book, a Mobile Infantryman fights in awesome combat armor which weighs a ton, allows him the option of hopping over a factory or crashing through it and features enough high-tech weaponry and comm gear to let him control a square mile or more at the close direction of an officer fifty miles away. The film's "starship trooper" fights in shirt-sleeves and a bicycle helmet, carries a single *slug-gun*—"futuristic" and loud but inferior in cyclic rate and firepower to an AK-47—and has no radio: commands are shouted to him. In the book, the Bugs build starships and have weapons technology as good as ours...in the film, they are mindless and have *no* technology except the mysterious ability to throw a rock from their star-system and hit Buenos Aires, for unimaginable reasons. And so on.

Why does Hollywood do this, over and again: recut the Crown Jewels? It's not just science fiction, either. If all you want is to make a braindead Val-Kilmer-as-high-tech-thief movie, why pay Leslie Charteris's estate a large sum for the right to pretend it has anything to do with his deathless character The Saint? If all you want is a Tom Cruise solo vehicle, why call it *Mission Impossible* and then kill off the whole team in the first ten minutes? Why title a movie *The Scarlet Letter* but change the ending? Why pay heavily for access to millions of pre-existing fans whom you plan only to insult and ignore?

Of course I'm happy that Robert's book has just jumped to number five on the bestseller list (again). But I fear that anyone who liked the movie and buys the book may find it insufficiently stupid and be disappointed—and thus unlikely to seek out other Heinlein titles.

There's still hope. Three other Heinleins are presently sold or optioned: *Tunnel in the Sky*, *Orphans of the Sky* and *The Moon is a Harsh Mistress*, the latter by the vaunted Dreamworks. Maybe one of them will have the sense to take more than a cursory glance into the goldmine they've bought. But I'm not optimistic.

Gone With the Wind. Destination Moon. Rosemary's Baby. 2001: A Space Odyssey. The Godfather 1&2. Lonesome Dove. Field of Dreams. These are about the only examples I can call to mind of popular books which were *faithfully* adapted to film. They simply put the author's story on the screen, with as little disturbance as possible. Please note that each was not just a hit, but an historic, record-breaking genre-changing classic.

Now note how few of them there are. And nearly all over twenty years old. It always works, so they've stopped doing it.

And we're talking about people with the power to risk many millions of dollars. You were right again, Robert: surely these are the Crazy Years.

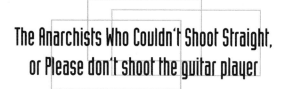

The Anarchists Who Couldn't Shoot Straight, or Please don't shoot the guitar player

FIRST PRINTED JANUARY 2001

THE TRICK IN LIFE is usually to find the balance point—the happy medium between incompossible extremes. Exactly where, for instance, lies the line between keeping an open mind...and being a sucker? Now that any quack with a modem can call himself an "alternative therapy healer" and no fact can ever be conclusively checked anymore, what should I do when cancer comes and mainstream medicine admits helplessness? Nod and die? Or try snake oil?

Exactly where is the border between editorial judgment...and censorship? I used to think I knew, but now that any fool with a browser can call himself a "journalist" and all accusations are true, I'm no longer sure.

Is there a stable balance point between discriminating against people and being indiscriminate? Between being racist and being reverse-racist? Between equal rights for women and no respect for men? Between the dread One World Government and World War Three? Or—to get even more basic—between order and anarchy? Now, there's a tricky one.

I've never been an anarchist myself. I read. But back in college, my circle of acquaintances included SDS leaders, Black Panthers, Weathermen, draft resisters, deserters and assorted other radicals. I got along with most, counted some as my friends. My knee-jerk sympathies often incline toward anarchy—most people's do, these days. Fight the power...rage against the machine...tune in and drop out...turn your poptop beer upside down and open it with a churchkey...I am not a number, I am a man!...information wants to be free....

Deep down, nobody really likes authority—except perhaps the few in authority. I don't think many of us were rooting for Nurse Ratched to break Randall McMurphy in *One Flew Over The Cuckoo's Nest*. We whose lives depend utterly on order and system all at least sympathize with the anarchist. Why? Because he's generally been the underdog, and his target a bloated oppressor of one sort or another.

Until today.

Science Fiction Writers of America, the professional organization to which most sf writers in the world (including myself) belong, is presently battling cyberpiracy—the posting online of members' copyright material without permission. But a recent issue of SFWA's journal *Forum* reprints an e-mail from someone I'll call CrazyEddie, proudly proclaiming a new cybernetwork I've renamed "ThiefNet." Think of Napster on steroids. It threatens the eventual end of all art and all professional-quality entertainment....

ThiefNet's creators describe it as, "a distributed decentralised information storage and retrieval system.... It provides anonymity [and is] totally decentralized: nobody is in control... not even its creators. This makes it virtually impossible to force the removal of information from the system." CrazyEddie makes clear what "virtually impossible" means: "It has been proven formally, by mathematical proof, that the system is immune to all attacks save for physical destruction of all host machines (spread across multiple jurisdictions)."

What's this bulletproof system *for*? "To allow the free distribution of information on the Internet without fear of censorship." Who could possibly quarrel with such a noble goal as ending censorship?

Me. And many others. Because what CrazyEddie means by "censorship" is "attempts to stop theft." The information that he feels "wants to be free" is my latest novel—and all its predecessors and potential successors. *All* novels, by anybody. Also my new CD—all recorded music—all films—pretty much anything CrazyEddie wants to enjoy without paying for it, really. He's quite clear: once a book... or CD, movie, documentary or dance video... is uploaded to ThiefNet, it's free, forever: Bill Gates and the CIA combined couldn't take it down again, "except by installing monitoring software on an Orwellian scale, utterly unacceptable to any democracy."

CrazyEddie's already personally stolen twenty-five novels, posted them on ThiefNet: works by Orwell, Arthur C. Clarke, Frank Herbert, Andre Norton and less famous authors. He plans to keep doing so. Why? "The explicit aim of ThiefNet from the outset was to destroy the system of copyright as we know it. A noble aim.... "

Got that? CrazyEddie's done his noble best to make sure nobody will ever write a book for you again, except the writers currently served by vanity presses. Nobody will ever compose or perform music for you again except the folks presently playing for free in the park. All software will be freeware. In order to wound Commerce, CrazyEddie is murdering Art and Entertainment. He and ThiefNet's supporters intend to starve an entire generation of creative artists and entertainers out of business, in the vague hope that something will replace them, someday.

And the vandals are proud of themselves. They think they're liberators. Like their fellow anarchists Timothy McVeigh and Ted Kaczynski, they are stunningly inept at target selection: they think writers, dancers, musicians and actors who eat regularly are oppressors.

Every one of the twenty-five writers CrazyEddie mugged happens to be strongly and loudly opposed to oppression, racism and economic exploitation. They are, without exception, eloquent champions of individual liberty. Six are personally known to me to be in difficult financial straits. CrazyEddie has no idea which ones and doesn't care. They all earn (at least some) money from their work, so they're all pigs. He's never read Dr. Johnson, who said, "No one but a fool ever wrote, save for money."

The irony is bone-crushing. Cyberspace anarchists have declared war—not on governments, banks or multinationals—but on *artists*, their traditional allies! And left artists only one thing they can possibly do to defend themselves: turn their talents of persuasion to selling the public on "monitoring software on an Orwellian scale." CrazyEddie may believe that's "utterly unacceptable to any democracy"—but he's never lived in a democracy whose artists are all *literally* starving. We stopped a war together, once. I imagine we could start one.

Some of my colleagues already react somewhat emotionally to ThiefNet, and call for measures I personally find extreme. I think it would be quite sufficient merely to torture the vandals to death, despoil their corpses and destroy their computers. Execution of their parents seems excessive—unless they're still of breeding age, of course.

Not all information wants to be free. My stories and songs aspire only to be reasonably inexpensive.

If You Take It ... We Can't Leave It

FIRST PRINTED JANUARY 2003

THE US SUPREME COURT rendered a historic decision regarding the Sonny Bono Act—I'm not making this up—and it could with some accuracy be characterized as a Mickey Mouse decision. But don't laugh too hard: what's at stake might just be the death of art, and the everlasting impoverishment of human life.

The Supremes upheld Congress's power to extend the term of copyright by twenty years. Until 1998, copyright protected a work for the lifetime of the author plus fifty years. Then the Sonny Bono Copyright Term Extension Act (named for the late congressman/entertainer), bumped it two decades, to seventy years.

Big whoop, right? Why would anybody get upset over that—much less push it all the way to the Supreme Court? I suppose Stanford law professor Lawrence Lessig might have decided to challenge the Sonny Bono Act, at his own expense, so we all wouldn't have to wait twenty more years to rip off the heirs of Gershwin and Frost and could immediately record "Rhapsody in Blue" or publish "Stopping By Woods on a Snowy Evening" without paying anyone a dime.

But I suspect what really got on Professor Lessig's wick was that a major lobbying force behind the Sono Buoni Act...excuse me, the Sonny Corleone Act...I'll have it under control in a minute...that one of the biggest supporters of the Sonny Bono Act was none other than Mordor itself: the evil empire men call Disney.

I've never understood exactly what's so vile about Disney. Every time I've ever given them a dollar, I got back a buck and a half of value. If the Sonny Boy Williamson...I mean, if the Sonny Bono Act hadn't passed, Steamboat Willie—The Mouse himself!—would have slipped into the public domain. Naturally the Disney corporation pressured Congress. If it hadn't, today we'd probably be paying half a buck for cut-rate Mickey Mouse gear that isn't worth a dime, and wondering why nothing good ever seems to last.

Granted: as far as I know, nobody who's currently a major player at Disney is a relative, loved one, friend or associate of Walt himself anymore. I doubt anybody getting rich on his genius today ever met the man. And I'll bet they all wear better clothes, drive better cars and have more aerobic sex than the average Stanford law professor. I'm not disputing that they're scum.

But they also jealously guard, and thus zealously preserve, old Walt's creations. To this day, every smallest thing in Disneyland is *perfect*. You can sneer at Mickey Mouse watches if you like, but they keep good time, and all the great Disney cartoons have been restored and reissued precisely because someone in a power suit could make enough money to lease a cool car to have hot sex in by doing it...because he held copyright to the material.

Lessig argues that Congress only has the right to permit copyright within limits: apparently in his view fifty years is a limit, but seventy somehow is not. To explore this, let's shift perspective 180 degrees from Disney, and focus on the exact opposite end of the financial spectrum: me.

Science fiction can have a fair shelf life, with a little luck: some of the biggest moneymakers in the field today have been dead for decades. The biggest, Robert A. Heinlein, died in 1988. I've written thirty-two books so far. I believe I've earned what money they've brought me (and then some!), and I hope they'll stay in print awhile after I'm gone.

So when I do snuff it, I'd like to leave them, and any money they may fetch (the wee percentage the publishers, producers and taxmen won't keep), to my daughter Terri—just like any other craftsman would. I don't think that's an outrageous, capitalist-pig desire: it's a large part of why the stories exist in the first place.

Terri's twenty-eight. If I hand in my lunchpail tomorrow, she'll hold US copyright on my works until she's ninety-eight. Again, that doesn't seem unreasonable to me. Lifespan is increasing. Her great-grandfather died last year at 100. I recently heard an eminent expert—Dr. Phil—say if you are alive in the year 2010, your life expectancy will be 125. If that's true, and I croak later today, Terri will be S.O.L. for the last quarter-century of her life, helpless to prevent slipshod pirate editions, bogus spin-offs or Hollywood rip-offs of her dad's legacy. So I'm fine with the Sonny Rollins...the furshlugginer Sonny Bono Act; I wouldn't mind extending it further.

Why this is unspeakably ironic is, twenty years ago I won science fiction's top international honor, the Hugo Award, for a story called "Melancholy Elephants"—which argued that firm limits will one day have to be placed on the length of copyright...because our technology now gives society an elephant's memory, and when was the last time you saw a happy-looking elephant?

Not ironic enough yet? You can read that story right now, for free, on-line—legitimately! It appears in my story collection *By Any Other Name*, and Baen Books publisher Jim Baen believes online samples are like rock videos: he figures if you like the free story, you'll buy the paperback. Maybe he's right.

I wish we were done with irony now. "Melancholy Elephants" was originally dedicated to Virginia Heinlein, Robert Heinlein's widow and one of the most remarkable people I've ever known. On Saturday, January 18, Ginny passed away in her sleep in Florida, surrounded by family and friends. She outlived Robert by fifteen years, not seventy. But she leaves several descendants—one of them three years old—and I don't see why they should get ripped off because "information wants to be free." We creative types are content for our information to be reasonably affordable. Whether we ourselves happen to be breathing or not, don't begrudge us that pittance, as long as someone we loved is alive.

Silver Lining

Valmiki's Third Reality

FIRST PRINTED DECEMBER 1997

ONE OF THE GREATEST LESSONS of my life came from a man I never met named Aubrey Menen.

In the summer of 1977 my wife attended the American Dance Festival at Duke University in North Carolina. We stayed in campus housing, cramped and sweltering. Every day Jeanne left at dawn and returned well after dark, utterly exhausted and creatively stimulated. All I had to do was survive the brutal heat. One thing that helped was Duke's splendid—air-conditioned—library, and one day I found a wonderful book there.

It purported to be a rogue translation of the oldest known work of literature, the *Ramayana*. Indeed, it claimed to be the only good translation. The problem with all previous ones, the author claimed in his preface, was that they'd all been made by Brahmins—and the *Ramayana* is, he said, essentially a sidesplitting satire of the whole Brahmin caste. I have no idea whether any of this is true—but I bought the premise, and enjoyed the book immensely. I can't recall many specifics—my principal recollection is of laughing so hard that sweat flew from my forehead and stained the pages—but twenty years later, I retain its final lines verbatim.

Prince Rama begins the story (this version, at least) much like Prince Siddhartha: rich, sheltered and naive. By the end, he's been stripped of everything: wealth, friends, family and worst of all, his ideals and cherished beliefs. Broke and banjaxed, he crawls across the world to the feet of the wisest sage in the world, Valmiki. "Master," he cries, "everything I ever believed is false; all my dreams were illusions. Is there *nothing* in life that is *real*?" And old Valmiki smiles, and speaks the sentences that changed my life:

"My son, three things in life are real. God...human stupidity...and laughter. But the first two pass our comprehension: we must do what we can with the third."

I had the wit to copy that down in my notebook. (No: I quoted it to Jeanne that night, and *she* had the wit to tell me to write it down.) But the Carolina sun had parboiled my brain, and I failed to note the author's name. By the time I got back home to Canada, it was gone from my head, and it took me years to find another copy of his masterpiece. (I presume it was his masterpiece.) His/Valmiki's words, however, just kept burrowing deeper and deeper into me in the meantime. I'd been a writer for *four* years, then, a published novelist for less than a year. I knew writing was what I wanted to do with my life...but those words helped me understand what *kind* of writer I wanted to be. The more I thought about it, the more it seemed the most pressing problem on Starship Earth is rotten morale, and the best thing I could do about it was to try and make people giggle. Twenty-three books later, I'm still trying .. because it only hurts when I don't laugh.

I once had surgery to correct a tendency of my lungs to collapse. It worked...and nearly killed me. I learned only recently that the procedure is considered one of the most painful a human can survive. When they sent me to my parents' house to recuperate and weaned me off narcotics, I spent a ghastly ten straight days awake, in so much agony Seconal couldn't touch me. Every time I started to drift, I would shift position slightly—wiggle a toe, say—and shocking pain would wake me. I began praying for the strength to kill myself. Finally, a movie I'd never seen before came on TV: *The Marx Brothers Go West*. It's probably the worst movie they ever made, and it was torture to laugh, and I laughed so hard I exhausted myself, and my eyes closed....

I awoke to total darkness, bright pain and insoluble dilemma. Somehow I'd managed to fall halfway out of bed. The only thing holding me up was the bad arm, the one too weak to lift a cup. I bleated in terror.

From the next room I heard, "Huh? *Weebis*? Snorkfarble." And then, in succession, *thump!...bump!...*CRASH *tinkle tinkle tinkle...*"Baggerin' jagfabble!"...*clang! clang!...*CRASH *scrape!...*"Holomcummen'!"... *thump!* CRASH! *scrape...thump!* CRASH! *scrape...thump!* CRASH! *scrape...*and the door flew open and in lurched Mom, in her pajamas, eyes glued shut, one foot inextricably wedged in a wastebasket, mostly asleep but coming to rescue her injured child. She stopped, pried one eye open,

discovered she had come within an inch of impaling it on the TV antenna, refocused past it, our eyes met...

...and we both laughed so hard we fell to the floor, and crawled to each other's arms, still laughing, and it was at *that* moment—not when I woke from the twenty-six hours of healing sleep that ensued—that I passed over the hump and decided to live. Maybe that's why Valmiki's words resonated for me.

God and human stupidity I can't deal with. It's laughter, if anything, that will get me through the Crazy Years.

The Ones with a Zero on the End

FIRST PRINTED NOVEMBER 1998

WELL, I TURNED FIFTY. According to Theodore Sturgeon, I've entered "the autumn of middle age." By the standards my cohort proclaimed in the sixties, I have been untrustworthy for twenty years now. If it is true that life begins at forty, I should be entering puberty soon.

Actually, I spent several days turning fifty. We had the party the Saturday before. My wife Jeanne and I had recently moved from Vancouver out to the Islands, and I couldn't ask my friends to ferry out on a weekday for a party. The last ferry back to the mainland pulls out at 9:30 P.M.: by the time they could get here from work, it'd be time to turn around and go home again.

So we celebrated my birthday a few days early, maybe fifteen of us, all day Saturday, and we had us a *good* time. Steve Fahnestalk and Tam Gordy and I played and sang damn near every song the Beatles ever wrote, played until the fingertips of our left hands threatened to split, sang until our upper registers were shot and quit only when our faces hurt from grinning at the beauty of the harmonies and the memories. Everyone gorged on the gourmet feast Jeanne and our friend Anya Coveney-Hughes had prepared. The coffee flowed like water. The jokes were toxic. I got nice presents, including a framed blowup of the *Revolver* album cover with myself digitally inserted as the Fifth Beatle, the memorial John Lennon boxed set I'd been hoping for (the last of the wine!) and another four CD box, an anthology from Verve called *Jazz Singing* which is so supernaturally wonderful that it is, all by itself, almost enough to be worth fifty years of sweat and aggravation. I got several birthday cards, all hilarious.

And we all talked of many things together: some serious, some funny and some both. For instance, a majority of us are Boomers (what an ironic name for the generation that wanted to stop the bombing!), and so we spoke of the recently-acquired syndrome Baba Ram Dass calls the "organ recital": the tendency, when meeting a friend you haven't seen in a while, to open the conversation by listing the organs that have begun to betray you since last you spoke. Funny and serious both, see? For awhile we listed Geniuses Who Got Screwed: people whose inventions created the world we live in, and whose names almost nobody knows. Nikola Tesla, of course, the most

shafted man in the last century, who gave us practical electricity, the electric motor, the transformer, the condenser, radio, the vibrator and (if you want to talk about things fundamental to our culture) the remote control...and died broke and is forgotten. Elisha Gray, who patented the telephone *the same day* as Alexander Graham Bell...unfortunately, two hours later. Many others more recent, too—just about *all* the pioneers of the Internet. (Do you know the name of the man who invented e-mail? Want to guess how much money he got for it?)

Perhaps I sang so long and talked so much because I did not want to leave an opening in which someone could ask me, "So...how does it feel to be fifty?"

As it happened, nobody did.

A few days later, on my actual birthday, Jeanne *did* ask me, late in the evening as we were cleaning up the kitchen together. "So...how does it feel to be fifty?"

I had been pondering the question for weeks, in odd moments. I'd spent most of the party wondering what I would say if asked. I'd been thinking about it ever since, and had devoted at least a solid hour to the question that morning in bed, before arising. When my wife asks me about my feelings, I generally think about twice as hard and fast as usual. And I put down the dishtowel and opened my mouth, and after a long while answered honestly, "Beats me, love." I had, and have, no answer.

It doesn't feel like *anything*. Really.

I don't *think* I'm in denial. I know that I have, like many men and some women, a tendency not to notice my own feelings going by until enough of the sludgier ones clog up in the pipes to cause some kind of bursting or spillage. But I know a lot of my own tricks by now, and I've employed my little interior flashlight in all the corners of my skull. And I don't feel one bit older than I did last year—nowhere *near* as old as I did back in the eighties, when I went through a horrid eighteen months of clinical depression. My fear of onrushing death has not increased by any detectible increment. I may not be the man I was...but hell, I was always more man than I needed to be, anyway. I'm not looking forward to retirement because writers *can't* retire. I've lost a few notes off my high register...but I've gained a few on the low end. Just tune the guitar down a step or two, and I won't even have to relearn everything in new keys.

Over the last few years I've seen friends, relations and colleagues experience their fiftieth birthday as a major trauma. Some got weeping/laughing drunk or hopelessly stoned. Some quit their jobs, or bought a motorcycle, or traded in their spouses and kids. Why am I, after much self-scrutiny, apparently unaffected by the dread occurrence of a zero on my odometer?

I began this essay with the hope that I might come up with an answer by the time I got to the end—and I think maybe it just now came to me. About three sentences ago. The answer is: dumb luck. I am fortunate enough to love my job, and to love my wife and daughter, with all my heart. I always have, and I believe I always will. I still think I can keep all three, if I work hard enough and am lucky. So nothing important has changed.

Bring on those Crazy Years—even the one with the zero at its end!

Precious Are the Eggs of the Sturgeon

FIRST PRINTED MAY 1999

I WAS GUEST OF HONOR at the science fiction convention DemiCon X back in 1999, and while talking with a knowledgable twenty-something fan at a party, I mentioned the late Theodore Sturgeon. And the young man said, "Who's that?"

It was as if a contemporary baseball fan had failed to recognize the name Willie Mays, or a hockey fan had said, "Rocket *who*?" Only two decades after Ted's death, a reputation that should stand for two *millenia* is—somehow—apparently already fading. I cannot permit this. Just as Robert Heinlein used adventure to teach me the love of reason and science, my friend and mentor Ted Sturgeon used words, the terrifying beauty that could be found in their thoughtful esthetic arrangement, to teach me the love of... well, of love.

He sometimes wrote entire chapters in iambic pentameter, for the sheer hell of it, and reviewed sf for the *New York Times*. When I was sixteen—barely in time—I read a story of his called "A Saucer of Loneliness," and decided not to kill myself after all. Years later I read another Sturgeon story called "Suicide" aloud to a friend of mine who had made five increasingly serious attempts at self destruction, and she has not made a sixth.

It's customarily said that all Ted's work was about love. He himself didn't care for that description. He accepted Heinlein's limiting definition of love: "the condition in which the welfare and happiness of another become essential to your own." Ted wrote about that state, but about much more as well. If he must be distilled to some essential juice, it might be least inaccurate to say he wrote about *need*. About all the different kinds of human need, and the incredible things they drive us to, about new kinds of need that might come in the future and what they might make us do; about unsuspected needs we might have now and what previously inexplicable things about human nature they might account for. (Consider his famous *Star Trek* script, "Amok Time": the one in which poor Spock goes into heat.)

Or maybe what Ted wrote about was goodness, human goodness, and how often it turns out to derive, paradoxically, from need. I envision a mental equation I think he would have approved: Need + Fear = Evil, but Need + Courage = Goodness.

One of his finest stories is actually called "Need." It introduces one of the most bizarre and memorable characters in literature, a nasty saint named Gorwing. How can a surly rat-faced runt with a streak of cruelty, a broad stripe of selfishness and a total absence of compassion be a saint? Because of an unusual form of telepathy. Gorwing perceives other people's need, *any* sort of need, as an earsplitting roar inside his own skull—and does whatever is necessary to make the racket stop. Other people's pain hurts him...so for utterly selfish reasons, he does things so saintly that even those few who understand why love him and jump to do his bidding. Whenever possible Gorwing charges for his services, as high as the traffic will bear—because so many needs are expensive to fix, and so many folks can't pay—and he always drops people the moment their needs are met. Marvelous!

Ted's own need, I think, was to persuade the post-Hiroshima generation that there *is* a tomorrow: that there is a point to existence, a reason to keep struggling, that all of this comic confusion is progressing toward something—and although he believed in his heart that this something was literally unimaginable, he never stopped trying to imagine it, and with mere words to make it seem irresistibly beautiful. He persisted in trying to create a new code of survival for post-Theistic man, "a code," as he said, "which requires belief rather than obedience. It is called ethos...what it is really is a reverence for your sources and your posterity, a study of the main current which created you, and in which you will create still a greater thing when the time comes, reverencing those who bore you and the ones who bore them, back and back to the first wild creature who was different because his heart leaped when he saw a star."

Ted's classic "The Man Who Lost The Sea" concerns a man who, as a boy, nearly died learning the lesson that you *always* spearfish with a buddy, even if you wanted the fish all to yourself—that "I" don't shoot a fish, "we" do. Now the sea-sound he seems to hear is really earphone-static, caused by the spilled uranium which is killing him:

> The sick man looks at the line of his own footprints, which testify that he is alone, and at the wreckage below, which states that there is now way back, and at the white east and the mottled west and the paling flecklike satellite above. Surf sounds in his ears. He hears his pumps. He hears what is left of his breathing. The cold clamps down and down and folds him round past measuring, past all limit.
>
> Then he speaks, cries out: then with joy he takes his triumph at the

other side of death, as one takes a great fish, as one completes a skilled and mighty task, rebalances at the end of some great daring leap; and as he used to say "We shot a fish," he uses no "I":

"God," he cries, dying on Mars, "God, we made it!"

Not *all* Ted's influence on my own writing was benign. He was a terrifying punster: the man who said H.G. Wells had "sold his birthright for a pot of message." He and I were once forcibly ejected from a Halifax restaurant called Chicken Tandoor for persistent punning.

"There is really only one sense," he told me once, "and that is touch; all the other senses are just other ways of touching." North Atlantic Books is currently partway through a ten-volume hardcover reprinting of all of his short stories, edited by Paul Williams; I urge you to seek them out, and his novels *More Than Human*, *The Cosmic Rape*, *The Dreaming Jewels* and *Godbody* (an astonishing and audacious contemporary rewrite of the New Testament), and let him touch your eyes and heart and mind with his extraordinary fingers.

Thanks for the Music

FIRST PRINTED JUNE 2000

I READ AN ARTICLE IN THE NEWSPAPER a couple years back that had my jaw dragging on the floor. It was a very little item, on page B-14, about extremely premature newborns. So premature they haven't had time to develop the sucking reflex. Such infants are literally too dumb to eat. What caused me to spend the rest of that day staring at the wall was the statement that doctors have lately learned to *coax* such preemies into sucking...by rewarding them.

But what could constitute a pleasurable stimulus for a critter too primitive to even crave nourishment?

Music.

Think about that. Here's an organism potentially human—but so underdeveloped that right now it isn't really even a functional *animal*. Yet it enjoys music. Enough to work to get it. We are hardwired to love a tune even more than the teat. Music is more basic to us than food.

(Naturally, musicians are among of the poorest and most ruthlessly exploited members of our society. Even the 1 percent who are superstars don't live nearly as well as you think they do. The list of rich retired musicians pretty much begins and ends with George Harrison.)

Now I begin to understand why Georgie Fame's Walking Wounded albums have such a powerful emotional impact on me....

Georgie Fame is an English singer/keyboardist, born in Lancashire in 1943. He's most often pigeonholed as a rock or pop guy, but he has worked in just about every genre except punk and rap, and I've always thought of him as a jazz musician who isn't pretentious about it. He has a voice reminiscent of an alto sax, warm and smoky, and sings like Dexter Gordon plays.

His first international hit, "Yeh Yeh," was written by Jon Hendricks of the legendary jazz "vocalese" ensemble Lambert, Hendricks & Ross. That single made number one in December 1964, dislodging the Beatles for the first time ever. They sent Georgie a telegram of raucous congratulation. To this day Lord McCartney says Georgie is his favorite nightclub act...and not just because Georgie was onstage at the Bag O' Nails, playing "Yeh Yeh," at the moment when Sir Paul met his late wife Linda....

Georgie appears regularly at a London club called Ronnie Scott's. In December 1995 his band Walking Wounded included trumpeter Guy Barker and alto sax man Peter King (who can both be seen in the movie *The Talented Mr. Ripley*), vibraphonist Anthony Kerr, tenorman Alan Skidmore, bassist Geoff Gascoyne and the Powell Brothers, Tristan and James, on guitar and drums. Led by Georgie's nimble Hammond organ they spent 133 minutes casually performing musical miracles, which were captured on the CDs *Name Droppin'* and *Walking Wounded*. If you're a musician, *this*, right here, is where you go to surrender.

If not.... Look, every time you ever put your glad rags on and went out to a club, *this* is the show you were hoping to catch. The magic perfect night. That time you and someone you love transcended time together in some smoky dive...got so high you forgot to drink...had so much fun holding hands you forgot to go home...rode the music straight off a cliff together, and for a few shining hours just finally *dug it*, grokked the universe in fullness and forgave the well-intentioned clown who thought it all up.

It's not simply the material—it's the provenance, too. Georgie's the Real Deal. All the blessed golden sainted names he drops—Mose Allison, King Pleasure, Nemoi "Speedy" Acquaye, Harry "Sweets" Edison, Stan Getz, Lionel Hampton, Chet Baker, Phil Woods, John Coltrane, Fats Domino, Betty Carter, Chris McGregor, Clark Terry, Hoagy Carmichael—these are all cats and kitties Georgie has known and blown with over the years, and every one of them alive or dead must regret having missed this session.

Together the two CDs constitute a millennial summation of the very hippest music made on planet Earth in the past century. More than that: it was a summing up of the sensibility, the vibe, the spirit, the chronically laconic but rarely sardonic, spastically iconoclastic but seldom drastic, cool but never cruel approach to the universe and the Human Dilemma which produced that music, and thereby justified that millenium's existence. When history judges the twentieth century, these two albums will be major exhibits for the defense.

The band absolutely cooks—if this is truly Walking Wounded, they'd kill you running flat out. Saint Bernards should carry CD players with these two albums strapped under their necks: even the most frostbitten toes would involuntarily tap themselves back to life. You've probably heard a *lot* of people take a hack at "Moondance"—but Georgie Fame was Van Morrison's musical director for years...and has a better voice.

And I hope I haven't given the impression I'm talking about preserved fossil music, a picking of the bones of a century of dead hipsters by some aging dilettante Brit. Better than half the tunes on these albums are Georgie

Fame originals. It's just that he's a contemporary and peer of all those gone great ones, producing music that fits seamlessly into an evening of classics. He's *entitled* to drop names.

In the midst of an instrumental solo, he'll suddenly call out "Thank you for Sam Cooke!" or "Thank you for Sweets Edison!" I don't know who he's thanking, but I thank him for doing it. In addition to being 133 minutes of relentlessly cool music, this set is a detailed Treasure Map, pointing the astute student to some of the very finest forgotten geniuses of the twentieth century, some of the greatest musicians who ever inexplicably failed to become household words—people who deserve to be as famous as Pops or Bird, Ella or Lady Day, but aren't—giants whose trail-breaking footsteps have sadly begun to erode. If you don't already know the work of, say, Jimmy Smith, Richard "Groove" Holmes, Percy Mayfield, Clifford Brown, Eddie Jefferson, Richard Tee, Gene Ammons, Joe Zawinul, Benny Golson, Kenny Gordon, Bobby Timmons, Zoot Money, Kenny Drew, Ezra Ngcukana, Chris McGregor or Karl Denver... well, listen to these two CDs, and you'll see.

Now, I've been a *serious* Georgie Fame fan since 1964. These two albums were recorded in December '95, then released in '97. Until a few months ago, *I didn't know they existed.* If any attempt to market or publicize them in North America was made, I managed to miss it....

...until it finally dawned on me, about a year ago, that I could use my computer to hunt down music.

Especially the weird stuff I like. I've spent thousands of hours of my life combing through remainder bins and cut-out stacks, hoping to find a rare Charles Brown side or Betty Carter reissue. I was slow to realize that an online source like Chapters, Indigo or Amazon can stock *everything* in its virtual catalog. I made a list, went a-mousing... and Georgie's Walking Wounded CDs are only one of the happy discoveries I've made as a result.

For those of us who'd like to keep the footprints of the great ones from eroding, who hope to preserve the memory of the pioneers on whose shoulders all contemporary musicians stand—not merely the handful who'd make it onto a *Time* Magazine Ten Best list, but *all* of them—the Internet is one of the best tools we ever had. It's actually easier to find a copy of Ray Charles' classic 1964 album *Sweet and Sour Tears* today than it was in 1968.

Cyberspace as cultural cryogenics. That's the kind of technology use I like.

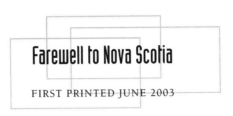

Farewell to Nova Scotia

FIRST PRINTED JUNE 2003

We wanted spirituality
on other days than Sunday
so we made our homes in shacks and domes
on the shore of the Bay of Fundy
on a mountainside that the Fundy tide
has been poundin' on for ages
and we lived for years on homebrew beers
and the wisdom of the sages

We lived in ruins in huge communes
where no one did the dishes
We lived in huts and froze our butts
and fed ourselves on wishes
We lived in shacks and broke our backs
to keep ourselves from freezin'
We lived on hope and grains and dope
and vegetables in season.

—"NORTH MOUNTAIN CRAZIES"

MY FIRST FIFTEEN YEARS in Canada, I lived in Nova Scotia. Now I've been here in BC for sixteen. But you don't get over Nova Scotia, not really. It's where I met and fell in love with Canada and then my wife and then our daughter, where I wrote my first dozen books, where I started to believe in magic because there it was under my nose. I'll go back there any time I can find someone to pay the airfare. I've just returned from my first visit in well over a decade, thanks to "Open Book with Mary Walsh," a CBC-TV show on which—I'm not making this up—people discuss a book which they've read. It was a week that stirred up old memories, then revised them.

I expected change, but paradoxically there was both more and less than I'd anticipated. Crow's Hollow, the parcel on which I courted my Jeanne, lies below what used to be a dirt road. It's paved, now, and in paving it, they raised the roadbed some eight meters just where it passes the Hollow. They swore they'd restore our access and provide parking. Turns out they lied. It took three passes to even locate the Hollow, then a desperate scramble down a scree slope to reach what used to be the head of the trail.

A few hundred meters downhill it got worse: both of the hobbit houses we left behind—the TA (for Total Anarchy) and the Five-Sided House down past the waterfall—are now wrecks, way beyond salvage. We, and our marriage, are holding up a lot better than the dwellings in which it was born. We wandered back uphill in a thoughtful mood until we suddenly noticed that, since our day, ticks have come to the North Mountain. In great numbers. See the funny old hippies parked on the road, dancing vigorously around their car, singing loudly if incoherently, and tearing off their clothes. Just like old times.

Still slightly ticked, we drove half a klick east, and found that our magnificent old neighbors Myrna and Johnson Sabean have not aged a day since 1987. Myrna has finally retired from taking in the foster kids nobody else wants—but there were so many, just keeping track of them all is a full-time job now. Johnson, in his eighties, still goes up into the woods with a chainsaw and comes down with finished boards. No change at all there.

That helped us come to terms with the decay at the Hollow—only wood was rotted, the important stuff was unchanged. And surely we'd have better luck at the next landmark down the road, Moonrise Hill. It was the main headquarters of our spiritual commune, our most together building, not a funky hippie hovel but a real fifty-year-old farmhouse. It sat right beside the road, so it had electricity (which we used to run the stereo) and two cleared acres of good garden soil. Someone would surely have moved in and squatted after we left, and that was fine with us.

We couldn't find a trace of the place. There's not the slightest sign Moonrise ever existed. Not a scrap of lathe, not a shard of broken window glass. The sills left no detectible impression on the earth. The root cellar has healed over and left no scab. We couldn't agree on where the outhouse used to be, or even pin down the former location of the front door with any certainty. Nothing anywhere but knee-high grass and snarls of alder. And 2 million more ticks.

We asked around. None of the hippies we knew still lives on the North Mountain. That brutal winter defeated all of us in the end, it seems.

But as Jeanne and I drove around the mountain last week with our grown daughter (who flew up from New York to revisit the places of her childhood with us), on at least four separate occasions we spotted new hippies, putting their garden in. Young kids in their twenties, like we were, sprouting curly hair in all directions, homesteading in the middle of nowhere with bright eyes and mysterious smiles, looking to get straight. That cheered us. When the next generation of kids suddenly realizes that the city sucks, and goes looking for someplace that isn't totally insulated from reality, there'll be a few country-competent folks waiting there to welcome them, teach them important things like how to build a fire and where to put the privy and why you should never sneeze in the goatshed.

I reckon that'll do.

And there may not be a hippie left
on the goddamn Fundy shore
Or it may be true that there's one or two
but there can't be many more
And we don't write much but we keep in touch
in a casual kind of way
We pass the word, and last I heard
we was all gettin' by okay

We've mostly found our way around
the things we were afraid of
The Mountain taught us what we sought:
we know what we are made of
We share one quirk: we've all found work
that doesn't hurt the planet
And it sounds like myth, but we're mostly with
who we were when we began it

Our kids are growin', our ages showin'
our memories gettin' faint
But I'm mighty glad for the times we had
and I won't pretend I ain't
The memories will bring me ease
when it's time to push up daisies:
I've had my fun—I once was one
of the great North Mountain Crazies

Why Pamela Wallin Is Dangerous

FIRST PRINTED NOVEMBER 1998

N 1998 I WENT ON A two-week triple-crown marathon of literary festivals: Calgary, Banff and Harbourfront in Toronto. Amid the endless readings, signings and interviews, there were many high spots—among them, meeting in person at last my esteemed editor at the *Globe and Mail*, Warren Clements; singing onstage with my wife Jeanne, accompanied by Amos Garrett and Ron Casat; and being interviewed by Pamela Wallin.

Ms. Wallin is unique in at least two respects. First, she appears not to have an adrenal gland: she is the only on-camera TV personality I've ever met who displays not even the faintest trace of stage-fright, who does not change in any detectible way when the red light goes on. Second, she actually listens to what you say—and is perfectly capable of dumping her next scripted question—or all of them—if something you say suggests a more interesting question. This makes her roughly as rare as a compassionate Republican, and even more precious.

It also makes her dangerous. If she doesn't recite canned questions, you won't get away with canned answers. And she doesn't let up: her last question will generally be as provocative as her first—which almost guarantees that you'll leave the studio with a bad case of *esprit d'escalier*. ("The wit of the staircase," meaning the brilliant conversational bon mots you think of too late, halfway down the stairwell on your way home.)

Toward the end of our session, she hit me with just such a question. Noting that the column I was writing at the time for the *Globe and Mail* forced me to focus rather obsessively on human insanity, she asked: what keeps you sane in the Crazy Years?

Nobody ever asked me that before. The first thing that came into my head was writer Donald E. Westlake; I began babbling about why he is superior to Prozac in reconciling God's ways to Man, why I always finish one of his books a little gladder to be a human being. That reminded of Laurence Shames, who like Mr. Westlake is capable of making you delete Dr. Kevorkian from your Rolodex, using only ink stains on paper. From Shames I began to segue to Lawrence Block, Carl Hiaasen, W.P. Kinsella, Don Winslow—and would doubtless have gone on from writers to cite musicians (Amos Garrett), dancers (Jose Navas) and other artists who have helped me stay sane.

But then Ms. Wallin did something I can't explain. Without, I swear, so much as twitching a single muscle in her face or body, she somehow conveyed the clear message that I had less than thirty seconds left. In desperation, I groped for a unifying theme, asked myself what all those writers I've named have in common...and came up with humor: the precious gift of laughter. I said as much, and quoted Aubrey Menen's *The Ramayana*, then the red light went out and they took away my microphone. And on the staircase, I realized I could have used another hour to answer her final question...or even to begin.

One thing I wish I'd had time to mention, for instance, is the first day I ever spent in Toronto, some twenty years ago.

I was visiting Steve Thomas, a friend who then lived in a walkup on Bathhurst Street. We were out on his balcony at the shank of the afternoon, preparing to hibachi a steak, when suddenly Steve screamed, dropped the meat and pointed at the sky. I assumed he had gone insane, decided to humor him by looking where he was pointing...and dropped the hickory chips and screamed myself. There, filling the whole sky, more vivid and vibrant than DVD, was the first (and so far only) complete and perfect end-to-end rainbow I've ever seen. Above it, like a Technicolor shadow, was a second, ghost rainbow, about half as bright as the first. Twice as far above that a third echo half as bright as the second shimmered in and out of existence, leaking tears of colour into the dome of the sky.

Steve and I gaped...turned to one another (Do you see it too?)...then together we leaned over the balcony and began hollering. "*Hey—dig the rainbow!!*"

At first only a few people looked up at us. Tough street, Bathhurst, in a tough town, with the dinner hour at hand. Then those few looked where we were pointing, became thunderstruck...and at once took up the cry, tugging at their neighbors, gesturing. Within thirty seconds I probably heard the word "rainbow" shouted in two dozen languages. Pedestrian traffic ceased. People ran indoors, dragged out protesting friends and relatives, who soon fell silent with awe. People appeared on neighboring balconies on all sides of us, many of them frantically telephoning friends, the rest exchanging grins with Steve and me. A Sikh mad with joy ran right out into rush hour traffic and forced it to stop in both directions. People rolled down their windows to curse at him, heard what he was bellowing, followed his pointing arm...then smiled, shut off their engines and got out for a better look. The ambient background noise of the city diminished perceptibly. Strangers smiled at one another; lovers held each other close;

children were silent; bent seniors giggled uncontrollably. The city ground to a halt, and focused its attention: for perhaps five eternal minutes junkies stopped needing, fanatics stopped fearing, cops stopped suspecting, brokers stopped coveting, students stopped worrying, pickpockets stopped working. For a timeless time, we all did the same thing, as one: we wondered. We shared our wonder, and took nourishment from it and from the sharing of it. And then finally the last lambent trace of rainbow faded and was gone, and a minute or so after that, we all turned back into ourselves and Oz turned back into Toronto again and reality rebooted.

Lagniappe

What's All This Brouhaha? Ha Ha...

[With insincere apologies to my esteemed colleague Silver Donald Cameron (*www.islemadame.com/sdc/*) and to legendary Vancouver bluesman Long John Baldry.]

DOCTOR SILVER," I SAID, "I'd like you to meet Donald Q. Public. Don, allow me to present Dr. Hyland Orenthal Silver. Dr. Silver was a distinguished oncologist for many years before becoming Canada's leading specialist in cloning."

Dr. Silver rose behind his desk and extended his hand. "Good afternoon, Mr. Public. Do you have a mi—I'm sorry, is something wrong?"

Don was staring, awestruck. "It just hit me," he said. "You're Hy O. Silver, the clone arranger, in T'ronto...."

There was a stillness, as complete as that which must exist on the moon now that the tourist season is past. I could hear dust motes collide. Dr. Silver took his hand back and sat down.

Well, I have a certain reputation to uphold, myself. "And if I were a great Nova Scotian writer videotaping you both," I said finally, "I'd call the result 'Silver/Donald, Camera On.'" Now I could hear dust mote near-misses. "I'm sorry, Doc, I should have warned you: Don here's a fellow paronomasiac. Look, can we move things along a little, here? We're already 182 words into this column with little sign of a theme yet."

"Certainly, Spider," he agreed. "As I was saying: Mr. Public, do you have a million dollars?"

Don blinked. "As a matter of fact, I do. Won a lottery."

"Good. Then you're not wasting my time. Continue."

"A megabuck is table stakes in your game?"

Dr. Silver merely nodded.

Don looked impressed. "Okay. I just turned fifty, I have this million bucks and since I have no family responsibilities I've decided to blow the whole wad on something eye-poppingly evil. Ideally I'd like to make the hair of everyone alive stand on end. All technology is intrinsically vile, of course...so I asked around, and everyone seems to agree that this cloning is simply the most horrifyingly wicked, morally revolting and ethically dangerous technology around. So t—"

"Wait a minute," I objected. "What about the time that Frankencarrot snapped its chains, killed its maker and raged around the countryside strangling little girls and raping the Burgomeister, and we all had to get our torches and pitchforks and march on the—"

I trailed off, and Don put the knife away. "—ell me, Doctor," he went on as if he had not been interrupted, "how can cloning help me subvert basic human decency and shock the world? Let's talk abomination, here."

Dr. Silver pursed his lips, then took out a wallet made of marzipan and lipped his purse. "First, of course, we can clone you."

"Walk me through that one."

"You give us a DNA sample and go away for a long time. We make a few hundred clones, of which a few will become viable—and non-mutated—blastocysts."

"So I could create several of me?"

"Maybe—at a million dollars per attempt. Turning an invisibly small clump of stem cells into a live baby is a nontrivial problem. Nobody's ever done it yet. Stick with one is my advice, unless your financial condition improves."

"Okay. So then...what?"

"With luck, a year or so from now, I hand you a squawling infant with no birth certificate to raise by yourself."

Don frowned. "But he'd be absolutely identical to me? To me when I was a baby, I mean?"

"No more than an identical twin. Different fingerprints, for example."

"But he'd be *real* close, right?"

Dr. Silver nodded. "Close enough that if you found him parents identical to yours, raised him like the kid in *The Truman Show* in an artificial environment that perfectly reproduced the one you grew up in, and arranged for his life to play out exactly as yours did—"

"—then in only fifty years, I'd have—"

"—someone very much like you are now. A man with no loved ones

who feels a powerful yearning to do something really evil, but has not won a million dollar lottery. And who doesn't know anything that's happened in the real world since 1951."

"If he ever meets you," I added, "and finds out what you did to him, he'll kill you."

Don suddenly got a sinister look. "Hey…what if I got hold of some of Hitler's DNA, somehow, and recreated *him* in his prime?"

This time Dr. Silver pursed his teeth. "Pretty much the same result…except you end up with a man perfectly designed to flourish in 1930s Germany. He'd end up playing bass in a Goth band, I expect."

"At a cost approaching forty megabucks," I added. "Clone Vancouver's greatest bluesman, instead: then at least you've got a terrific pair of Long Johns."

Neither heard me. "I must say I'm a little discouraged," Don said.

"It's not the cost," Dr. Silver agreed. "It's the upkeep."

"If all you want is genetic copies of you, fifty years younger, and you don't mind if they think or behave differently than you," I offered, "grow as many as you can afford, and just leave them outside orphanages. Social services fraud: now *that's* evil."

Not enough for Don. "Suppose I cloned an army, Doctor? A thousand copies of some great warrior?"

"Then for the price of a hundred submarines you get an army whose every action is utterly predictable and every weakness magnified a thousandfold. Every private will think he's as competent as his officers—and be right. But their uniforms should all fit perfectly."

Don frowned. "Not very frightening." He brightened. "Wait. What about cloning my organs for transplant?"

Dr. Silver looked puzzled. "It'd be infinitely cheaper to bribe your way to the top of the transplant list, or buy organs from the Third World, like other millionaires do. Seems to me cloned organs would be far *less* immoral. And better for you."

Don was visibly disappointed. "I don't get it. What's so evil about cloning?"

"Beats me," the doctor confessed.

Suddenly Don grinned broadly, leaped to his feet and pointed at the doctor. "Spider said you used to be an oncologist," he said accusingly.

"Yes, why?"

"You're the clone arranger in T'ronto—chemo savvy!"

That's when he threw us out of his office. Apparently scientists *do* have at least some scruples about who they clone.

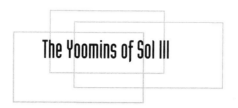

The Yoomins of Sol III

JOIN ME NOW as we beam down to a strange new planet. Our five-minute mission: to determine whether intelligent life exists here. And since we only have five minutes, there is no time for a proper study of the large-scale organization or behavior of the planet's dominant species—we must simply drop in, take one quick technology sample at random, assume it is representative and draw the best conclusions we can. Ready? CUE THE SPECIAL EFFECTS—

God, that always tickles.

Okay. We're in a typical dwelling of this race—*yoomins*, they're called. We've tried to bias the test in their favor as much as possible, by choosing our sample from one of the most affluent regions of the planet; surely here will be found their most intelligent technology. Tricorders ready? Let's look around.

The room we're presently in—the name sounds like a sneeze—is the one in which yoomins store and prepare their food. The largest two items in the room are a heat-making machine and a heat-losing machine. They sit side by side—yet careful sensor readings indicate they are not connected in any way. Hmmm.

Let's look closer. The heat-loser is—bafflingly—designed to stand on its end, so that you *must* spill money on the floor every time you open it to access or even inspect its contents. And they put the coldest part *on top*.

The heat-maker is complementarily designed to spill money on the ceiling. Not just the four elements on top (one of which is *always* defective): the central module, called an *uvvin*, has a door which—inexplicably—opens *from the top*, so that you cannot touch the contents during cooking, even momentarily, without wasting *all* the heat. The whole unit is utterly unprogrammable, and lacks even the simplest temperature readouts: everything is done by guess.

Perhaps some sort of cultural blind-spot is at work here. Let's examine the water-recycling facilities.

Uh, there are none. Yoomins throw potable water away. They throw *hot* water away. And look at the temperature control system: there is none. No sensors, no thermocouples, taps completely uncalibrated—though all these

technologies are trivially cheap here. They keep a large, almost-uninsulated tank full of water heated at all times to skin-scalding temperature (using none of the waste heat to warm the pipe, so that hot water will always be slow in arriving when needed), and then mix it with cold water to a safe temperature, by hand, adjusting the result *by testing it with their own skin*. With every use.

Well, perhaps yoomins customarily eat in restaurants, and this room is only intended as a fallback—in case, let us say, a wave of psychosis passes through the restaurant industry and they all start turning away a quarter of their customers rather than run a fan. Let's try another room.

And let's make it as fundamental and essential a room as we can. A yoomin need not necessarily sleep in its bedroom, nor relax in its living room, nor work in its study—but there is one room in which every yoomin *must* spend some time at least twice a day. Surely there, if anywhere, we will find the most thoughtful applications of intelligence.

The first and largest thing we find is a combination shower and bath. It cannot be used comfortably to bathe and cannot be used safely to shower. Its principal purpose appears to be to kill the elderly, unfit and unlucky, which it does with ruthless efficiency. The shower head is generally fixed, impossible to train on the areas where it is most needed. It has *worse* temperature control than the sink in the other room and is tested with the whole body. No provision is made for hair accumulation in the drain—or, usually, for venting of steam or gradual equalization of ambient temperature after a shower.

Let's move on to the central fixture: the commode. It enforces an unnatural, inefficient and uncomfortable posture, presents about the most uncomfortable sitting surface possible, has absolutely no facilities for cleansing or disinfecting either the user or itself—and after use, it takes the precious irreplaceable fertilizer and *throws it away*, using *gallons* of potable water to do so with no attempt at recycling. The obvious one-way valve, to prevent it backing up, is not present. And for a full 25 percent of its purported purpose—as a male urinal—it is completely and manifestly worthless, a constant source of domestic strife.

But if you think that's odd, keep going. There *is* a perfect, rationally designed male urinal, right here in this room—less than a meter away—but for some reason, no male human will admit to ever having used it for that purpose. That would somehow desecrate it, soil it. Officially it is reserved for saliva, nasal mucus, toothpaste spit-up, beard-hairs, blood, assorted skin-paints worn by females and the truly disgusting things humans seem to have to rinse off their hands all the time. Needless to say, it too must have its water-temperature laboriously reset by guess with each use.

Above it, on the wall, hangs another curious thing: a cabinet designed to spill its contents. The spice-rack in the last room, meant to hold items of uniform size and shape, has retaining walls for them—but these shelves, intended to hold items of varied size and shape, do not. And they are always too small and shallow to hold what is required; the overflow goes under the sink where it can grow mold faster.

Let's go back to the commode. Does it come with a reading lamp? No? Not even a magazine rack? Good God, Spock, are these creatures *savages*?

There are stereo speakers built in, surely? Power and data-feeds for a laptop? *At least* tell me there's a built-in deodorizer—

Let's stop. It's time to beam back up. These hominids may have developed some clever technology—but they are obviously not bright enough to have given the slightest thought to applying it to their own most basic personal comfort, and so they cannot possibly be regarded as sentient.

We'll check back in another century or so. It's possible yoomins are going through some sort of temporary cyclical madness—every adolescent species has its Crazy Years.

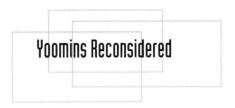

Yoomins Reconsidered

To: Kames T. Jerk, Commander, Starship ExitPrize
From: Academician Npolfz Tuvefou, University of Aldeberan
Subject: Your Report on Sol III

Dear Captain,

I don't think you're being entirely fair to the yoomins of Sol III. I've read your recent assessment of their intelligence, as exemplified by the personal-comfort technology found in their fuel-intake and -exhaust chambers, and I cannot fault your data. But I think you've missed a subtle point, which colours your conclusion.

There is about yoomins a quality so profoundly strange that it renders questions of intelligence or stupidity simply irrelevant. I have spent some time in that sector of the Lesser Magellanic Cloud—not by *choice*, of course; a breakdown—and ask you to believe that this is true, however improbable it may seem.

Yoomins believe at their core that life is not tough enough.

A primary example: like any sentient species, they recognized a need to transmit information nonverbally with high reliability over distance. Like most, they developed a symbol system: in their case, dark stains on leaves of whitened plant matter. (An unstable medium—but then, their lives are short.) They called theirs an "alphabet."

So far so good. But yoomins believe life is not hard enough; they could not stop there. The most advanced tribe of them developed not two but *three* alphabets, almost but not quite identical—called "upper case," "lower case," and "script"—*for absolutely no reason at all.* These yoomins require their young to master all three, and an endless series of self-contradictory rules for when each may/must be used. The *largest* tribe of yoomins, on the other hand, uses an alphabet that has endured, essentially unchanged, for millennia... which contains *hundreds* of characters, of surpassing complexity, and is nearly impossible for most yoomins (even of that tribe) to learn, write, type or translate.

Consider language itself. The purpose of language is to encode reality and communicate useful observations regarding it. Obviously, the more languages you construct, the more ways you have of looking at reality; integrate enough of them, and the noise should filter out, leaving a refined approximation. Yoomins have a reassuring plethora of languages—and much urgent reason to want to communicate with one another. *But almost no yoomin learns more than one language.* Bitter emotional debates often rage on whether it should be permissible for the young to be schooled in as many as two. This requires that *every message* between different tribes be laboriously translated by a single freak-expert, whose work can not practically be checked. Attempts at establishing a planetary pidgin—the very first sign of a civilization—have been made, but never seriously; yet yoomins maintain a planetary civilization. They do not believe life is hard enough.

The yoomin ecosystem *teems* with substances containing neurochemicals which induce pleasure in them. Nearly *all* yoomins show clear need for at least some such pleasure above that provided by simple successful survival. Most of these chemicals have societally-damaging side effects, some great, some small. Dealing with those would be a large but entirely manageable problem.

But yoomins don't think life is tough enough. Their response is to absolutely forbid use of any such substance, punishing violators with death, torture, imprisonment and disgrace. I swear. Excepted, of course, are substances that do not make a yoomin feel good *enough* to arouse anyone else's envy (e.g., "sugar," "chocolate," "caffeine"). But the *only other* exception—one made almost universally around the planet—is for the single substance which demonstrably and unmistakably has the most destructive effects (ethanol). All substances in between tend to be demonized in direct proportion to their relative harmlessness, and the strength of the user's need for them.

This clearly does not work: it produces a daily spectacle of slaughter, waste, corruption and degradation which has continued for several centuries. They simply do not see it—they acquire a blank look when you point it out.

Yoomins reproduce sexually, and at high efficiency. At present, they are confined to a single planet (for no explicable reason; apparently by choice), and thus suffer an overpopulation problem so intense it must be immediately apparent to the meanest intelligence among them. They are extremely blessed by nature in that a) contraception itself is trivially simple for them, and b) there are a number of alternative sexual recreations that offer no possibility of impregnation and are even more pleasurable than the procreative act itself. So what do yoomins do? *They deify ignorance.* They do

their level best—*knowing* in advance that they cannot possibly succeed—to ensure that their young learn *nothing* about sex (not even simple hygiene) for as long as possible. Indeed, sexual ignorance in children is given the special name "innocence," and considered not only a virtue, but the ultimate virtue. Yoomins deliberately go to enormous trouble to guarantee that their own young will begin their sex lives incompetently, with maximum possible emotional trauma, *just* as they are most fertile.

Recently yoomins developed technology which makes unintended conception a correctable mistake, long before a developing fetus could possibly possess a single functioning nerve cell or pain receptor—and so now, inevitably, the most revered and popular religious leader in the history of their planet tells them such technology is evil. He himself is a celibate. Life is nowhere *near* tough enough for the inhabitants of Sol III.

Yoomins made a terrible historical mistake. They destroyed or tamed every single predator that threatened them, from saber-tooth to smallpox, and gained control over most natural catastrophes—long before they were emotionally prepared to do without them. They have become too accustomed to the regular sound of ringing alarm bells in their heads, and so will manufacture emergency if none arises naturally. In between emergencies, they fantasize about them. They are addicted to fear, and for some reason cannot admit it. They are neurologically wired up to deal with a more hostile environment than presently presents itself...and are undone by the lack of competition. They turn their own intelligence to making life difficult enough for their own comfort, for their innate sense of the rightness of things.

Thus, the brighter they are, the stupider they appear to be.

It is what makes them happy. We can judge it only as art. And they are clearly great artists...currently shaping their greatest collaborative creation yet together, a masterpiece known as the Crazy Years.

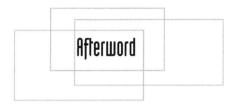

Afterword

Your most royal swingin' majesty:

I've been on a lot of sad tours... I been on a lot of mad beat bent-up downgradin' excursions... I been on a lot of tilted picnics, and a lot of double un-hung parties... I suffered from pavement rash... I been bent, twisted, spent, de-gigged, flipped, trapped and ba-bapped... but I never was so drug in my life as I was with this here last gig you put me on....

—Alvar Nuñez Cabeza da Vaca,
writing home to Ferdinand I of Spain from America
in the paleorap "The Gasser," by Lord Buckley

I
N 2004, the *Globe and Mail's* Comment editor abruptly stopped buying my columns. I could not say why, since he also stopped answering my e-mails and voice messages. I suspect budget cutbacks, but for all I know he heard something about me and his wife and found it plausible.

This sudden partial unemployment came as an enormous relief, which has been growing ever since. For the first time since 1996, I have the glorious luxury of ignoring the news once again. Sometimes I don't get Doonesbury, now. My disposition has already begun to improve, not to mention my digestion. I have not noticed that the world has suffered measurably from the lack of my commentary. And I have a lot more time and energy to write novels, stories and songs, which is why I was placed in this skull.

But it *is* a shame, artistically speaking, that I ceased chronicling the Crazy Years just as they reached their apotheosis. Even Robert A. Heinlein himself could not have imagined just how horrible the madness would become, only fifteen years after his own death. Even he, the bravest man I ever knew, would have paled at the depth and malignance of the sickness that has beset his beloved United States of America today.

That may sound like hyperbole, and a lot of people have made chumps out of themselves by claiming to know what Robert Heinlein would have believed, thought or felt about this or that subject. But I believe I can show what I just said to be a factual statement, using his own words.

Robert made a great many fictional "predictions," and a surprisingly high percentage of them happen to have come to pass. Only once, though, was he talked into making actual factual real-world predictions for the future, in a magazine article. As he later recounted, it "appeared with the title 'Where to?' and purported to be a nonfiction prophecy concerning the year 2000 A.D. as seen from 1950. (I agree that a science fiction writer should avoid marijuana, prophecy and time payments—but I was tempted by a soft rustle.)"

He later updated its nineteen specific predictions—twice, in 1965 and finally in the 1980 collection *Expanded Universe*—by which point he was showing a success rate of about 66 percent, or about 65 percent higher than the average fortuneteller, psychic or horoscopist. Of course, his predictions were more conservative. Jeanne Dixon and Edgar Cayce both prophesied the utter collapse of civilization by 2000; Robert merely foresaw that people would, for some reason, still be reading both of those prophets in 2001.

As this book goes to press, I have the unique honour to be writing a novel, *Variable Star*, based on a detailed outline drawn up by Robert in 1955, and recently entrusted to me by his estate (the Heinlein Prize Trust, which gives away half a million US dollars a year for achievement in commercial manned spaceflight; visit www.heinleinprize.com for details). So I recently found myself with ample reason to go back and carefully reread *Expanded Universe*, a wonderful collection of Robert's work that sheds much light on what readers of the fifties expected the far future world of the 00s would be like one day. I was having a wonderful time. Then, halfway through the book, I came to the article "Where To?," smiled in fond general recollection and continued reading, curious to see whether his success rate would hold, or if not, whether it would go up or down this time—

—and eleven pages in, I slammed the book shut, let it fall to the floor, put my head in my hands and burst into tears.

I sat there crying a while. Then, because it is our agreement, I brought my sorrow to my wife and shared it with her, and we comforted each other as best we could. Now I share it with you.

Page 266, prediction #4: *"It is utterly impossible that the United States will start a 'preventive war.' We will fight only when attacked, either directly or in a territory we have guaranteed to defend."*

Even as late as his final update in 1980, Robert modified that only to the extent of saying, *"it is no longer certain that we will fight to repel attack on*

territory we have guaranteed to defend; our behavior both with respect to Viet Nam and to Taiwan is a clear warning to our allies."

I read that prediction—it is utterly impossible that the United States will start a "preventive war"—and all at once I realized that the United States Robert A. Heinlein and I knew and loved, the one that does not, will not and never ever could first-strike, is *gone*. In a lousy fifteen years, somehow its most fundamental principles have vanished in the night, some of its most basic tenets have been smashed, trashed and pissed on, and nearly everything great it once stood for has been replaced with things for which it now crawls on its belly like a reptile.

Robert grew up in a literate and educated America, where people were aware of the existence of other countries and other cultures, or at least required their national leaders and policy-makers to be so, or at the very least required them to pretend to want to be so. He could not have imagined how quickly the U.S. would degenerate into a nation of mouth-breathing TV addicts proud of their ignorance and provincialism and happy to be led and represented by someone dumber than they are.

Robert lived his life in an America where most people were wise enough to understand, intuitively, without even needing to be told, that if it were ever to come down to it, it would be better to be defeated by Nazis than to become Nazis. He simply could never have conceived of an America that defecates on the precious Geneva Convention—much less its own magnificent Constitution and Bill of Rights—in the belief that it's defending freedom.

Robert wrote his books in an America where everybody—not just a handful of crackpot liberals, but everybody—understood, without it even needing to be said, that *John Wayne doesn't hit first.* That John Wayne particularly doesn't hit a little puny guy first. That John Wayne most especially doesn't shoot a little puny guy through the head, and then keep insisting the deceased had a gun after careful search has proven otherwise, like a child jamming his fingers into his ears and shouting "Neener neener neener" until he gets his way.

Robert thought America was made up of men and women of, if not high average intelligence—he was never that naive—at least of high average courage. He imagined them possessed of the same kind of quiet bravery that had allowed the common people of Great Britain to hunker down under *Blitzkrieg* and fucking carry on...counting their losses and with good reason to fear total doom, but moving forward. He probably assumed the citizens of a country that had fought an evil empire for half a century, with nuclear apocalypse as the stakes, had enough guts for anything the future could throw at them.

It would have been beyond his comprehension, I think, that fifteen years after beating that evil empire, America could possibly turn into such a stupendous collection of sissies, chickenshits, wimps, ninnies and weenies; that the loss of fewer than three thousand lives and two giant piles of ugly poorly constructed hubris would panic the greatest nation in history into abandoning both its brains and its honour; that even after three full years without a single follow-up attack by al-Qaeda, without a single injury let alone fatality on U.S. soil, most of the nation would still be quivering in genuine stomach-churning terror of the memory of nineteen dead savages with box cutters, so uncontrollably freaked out that they will willingly send their sons and daughters off to be killed or maimed and tolerate profoundly unamerican obscenities like Guantanamo and Al-Ghraib in their name, in return for even an obviously phony promise of "homeland security" made by people who, as Bill Maher so eloquently puts it, "are clearly still eating paste."

Robert respected the scientific method, and probably felt that America, whose success was based on it, would always agree that when it has been proved something is false, and everyone can see and test the proof, then you have to stop saying it is true. An administration impervious to facts, infallible as a Pope, would have seemed to him a contradiction in terms— how could you ever *get* that far, if you kept consistently ignoring reality? It might have boggled his mind that half the nation could possibly continue to believe Saddam Hussein was al-Qaeda's friend, even after it has been *proven* to them that he was al-Qaeda's enemy—just because they want so badly to beat up a friend of al-Qaeda and can't actually find any. He'd probably have been sourly amused to learn, as we just have at press time, that in fact, al-Qaeda's biggest friend in that part of the world at the time of the September 11 attacks was…wait for it…*Iran, Saddam Hussein's hereditary mortal enemy.* Considering that President Bush can't (or perhaps simply won't) read, I think he did remarkably well to come within a single letter, and only a few miles, of attacking the right country.

Robert, a graduate of Annapolis, greatly respected the military and stood up for them so eloquently in the dark days of Viet Nam that he even managed to persuade raggedy-ass hippies like me that I should respect them too…whatever I or he might think of the fatheaded chair-warming paper-shuffling cementheads who gave those brave soldiers, sailors and fliers their orders. I think he would have wept aloud to see a great military force so criminally misused, to see so many good men and women killed or crippled for absolutely no reason at all but one man's blind pig-ignorant obsession, spilling their blood and leaving body parts in the hot sand without having succeeded in avenging a single Twin Towers death or in postponing the next such Jackass Jamboree by so much as an hour. I know he would have cursed sulphurously to see not just America's soldiers, but all soldiers everywhere from now on, placed in ghastly danger by the completely gratuitous obliteration of the Geneva Convention and the disgraceful official sanctioning of torture as an allegedly acceptable policy of allegedly civilized peoples.

As if we couldn't possibly win without cheating! As if the ghosts of the Nineteen Numbskulls—and those friends and supporters who didn't have the guts to accompany them to battle last time, even though Mohammed Atta begged for more manpower—were really so terrifying that we dare not handicap ourselves with Marquis of Queensbury rules in fighting them. As if a nation of over 300 million people truly needed to fear a handful of cowardly psychopaths; as if Japanese kamikazes had actually defeated the US Pacific Fleet, let alone defeated the atomic bomb.

I think Robert would have found it just as astounding as I do that anyone, anywhere—much less everyone, everywhere—could possibly believe Osama Bin Laden is still alive. What are all you people *smoking* out there? Do you all honestly think for three years he's had constant access to extremely low-fi audiotape, but has never once managed to get his billionaire hands on a camcorder or even a new cell phone? (If he can't afford one, why are you afraid of him?) Or can you conceive of some reason he would *not* want to conclusively prove he's survived the worst the Great Satan could throw at him?

I believe Robert would have been as appalled and heartsick as I am to find that America's response to murderous assault by fewer than twenty terrorists would be to recruit untold thousands more. That instead of demonstrating to the world that those religious fanatics were wrong, murderously wrong, we would do our best to make it appear that they were right: that we here in the west *are* a civilization of arrogant bullies and self-righteous ignoramuses as they claim, that democracy *is* just the rich and powerful conning the poor and weak. For this, Americans went half a trillion dollars in debt?

When I first moved from the United States to Canada, I put in a lot of hours defending my native land to the residents of my adopted land. You have to: Canadians bitterly resent America because it not only has everything they want and don't have, it *doesn't* want what they *do* have, even though it's better. The stupid bastards down there don't seem to *want* free health care, good manners, safe streets and schools, clean cities, racial integration, intelligent radio, tasty beer or good marijuana, for instance. So I spent a lot of time telling fellow Canadians, "Look, America has sometimes failed to live up to its own ideals. If you want to upgrade 'sometimes' to 'often,' I won't argue with you. Well, the same is true of Canada, let's face it—and of every nation there ever was, if it comes to that. But remember this: America has, far and away, the most magnificent set of ideals that any nation in history ever failed to live up to."

Well, it used to. Apparently, America has found the strain too much, and has chucked its ideals into the dumper. They are just too much of an impediment, given the deadly urgency of defeating a worldwide terrorist conspiracy so vast, so well funded, so brilliantly organized and led, so terrifying in its implacable wrath, that the evil mastermind behind it has not killed a single American in three solid years of fighting. I speak, of course, of Michael Moore.

I used to wish, passionately, that Robert A. Heinlein had lived longer, much longer. But maybe it's just as well that he took his leave before the Crazy Years reached their peak intensity. It's going to be a while before anyone can again be as wholeheartedly proud of being an American as he—and I—used to be. I only hope I live to see the day America remembers its own splendid ideals, and decides to respect them again. And I really hope my nephews, nieces and grandchildren live to see the day.

Enough Crazy Years. Time, long past time, for some sane ones.

That's *my* prediction for the future: sunny skies, with increased chances of intelligence showers in the afternoon, and major brainstorms expected by early evening. The Sane Years—at long last. If it turns out I was right, terrific. And if not, we'll all have a lot more to worry about than the accuracy rate of some scribbler from

— Howe Sound, British Columbia
19 July, 2004 (my 29th anniversary)